DOWN BEAT

Max Henry ♡

WWW.MAXHENRYAUTHOR.COM

MAX HENRY

DOWN BEAT
Copyright © 2018 Max Henry
Published by Max Henry

Cover image: Serge Lee Photo
Model: Aykhan Shinzhin

For those who have always found

more comfort in the darkness

than the light.

PREFACE

Two things:

1.

DOWN BEAT deals firmly with the subject of mental illness and its associated effects on not only the sufferer, but those around them. If this is something you feel may be a potential trigger for you, I advise you stop, consider if you should continue, and if you choose to do so, ensure you have a support person available.

Rey's story is an immensely personal one for me and I would love for you to experience it, but not at the cost of your own health and wellbeing.

2.

I always include a link to the book's playlist—the songs that inspired the words—at the end. But this time, I've noted the songs that match the chapters so you can experience the soundtrack as you read.

The playlist can be found on Spotify here:
https://spoti.fi/2rdO7La

Now let your hair down, smudge that eyeliner, and get ready to rock, because the tour starts NOW!

ONE

REY

"Got the Life" - Korn

Fuck, I hate this city. Seems only appropriate the goddamn sky has seen fit to piss all over my arrival.

"How long do we have to layover here?" I scowl at our useless fucking manager, Rick, as he steps off the plane.

"Four days." His jaw works the same piece of gum he's chewed for the past three hours as he stares down at the puddles underfoot.

Cocky little shit only has his goddamn job because Daddy didn't have enough balls to stand up to Mommy when she demanded her baby boy get a position in the family business.

"Better have us staying in a hotel with a fuckin' five star rating this time," I toss over my shoulder as I shrug my jacket higher and leg it for the terminal. "I swear to God if some illiterate cunt wakes me up because they can't read the 'do not disturb' sign again, I'll murder them with it."

My brother Toby, our drummer, sighs as he passes a

seething Rick. His denim vest is pulled high over his bright orange-and-red hair in an effort to protect the goods. "Fuck off and have a smoke, would you?"

I flip him the bird, aware that we've already drawn a crowd at the terminal windows above. It's not all that often that a chartered plane comes in during a storm and regurgitates five denim-clad heathens and their cargo hold full of hard cases.

If Rick did his goddamn job right, we wouldn't be here all together. But apparently scheduling isn't his finest attribute. We were supposed to fly in tomorrow, ready to rehearse the next day prior to our two-show stopover, yet Rick, the goddamn legend, missed that flight entirely from the itinerary. He booked everything else: the venue, the accommodation, but not our fucking flights to get here. And being the middle of school vacation, the commercial liners were stacked.

I could hear his old man scream down the phone from ten feet away when Rick gave him the cost of our private plane.

"Hey, Rick." I turn and walk backward so I can jerk my chin at the asshole. "What exactly did Daddy say when you told him how much this flight set him back?"

His nostrils flare before he answers, water kicking up around his polished, pointy-toe boots in a fine mist. "He's making a few calls."

"To Mommy?"

His jaw sets hard. Toby punches me in the arm as the rest of the guys pour off the plane. Our bassist, Emery, skips the second to last step and narrowly misses face-planting his drunken ass.

"He might have a solution," Rick pipes up, drawing my focus back to him. "The added day could work out in our favor as far as recovering costs goes."

"Yeah?" I spin back around to face forward and shake my head. "Struggling to see how, my good man." The fuckhead's delusional. We're three shows into a twelve-stop tour. We're supposed to be gaining momentum, not derailing the fucking train before it's even reached full speed.

Some guy in a high visibility jacket opens the lower terminal door to let us in a private room they've set aside. Toby gives the guy a raised palm in thanks while I bowl on in to the heated haven. Rain and I don't mix. Pretty sure I had some traumatic experience with water as a kid; nothing else explains why I hate it so much. Swimming, baths, rain, and even a shower if it goes too long, all get me twitchy. Don't get me started about the pitchers of water the swanky hotels leave around the place. I only consume the wet shit because my vocal chords would dry up otherwise.

I shake my black denim jacket off and throw it over the nearest armchair. Toby makes a beeline for the coffeepot while Rick stands in the center of the makeshift room with his phone in hand, useless as a foreskin on a Jewish kid.

"Thank fuck that's over," Emery hollers as he tumbles onto a sofa. "Hostess wouldn't give me any more alcohol."

"Pretty sure you drank the plane dry," Kris, our lead guitarist, murmurs. The sullen fucker finds the darkest corner in the room and makes his emo ass at home.

I pull what's left of my smokes out of the pocket inside my jacket, and then shake out a stick. The tobacco teases my senses as I pinch it between my lips and check my pockets for my lighter. The chain on my belt rattles while I pat my way around my jeans, my frown growing deeper the more it becomes apparent I've lost the fucking thing. *Perfect.*

"Excuse me."

I look up to find the source of the sickly sweet voice. "What?" Some hostess that's young enough to still shit yellow gives me a well-practiced smile.

"I apologize, but this lounge is nonsmoking."

Toby laughs as he dumps sugar in his brew.

I throw a middle finger his way, gaze still on the baby deer in my headlights. "Got a flame for me, princess?"

She frowns, thrown by my question. My guess is that my kind of arrogance wasn't covered in her standardized training. "If you'd like to smoke, Sir, you'll need to exit the terminal building."

"Are you fuckin' jerking me?"

"Take it easy on the poor thing," Emery tosses up from his position laid out, eyes closed. "If my head didn't hurt so fuckin' much I'd take a look at her, but I'll judge by the voice alone she's a pretty little thing. Probably not used to assholes like you, Rey."

"I can show you to the exit, if you like," she says with a smile.

Oh, she's good. Young, but determined. "Nope. Pretty sure I can find my way out of here."

"You couldn't find your way out of a paper bag," Toby scoffs.

He has a point: my sense of direction is shit at the best of times. Swear that's some side effect of the tragic water incident; my inner ear has to be fucked or something. Still….

"Watch me."

I smirk at the hostess and reach out to bop her on the nose with my fingertip.

She jerks backward, personal bubble violated, and allows me space to head for what has to be the door out of here considering we walked in the only other one.

"Rey." *Fuck.*

"What, Rick?" The door handle mocks me with its brushed steel.

"Got our silver lining."

I sigh through my nose and turn to humor him. He smiles at me like a puppy proud for remembering to take a shit outside. "I'm waiting."

"We've got a venue for an intimate show day after tomorrow. IT put tickets up on the website while we were in the air, and they're already 60 percent sold. We shuffle rehearsal times around, and we add this in as a fan bonus."

"Rick," I say, jerking my head to the side with a wink. "I may just keep you on, you dashingly handsome bastard." Kris crosses the room and snatches the packet of smokes from my hand before busting through the door. "I'm off to find a sheltered spot to chain smoke with that moody fucker." I thumb over my shoulder. "When I get back, you can fill me in on the details."

The moron grins as Toby slings an arm around his shoulder, dwarfing him, and takes a swig of coffee.

Yeah. Rick pisses me off no end, but I can't deny one thing about him: his old man is what keeps my name on the end of everyone's tongue, and for that, I'd forgive the fuckwit for damn near anything.

TWO

TABITHA

"Symphony No. 7 in A Major"
– Ludwig van Beethoven

"What about this one?" I run my palms down the corset, a little uneasy at how tight it is once on.

The leather and lace ensemble looked kickass on the website I bought it from, but after seeing my short ass squeezed into it I'm convinced the model must be some six-foot Amazon princess. I qualify for one of those fail memes that float around Facebook daily.

"Ooo. That's hot. Where the hell did you get that?" My roommate, Kendall, kicks her boots over the end of the stubby two-seater and pivots to see me better. "I love the detail under the bust."

"You don't think it makes me look desperate?" I sidestep to catch a glimpse of my reflection in the living room window.

"It makes you look trendy."

"I don't want to be trendy."

She rolls her eyes. "Not in a following-the-herd kind of way, but an alternate I-don't-give-a-fuck-what-you-think way." Her black-rimmed eyes narrow. "Does that make sense?"

"I think so." My lips twist as I frown at her.

Thursday night is the turning point of my life. What I wear won't only show the people there to watch me play who I am, but it will set the tone for my brand. I've never had such a hard time choosing what to put on for a performance.

Fuck this shit.

"You're overthinking." Kendall reaches to the bowl of popcorn on the floor and grabs a handful before popping a few in her mouth. "I can see it."

"Yeah, well I can see your food when you talk with your mouth full."

She smirks at my cocked eyebrow. "How many tickets you sold now?"

"One hundred and eight."

"Hell yeah!" She lifts her hand for an air five.

I give it an air slap, yet my lack of smile gives away my true feelings on the subject. It's a good number, sure, but it's not even a fifth of the venue's capacity. I'm going to be competing for attention with the tumbleweeds that'll drift through the empty seats.

"Again," Kendall scolds. "You're in your head. Get out here. Stop it."

"It's just..." I pop the snaps on the corset. "It could be more."

"Your last performance was sixty-something, right?"

I nod.

"So, you've almost doubled your last event sales."

"That was close to a year ago." I ditch the torture

device and drag in a lungful of air. *Wonder if I can breathe enough to play with that thing on?*

"And in that time you've hustled your ass off to get more fans." She drops her feet from over the arm of the sofa and twists to sit upright. "Without making you feel shit, classical violin isn't exactly a hot genre of music, babe. You're doing well considering the uphill battle you have to get noticed."

She's right; I couldn't be more obscure in today's market of pop rock and R&B if I tried.

"Shit." My ass hits the sofa next to her. "My parents are fucking right, aren't they?"

"Pfft." Kendall slices a hand through the air. "Ignore them. You've already proved them wrong when they said you'd never be able to support yourself playing music."

I level her with a hard stare.

"Right." She chews her bottom lip, fighting a smile. "I never said you lived in luxury. A steady diet of ramen noodles is a thing."

"Bitch, please." I bury my face in my hands. "I think I'm going to be sick."

"It's just your nerves talking."

"Are you sure?" I moan as my phone rings out across the room. "Ugh."

Kendall's weight lifts from beside me, her footsteps heavy on our hardwood floor. "Screen says it's John."

"Ugh." I moan louder as I rise to my feet. "Now I'm certain I'm going to be sick."

She swipes across to answer before the call is lost and hands me my phone. I close my eyes and give the guy I took a chance on for publicity a greeting. "Hey, John."

"Hey, Tabitha. Sorry to call you so late, but I needed to get in touch before rehearsal tomorrow."

My gut bottoms out. "Why?" I can't keep the worry from my voice.

"Um, something came up at the venue. We've got a major issue."

"Tell me you have a solution." I meet Kendall's worried gaze and shrug.

"Not quite." He hesitates; the sound of what seems to be a pen tapping on a desk echoes down the line. "We have to reschedule."

"As in later in the night? The next day?"

"As in they're booked out for another two months before we can get in again."

I swallow hard, fingers pinched to the bridge of my nose as I squint my eyes shut. "Why 'again'? We're all ready to roll for Thursday. We've pushed this for—"

"I know. I know," he placates, cutting my complaints short. "But this is out of my hands."

"I paid you to set this up, John. How can it be out of your hands? This is your job," I damn near shout at the fucker.

"Yeah, well, sometimes the big dogs come and shit all over the small breed's yard, Tabitha. I can't do anything about it. The venue's been taken over by somebody with more money, more influence."

I spent every dollar I saved on this guy, adamant that representation would open the doors I couldn't. This isn't happening. *Nope.* Not believing it.

"Who?"

"Does it matter?"

Kendall slides a glass of wine across the counter to me. "Of course it fucking matters. You're telling me that we have to reschedule my biggest performance yet. You know how many of those people probably won't bother to come again if they have to rearrange everything?"

"Yeah, I know we'll lose a few."

"I can't afford to lose anyone!" My hand shakes as I throttle the stem of the glass. "Who did it? Who kicked me out?"

He pauses; the tapping stops also. "Dark Tide."

"You've got to be kidding me." I knock back half the glass before continuing. "I'm being ousted by a damn rock band?"

"A charting rock band. A top forty rock band. A rock band that shits gold. What did you expect me to do?"

Fuck—he's right. What the hell could a publicist such as John do? The kind of publicist a broke bitch like me could afford?

"I'm out of pocket on this too," he says quietly, as though testing the waters. "I'm frustrated as well, but I also know there isn't a damn thing I can do about it."

Not if he wants to keep his connections in the area happy. Not if he doesn't want to stir the pot. Me on the other hand? What do I fucking care about what a rock band think of me?

If they want to forget what it was like to start out, to have to drench yourself in sweat, blood, and tears to earn a name for yourself, then like hell I'm going to lie back and let them walk all over me.

Fuck that. Nobody sets fire to my dreams and gets away with it. Not when I've sacrificed so much to get where I am, even if that's relatively nowhere compared to the likes of them.

"Thanks for calling, John." Guess I can hang up the corset again. "I'll ring you tomorrow to go over what we do from here."

"I'm sorry. If there was something I could do, you know I would."

"It's not your fault. I appreciate you letting me know." I end the call and slide my phone across the counter.

"Tell me what the hell is going on," Kendall demands. "Why do you have to cancel?"

"Because Dark Tide have taken over the venue," I say in a daze.

She tops up my glass with what's left of our coveted last bottle. "What do you do now?"

I take a sip, still focused on the wall behind her. "Make their life hell."

THREE

REY

"Headstrong" - Trapt

"Will that rig stay up there?" Toby squints at the pipe steel that's mangled into what resembles a lighting bar over the auditorium. "It doesn't look certified."

"Not our problem," Emery states as he takes long strides down the aisle, hands trailing over the top of the red velvet chairs.

Arms folded, I stand at the double door entrance and frown at Rick. "This place is kind of posh, ain't it?"

"You mean, it's not a stadium with plastic fold-away chairs?"

"Yeah. That too."

Emery launches himself with a hop and a step onto the seats, balancing like an acrobat on the high wire as he steps across the backs to head for the stage.

"Get the fuck off," Kris grumbles, trying and failing to push him face-first into the seating.

"They usually hold theater productions, small classical concerts, that kind of thing here." Rick unwraps a stick of gum, popping it in his mouth as I walk a little further into the place to check out the balcony above us. "But like I said, it's an intimate performance, so this suits the vibe."

"The vibe?" I snarl my lip as I mimic the moron. "What exactly is our *vibe*, Rick?"

"The tickets were invite only to the Ultimate Fans. An email went out, and a text alert for those who'd signed up to let them know about it."

"Why the fuck would they want to come here when they can watch us at a fucking stadium with all the pyro and shit?" I drop a sigh as Toby steps between Kris and Emery, attempting to split them up before fists are thrown.

He shouldn't bother—Emery couldn't hit the broad side of a barn while he's sober. Give the fucker an hour or two, and we've got cause for concern, but it's barely after breakfast—he hasn't finished his first bottle yet.

I turn to scowl at Rick when he doesn't answer my question. Asshole has his phone in hand, scrolling what looks like one hell of a skin-orientated Instagram feed. *Must remember to check out what accounts he follows, later.*

"Ahem."

His head snaps up, the screen black in a flash. "What?"

"You were telling me why our diehards would waste their time on this museum-smelling dump."

"They get first access to the album when it drops."

"They what?" Toby joins in our cryptic conversation.

"Yeah." Rick eyes the two of us as though *we're* the crazy ones. "They get a code to download it for free."

"Fuck off." I feel around for my smokes. "And what's stopping them sharing it with friends?"

"Each one is specific to the fan, and only works once." Kid looks proud of himself.

Toby lifts an eyebrow. "That's pretty smart, really."

"If it works." I rip my pack out and stuff a stick between my lips.

Yeah, it is smart. Any asshole decides to hock off our album free, or pirate it, and the file gets traced back to them. Still—I'm not about to rub Rick's ego and let him know he's done well in a hurry.

Especially when it was probably his old man who thought up the clause.

"Do we get to choose the set list?" I locate the lighter I picked up from the airport souvenir shop.

"I think so." Rick frowns, lifting a finger to Toby. "Be right back."

I roll my eyes as he ducks to a quiet corner to phone Daddy. Seriously. Some days I wonder if he shits on his father's schedule, too.

Totally never having kids if that's how rich brats turn out.

"Can we help you?" Toby squints behind me.

I spin to find a distinctively feminine form silhouetted against the blinding morning sun that fills the foyer. *Great.* A fucking groupie who's sniffed out an opportunity to get close.

"Where the hell is our security, Rick?" I holler across the auditorium.

Kris and Emery quit their bellyaching on-stage and turn their attention to the newcomer.

Rick hustles between the seats as he pockets his phone. "You can't be in here, love. I'm sorry."

He reaches for the shadow of a girl, presumably to guide her out the way she came in. Yet the sassy little thing whips her arm away and marches her pert little butt down the aisle, right past Toby and me as though we don't exist.

Who the fuck even does that? Acts as though we don't exist, I mean.

"I'll only be a minute," she throws out to nobody in particular.

"Lady, this is a closed rehearsal." I track the woman down the aisle, ignoring the fact she has one hell of a set of legs on her, and try to get the bitch to stop walking.

"Rehearsal?" She shoots a pouty-lipped smirk over her shoulder, and then promptly launches herself onto the stage. "Where are your instruments?"

"Coming," I lamely protest. *Losing your touch, boy.*

Kris and Emery split, backing up a step each as she plows a path between them to a small road case shoved in the dark recesses of the stage.

"You can't just walk in and take what you want." I jab a hand at the trunk as she lifts the lid. "Woman, just stop fuckin' messing with other people's shit for a second would you?"

She snaps the locks closed again, and then hefts its bulk into her arms.

"You want a hand with that?" Kris murmurs. *Ever the fucking gentleman.*

"I'm fine." She forces a smile for him. "Thank you."

"You shouldn't be helping her steal shit, you douche,"

Toby teases from beside me.

"Can't steal it if it's mine, right?" Her slightly raised eyebrows dare any of us to challenge her.

"What the fuck is your shit doing in here?" I ask. "And how do I know it's yours anyway?"

The svelte little thing dumps the case down on the stage between Kris and Emery with a loud thud. The metal corner brackets scratch on the painted surface as she spins it around to show a name etched into the panel above the lock.

Tabitha Reeves

"Am I supposed to know that's you, let alone who the fuck you are?" I cross my arms, ignoring the elbow from Toby.

Small and petite Tabitha reaches into her back pocket and produces a wallet. *What chick stashes her wallet in her back pocket like a guy?* Weirdo. She flicks it open and then throws it down on the edge of the stage.

Like I'm playing into her game. *Pfft.* I turn my head to the side, refusing to look at the ID.

Toby does instead. He retrieves the wallet, nodding as he holds it out for me to see. "Legit."

Like the petulant fuckhead I am, I lift my chin to avoid making eye contact with it. "Take your word for it."

Toby hands the closed wallet back to our mystery chick, and then steps back from the stage as she shunts it back in her pocket. I eyeball her as she bends to retrieve the road case. If she hadn't barreled in here like a snowball starting an avalanche, I might have been more interested at the start. But it's only now when she's distracted that I let myself steal a good fucking look.

She's small—I noticed that much already. But she's also tidy as fuck. Short, bobbed hair that frames her sharp jaw, slim waist and hips that hold more cushion than most of the stick-thin groupies we see backstage. A man has to appreciate a woman who can rock a little meat on her bones. She wears a plain enough outfit: black skinny jeans and a dark gray tank, but what makes her stand out are the boots loosely laced around her ankles: they have lilac music notes literally stitched into the leather. *Cool.*

"Why was your shit here, anyway?" I ask again.

Tabitha hesitates halfway to the side of the stage and levels me with a cool glare that could fucking freeze the balls off an Eskimo. "I *was* playing here." Her gaze drifts over my head, her focus scary as she eyes what I can only assume to be Rick. I half expect her to drop the road case and whip a semi-automatic out of it. "You don't look like one of the band."

Rick steps forward, hand wringing his phone. "I'm their manager."

"You set this concert up for them?"

"I might have," he murmurs.

All eyes switch to me when I bark a laugh. "You lost your balls there, Rick?"

"What's your cut of it then?" Tabitha asks, unfazed by my remark.

"Oh, I don't get a share of profit," Rick splutters. "My fee is fixed."

"No bonus then?" she presses. "No incentive to add more shows into the tour?"

He shakes his head while I rest my ass against the edge of the chair behind me.

"Interesting." Her lips curl down at the corners.

"Wh-why do you ask?" Rick frowns a little at her.

Kris motions for the smokes. I pull the pack out and toss it to him. Tabitha watches the interaction before answering.

"Just wondered what it took to buy out your conscience is all."

Kris drops off the edge of the stage as she makes her way down the steps on the other side, and then hands me the pack while he watches her leave.

I shove it in my pocket and follow the fiery little thing as she heads out of the auditorium. "What do you mean by that?"

"Ask *Rick.*" She spits his name, refusing to look at me as I catch up.

"Rick?" I holler back to where he still stands by the stage. "Why is she pissed at you?"

"Because I doubled what she paid to take the venue."

That's cold. Even I wouldn't be that much of a cunt. At least, I don't think I would. "Fuck, man."

I turn to go after Tabitha and dig a little deeper, find out a bit more about this ballsy fucking woman, but as quickly as she appeared, she's vanished.

"Sucks to be her," Kris mumbles.

I shunt the fucker in the back of the shoulder with a flat palm. "No shit. Now come on. I need something to go with this smoke."

FOUR

TABITHA

"Zero" – The Smashing Pumpkins

"You did what?" Kendall slides a latte in front of me, and then promptly drops into the seat on the opposite side of the table.

"What the hell are you sitting down for? You're working, buddy."

She rests her chin on the back of one hand. "Yeah, and you have gossip. So make it quick before I'm busted."

I take a sip of the caffeine goodness, and then lick the foam off my lip before I explain. "I figured if they want to jerk my dreams out from under me, then they may as well see the very real, very human face behind the name they fucked over."

"So you stormed in the venue to play the guilt card?"

"I retrieved my equipment," I say primly.

Kendall hooks an eyebrow. "You didn't have anything there."

"Yeah I did." I pat the box at my feet. "This trusty old case here. Gave me reason to walk in when they arrived."

Kendall leans back in her seat, eyes narrow. "Is this why you left the apartment early?"

I nod.

"You stalked them?"

"I studied them."

"You're a nutter, you know that?" She smiles. "So, what did they do?"

"*Kendall!*"

"Fuck." She jolts from the seat, standing at my side as though she takes my order. "Give the rundown to me in ten seconds or less, otherwise I'll be sharing your noodles."

"What do you think the guys did?" I scoff. "They acted like the stuck-up assholes they are."

"Jesus, baby." I freeze at the husky voice behind me. "That's a bit harsh."

Kendall stands with her notepad in hand, eyes wide. The nib draws a squiggly line across the paper as her arm drops, along with her jaw.

I extend my leg under the table to kick her shin. "He's behind me, isn't he?"

"You're on your own with this one, babe; I have to get back to work." She pulls her jaw back, lips tight with an "oh shit" grimace, and then darts across the shop to serve an old couple in the back corner.

"You started without us." The dark-haired cocky bastard from before makes a show of moving my road case so he can sit in the seat adjacent to mine.

The quiet guy who offered to help me carry it heads for the counter, and is immediately assailed by some desperate woman with a napkin.

"You're really something, huh?" I muse as I lift my coffee to take a sip.

"I like to think so." His gaze bores into mine despite the fact the horn bag with the napkin is lining him up in her sights. "What kind of music do you play?"

"What do you care?"

We enter what appears to be a staring contest while he formulates his answer; piercing eyes fix firmly on me as I hold my coffee to my chest. His black hair is spiked haphazardly, yet a few loose tendrils across his face give him the mysterious edge that I imagine his groupies love. The T-shirt he wears is torn, fashionably so, and just enough that I can get a glimpse as the ink he hides below.

I sip my coffee with a smirk.

He leans forward, the studded cuff on his left wrist making a soft clink as it hits the timber surface.

"Ohmygod," the horn bag breathes in one rushed syllable as she arrives at my table. "I can't believe you're in here."

The cocky asshole drags his gaze from me and smiles at her, laying on the charm. "Good place to get a coffee, right?"

"The best," she gushes, oblivious to the intense standoff she interrupted.

I sit back and sip my latte, sizing up the woman. She seems to be in her late twenties, early thirties at most. What surprises me is that she's dressed like a soccer mom. Not exactly what I'd expect a fan of a man kitted out in denim, leather, and enough chains to rival a prison warden to look like.

"Can you sign this?"

"Kris leave me any room?" He takes the napkin from her, brushing his fingers over hers.

The woman damn near comes on the spot. *Slick move, asshole.*

"I think there's a space up here." And in one swift move, Soccer Mom transforms to Desperate Housewife with the tilt of her hips. The blouse that mere seconds ago demurely hid her assets now hangs like a slack sail in the Dead Sea, giving the cocky asshole to my left the perfect view of her ample tits.

Shoot me if I ever turn into one of those.

"Thanks." He takes the pen she offers and then scratches a quick message for her like he probably has a million times before.

She leaves with her smile a little wider, and her panties more than likely a darn sight wetter.

"Excuse me." I pull my phone out, amused to find him frowning at me in my periphery.

"What are you doing?" He leans closer to see my screen, wafting what has to be pure pheromones under my nostrils. *How the fuck do they make men's cologne so addictive?*

"I'm googling your name, since you won't introduce yourself properly."

He laughs, the rich sound traveling throughout the shop as his bandmate, Kris, returns with a table number.

"Shouldn't you have like a private coffee shop, or something?" I sass. "Don't celebrities like you get places shut down so they can drink in peace?" The result comes up on my screen, along with an assortment of very hot performance shots. *Damn, this man can rock studs.*

"She's kidding right?" Kris mumbles to the cocky asshole.

"I don't think so." He smiles at me, leaning back casually in his seat. "I can't believe you don't know my name." The jerk spreads his legs wide, a denim-clad knee perilously close to my thigh.

"Do you know every stranger you meet's name?" I lift an eyebrow at him. "*Rey?*"

"Babe, I'm not a stranger." Fucker still smiles. "I haven't had to introduce myself for the past four and half years."

"Since we first made Billboard," Kris adds quietly.

I like him. He's not in-your-face like this jackass to my left. He's quiet, humble even. *He* actually makes me want to hold a conversation with him.

Rey, on the other hand…. "You're a little full of your-self, aren't you?"

Kris smiles behind his linked hands, elbows on the table.

"Would *you* prefer to be full of me?" Rey wiggles a pierced eyebrow.

"You have to be shitting me," I mumble, looking away.

"You never answered my question, *Tabitha*," Rey taunts. "Or can I call you Tabby, since you're like a wild cat, all claws and snarl?"

I almost smile at his comment… *almost.*

"Tabitha." I look back at the guy, pissed at myself for recognizing that he is in fact pretty damn good-looking. *Bastard.* "And I play classical. A little bit of crossover."

"Classical." Rey looks like he's fit to burst. "People still listen to that?"

"They do." I give him a hard stare, and then shift focus to Kris. "In all honesty, I am surprised you two don't have security or some kind of protection if you're that shit hot."

He lifts an inked finger and points to a burly guy outside the shop. If I didn't know better, I'd think the man was Joe Public. He's big, sure, but he's dressed in sweats and a T-shirt. No earpiece, no Secret Service-style shades. He just looks... normal.

"I think his name's Pete," Kris mumbles. "He turned up late. Hence why you got in."

"You *think* his name is Pete?" I snort a laugh.

"He's not our normal crew," Rey fills in. "Hired while we're in town."

"Oh." Frustrated by how quickly the conversation has turned comfortable, I redirect back to the issue at hand. "Can I ask why you're at my table?"

"We need coffee." Rey shrugs.

"At *my* table, though?"

"Figured we got off on the wrong foot." He wrinkles his nose. It's cute. *No it's not. Focus, Tab.*

"Can't blame me for that." I take a nonchalant sip of my coffee... and promptly choke on a bubble of foam that gets stuck on the roof of my mouth near my throat. *Slick.*

"Can't blame us, either," Rey retorts.

It's okay, asshole. I don't need a pat on the back or anything. Just unable to breathe for a beat there, but you just take it easy, okay?

"Rick organized the whole thing," he finishes, unfazed

by the tears teetering on the rims of my eyes.

"You okay?"

"Yeah, Kris. I am now. Thanks." I wipe the moisture away before I end up looking bat-shit crazy with mascara down my face.

"Where you from?"

"Pardon?" I glare at Rey.

"Your accent. You're not American."

I give the muppet a slow clap.

His nostrils flare when a few customers look across at our table. "Are you Austral—"

I lift a palm to stop him. "Don't say it."

"What?"

"Don't you dare assume I'm Australian. There's more than one country down there, you know."

He stares at me, blank. *Fuck my life.*

"Kris, help him out here." I down the last of my coffee.

"New Zealand," he murmurs to Rey.

"Oh." His face stays blank as a clean slate.

"You've heard of it, right?" I ask.

"Of course I have," he scoffs.

"But you didn't know where it was."

He smiles, and damn it all if that doesn't make me do so too. *Stay strong.* I can't fawn over this guy like every other female on the planet, not when my objective is to make his life hell. *Not that I know how I'm going to do that just yet.*

"Geography was never my thing," he explains as Kendall brings their drinks over.

She sets Rey's down first, and then throws me a sneaky look behind his back before setting Kris's before him.

"Later," I mouth while both boys are distracted adding sugar.

She gives me her *don't test me* eye, and then leaves.

"Well," I announce, pushing my empty cup to the middle of the table. "This has been swell, guys, but I really must press on."

I get halfway to my feet before a strong hand to my thigh shunts me back in the chair. *Holy hell, that was intense.*

"Sit." Rey stirs his coffee, eyes on the amber swirl. "I'm not finished with you yet."

Kris shrugs and then promptly lifts his drink as though I haven't just been ordered around like one of their staff.

"Last I checked," I say, "I'm free to leave when I want."

"Guess you got it wrong, then." He lifts both eyebrows before shifting his dark eyes toward me. "How many tickets had you sold?"

"A bit over one hundred."

I avoid his gaze, waiting on the laugh that's sure to follow.

"How many over?"

To my surprise Rey watches me intently, eager for my answer.

"Nine. I sold one more right before you officially dropped the anvil on my dreams."

He frowns at my sarcastic smile, and then looks toward Kris. "Rick said he left the top empty, huh?"

"I think so."

"Cool." Rey rolls his lips, seeming to think something over. "I'm sure we could swing it."

"Swing what?" Kris frowns.

"Yeah. What?" I settle back into my seat.

"Don't you worry yourself, little lady." He reaches out and bops his index finger on the tip of my nose. "I've got you covered."

REY

"Still Counting" - Volbeat

Rick drops his feet off the coffee table as I walk into the hotel room, Kris in tow. Our new buddy, Pete, gives a mock salute before shutting the door behind us as he leaves.

"Got a job for you, Momma's boy." This shit is going to be epic.

Rick straightens in his seat, arm slung over the back as I toss the napkin down on the table.

"Ring this guy. Like, now. And make sure Tabitha's tickets don't get refunded."

"Um. Why?" He leans forward to retrieve the number Tabby wrote down for me.

Yeah. I know she said not to call her that, but damn. *Meow.* Hot little thing suits it.

"She's opening for us." And proving my point while she's at it.

"Uh, Rey," Kris murmurs, "you never told *her* that."

I throw my hand up in a mock pistol at him. "That's because she would have said no." I bop the thumb hammer.

"She's kind of a key ingredient, if you could even pull the whole thing off."

"Pull what off?" Toby wanders into the room, shirtless and barefoot.

The man would get around nude if he had half the chance.

"Little Tabby-cat is opening for us. That way she gets her concert, and we do this publicity thingamajig for the fans." I give him a wicked smile. "And when our fans boo her Beethoven-loving ass off the stage, then we get free entertainment too."

"You're an asshole." He frowns. "What does she play exactly?"

"Violin," Kris mumbles.

"Vi-what?" Toby laughs. "Violin and rock? Mm-kay. I can see why you think this would be a disaster." He lifts an eyebrow and wanders over to where Rick frowns at his phone. "What does Daddy say about this?"

"He doesn't know yet," Rick answers absently, thumb tapping the screen. "He's about to find out... now." He beats the screen with finality and tosses his phone down.

I retrieve it and throw it back in his lap. "Ring the publicist dude. Now."

"I need the go-ahead before I can jack something like this up," Rick protests. "I can't just change everything on a whim."

"Why the fuck not?"

"There are things you need to do first. Rules to follow."

"Fuck rules." Since when have we got anywhere by obeying the rules? "Just call the guy and get him to hold off on canceling everything in the very least, okay?"

"Rey, man?"

"What?" I snap my gaze to Toby.

"What does it matter if it's canceled? She'll get another spot. If you're doing this just to fuck with her—"

"Place is booked for three months, or some shit," Kris explains as he pops his earbuds in. "She needs the cash before then."

"How do you two know all this?" Toby drops onto the arm of the seat beside Rick.

"We had a chat." I shrug, turning for the mini bar. "Just ring that fucker, Rick, and let me know what your old man says when you get a reply."

I reach over and snag a whiskey, thankful the assholes in this pricey place include full-size bottles, and head for the balcony. Toby skids between the door and me, bare feet grazing over the plush carpet.

"Nope."

"What the hell, man?"

He bars the slider with his arm. "Last time you went out on a balcony to drink, you tried to jump off it."

"I was in a dark place," I level. "Now move."

"Mm-mm." He shakes his head. "How do I know you're not in a dark place now?"

I stare at the well-meaning asshole impassively. "Because I haven't just finished writing lyrics for an album. I've had a break already."

"A few months." He stays rooted to the spot. "Is that enough?"

"If I wanted to jump, I'd do it when none of you cunts are here to stop me."

"Good to know." He lifts both eyebrows and snaps his fingers to get Kris's attention. "We're on Rey-watch."

"I don't need a babysitter, man. Now move. I'm dying for a fucking cigarette."

"I'll join you then." Toby twists and opens the slider, gesturing for me to go first. "And for the record, we're not babysitters—we're caregivers."

"So much better." I roll my eyes as I set the bottle on the small table and retrieve my smokes.

"Plus," he continues, "you bite the big one and we all suffer. Can't play a fucking set without our singer, can we?"

"Kris can sing," I point out as I spark my stick.

Toby grins. "He won't fucking speak up around us, let alone do a goddamn solo interview. And you think he'd stand in front of five thousand people and sing?"

"Turn all the lights off." I point my smoke at him. "He sings in the dark. You've heard him, right?"

Toby nods.

The slider scuffs as it opens, Rick poking his head out. "Dad wants numbers."

"Numbers for what?" Toby asks.

"And for fuck's sake," I add, "call him Wallace. It's just fucked when you call him dad with us."

"Wallace sounds weird, though." Rick curls his lip.

"Dad sounds like we're playing a concert in your garage."

He tips his head in assent. "I guess."

"Numbers for what?" Toby repeats.

"Oh." Rick checks the message on his phone. "How many tickets she'd sold."

"One hundred." I drag the smoke almost to the filter.

"Thanks." Rick shuts the door behind him, tapping as he walks away.

Kris sits in the distance, head over the back of the sofa as he loses himself in the playlist. It's a ritual of his: listen to our set list in order three times each day before the show so he doesn't feel as though he'll fuck it up on stage. Anxiety. Fuck knows how the asshole functions some days.

Still—he's killer with an axe, and that's what matters most.

"Why you doing this?" Toby eyes me as he turns the bottle on the table between his pinched fingers. "When are you going to start giving a fuck about the people you trample on to get where you are?"

"Ouch, bro."

"I'm serious." He cocks an eyebrow. "If there's one thing that's kept me busy in our journey to where we are, it's making sure you don't stick your neck out a little too far. You're an arrogant asshole man." He smirks. "Said in the most loving way."

"Compliment taken," I murmur, giving him the side eye. "Somebody in the family had to be the jackass so you'd get all the charm." He rolls his eyes. "I don't know why I'm doing it though." I tap the end of my cigarette and watch as the last of the ash falls to the balcony floor. "She just...." I shrug. "It doesn't matter."

Truth is, I don't know. Not like she's done anything to me to deserve it. I just have an inane need to prove that my epic music is what the people want, not her vintage bullshit.

"Buddy." Toby punches me in the arm as I swipe up the bottle of liquor. "Everything matters when it comes to you."

"What you trying to say?" I tease, opening the sliding door.

"You're high maintenance, man. Fucking high maintenance." He smirks. "You're lucky we're related, otherwise I probably would have told your diva ass to get fucked years ago."

"I'm the lead, brother. It's in my job description to be a diva."

"Lucky it comes naturally then, huh?"

SIX

TABITHA

"Enemies" - Shinedown

The number displayed on my phone's calculator taunts me with its three figures. I worked out what would be brought in from the ticket sales, took the expenses off, and then subtracted John's share to find what I would have earned out of this show.

I couldn't even make it into the thousands.

Fucking Dark Tide would probably be able to sell an empty toilet roll for a grand. *Bastards.* At least if they do what I'm guessing Rey plans to, it won't put them out much to reimburse me lost earnings.

"What are you doing?" Kendall snatches my phone from my grasp, leaving it on the counter where she enters the kitchen. "Put this fucking thing away for a bit."

"I could have been sending an important email, you know." I reach for the device, only to have her slap my hand away.

"You were in the calculator. Again."

"So?"

"So stop pining over the money you don't have, and focus on earning the real thing."

I glare at her as she pulls yoghurt from the fridge. She makes it sound so easy. "That concert would have been the real thing."

"But it's not, so face forward and work on the next gig."

She means well, but, "Are you always this bitter in the morning, or is it just because you haven't had coffee yet?"

Her lips curl on one side as she pours the yoghurt into a bowl. "I'm dishing out tough love, babe. You shouldn't sulk about what you can't change. Didn't you tell me that John said he would have fixed things if it were possible? You had your fun with the rock star guy, now leave him to be an entitled douchebag and rise above."

Fuck's sake. She's right, but I'm not ready to "rise above" yet. I want to wallow in my anger and bitterness a little longer.

"We're going out today." Kendall shovels a spoonful of creamy mixture in her mouth.

I lean over and replace the lid on the container, and then slide off the barstool to take it back to the fridge for her. "Where?"

"I dunno," she mumbles around a mouthful before swallowing. "We'll go sit at the mall and try to guess what people are there to buy."

As much as the thought of our favorite cost-free pastime makes me smile, I shake my head and face her with a lifeless stare. "I'd rather hang out and binge whatever's on TV."

"Nope." She finishes her last mouthful. "Not having it."

"We're broke, Kendall. What the fuck do you propose we do?"

Her eyes light up, and I just know it's going to be insane, whatever she thinks.

"We'll go stalk your band buddies."

"Ugh. No. I did that yesterday, and it backfired."

Her nose crinkles. "Then we do it better. I didn't say we'd do it to get revenge on them like you wanted to, anyway. We're doing it purely because we're bored, you need to get out of the house, and I think they're fucking sexy." She bites her bottom lip before adding, "Especially that quiet one."

"I think he's socially stunted or something." I drop my head back with a groan, staring up at the watermarked ceiling. "We're not doing it, okay? The sight of them is liable to make me murderous. Besides, didn't you just tell me, like a second ago, to leave them alone?"

"I said to leave that Rey guy alone, not all of them." She rolls her eyes. "Fine. We can go see if that cute guy is working the panini stand at the park today."

"Why does every plan of yours involve going out, and men?"

She looks at me wide-eyed as though the answer is obvious. "Vitamin D is good for you, babe. So is admiring hot guys."

"For you maybe." I shoot her a displeased frown and trudge from the room. "How long do I have?"

"Half an hour." She sidesteps to see me down the

hallway. "Put something short and sexy on."

"Short how?" I holler back as I step into my bombsite of a room.

"I don't care. Short top, short skirt, short shorts: whatever makes you irresistible. We'll see if we can get free paninis."

"Kendall," I whine, flopping onto my bed face-first. "Why? Why do you do this to me?"

She startles the fuck out of me when she speaks from my doorway. "Because you're young, you're pretty, and its just downright sad watching you waste away like a bitter old spinster."

"I like being a spinster," I groan into the bedding. "Let me wallow in my self-pity."

She takes hold of my arm and rolls me over. "Harden the fuck up, princess."

"Your hands are like goddamn ice." I swat them away, fending off the slouch top she tosses at me.

"Put that on. And your faux-leather booty shorts. Sexy, yet demure. You can't go wrong with that."

Ugh.

I emerge from my room fifteen minutes later to a dissatisfied sigh from Kendall. "What the fuck is that?"

"It's comfort in troubling times, is what it is." I readjust my baggy sweater so it covers my ass a bit more. "I have the shorts on. I compromised."

"You look like a hobo in those worn boots."

"And you look desperate," I counter, gesturing to her tube top and tight skirt.

She scowls, and then thrusts my phone at me. "You

missed a call, little miss sunshine."

"How the hell did I not hear it?" I check the display to find John's name.

"You left it on silent." Kendall snatches up her purse, and then steers me to the door with a hand on my shoulder. "Ring him on the way."

"Why?" I pocket the device and open the apartment door. "He probably wants to tell me when the next available booking is. I don't want to know how far away it is, yet."

Yep. I'm still sulking. What of it?

"You're so fucking depressing," Kendall moans as she locks the door behind us. "You need to lighten up."

"Give me reason to."

As though on cue, my phone vibrates in my pocket. I slide it out and pick up John's call before it goes to voice mail again. "Hey."

"Good. I got you this time."

"Why? What's the urgency?" I sass.

Kendall leads us out onto the street while I talk.

"Tell me you're still in the city," John asks.

"I'm still in the city."

He sighs at my smart-ass response. "Are you really?"

"Yes." I roll my eyes as we turn right and head downtown. "Why?"

"You're still on."

I halt, earning a frown from Kendall. "I'm what?"

"You're still playing." He can barely contain his excitement.

"Stop fucking with me, John. When? When am I playing?"

"Tomorrow night."

My silence urges him on.

"I got a call from Dark Tide's manager, and he said they want you to open for them."

"Look," I snap. "I appreciate you're trying to break me out of this mood with black humor, but fuck it, John, I wanted that concert. Playing a prank isn't going to cheer me up."

"It's not a prank," he levels. "They're serious. I don't know what the hell happened—maybe they looked you up on YouTube—but they want you to open for their concert. It's only a few people, not as big as they're used to, but it's good for you."

"And the tickets we sold?" I slouch against the front of the building.

Kendall stands before me, hands on hips.

"They get transferred over."

Holy shit. "How does that even work?" I ask. "I play classical, they're rock."

"I don't know. I'm the messenger, that's all. You need to talk to them about the logistics. I'll email you their contact details in a few."

"Thanks, I guess." I'm still hesitant to believe it. None of it makes sense.

"I'll be in touch later."

John disconnects, leaving me staring at the phone in my hand.

"What's happened?"

I look up and meet Kendall's concerned eyes. "I'm still playing."

"Huh?"

"I'm opening for Dark Tide."

"Holy shit."

Yep. Holy shit.

SEVEN

REY

"Self Esteem" – *The Offspring*

"Did she get the news?" I crowd Rick into a corner while we wait on the lift.

He gently urges me back a step with a finger to my shoulder. "I spoke with her publicity guy, so I guess so."

"You didn't talk to her yourself?"

"No," Rick drones. "I didn't exactly ask for her personal number."

I stare the fucker down as the signal dings to say our ride has arrived, working out whether I'd get punished for laying him out or not.

"Come on." Rick steps into the lift as the doors slide open. "The others are waiting on us."

I follow him in, pulling a face. Fuckers can wait as long as they have to. Not as though there's any practice without me to sing, is there?

"We've got two hours there, and then I have to rush you guys over to a radio interview at four." He drops the facts while staring at his phone.

"Epic." I fucking hate radio interviews.

At least when there's a camera on you, you can act up and show personality through gestures. Clown around. Radio... I hate it. Listening to myself afterwards always gives me hell; I sound dull as an unstrung drum.

"Find out if she knows," I instruct. "She'll need to come in and do a sound check."

"I've got the guys jacked up to do that in the morning."

I nod, aiming for nonchalance, but eh, kind of hoped she'd show this afternoon.

"About time, fuckers," Toby exclaims as our lift opens on the lobby.

Kris rises from one of the plush sofas with his phone in hand, our bassist nowhere to be seen.

"Where the hell is Em?"

Toby's face falls as he thumbs in the direction of the hotel bar. "Pete's gone to get him."

"And here you are bitching about waiting on me." I join Kris as he drops back into the seat. "How long has he been in there?"

Now that I think about it, I haven't seen him since we checked out the venue yesterday.

"Can't be sure." Toby rubs the back of his neck. "Possibly this morning?"

"Possibly last night," Kris mumbles.

"Fuck it." I push to my feet and head off in the direction of the alcohol. If a hulk of a man like Pete hasn't got the idiot out here yet, then it ain't happening anytime soon without some not-so-gentle verbal persuasion.

I make it as far as the door to the dimly lit lounge before I'm recognized. *Fuck fame.*

"Rey!"

I ignore the blonde thing and keep hustling.

"Rey, you goddamn moron."

Hey, now.... I whirl on the woman and get a weird sense of déjà vu. "What did you call me?" Where the fuck is Pete when you need him?

Oh, yeah... thanks, Em.

"Seriously? Is your memory that lousy?" She lifts a perfectly shaped eyebrow.

Curvy little thing looks quite delicious in a figure-hugging skirt and top thingy.

"Have we...?" I flick a finger between us. Her lips flatten, and it dawns on me where the fuck I've seen her before. "Café girl!"

"Yeah," she drones. "Café girl. Anyway—"

"I'd love to stop and chat, but babe, I'm a little busy. Another time, yeah?"

Her hands stamp her hips. This bitch isn't amused. "Busy doing what?"

A holler drifts from inside the lounge bar. Her darkly made up eyes shift in the direction of the ruckus.

"That." I thumb toward the bar. "Nice seeing you again, though."

She catches my arm as I step away. "No. You're not blowing me off that easy. Tabitha's looking for you."

"She's here?" *Fuck.* Did that sound as eager as I think it did?

Judging by the wide-eyed stare I'm currently receiving, it did. *Damn.*

"Yeah. She's at the reception, trying to get ahold of you."

I snort. "Good luck with that." We don't pay extra under the table for the hotel staff to give our whereabouts out to any old person off the street.

The doors to the lounge bar burst open, Pete hustling one very inebriated Emery out of the place in an arm bar while the moron sings Offspring's "Self Esteem" as loud as he fucking can.

Shit.

"Follow." I gesture for Café Girl to tag along, half-jogging to catch up with Pete so I can clip Emery around the back of the head. "What the fuck, man?"

"Hey," he greets with a huge smile. His free hand fumbles against his jeans, his fucking feet tangling in themselves. The only thing that saves him from going down face-first is Pete's hold on him. "Check this out." Somehow, amongst the tangle of limbs and scuffed feet, he manages to pull his phone out.

I take it from him, wrinkling my nose at the home screen. "You rearranged your apps?"

"Nah." He chuckles as Pete dumps him on the sofa beside Kris's. "Open Messenger."

"Don't go anywhere," Café Girl murmurs, leaning in close. "I'll go get Tabitha."

"Tabitha?" Toby asks, watching the tidy thing as she hustles across the lobby.

"Yeah, Tabby." I fight the urge to look up and search her out, focusing instead on the most recent message in Emery's inbox. *Bitch.* No wonder he's a fucking mess.

"I'm going to buy her a ticket, man," Em rambles, spread-eagled over the cushions. "Bring her out to join us for the rest of the tour."

"Fuck off," Kris mutters.

He hates the manipulating piece of shit as much as I do. Fuck, as much as all of us do.

"She's not coming anywhere near the tour," I snap, tossing the phone back at him.

It ricochets off his arm, leaving him in a heap on the floor as he tries to retrieve it. "Come on, Rey."

"Come on, nothing. If she wants to play fuckin' mind games with you when we're home, then fine. But you're not flying her here to do it."

"Jesus, man," Toby says with a frown. "You'd spend a grand to bring the bitch here?"

"We're getting married," Em states as though it's the solve-all for his love fiasco. "I haven't asked her yet, but she'll say yes."

"And I thought *I* was a suicidal masochist," Kris mumbles, still engrossed in his phone.

"We all done here?" Rick looks hopefully toward our ragtag bunch, completely unaware of the storm that approaches behind him.

"What's the end game, Rey?" Tabitha blazes past our manager as though he's not even there. "Why would you have me opening for you?"

"Hi, Tabby." I grin at her, thumbs hooked in the pockets of my jeans. "Nice to see you again, too."

"Fuck hellos." She thrusts her arms across her chest, enhancing the ladies. "Why are you doing this?"

I shrug. "Seemed like a fair compromise."

"Was it your idea?" She takes a look around at the group, scowling when her gaze lands on Emery and his goofy grin. "Or did one of these muppets come up with it?"

"Muppet." Emery dissolves into girly giggles on the floor.

"My idea." I hook a hand around her elbow, ignoring the buzz it leaves in my palm. "Now hustle. We're late for sound check."

"What?" Her boots dig in to the carpet. "Sound check?"

"Yeah." I wink at Toby as he slings an arm around Café Girl's shoulders and guides her toward the exit. "You know how it works, babe. You sing, the sound geeks do their shit, and we all come up smelling of roses on the night."

"I know what a sound check is," she bites out. "I don't have my violin, though."

"Easy." I give Emery a kick in the shin to get him moving as I walk us by. "We'll go pick it up."

"This isn't why I came here." Tabby jerks her arm free of my hold.

I catch the warning stare Kris gives me as he sets himself in motion.

"Why *are* you here, then?" I ask. "Can't be just to ask me why I'd let you open for us."

Her eyes stay focused on me, and yet her thoughts seem to be a thousand miles away as she stays mute.

"You don't know, do you?"

Epic. Girl's stuck on me already; she just doesn't realize it yet.

EIGHT

TABITHA

"My Fight" – From Ashes to New

The SUVs that we're packed into are nothing short of pretentious penis extensions. Who the hell needs twenty-inch brushed metal rims just to get from A to B? I mean I get the whole upkeep of the image thing, but really.

"You want help to get your stuff?"

I snap my head around to glare at Rey where he sits on the opposite end of the seat, legs spread wide in an arrogant show of power. "I can manage, thank you."

Two black behemoths turned up outside the hotel, and considering there are eight of us who needed a lift, I assumed we'd split the group evenly between the two. No such luck. Kris called shotgun on the second vehicle, a guy who I've learned is called Toby hustling Kendall into the back seat, before their manager Rick decided to forgo the fold-out rear seats and piled a very drunk Emery into the cargo area.

That left only Rey and the bodyguard, Pete, to travel in the lead vehicle with me.

Yay. Seriously. Could this be any more awkward?

"It's the next block up, so wherever you can find a space to pull over," I tell the driver.

"What number?"

"Two eighty-five. It's the one with the patisserie on ground level there."

He gives a curt nod, and then proceeds to block the lane of traffic as he double parks. The two SUVs sit with their hazard lights flashing, cars honking at them, as I launch myself out the open door.

"Loop the block," Rey tells the guy as he proceeds to scoot across the seat.

"Hey." I lift a hand. "I said I can cope. It's a violin. Hardly a struggle to carry on my own, you know."

"I know." He thrusts both feet toward me, launching himself out the door. "But I want to see where you live."

I don't get a chance to protest before he has the SUV door shut, and some guy hurls abuse as the convoy starts away again.

"Sheesh." Rey lifts his top lip at the disgruntled motorist. "Little bit of patience, buddy."

"Yeah, well, not everyone takes it upon themselves to stop wherever the hell they want around here." I pull my phone out as we approach my apartment building, noting a new message from Kendall.

K: Take your time ;)

A selfie accompanies the message: her reclined against that Toby guy as he leans on the car door, tossing devil horns.

Ugh.

"Ladies first." Rey holds the door open, throwing me a wink as I pass by with a frown.

He follows me up the stairs, hands in pockets as he silently takes in the details of the worn yet tidy complex.

"What are you thinking?" I shouldn't ask, but the observations that rest on the tip of his tongue are damn near readable in his eyes.

"Nothing, really." He shrugs.

He's thinking how horrible it would be to live here.

He's thanking his lucky stars that he doesn't have to be one of us—the common people—anymore.

He's regretting his decision to come up with me.

At least, I know that's what I'd be thinking if I was used to flash five-star hotels and being waited on hand and foot.

I give him an once-over as I punch the code in our door. He bends over the balustrade, both hands braced on the painted rail as he stares down at the ground floor. Rey's lean, but not lanky. Just tall and not overly muscular or built, although the lines of his arms suggest that playing keeps him fit enough. Regardless, his clothes hang well from his frame, and I find myself staring a little too long at where his black jeans hang from his ass.

"Home sweet home," I say dryly to gain his attention.

He pushes off the rail and spins my way, face impassive as he takes the lead and strides through the door. *Make yourself at home, why don't you?*

His head tilts to take in the modest apartment. "Holy fuck. There's like nothing in here."

"There's a sofa, and a TV," I point out. "What else do

you want?"

"Aren't chicks supposed to have a million cushions, and like, little knickknack things everywhere?" He wanders across to the windows to check out the view of the street.

I glance around at the space with new eyes, trying to see it from a stranger's point of view. I guess he's right; there's nothing that's uniquely Kendall or me in here. "If I had free cash at the end of the month then maybe there'd be more *knickknack things*," I surmise. "But I suppose we've got all we need."

"We?" His brow is hard when he turns to face me. "Do you live here with Café Girl?" His gaze darts to the few photos stacked on our short kitchen counter as though to analyze them for clues.

I chuckle at his nickname for her. "Kendall. Yeah."

Rey returns his focus to me, seemingly satisfied. His eyes soften, holding mine a beat too long. The gentle *andante* of my heart quickens to a definite *moderato*.

"Anyway." I turn like the boy-awkward introvert I am, and get my ass in motion. "I better grab this damn violin so they don't start a riot down there, right?"

"I guess." He calls after me as I step out of sight. "Are you nervous?"

"About opening?" I slide the vinyl case from beneath my bed.

"Yeah," he shouts, his footsteps moving around the living room.

"I guess." I'd be peculiar if I wasn't, right?

After all, it's not every day you get to step out in front of an audience that size ... unless you're Rey.

"They're just people, Tabby." He startles me from my door, shoulder casually rested on the frame, hands slung in his pockets again. "If you don't give a fuck what they think, then you'll be fine."

"Easier said than done." Especially when I still play the popularity game.

I can't afford to throw caution to the wind. I still have to do whatever will please the masses until I can build that dedicated following. *Then* I can step outside my comfort zone.

"Why does their opinion matter?" He strides into the room while I fuss pointlessly with my case.

I turn my head and take a moment to look at him as he stands beside me, watching intently for my answer. His arms are folded across his chest now, head slightly cocked. His eyes ... God, they're so intense. They're the kind that strip away all the layers of bullshit and take a peek deep inside your soul.

I feel bare. Naked. Totally exposed and utterly vulnerable.

"If I want to make it big I have to make the crowd happy, right?" I lift an eyebrow. "Are you telling me that you don't care what your fans think?"

He shakes his head as he shifts to the foot of my bed and takes a seat. "Not always. No matter what you do, you can't win over everyone. As long as you're confident you brought your best game, then so what if you get a shitty review or some troll on your social media the next day? Make yourself proud, and then the confidence will come naturally."

"Is that what you do?" My thumbs stroke the silver

latches on my case while I study his reaction.

His eyes fall to my bedspread, his mouth twitching at the corner, the slightest crinkle to his eyes before he answers telling me he withholds the whole truth. "In a way, I guess."

What is his deal? If I hadn't googled Rey Thomas like a total creeper last night, if I didn't know he was a rock star worth a pretty penny, I would be mistaken for seeing nothing but an everyday—albeit alternate—guy sitting before me. Yet I did look him up, and having read some of the stories I did about him, I can't connect the two seemingly opposite personalities.

Womaniser.

Loud.

Arrogant.

Driven.

Some of the words journalists used to describe the self-made musician who packed up everything he owned at age nineteen and moved halfway across the country with nothing but his like-minded brother and a dream. His attitude makes you think he's been gifted everything on a silver platter, but reading his biography shows his history has been anything but easy.

Seeing the sad reflection in his eyes as he traces the fold of my bedding with his finger is proof enough that something dark lurks beneath the surface.

"I think I have everything I need."

He nods, snapping out of his trance to look at me. "Cool."

"Why did you do this? Really?"

He frowns, and then stands to move to my bedroom

window before he answers. "It seemed like the best I could do after Rick fucked you over." He keeps his gaze trained on the street below, but I don't need to see his eyes to know. I recognize a lie when I hear one. "They're back out the front again."

"I'm good to go." I snatch up the handle and wait for him to exit first.

Like hell I'm leaving him alone in my bedroom where he could pry through things. For all I know he's one of those celebrities who feel they're entitled to anything they want, that boundaries don't apply.

He walks ahead of me, hands in his pockets as though the stance is his fail-safe, as we head for the door. "Do you really think you'd be no good as an opener?"

Isn't it obvious? "Rock fans don't usually dig classical music."

"So sell it to them." His eyes are hard and full of challenge as he waits for me to do the usual once over of the apartment before I lock up. "You must be okay if you can sell a hundred tickets on your own."

"Gee, thanks," I sass as I shoo him out the door.

He shrugs. "Just stating facts."

Could I do it, though? Could I sell his audience something so vastly different to what they like?

"What else?" I frown a little as he continues to stare at me while I check the door's locked.

"Nothing you need to know right now." He grins, leaning his shoulders against the wall, head turned to look at me. "You ready to practice?"

"To an empty auditorium? Sure. To you? No."

He huffs a laugh, taking my violin from me. "And

there you go again, doubting yourself."

"You're asking me to basically audition before *you*, Rey. I think nerves are a natural response to that."

"And playing for me would be an issue because ...?" He gestures for me to go first down the stairs.

"You're like, super successful compared to me. What I think is good is probably shit to you."

"And yet I'm a nobody compared to the likes of Metallica or The Rolling Stones." He sighs behind me as I start the last flight. "We're all somebody and nobody all at once, Tabby."

I might have only known this guy twenty-four hours, but it doesn't take a rocket scientist to work out the Rey the world knows and the Rey his bandmates are privy to are two entirely different people. Something tells me that the more time I spend with him, the more I'll get to know the real Rey.

A part of me worries that I might like it.

"You've got an answer for everything, huh?"

"When it's not about me, yeah." He reaches up to slip his shades on before we exit into the sunshine. "Come on, kitty. Your entourage waits."

I chuckle as I follow Rey into the street, the vehicles parked obnoxiously in the traffic again. He passes my violin to Pete, who holds the door for us, and then climbs into the SUV.

Just play the concert, Tab. It's one night. By next week, Rey will be back on the road, and I'll be a fading memory of some girl he met along the way.

I don't have to like the guy. He doesn't have to like me.

Don't overthink things.

For all I care Rey could cross-dress in his spare time and sing nursery rhymes to an array of teddy bears. All I need to know is regardless of the fact my music style couldn't be further from his, he's more than quadrupled my audience tomorrow night.

And for that, I guess I could be a little less whiney and a little more grateful.

REY

"Invincible" – Adelitas Way

There's nothing like the crisp sound of money as it rolls between your fingers, especially when that movement will eventually satisfy an intense craving.

"Anything full-strength," I instruct Pete, handing him the two twenties. "And get something sugary with the change."

I ran out of smokes half an hour ago, and with the diva shots Emery calls, I'm about ready to gut the next fucker who asks me to "stand there for a moment and give me a few lines."

"Can you hear that echo?" Toby hollers from behind his set. He smacks the snare a couple of times, head cocked.

"Yeah." I lean on the front of the stage, facing him, with my elbows near my head. "It should sound different with a full house, though."

Our sound tech nods from behind his desk as though to agree. Pack a venue with a thousand sacks of flesh and bone, and the acoustics change notably. That's why we pay these fuckers who operate the board: they know how to predict that change and to adjust the levels for it.

I tuck my chin between my outstretched arms as Toby strikes the drums a few more times, using my peripheral vision to watch Tabby-cat. She sits in the front row with Café Girl, chatting. You'd be forgiven for thinking she's relaxed by the way she talks, yet her incessantly tapping foot says otherwise.

I took two steps inside their apartment and the raw reality of her situation hit me smack in the face. I've been there. I've lived with only the bare necessities while I fought to get where I am today. *Shit*. One look in her eyes when I opened my goddamn mouth and stated the obvious, and I was thrust back to the good old days when that was Toby and me.

Beaten down. Embarrassed. But too fucking stubborn to quit.

I jacked this thing up and told myself it was because I wanted to humiliate the woman who stormed into my rehearsal and made me feel insignificant. But ten minutes in her apartment and I realize how much of a fucking liar I am, even to myself.

I want to help her because she deserves better than this.

"Where the fuck is my stand?" Emery hollers from the side of the stage. The crash of metal on wood precedes a growled "Fuck!"

Should have given Pete money to get alcohol, too.

Toby tips his head back, jaw slack as he makes a strained face. I chuckle into my arms, fingers tapping out a rhythm on the stage to fend off my cravings.

Idle hands ...

Some bands hate this part, the setup. It's tedious, broken practice. But I love it. Throw the four of us in a room, banging around pointlessly, and it's as though we're twenty and jamming in Emery's games room again. It's the fun before the bullshit. It's the essence of why we all embarked on this fucked-up ride of lights, sound, and motherfucking publicity.

Fuck, the publicity.

Apparently we can't market the band without being involved—who would have thought? Swear to God I'll find a way, though. Bring it back to the music. I didn't move out of home to get a career in style and opinion pieces. I hit the road to make a living doing what I love, what brings me alive.

What's almost killed me several times over.

"We're set for you now, T," our sound tech calls across the auditorium. "Can you guys run through a couple of songs? We'll see how it mixes."

I cast a glance Tabby's way to find her quiet, focused, and seemingly eager to hear us play. Fuck—it's never crossed my mind to ask the woman if she's heard our music. Does she live and breathe classical, or do her tastes vary?

Time to find out.

I jog up the steps side of stage, two at a time, and head across to grab my guitar. I saved for what felt like a fucking lifetime to buy this baby at the start: a PRS SE custom. No matter how much money I make, how many guitars I get gifted by sponsors, this girl will always be my baby. The strap rests across my shoulder, comfortable and familiar, as I lean in to check song choice with Toby.

"Think we should start with 'Descent of My Mind'?"

Emery strides on from the side of the stage, mumbling under his breath.

Toby flicks his eyes across to the moody fucker, and then back to me. "Think he'll break his guitar if he fucks up the end again?"

"Should we find out?" I pull the pick from my strings and give a couple of warm-ups.

"What we playing?" Em asks, brow furrowed.

"Descent of My Mind." I shift my gaze to Kris as he settles his favorite ESP against his hips. "You catch that?"

He answers with the first chords of his solo.

"Right, guys," I call, taking my spot at the mic. "Let's give these lovely ladies a good show."

I earn a giggle from Café Girl, yet Tabitha stays impassive, simply lifting an eyebrow. I blow that bitch a kiss as Toby taps out the beat with his bass, and then rip her mind apart with the opening riff.

She sits still as a statue while I build the power chords, working up to the best part of the intro, and by the time I drag my pick down the strings to slide into where Kris takes over, she's leant forward in her seat, elbows on knees as she takes the music in with un-blinking eyes.

That's it, Tabby-cat. Lap it up. I'll have this woman addicted to rock and laying that violin down for good in no time.

The song feels good, the lyrics pouring off my tongue with ease as Emery settles, his earlier frustration seemingly lost. Empty or full, it doesn't matter what that goddamn theater is, I enjoy the moment all the same as I work the stage, putting the sound guys through their paces.

Five minutes and forty-two seconds of pure, un-checked emotion pour from me. My throat hurts from the strain the song demands, my neck stiff as I lay the final chords, but fuck it all, isn't this why I live?

"Nailed it." Toby taps the end of his stick to my raised palm, giving me one of his extended high fives.

My chest rises and falls as I catch my breath, Kris's smile infectious. *Fuck yeah.* That song alone will sell our next album.

"What did you think, ladies?" Emery struts to the front of the stage to accept the bottle of energy drink Pete passes up.

That guy's a goddamn legend. I make a mental note to see if he wants a full-time gig.

"Holy. Shit," Kendall gushes. "I mean, I felt the vibrations in here." She taps a closed fist to her chest. "That was loud. Awesome, but loud."

She continues talking to Emery, the grizzly fucker lapping up her adoration the same as he does that bottle of guarana. Yet I hear none of it, my focus squarely on the girl who reclines in her seat as though she's seen performances like ours a thousand times over.

Maybe she has? Not as though I've bothered to find out much about her.

I lift my guitar off my shoulder and set it in its cradle before hopping off the front of the stage with a loud thud.

"Talk to me, Tabby-cat."

She shrugs. "It was good."

"Just good?" *Way to kill a buzz there, little lady.*

"What would I know?" She narrows her critical eyes on me. "I play classical, remember?"

Gonna be like that, huh? "Suppose." I drop into the seat beside hers and watch the guys as they talk amongst themselves.

Kendall takes her seat on the opposite side of Tabitha again. "I can't believe you're opening for these legends, Tab." She nudges her friend in the arm.

I watch her keenly in my periphery, frustrated when she doesn't react other than to say, "Lucky me, huh?"

I picked her as the guarded type when we met yesterday. But that's a damn understatement. This girl isn't just guarded, she's estranged from her fucking emotions altogether. Would it kill the woman to be excited about something?

She hasn't put the bow to the strings yet, but she's already convinced she's failed. What the hell has this girl been through to make her so damn pessimistic?

Fuck. And I thought I was a moody buzz-kill at the best of times.

"Rey! Get your ass up here," Emery calls. "We've got time for 'Succession' and then we've got to split."

I slam my hand down on Tabitha's knee and pat her leg twice. "If you thought the last one was 'okay', baby, then you might struggle to stay awake during this belter." I flash her a cocky wink as I rise. "Fair warning, and all."

If I'm not mistaken, that was the hint of a goddamn smile.

Girl might not be so cold after all.

TEN

TABITHA

Theme from Schindler's List
– John Williams, Itzhak Perlman

I said he was good to save inflating his ego to dangerous levels. I lied.

It. Was. Fucking. Phenomenal.

I'd come across the name of the song in the press pieces I read that were published pre-tour, but because the track was a key selling point prior to the new album dropping, they'd decided to keep the song relatively under wraps. No YouTube video, no Spotify upload. Nope. "Descent of My Mind" is the dark horse of the tour.

And I can see why.

"I've got to take these guys to a radio interview," Rick says as he stops beside where I unpack my violin. The guy is attractive in a clean-cut corporate way. "But I've asked one of the cars to stay behind for you and your friend." He hands me a business card, which I promptly drop into my open case. "Phone me if you have any issues, otherwise we'll see you back here tomorrow night, an hour at least before you're due to go on, okay?"

"All my ticket holders have been notified of the change in time?"

He nods. "An alert went out through the seller."

"Cool." I lift my tried and trustworthy Cremona from its case and force a smile.

I need a better violin. This one has done well—hell has it done well—but if I want to notch my performances up that bit higher I need a better tool for the job. Only problem: that tool costs in the vicinity of two grand. I can't afford to feed myself properly, let alone save enough to buy my ideal instrument.

Talk about a hell of a catch-22.

"Keep these guys here as long you need them," Rick instructs. "They get paid by the hour, so don't let them bitch out on you, okay?"

"Sure." Not 100 percent sure how I'd feel about ordering around people I don't know, let alone pay, but okay.

He gives me a curt nod and then turns for the exit. I cast my gaze across the room, violin tucked under my arm as I check the tension on my bow. The band hangs near the doors that lead through to the lobby, Toby chewing everyone's ears off. Kris leans his shoulders against the wall, hands in pockets as he listens. Emery clutches a new can of energy drink like his life depends on it.

Probably does.

Rey, however. Rey nods at what Toby says, yet his gaze keeps cutting across the enormous auditorium toward where I set up. Seems I'm not the only curious one.

I shy away, same as I always do when people are fascinated by me, and swallow back my nerves. *Like you have a million times before, Tab.*

"You got everything you need?" Kendall drops her ass to the front of Toby's platform, legs crossed as she watches me apply rosin.

"I think so." I flick my eyes toward the band. "Be better when they leave."

"Babe." She sets her lips in a firm line. "If you're nervous about playing in front of them, then how the hell will you handle it tomorrow with a full house?"

"Let's not talk about that, okay?" I wince at the thought, and then bring my violin to rest on my collarbone.

The bow glides over the strings perfectly until the final inch where it snags. I huff and drop the instrument back under my arm to apply a little more rosin to the end of the bow hairs.

"Breathe," Kendall coos. "You got this."

"I have to play classical to rock fans. I don't have this."

"You don't *have* to do anything." Her gaze flicks to the rear of the room as the guys head out. She gives Toby a cute finger wave. "If you don't want to play, don't."

"And how would that look to the people who wanted to see me?" I ask, noting Rey leave without so much as a backward glance. *Asshole.* "First I change the time, and then I bail altogether."

Kendall smiles. She has me in her little trap.

"That was your point, wasn't it?" I drone.

She nods with a smug smile, hands tucked between her legs.

"Ugh." I retry the bow, and satisfied that it's ready, head for the mic.

The sound guy waits patiently at his desk for me to start.

"Um." I lean a little too close and wince at the feedback. "Do you want me to do a whole song, or...?"

"Whatever suits," he calls. "We'll work around you and let you know if we need more."

Okay. I nod and pull in a deep, cleansing breath. *Go with your favorite.* I lift my violin and close my eyes, letting my senses guide my bow to the strings.

The room falls silent, enough so that a pin drop would be deafening. My breath escapes on a long exhale as I pull my bow across the strings and begin.

There it is. My heart calms, my mind at ease as I visualize the sheet music, preempt the next note. I fall back on the piece that cemented my love of violin: the theme from *Schindler's List.* A beautifully emotive and sad tale. A perfect piece to play solo.

I sway as the piece builds, feeling each note rather than hearing it, completely and utterly immersed.

So much so that I don't realize the entire theater remains silent while I bring my violin to my side and pull a deep breath to open my eyes.

Kendall sits speechless, nothing short of pride on her face. "*That* is why you're supposed to do this shit." She beams. "That right there."

I glance across to the two sound techs. One sits perched on the back of a chair, his feet on the seat and jaw slack. The other, the guy who works the levels, stands with his hands immobilized on the board.

"Wow." He snaps out of his trance, lifting one hand to scratch the back of his head as he looks down at the controls. "I think we're good, but if you want to do another...."

"Something a bit faster?" I ask. "I've got backing tracks for a few of my pieces, but the USB for it isn't with me." I was so thrown by Rey at our place that I forgot to grab the damn thing.

"No issue." He waves his hands before him. "Turn up early tomorrow, and we'll run over them before everybody else gets in."

"How early?"

He looks to the guy who's now managed to shut his jaw. "What do you think?"

"Um." He climbs off the chair. "How many tracks are we talking?"

"Four." My hand flexes on the neck of my violin. "I can find out who was supposed to do the sound for me if it helps?"

"No, no." He shakes his head, scratching around for something on the desk. "No need. We took over before they were scheduled to come in." He pauses to look up at me. "You would have practiced today with them, right?"

Of course. I roll my eyes upward. "Yeah. I would have." *Duh, Tabby.*

"Um. Come in three hours before the doors open and we should have plenty of time to get through it before the pretty boys rock up for their tuning."

The first sound guy lifts a palm. "Don't tell them we called them that."

I chuckle, liking these two already. "Secret's safe with

me."

"So, do you want to do another?"

I look to Kendall. "Do you need to go?"

"I'm right where I belong, babe." She grins, flicking the back of her hand at me. "I've got time before I have to be at work. Play away."

I turn back to the sound guys and give them a smile. "One more then."

"Stage is yours, pretty lady."

ELEVEN

REY

"Fell On Black Days" - Soundgarden

I stayed. Tabby-cat thought we all bailed on her, but truth is I got into an argument with Rick and shoved him out the door onto the sidewalk before I let Kris know that if he so much as opened his mouth to cough he'd be dead.

All I wanted was a minute's fucking silence so I could listen.

Holy shit.

I felt it.

In. My. Fucking. Soul.

"I think we've got a problem," I murmur to Toby as I flip Rick the bird in response to his glare.

"Like what?"

I tug on my brother's sleeve so he drops back behind the group. "You heard her, right?"

Rick gets in the front seat of the vehicle, Kris and Emery clambering into the back. Toby frowns at them before shifting his focus back to me. "Nope. I was out here reminding Rick why we need a fucking vocalist."

Okay. So I may have pushed him a little hard.

"She's good, man."

"So?" He leans in the SUV and gives Emery a shove, gesturing for our bassist to get in the back.

"So, she's supposed to be awkward and shit. She's supposed to bore everyone half to death so they're gagging for it by the time we come on stage."

"You were using her to amp up our performance?" He scowls at me as he slides into the middle seat.

"You say that like it's a bad thing." I had her pegged as good publicity: *Charitable Dark Tide Give Solo Artist Golden Opportunity.* But with a performance like that, she could damn well rival the shit we've got planned to steal the show.

"She's classical." Toby states the obvious while I get in behind him. "The only thing our fans will care about is how long she hogs the stage before they get to see us."

"True." I tug the door shut behind me, and then hang on as our driver reenacts his youth. "Easy on the pedal, man."

"We're late," Rick clips. "No thanks to you."

Fuck off. So we're ten minutes behind his perfect schedule. It's not that much of a big deal, is it?

It is. By the time we get through reception at the radio station and are directed to the studio, the murderous stares we get from behind the soundproof glass could strip paint.

The DJ wriggles around animatedly as he announces the next song, smacking the button at the exact same time as his fake smile falls clean off his face. He shunts the chair out from underneath him, and stalks to the door as Led Zeppelin plays.

"I can't fit you in now." He tosses his hands in the air. "My show wraps up after this song."

"Can we shift across to the next one?" Rick asks hopefully.

I shrink into the shadows, suitably guilty. *Fucking traffic.* Our ten minute late departure became a twenty-five minute late arrival.

"The next show is a fucking preprogrammed count-down," the guy grits out though a stiff jaw. "We don't do live slots again for another eight hours."

He's tall with curly hair. Kind of reminds me of Jeremy Clarkson. I look around to see if the Stig is hiding somewhere nearby.

"Come on." Toby rests his hand on my shoulder, jerking his chin at Emery to turn him around. "Leave Rick to it, hey?"

Kris sighs out his nose, head shaking as he takes the lead on our retreat. "He's going to be fuming, man."

"I know." For once Rick would be justified in tearing strips off me. "It's only a radio show, though, right?"

The unimpressed glare I get from Kris says it all.

"Yeah, I know. We need all the publicity we can get to keep momentum."

Our dream is to be the headline act at one of the many epic music festivals held around the country each year. Fuck, our mini goal is just to be high enough on the poster that our band name is printed in the correct font, not just what fits under the big guns' names. Carry on how we are, and we just might get there. But one too many screw-ups like this and we might not, too.

The four of us get situated in the lobby to wait Rick out. Toby stands with his hands in pockets to read the posters framed on the wall. I sink into the plush two-seater with Kris, while Em drums a beat on the receptionist's desk with two pens.

My head hits the back of the seat, and I stare up at the tiny holes in the ceiling panels. We've got eight stops and sixteen shows to go, and that doesn't include this bonus performance. We play tomorrow night, and then it's back on schedule with two shows at the stadium across town before we catch a red-eye to the east coast.

We've played 335 times in the last six years, varying from gigs with a dozen bar patrons, to joint shows with other local up-and-comers. This tour? It might be our first structured trip, but prior to it kicking off we had one month's downtime to record the new album. Before that we were on the road in our shit-box of a van, playing anywhere and everywhere we could.

I wrote every single lyric on this album either crammed in the van's bench seat, or in the semidarkness of a gig. You learn to adapt when luxury isn't a choice.

"Well," Rick announces, joining us in the foyer. "I managed to get them to edge 'Succession' in before the countdown starts. Threw a free double-pass in as an apology."

"No interview then?" Toby asks.

"Not today." Rick holds my eye as he answers.

Damn. "Guess that means we're free to go get an early dinner, huh?"

"Fuck, Rey." Toby rolls his eyes. "How about we head

back to the hotel and decide on the set list order? Or I don't know, run through our bookings to make sure Rick hasn't fucked up any more stops?"

"Hey." Rick frowns.

"It's a legit idea," Kris mumbles.

"Come on, Em." Toby clips him around the back of the head to grab his attention. "We're out of here."

The Casanova leans over the reception desk to whisper something at the woman who looks old enough to be his mother. She blushes and laughs, ducking her chin to hide her face.

Unstoppable. That guy is off the charts ridiculous.

"Really?" I ask Em as we head outside.

He shrugs. "No harm in having a little fun, is there?"

"This morning you were crying into your milk over Deanna."

He scowls at the mention of the bitch's name. "Yeah. Well what she doesn't know won't hurt her."

"She should know," Toby adds, overhearing our conversation as we cross the parking lot to the SUV. "Maybe then she'd leave you the fuck alone and you'd move the hell on."

"I don't need to move on." Emery charges ahead, wrapping his arm around Kris's shoulders.

"He's a lost cause. You know that, right?"

I nod at Toby. "If we keep our asses on the road, then he'll be fine." I catch his quirked eyebrow in my periphery. "She'll never tour with him."

"True that." He nods to one side. "She'll also never let him go. Not as long as she has a shot at being Mrs. Rich Rock Star."

"We need a lawyer."

He huffs a laugh as we arrive at the car. "We need a hit man, more like."

"Amen to that."

TWELVE

TABITHA

"Go To War" – Nothing More

"It's not going to be enough." I grip my hair with one hand, resting my head in the hold. "I won't win them over with this."

Kendall groans from her spot stretched out on the sofa, one arm thrown over her eyes. "Just stop. Please."

"Excuse me for wanting to not fuck this up," I snap. "It's not every day I get an audience that big, is it?"

Eight hundred and forty-three. Turns out Dark Tide have quite the super fan base, there.

"What have you got so far?"

I slide off where I'd been perched on the end of the kitchen counter, and carry my scratched and rescratched playlist over to her.

Kendall skims the names, mouth twisted as she reads. "This one." She points to my third choice. "Is that the one that goes…"

I do everything I can not to grimace at the way she butchers the piece by trying to sound it out with her voice. "If we're thinking of the same one, then yes."

"Put it second to last."

"Why?"

"It'll make them think you're winding down and then, bam! You'll hit them with this one."

I snatch the notepaper from her and mentally shuffle the songs. "I think you might have a point."

"Babe. I haven't hung around with you the past six years without picking up a thing or two about your music."

She giggles as I crush her in a hug, and then pull back to read the list one last time. Kendall's my rock. It's crazy when I think back to the first time we met, how badly we couldn't stand each other.

"I still think it's flat," I complain. "I'm competing with this, for crying out loud." I dash over and retrieve my phone, smacking the passcode in to unlock the screen.

It still shows the YouTube video I watched over and over while Kendall showered.

She takes the device from me and hits Play. "For starters, they're in a huge arena, Tab. They won't have as many lights and fire and shit in that theater."

I know she only tries to placate me, but I can see the same look in her eyes as I felt in mine watching Dark Tide perform their breakout song on the first stop of the tour: awe. All the light effects and pyrotechnics in the world can't outshine Rey's raw magnetism.

He draws you in to him by just *being*. The man could be bent over, thrashing out the chorus, or static while he serenades a softer verse. It doesn't matter; you're captivated all the same.

He's what they call natural talent. Marketable

material. He's a promoter's dream. No wonder the band blazes a trail through the rock world.

"What do you propose then?" Kendall hands my phone back, her lips set in a flat line.

I shrug. "That's the problem; I don't know."

"Do you need a piece with more oomph? Something original?"

I level her with a hard stare. How in hell does she expect me to come up with an original piece in twenty-four hours?

"Okay," she cedes. "Maybe not original, then."

Although. My index finger taps my lips as the idea forms. "Maybe I can't do completely original," I say. "But I could do an original *take* on a favorite."

"You mean make one of these old pieces more modern?"

I shake my head, my veins charged at the thought. "Nope. Make something modern sound like an old classic."

She frowns.

"I'll play one of their songs."

Kendall jackknifes into a seated position. "Now you're talking."

"It shouldn't be hard," I muse aloud. "All their songs are basic when you break it down; easy chords and progressions. It's just how they put it all together."

"What one are you thinking?"

I open my Spotify app and thumb through their song list. "This one might translate well." I tap the little triangle. "You have to remember that I'm replacing his voice with my violin, so it needs to be a melodic tune for me to carry it."

She nods as Dark Tide's "Pull Me Under" begins. The two of us sit in silence, listening to the ballad as it plays through the small speaker. The song wraps up with a long guitar solo, but I'm pretty sure I can wing it if I cut that out.

"Do you think you can do it?" Kendall asks as the next song auto plays.

My heart beats heavy in my chest. "Only one way to know." She still sits where I left her when I return a few moments later, my violin in hand. "Play it again."

I listen to their signature track upwards of forty times, scratching a few notes to guide me, before I'm confident enough to attempt it start to finish. The clock on the microwave shows we're already into tomorrow as Kendal cradles her cup of coffee and sits cross-legged to hear me out.

"Are you ready?" I lift the violin to my shoulder.

She nods, one hand splayed. "I think I've memorized how it should sound by now."

We both chuckle before I pull in a deep breath and let my eyes close. *You can do this.* I fuck up the start three times before it sticks. *Easy chords, remember?* I pull a deep breath, and to my relief play the ballad start to finish, all four and half minutes of it.

Kendall stares at me with her lips twisted as I set my instrument aside.

"What?"

"It's missing something."

I flop onto the arm of the sofa. "I know." I jerk my

chin toward my phone beside her. "Play it one more time?"

She taps the icon and we both sit staring off into space as the tune plays.

"I need the drums," I say with a shake of my head. "That's what makes it flat on my own."

"Shit."

"How am I going to do that without giving it away?"

A wicked smile creeps across her lips. "I have his number, you know."

"Toby?"

She nods. "I could ask him to play drums for you, but not say what song it is."

My shoulders drop. "He'll want to know."

"So tell him tonight before the thing kicks off."

She might be on to something. It's not as though he needs practice; he's playing his own music. All I need is to be able to divert him from the details until the concert starts. And looking at the blonde knockout next to me, I think I have just the thing.

"Message him." I give a nod. "Tell him I need a drummer to back me up on my final track and that I'll give him the details when we get there. If he asks, tell him it's an easy beat so he can play it from the sheet."

Kendall remains silent beside me, drawing my focus to her. She sits with pride in her eyes, and what could almost be read as satisfaction in the way she relaxes into the seat.

"You okay?" I ask with a hint of a smile.

"You've totally got this, Tab. You're going to show that arrogant bastard what's up, that's for sure."

And if not, then damn it all if I'm not going to have fun in the process.

THIRTEEN

REY

"Bottom of a Bottle" – Smile Empty Soul

"What the hell?" Toby exclaims as the first notes of Tabby-cat's performance play above us. "Is she on stage already?"

"It's eight," I tell him, feet kicked up on the small coffee table in the dressing room. "Time for her to start."

"Shit." He pushes to his feet.

Toby's always the cool, calm, and collected one. It's odd being in a role reversal situation. "What's the deal, bro?"

He frowns at Emery as our resident drunk brings a hip flask out for a swig. "She said she had some music for me."

"What?" I drop my feet and lean forward, elbows on knees. "What do you mean, music for you?"

He slices his gaze my way. "As in, she asked me to play for her final song. Said it was just a basic backing track, and that I could follow the sheet music easy enough."

Kris pauses in his application of eyeliner to look at

Toby in the mirror. "She wants you to play drums for a classical track?"

He's on the money; it doesn't make sense. Unless he's literally banging his bass a dozen times in the climax, a drum set like Toby's has no place with her music.

"Hey," Toby protests. "I didn't ask questions. I just thought it was cool she had enough kahunas to ask."

Fucking little minx is up to something. "Where's that pal of hers? Café Girl?"

He shrugs. "Haven't seen her since before we warmed up."

"Message her. Ask if she has it." *Fuck.* "Do you even know when you're going on?" I stifle a laugh.

He's so royally messed up it shouldn't be funny... but it is. It's downright hilarious watching the normally collected band member lose his fucking shit.

"Christ, man," he hollers, jerking his head. "What the hell do I do?"

"Get your ass side of stage," Em offers, "and wait until you get your cue."

Not much else he can do. I push out of my seat and chuckle under my breath as I turn for the mirror. Kris twists his head left to right, checking his makeup. We'd give him shit in the early days about prettying himself up like an eighties glam rocker, but I have to give it to him: his look is his image, now.

Black eyes, smudged so he looks like some child of the devil. Team it with his undercut black hair that's forever in his fucking face, and he looks like some hot mess cross between emo and goth. He's too pretty for one, and not skinny enough for the other.

He's just Kris, and people seem to love that.

I lean over him to grab the tub of hair wax and then swipe a little out on my index finger. It warms between my palms; just enough that I can make sure the ends of my spiked hair stay rigid. I finish it off same as I always do with a cloud of extra-hold lacquer, making Kris cough in the process.

"Swear to God," he chokes. "If I get cancer from breathing in that shit, you're paying for me to go to some fancy Swiss treatment center."

"Deal." I pinch a wayward spike between my fore-finger and thumb. "Come on, fuckers. Let's go see when Toby has to get his ass on stage for the mystery song."

"You know," Em says, a little too rosy-cheeked already, "you could get a runner to shoot out to the sound guys and find out what it is."

Damn man is a genius.

"There you go," I tell Toby, arms wide. "Problem solved."

He dashes out the door without a word, clearly off to torment or bribe some poor fucker on the road crew.

"Where are you going?" Em asks as I head for the door.

"The side of stage." I thumb toward the stairs.

The sudden silence indicates Tabby has finished her first song.

"Oh." Emery kicks back on the sofa, frowning at Kris who touches up the smudge under his eye. "I thought we weren't bothering anymore now Toby's off to sort it out."

Truth. I have no reason to go hang out up there until

we're called to play, but I still want to. "It gets boring in here with you fuckers," I quip, and then stride out the door before he can question me further.

I want to see her play. I want to know how she looks, what the audience do. I want to absorb and analyze it all.

I make my way up the stage stairs slowly, careful not to let my boots slam down on the wooden steps. Two of the crew straighten their backs as I pass where they sit on one of the road cases, watching Tabby play. They look sheepish as all fuck, being caught out chilling side of stage, but I couldn't give a fuck what they do during sets as long as everything runs smoothly on stage when I'm there.

I edge out into the wings, careful not to step too far. Golden rule of theaters like this: if you can see the audience, they can see you.

Tabby settles into her second song, her hips slightly swaying as she pushes through the notes. She gives her performance an edge, kitted out in a fitted tee, a tutu-like skirt, and those boots with the notes on. The woman looks at ease, comfortable even, but I can fucking guarantee she's anything but.

As it was, her hands shook too hard to get her practice song right when we first rocked up at the theater this afternoon. Her bow had screeched over the strings, those of us in the auditorium covering our ears as the microphone amplified the head-splitting tone.

I was convinced she'd bail right then and there, but the fiery little thing simply took a deep breath, muttered something to herself, and then puffed her chest out to try again.

The top seats are mesmerized. I inch further than I should so I can see her ticket holders up in the balcony. They sit motionless, eyes glued to her as she plays a more mainstream piece. The kind of classical I'd expect to hear in a car commercial or some shit.

My gaze drifts south. And just like that, I'm ready to choke a motherfucker. Some dickwad in the third row talks animatedly to his girlfriend, twisting to throw a comment or two at what must be his buddies in the row behind. *Watch the performer, fuckhead.* Why do I care? I can't really say. Maybe it's because I like Tabby—there, I said it. Or maybe it's because as the guy who stands front and center in the stage, I know how much it fucking burns when people can't give you some simple goddamn respect and watch the show.

Tabitha finishes her second song, seemingly oblivious to the asshole. I catch the runner Toby sent, skim back up the aisle to loop around backstage from the foyer. Tabby gets into her third song, and it's only when she opens her eyes to move to the quicker tempo that she spots him—the asshole in third.

Her bow falters. She misses a note. At least, to my ears, it sounded like she missed one. The whole fucking scenario throws her right off before she manages to compose herself and carry on.

I should laugh. After all, the exact thing I wanted to happen just did.

But I don't. Instead, I drill my fingertips into my thighs to save from marching into the auditorium myself. *Where the fuck are those crew?* I spin and wave my hand at the pair to get their attention. The shorter and stockier of the two approaches.

"Yeah, man?" He leans in close enough to whisper that I catch the stale smell of smoke on his breath.

Fuck yeah. A smoke right now would be epic.

"I need you to do me a favor."

He nods.

I take the guy by the shoulders and position him where I was. "See that douche in the third row, talking to fuckin' everyone around him?"

He nods again.

"Get his fucking ass out of this goddamn theater, and tell him if he so much as tries to reenter while this gig still plays, he gets blocked from our fan site."

"Um, I'm not sure if I have autho—"

"This is my show." I level with him, eye to eye. "I give you authority. Anybody questions it, they come see me."

"Just him?" The guy frowns.

"Just him. Not his friends' fault he's a cunt."

He scurries away, passing Toby on the stairs. My brother looks as though somebody just left him an ounce in the dressing room.

"You will never believe this."

"What?" I position myself so I can witness this takedown when it happens.

I want to see the utter look of devastation on that asshole's face when he's dragged out.

"She wants me to play 'Pull Me Under.'"

I stare at him as though he has two heads. "What the fuckity-fuck?"

"Right?" His gaze flicks over my shoulder.

I turn back in time to see the crew member hustle

down the aisle. The jackass ignores him the first time my little buddy taps his shoulder, only turning on the second more forceful tap. I might not be able to hear the words exchanged, but the mime is funny enough. The guy refuses to leave.

My little gopher looks absolutely devastated.

"Be right back."

I leave Toby side of stage and literally float over the floor as I run quiet as I can down the stairs, along the back hallway, and then up into the side alley. Yeah, there are a few curious looks thrown my way as I emerge around the front of the theater. The few people who hang out in the foyer buying snacks, or heading for the bathrooms, all appear stunned as I rip the auditorium door open.

Heads turn like a goddamn Mexican wave, the gossip train making its way down the aisle faster than I do. By the time I reach the asshole in Row C, Tabby has finished her third song, and I have the captive attention of everybody in a ten-seat radius.

"Excuse me."

The girlfriend gasps as the guy twists to see who spoke. He turns so damn fucking white I expect him to pass out from the sudden blood loss. "Hey, Rey."

"Get the fuck out of my show," I hiss.

His brow pinches. "Look, man. I didn't mean any disrespect. She's boring as all fuckin' hell."

I reach over the guy sitting in the aisle seat, and take a fist hold of the cunt's collar. "Move."

Tabby's chipper voice carries through the auditorium as she announces her special guest. Eyes on me, she welcomes Toby to the stage.

The lower seats roar with excitement.

It dawns on me that I still have this guy in a hold. One vicious stare, and he rises to his feet. The girlfriend starts to follow, yet I hold a hand out to stop her. "Sit."

She blinks a couple of times, and then snaps out of her daze as Toby's sticks hit skin.

Her ass hits the chair while I palm her boyfriend off to my gopher. "Make sure he doesn't come back in."

"Rey, man. I'm sorry," the guy begs. "Let me stay, huh?"

"Out," I whisper-yell, pointing to the foyer doors.

Toby taps his way through the song's intro and then, the magic happens. Right where I usually take my first breath, Tabby lifts her bow to the strings. And just like that, my lyrics become her sonata.

I stand entranced, watching this stubborn little woman as she absolutely slays my song. The audience rock out as she makes those strings sing. A lone person brings their hands together, and before any of us can comprehend what the fuck happens, half the lower floor has their arms over their head as they clap out the beat.

I took the mickey out of her for the genre she's chosen to play. I was damn certain she'd fail and make a fucking fool of herself.

But who's the fool now?

"Rey," my gopher whispers. "You're needed back-stage."

I nod, absently pushing him aside as Tabby reaches the climax of the song. My lips move of their own accord, and I sing along under my breath as she replays my favorite lines on her violin.

> *Your whispers, like ice.*
> *Your heart, like stone.*
> *You pull me under, pull me under,*
> *I'd rather die alone.*

 FOURTEEN

TABITHA

"Tomorrow" - Silverchair

Sitting on my damn hands won't stop them shaking. Probably doesn't help that my whole body vibrates with the rush I got when half the auditorium stood to give me... well, it wasn't exactly an ovation.

A cheer? Yeah. That would describe the thunderous noise they made whooping and hollering better.

A flash of cherry red catches my eye, and I turn to see Kendall sneak up the stairs side of stage.

"Where the hell were you?' I ask.

She points to the balcony. "I was making myself feel posh." She giggles. "Sat in the fancy-schmancy section at the side."

Crazy damn woman.

"How do you feel?" She sets her icy-cold hands on my arms and stoops to level our faces. "You killed it, babe."

"Nervous."

"Huh?" She cocks her head before gesturing for me to scoot over.

I jerk my chin toward where Dark Tide bang their

way through one of their more radio-friendly tracks. She perches on the hard case beside me, her knees bent and legs tucked to the side to accommodate her tight skirt.

"I didn't get a chance to gauge what they thought before they barreled on stage."

"Ugh." She rolls her eyes. "Who cares what they thought? You did your thing and the people loved it." Kendall's eyes go wide. "Shit. We didn't bring any promo stuff. Flyers, cards… hell."

My shoulders drop as I return to watching Rey own the stage. "I know. I realized that too."

How damn stupid could I be? *Or distracted.* Selling yourself 101: Always have promo material on hand. All these people in here who watched me perform, who enjoyed what I did, and they have no way to stay connected.

Take two groups of people and give one the information all laid out nice and neat for them to follow, while you leave the other group to search out the same for themselves, and one guess which group would be more likely to follow through.

I've lost so many potential supporters by not staying on my game. When the hell will I get an opportunity like this again?

Easy: never.

"How are we all feeling?" Rey belts out once the song ends. *"Still alive?"* The audience roars, the unmistakable thunder of drumming feet taking over. *"Still… sane?"* They absolutely lose it as he drags out the tease.

Rey's pick hits the strings and he leads the boys into the song they practiced yesterday—their next big hit,

"Descent of My Mind." The people go mad as he slides along the strings, leading into where Kris takes over.

"It's insane how much they love them, huh?" Kendall hollers as she watches Toby thrash the living hell out of his drum set.

"Totally."

I can see how addictive that thrill would be, how a person could come to live for the attention.

How it could make them lose their mind in the challenge to keep it.

I've slipped yet again, lying cradled on the floor,
Falling harder, deeper, faster than before.
I've gone too far, I've sunk too low,
Stay a while and catch the end of the show.

I rise to my feet as Rey begins to sing, pulled into the words I paid no mind to yesterday. At the sound check I was captivated by the music, my melodic mind dissecting how they'd put it all together, how you'd play such a song. Yet today I'm drawn into the lyrics.

I'm drawn into him.

Leave me on my own,
Yet don't walk away.

His pain fills the words, brings the song to life. He digs deep as he delivers the lines, the heartache clear in the strain on his face.

Where do I turn?
Who do I believe?

When the demons in my mind,
Wear my heart on their sleeve?

The music builds to an epic crescendo as Rey continues to sing the verses, before Toby stills his cymbals. The song cuts abruptly short to let Emery build it back up again with his deep reverberating bass notes. Only this time neither Kris nor Rey join in with their guitars. Rather Toby adds a quiet edge with the drums as Rey whispers the final lines into the mic.

Love me, hold me,
Tell me you're here to fix me.
Love me, hold me,
Tell me baby, please,
Tell me you can fucking save me.

The audience stays respectfully quiet as Emery strums the final note, waiting for a breath before they erupt into screams and cheers for more.

"You okay, babe?"

I look to my right to find Kendall beside me. She lifts a manicured hand and gently wipes the tear from my cheek with the side of her finger.

"He's so hurt."

She nods with a gentle smile. "Most moody artist types are."

"It's not right though." I return my gaze to the stage.

Rey stands before Toby's platform taking a sip of his water. His back is to the audience, his face hidden so they can't see what I can.

A man who makes a career out of his cry for help.

FIFTEEN

REY

"Jekyll and Hyde" – Five Finger Death Punch

Once, just for once, I'd love to finish a show and *do* *nothing.* No press ops, no backstage passes for the diehards, no rundown and recap of what and where we're playing next.

Just pure, unadulterated nothing.

"Fucking awesome as always, guys." Rick beams, yesterday's hissy fit at the missed radio interview seemingly dead and buried. "We've got your ten back-stage passes waiting in the second dressing room for you, but first I need you to do a five-minute interview with *Rocking in Rollers.*"

Fuck. "Why?" I snatch a bottle of water out of a roadie's hand before the bastard has a chance to get the first sip.

He grumbles and walks away to presumably find another. *Not my issue.* Not as though the fucker just spent seventy minutes on stage sweating his fucking ring out.

"What do you mean why?" Rick asks.

"Come on, bro." Toby nudges my arm with his elbow. "It's five minutes."

"Three hundred seconds," I grumble as Rick shepherds us toward where he's probably got the woman waiting.

Valerie "Vixen" Carrell is one hard-ass interviewer. She runs her music blog *Rocking in Rollers*, as a one-woman band, and considering the sheer volume of content she has on there, she must be one busy lady. Probably why she's developed a ball-breaker of a personality to go with her signature image: bright green hair in rollers, and pinup makeup that makes her look as though she's stepped out of a fifties print commercial.

"Five minutes," Rick repeats under his breath as he funnels us into a curtained-off section backstage. "Just kill time with the usual bullshit."

The usual, aka shit that doesn't give away any major plans of ours or lock us into having to do something in the future.

Emery takes a seat on top of a crate, earning a smile from the straight-up woman as she fidgets with her question sheets. Toby leans his hip against the side of the same crate, Kris dragging over a road case to sit next to him. I eye the tablet she has set up on a stand to record our interview, and fight the urge to bail.

Fuck. Six days ago I was on a high. We played a sell-out show to a packed events center of four thousand loud, interactive fans. I had faith in our music, was completely in love with life and thankful for where I am.

But then shit started to fall apart. We got stuck at our last stopover when we were supposed to be five hundred miles away, here; then the radio interview debacle made me feel like a right sack of shit; and then watching Tabby play the hell out of our track…. I'm a right cunt, really.

I set her up with the initial hope she'd fail, and she proved me wrong.

She proved what a coldhearted asshole I am. I mean, who the fuck hopes somebody will humiliate themselves like that? What the fuck was I going to gain out of it, other than rubbing my own ego by stomping on hers?

How fucking low do I have to be to make myself feel better by ruining others?

"Rey, man." Emery clicks his fingers at me, one eyebrow raised.

I cut my gaze to Valerie and find her watching me with a frown. *Fuck.* I can see it now: "Rey from Dark Tide affected by his demons during our interview"….

"We getting this shit done, or what?" I bounce across and shunt Emery to the side as I take a seat beside him.

Valerie smiles, reaching for her tablet. And just like that, my bullshit sells. "Ready, boys?"

We all nod like the good little puppies we are.

Her manicured finger taps the screen, and then we're straight into it. "I'm here tonight with the dashing boys from Dark Tide, straight off the back of their impromptu show here in the Regent Theater. Hi, guys."

We all echo our greeting, Emery's smile wide, despite the fact he hasn't had more than the half liter of bourbon he hid in the wings.

"First up—what an opener!" She gives us a "what the fuck" look before continuing. "Whose idea was it to have a classically trained violinist be your support act?"

Three thumbs all get hitched toward me. *Thanks for nothing.*

"Tell me about it, Rey," Valerie coos in her sultry voice. "What sparked that idea?"

I shrug. "We met Tabitha by chance, and I thought why the fuck not? It's different, right?"

"Amazing," she praises. "She really nailed her cover of 'Pull Me Under.' Toby, you were on stage with her for the song. Were you in on this?"

"I had no idea what was going down until seconds before I walked on," he says with a laugh. "Totally threw me in the deep end."

"Well, you did fantastic." Valerie glances to her sheet, back straight as a rod as she perches on the front of her foldout seat. "My next question is for you, Emery."

"Uh-oh." He laughs.

"Tell us about the incident in LA."

Bitch. Emery stiffens beside me before answering, "I don't think we have time to cover that in enough detail, love." He finishes with a wink.

Nice save.

"Maybe you and I could do a one-on-one later, huh?" She tilts her head to smirk at him.

He remains silent. Kris stares at the floor; Toby's eyes remain front and center despite the fact he looks a thousand miles away. *Smile and wave, boys.*

"Now, this tour," she carries on, unaffected by the fact she just derailed the mood of the interview by bringing up what was probably our worst PR nightmare to date, "you boys are playing things a little differently, aren't you? Always one to surprise, you've decided to release your next album *after* the shows wrap up. Tell me why that is?"

"Well," Toby answers, "in today's day and age of instant access, we wanted to make sure people still had an incentive to come and see us live. Not only that, but it's a reward for the people who do, getting to see us play the tracks before they're uploaded for streaming."

"Nice." She shifts her gaze to Kris. "What's your favorite from the album, Kris?"

He stalls at the mention of his name, glancing my way before swallowing away his anxiety and murmuring, "Cold Call."

Valerie tips her head to the side. "I don't believe you played that tonight."

"No," I say. "We didn't." The damn track fucks Kris up for days every time he plays it, so we're strategically spacing it out across the tour.

We all have the songs that we've poured our very being into, and for him "Cold Call" is it.

"Could you give me a little preview?" Valerie looks to each of us expectantly.

I could whip out my phone and play it if I really wanted to, but instead I answer with "No instruments, sweetheart." I pull my lips into a thin line and squint as I tip my hands palm up in the air.

Emery chuckles, Toby shifting from foot to foot.

"What's on the agenda once the tour is over? Obviously the new album will release." She looks down at her page, making a hum. "I don't believe we have a title for it yet. Can you let the fans know what to look out for?"

"It's a surprise," I say with a sly wink.

More like, we can't fucking decide. We have three options all drawn up, but the four of us can't pick which one we all like better.

"Well, I certainly look forward to finding out."

"You'll be one the first to know," Toby says.

"What is this?" Valerie asks sweetly. "The fourth time we've caught up now? I remember when you boys were starting out in the clubs with private gigs, and now look at you. In the short space of..."

"Five years," I fill in.

"Five years," she repeats with a nod. "It's not the fastest rise to fame I've seen, but definitely one of the most impressive. You've done all this with no major sponsor, and you've also retained your style, refusing to conform to what's more mainstream. Do you think that edge is what has helped you get where you are?"

"Nope." I shake my head, crossing my arms high on my chest. "We work hard. We live and breathe our music, drawing inspiration anywhere, anytime. This is what we want to do, and so we give it all we've got."

"An impressive work ethic, for sure."

"I'm sure you can relate, Valerie?" I cock an eyebrow at her.

She smiles, her gaze positively wolfish. "I sure can, Rey." The bomb detonates in her eyes before she even opens her mouth to spew the next shower of shit. "The stress has certainly taken its toll on you personally, though. Tell us, because we all love and care about you, are you better now after those unfortunate and traumatic events?"

"The events?" I level with a scoff.

She shrugs off camera, challenge in her smirk.

"You mean, after I tried to top myself?" Her lips fall as she fidgets. "Twice?"

Booyah, bitch.

"Rey has had excellent help," Toby chimes in, throwing an arm around my shoulders. "And we're doing great, thanks for your concern."

"It must have been hard on you especially, being brothers." Valerie goes in for the kill.

"Blood means nothing," Kris interjects. "We all felt it the same. We all suffered along with him."

She seems suitably stunned. Our normally mute band member has felt it necessary to speak up.

You could hear a hairpin drop.

I'm pretty sure one of hers does.

"As always you've been a real hoot," I sass. "Thanks for having us on the blog, V."

She scowls, aware I've probably shaved a minute off the time she was promised. "Likewise." Her tone doesn't show her frustration, though. "I'll catch up with you boys again after the new album is live. Best of luck with the rest of the tour."

We all give thanks, Emery adding in a shout out to the fans watching.

As soon as her finger hits that damn button to stop recording, my ass leaves the crate. *Fuck her shit.* Fuck her for bringing up last year, both for Emery and me.

What the fuck is the sabotaging bitch trying to do?

Rick's eyes go wide as I blaze past him on a mission

to get the VIP meet and greets out of the fucking way.

"We're never doing an interview with that bitch again," I toss over my shoulder as I hit the stairs.

"Huh?" Rick looks to Toby. "Why?"

My brother hangs back, presumably to fill our manager in on what a jerk she was, as Kris reaches the stairs behind me.

"You okay?"

I slow as I drop off the last step, and half turn to face him. "Yeah. Thanks, man."

"I can't believe that woman," Emery snaps as he barges past the two of us. "Bet the whore would dance on our fucking graves if it gave her a good view count."

"Don't let her get to you," I say, restarting toward the second dressing room.

"Pot, kettle," Kris murmurs.

I shunt the heel of my hand at the door, flinging it open on eight wide-eyed young women and two very out-of-place-looking guys.

"Who's ready to party, motherfuckers?"

 SIXTEEN

TABITHA

"Face Everything and Rise" – Papa Roach

"We totally could have hung around." Kendall shrugs her coat a little higher as we wait on the cab. "It's not too late to go back inside."

"No." I shift from foot to foot to try and keep warm, eyes on the road for any sign of our ride. "They're busy with fans. I'm sure if they want to say anything, they can get my email address, or some shit."

Kendall reaches into her purse as the cab emerges in the traffic. "I'm totally messaging Toby your details."

"No!" I slam my hand down on her wrist. "No, please. Just... ugh." I sigh. Just what? Don't make me seem so desperate to ride their coattails?

"Fine. But if you change your mind, just say the word."

I open the car door for her. "Trust me, I won't."

She slides across the back seat, giving the driver our address as I get in and shut the door behind me.

"When do you go back for your stuff?"

I stare out at Dark Tide's name all lit up above the

ticket box and frown. "Their roadies are packing everything up tonight because they need it all at the next venue by 2:00 A.M. to have it all set up again in time, so apparently I can come get my things tomorrow."

"It would have fit in the back, don't you think?"

I shrug. Probably. It was only my violin and small road case. But I guess deep down I had hoped that leaving it behind would give me an opportunity to "run into" the band again.

That was, until I learned Rey and the guys will be shackled to the next venue so they can be prepared for tomorrow night's much larger, much flashier show. You know, no big deal, just *five thousand fucking people.* Jesus. What would it even feel like to face an audience that huge?

"Get out of your head," Kendall grumbles, eyes narrowed.

"Sorry, hon." I slouch in my seat and roll my head her way. "Did you enjoy yourself?"

Her wicked smile says yes. "You do realize where I was while you did all that preshow stuff, right?"

"I can guess." Involves a guy that's six-foot-plus and pierced. Realization hits me like a slap to the face with a wet fish. "You didn't want to hang around to see if, you know...?"

She tosses a hand through the air between us. "No, don't be silly. Toby's busy with their VIPs, and besides, I'm sure they have all that special band stuff to do before they play tomorrow."

"Like sleep?"

"Do rock stars even sleep?"

She plays it cool, but I can see the disappointment in the set of her lips as she stares straight ahead.

"I'm sorry for being melodramatic."

"Pfft." The cab enters our neighborhood. "You've had a real roller coaster the last few days. It's okay."

I reach across and take her hand. "No, it's not."

Kendall looks down at the contact before she squeezes her fingers around mine. I'm not often the touchy feely type of friend, so for me to do this tells her how sorry I am.

"Look at it this way," she appeases. "Without you and your drama I would be doing something lame like binging Netflix at home and I *never* would have got to meet Dark Tide one-on-one. So I guess for that, I can put up with your shit a little."

She chuckles as I squeeze her hand and rest my head against her shoulder. "Love you."

We stay like that the rest of the cab ride, each lost in our own thoughts of the past couple of days. Midweek I thought I'd be playing a quiet concert to my loyal followers, hoping against hope that maybe, just maybe, there would be somebody influential out there in the audience. Now here I am, stepping out of the cab at home after not only playing to those same people, but opening for one of the hottest up-and-coming rock bands right now.

Still, I can't place how I'm going to feel about this one-night stand in the next five, ten, or fifteen years. Will I look back on this with warmth, happy that I got to experience something that will probably never happen again? Or will I look back on it with regret, wishing I had been ruthless and pushed for more through the kinds of connections a band like Dark Tide has?

Easy answer, Tab. I've never been an opportunist. Success born from somebody else's hard work always seems like such a cop-out. Yes, people can openly offer to help and I won't turn it down, but I'm not the kind to blatantly shove my agenda into somebody else's schedule.

I have to earn this myself. I have to become who I dream to be through my own hard graft, otherwise the victory seems hollow.

"Um, Tab?" Kendall stops on the landing for our apartment, blocking my view of our door. "You should see this. You've got a gift."

I take the last step and then move around her to search out what she cranes her neck at. *Holy shit.* A bouquet of flowers—no, not just flowers: long-stem red roses—sit in a glossy white ceramic vase.

"They're probably for you, you doofus." Makes the most sense that Toby would be trying to woo her after the way she's been throwing herself at him.

I carefully lean over the arrangement to punch our code in while Kendall stoops to pluck the card from its plastic sleeve. She gathers the arrangement in her arms and follows me in.

"Nope. Most definitely for you."

I frown as I set my purse down. "Who from?" Maybe my parents are finally coming around to the idea that their daughter can make a living from music. *No way.* Nope. Even if they had found out about the concert, they're not the kind to send flowers.

"One, two, three...." Kendall's counting fades as she bops her pointer finger above each bloom. "Man, this must have cost a packet. There are twenty of the little critters." She lets out a low whistle and passes the card over.

I lean my hip against the kitchen counter and flick it open.

Maybe next time I'll do it traditionally and throw them on stage one by one when you're done.
- R

"R?" My heart pitter-patters as I set the card down on the counter. "Do you think these are from Rey?"

Kendall shrugs with a silly smile on her face.

"No." I shake my head. "Has to be their manager, Rick."

"Awfully personal for him, isn't it?" she sasses as she heads up the hallway.

"Awfully personal for any of them," I call after her. "I mean, red roses?"

"Yeah," she shouts from her bedroom. "He said in the card about doing it traditional. I bet he's thinking about opera and stuff, how they toss the roses at the singer."

"Oh." *Ohh....* "What the hell do I make of this?" I dart up the hallway and swing into her room to find her halfway into her sleepwear already. "Don't abandon me with something like this. I need help." I fall onto her bed and stare up at the ceiling.

"Jesus, woman. You're twenty-what? And you still need help deciphering boys?"

"Twenty-four," I answer. "And he's not exactly a boy

at our age." I narrow my eyes on her. "How old is he?"

She shrugs before tugging her tank top on. "Fucked if I'd know." Her arms twist as she sheds her bra from underneath. "Google it."

I slide off the bed and onto the floor in true dramatic style and then get to my feet to retrieve my phone. A quick search pulls up his date of birth as three years before mine.

"How old is he then?" Kendall walks into the kitchen, suitably dressed for bed. Even her makeup has been removed.

"It really takes you no time at all to go into comfort mode, huh?"

She winks as she pulls a mug from the cabinet. "Girl, I love to go out. Don't get me wrong. But you know how much I love to bum around as well."

"True." She's spent as much time tearing up a dance floor since we met as she has bingeing TV on the sofa.

"So? Age."

"Oh." I check my phone again and redo the math in my head to be sure. "Twenty-seven. His birthday is the tenth of December."

"Ooo. A Sagittarius." She waggles her eyebrows.

I hop onto the counter and fold my legs. "Why 'ooo'?"

"Very outgoing, and very open-minded, if you know what I mean." She gives a thrust of her hips to cement the point.

I drop my head back and roll my eyes. "Ugh. As if it would ever get to that. They're flowers, babe. Flowers can be totally platonic."

"Do you want it to get to that?" She leans her elbows

on the counter beside me, popping her butt out behind her as the milk heats.

I frown, stuck for words. Would I? *Getting a bit ahead of yourself there, girl.* "I don't know."

"But you like him, right?"

"He's a jackass," I deadpan.

She turns her mouth down and wiggles her head side to side. "I can see that, I guess."

"He's arrogant, messed up, and not to mention totally out of my league."

"How?" she challenges, retrieving her hot mug. "You want one?"

I shake my head. "He's like famous and shit, and I'm...."

"Human? Like him?" Kendall cocks an eyebrow as she adds her cocoa.

I reach out with my foot and knock her in the arm. She responds with a "Hey!" as her hot drink sloshes over the side of the mug.

"Sorry." I pull my jaw back, giving her apologetic eyes.

"Look." She grabs the cloth to clean the mess. "All I'm saying is that boundaries are all in your head. It's a mental block, thinking he's some untouchable god just because a gazillion people know his name."

I lift an eyebrow at her.

"Take a horse for example." Now she's lost it. "Raise it in fenced paddocks all its life, and then place it on a patch of grass with nothing but a single line of tape around it. Know why it doesn't try to escape even though it could jump that single line, or knock it down?"

"Because it's stupid?"

"Because it believes it can't up here." She taps the side of her head. "It has a mental block that's been trained into it. Nothing physically stops it from leaving, just like nothing physically stops you from getting in touch with Rey to say thank you. It's all in your head, Tab."

"Do you really think they're from him?" I look to the bunch, suitably impressed with how full and symmetrical the blooms are.

"Who else would they be from?" She takes her mug across to her purse, and then retrieves her phone. "I'm messaging Toby now to say you want Rey to know the flowers were beautiful."

"Oh, no you don't." I slide off the counter and leg it for her.

She lifts her phone high with an, "Ah, ah, ah! I have a hot drink in my hand."

Ugh. "Seriously, don't though. What if Toby doesn't know he did this? Don't embarrass him."

Kendall narrows her gaze on me, lips firm. "Fine. But you have to promise me you'll get in touch with Rick to find out Rey's number so you can thank him yourself." Her eyes go wide. "Or even better, stalk him on Facebook and send a message."

"Probably be easier," I cede.

"Do it now." She takes a smug sip of her cocoa. "I want to see the message when you're done."

I return to where I left my phone on the counter with a groan. "Why do you always have to be so difficult?"

"Because it gets results, babe. It gets results."

SEVENTEEN
REY

"Paralyzer" – Finger Eleven

"How the fuck are we supposed to get him on stage for sound check in four hours?"

"Fucked if I know. You were the douchebag who brought out shots."

"Oh, so it's my fault now?"

"Did I say that, fuckhead?"

"Guys! Settle down, for fuck's sake. We'll drop him in the shower when we get back. Ice the fucker awake."

Oh, I'm awake, all right. Just that my body doesn't want to cooperate while we're in this goddamn tumble drier of a car.

"Hey. If you want to give him a cold shower, that's your deal, man. He almost knocked me out last time we did that."

Ha. I still remember that night. Fun times....

"How else do you propose having him awake enough to stand up, let alone play? We can't wing it, Em."

"Don't you think I know that? Short of giving him an upper, I'm fucking out of suggestions."

"None of us would be in this predicament if you hadn't let him leave the theater."

"Fuck up, Rick. Who asked you?"

The band tears themselves apart, and it's all because of me. *No surprises there.* Fuck an upper. Somebody pop me a downer. I need to sleep for a week to get over this shit. *Whoa!* Slow down there, driver.

"He's got some fucking talking to do when he comes around, anyway."

I cringe internally at the hurt tone in my brother's voice. *Fucking useless, drunk body.* I'd open my eyes and say something, but I'm pretty sure if I opened my mouth right now, all I'd do is vomit thanks to the constant bump and jolt of the car.

My chest tightens, but not from the effects of the alcohol. Nope. It's the self-loathing that I resent with every part of my being. *Nothing but a fuckup, Rey.* Nothing but a fucking selfish fuckup.

I tune out the voices around me and surrender to the black fog that swirls in my head. The dark has always brought so much more comfort than the light....

• ♭ •

Holy, ba-jesus! "What... ugh... fuckers...."

"There he is," Toby soothes before he backhands me across the goddamn face. "Wake up, asshole. We've got three hours until we leave for the venue, and some of us haven't slept yet."

Hard, unrelenting ceramic digs into my spine and the knobby bit at the base of my skull. *I'm in the bath.* That's right. "I'm awake," I slur.

Goddamn, these hotel fluorescents are fucking bright.

"Switch the light off, Em. Precious here can't handle it judging by that face."

The bathroom is plunged into darkness, save for the muted light filtering in from the adjacent bedroom. My eyes burn like two motherfuckers as I force them open again and wait for my focus to come around.

Shit. Toby's fair pissed judging by that scowl. "How bad?" I groan.

"Depends what you refer to," he says with a jerk of his head. "Damage to public property, damage to public image, or damage to band morale. Where should I start?"

"With the—" I pause to swallow away the bile ebbing in the base of my throat. "With the bit that hurts least."

"Guess I won't tell you a fucking thing then." He tosses ice-cold water in my face from a hotel mug, and then rises to his feet. "He's yours, Em. I stick around, I might kill him myself."

"Enough with the fucking water," I holler after him. "You know I hate goddamn water."

Shit. A shiver rips through me thanks to the icy liquid soaking my clothes, and now hair. I roll my head away as Emery squats down beside the bathtub, unable to face any more disappointment.

"You don't have to worry about me, Rey," he says quietly. "You know I'm not one to judge."

Thank fuck for that, because right now I feel like the accidental baby that nobody really wanted to begin with. *Oh, that's right. I was.* "What did I do?"

He sighs, moving in my periphery to settle on his ass.

"Got blind drunk in the space of an hour and a quarter at the VIP meet and greet."

Fuck. I kind of remember that.

"And then slipped out while everyone was distracted with one of the VIPs vomiting her guts all over the dressing room floor."

Epic. I had the whole room following me down the rabbit hole.

"Made it to a bar, where you decked the bouncer best you could when he refused you entry. I do believe you hollered, 'Do you know who I am?' at the guy."

I groan, closing my eyes again. *So much better in here.*

"And then you managed to get into the driver seat of the rented SUV and crashed it into a parked car while yelling something about being 'late for a very important date.'" He chuckles. "The cops started referring to you as 'Whitey,' after the rabbit in Alice in Wonderland."

Fuck my life. "Jesus."

"Pretty sure he can't help you with this one." Emery shifts. "Think you can get out of here without puking on me?"

"As long as we go slow, good buddy." I throw my right arm toward the side of the tub, and miss.

Way to get a start there, Rey.

Em manages to lean me forward, yet all that achieves is crunching my stomach. Not a flash idea when it's currently carrying enough liquid to see me through the Mojave Desert. I bend my legs and slide to my back again. What water remains in the base of the tub soaks the parts of my shirt that were still dry.

"No good?"

"Not unless you're real keen on seeing what I drank last night."

"Fucking novice," he mutters before rolling me to my side. "Get on your hands and knees, you fuckwit. You can crawl out of here."

It takes what feels like an hour before I'm starfished on the bedroom floor while Emery gets clean, dry clothes for me. Pete, the bodyguard, magically appears to help hoist me up so Emery can change me.

Not really the time to bitch about dignity now, is it?

"Where the fuck were you?" I ask Pete as he lifts me to my feet with arms locked under mine. "Why didn't you stop me making a goddamn ass of myself?"

"He had his hands full keeping a couple of touchy-feely girls off Kris," Emery explains. "We need more guys on deck with those nutcases."

I swing my gaze back to Em as he chuckles, threading my arm through the shirtsleeve. The two of them manage to assist me into what I guess is what I'll wear today, and then place me in the recovery position on top of the bed.

"Anything you projectile vomit around here comes out of *your* money, asshole," Em warns.

"Stop talking about vomit and I'll be fine," I groan.

He leaves with Pete, turning the light off as they go. I stay immobile, staring at the door until I'm sure I can move without sending my head into a spin. Sleep doesn't come; neither does any acceptable level of sobriety as I lie on the bed and count down the minutes. The guys talk out in the main living area of our suite for a while, before all the lights are switched off and the hotel room becomes eerily silent.

I roll to the side of the bed and navigate my way down to the floor with absolute minimal movement. My head pounds anyway.

It's warranted. Every fucking ounce of pain is less than I deserve.

Like a goddamn commando, I crawl belly-flat on the carpet across to where the guys have left my phone. The light stings my eyes as I wake it, forcing me to blink away the burn.

Time to evaluate the damage. I open the Google app and punch in "Dark Tide Rey." The results are exactly what I expected: images of me being hauled out of the crashed SUV, status updates and tweets by eye-witnesses at the bar where I assaulted the bouncer, and one picture that jogs my memory—a shot of me as I run toward the SUV.

I was going to see Tabby-cat. Holy fuck. I got blind drunk and thought it would be a shit hot idea to go see her, since she bailed early at the theater.

The swill in my stomach becomes a deathly eddy as I navigate through every damn post and every damn story on every one of the fucking trashy tabloid sites, to see if anywhere it mentions me saying where I was headed.

Steamrolling over my own reputation is one thing, but fucking ruining hers in the process is another.

My panic lessens with each story I skim through that mentions nothing about her. To be on the safe side, I google "Dark Tide Rey Tabitha" and feel instant calm when the results are the same; her name returns nothing extra.

Thank fuck for that.

I double tap the home button and swipe up through the apps to close each one, yet still when the red icon at the bottom of my shrunk Facebook page catches my eye. *Fuck it.* If I can't sleep, I might as well fuck around on Facey. I thumb through to the notifications, closing my eyes a couple of times to get them to refocus. *Fuck headaches.* I'd eat something, maybe search out an Advil or two, but I'm not so certain my gut can take any more intrusion just yet.

Tabitha Reeves wants to connect with you.

What the ever-loving fuck? I can't smack the notification fast enough. Messenger opens, and there, right before my goddamn eyes is a message from the little tabby-cat. *Hello, kitty.*

I stretch out on the carpet, head braced on bent arm, and hold the phone out to the side to read it.

Thank you for the flowers. (Tell me they were from you, right, otherwise this is awkward as hell, LOL). It was a really nice gesture. I hope I didn't cross any lines playing your song. The audience seemed to like it ☺ Anyway, thanks again for an amazing opportunity. Best of luck with the rest of the tour.

The flowers. *Fuck, the flowers.* I forgot I'd ordered those. Damn near scared the living shit out of Pete when I demanded he get in touch with the driver and find out what the address we stopped at was, and then instructed him to order the bunch online while we played.

Yeah, I like that Pete. He's a good sort.

I roll to my elbows, laid out on my stomach, and hesitate while the sickness eases. Sure I'm not about to make a mess of the hotel floor, I tap out my reply, grinning like a right fucking tool as I do.

They were from me, so you can stop panicking about some other creepy stalker with the initial R now. Send me a picture. I want to know that I got what I paid for.

I send the phone to black and toss it aside. She'll be all tucked up sound asleep at this time of the goddamn morning. Fuck, so should I be. I tap the home button again to check the time. Roughly an hour and Rick will be kicking our asses into the car. *Wonder if Pete can shoot out and get me a bucket for the ride?*

My temporary high fades as I roll to my back and stare up at the ceiling. The press will have a field day when this latest stunt slides across their desks in the morning. Rick's old man will have his work cut out smoothing the edges, trying to turn my goddamn tantrum into something manageable.

Whatever happens in the next few days, I know one thing for sure: I can't keep doing this.

I can't tumble off the damn wagon every time somebody throws shade my way, least of all me.

Because pretty damn soon I won't recover from the fall.

EIGHTEEN

TABITHA

"Stupid Girl" - Cold

His response: blunt and to the point. Still, I smile like a giddy schoolgirl at the knowledge that I, mere Tabitha Reeves from a small town in New Zealand, got her very own personal message from Rey Thomas, lead singer and guitarist for Dark Tide.

I set the phone on my nightstand and then roll out of bed to get dressed. The apartment rests in darkness, which indicates Kendall still sleeps. I pad over to my set of drawers and tug out a comfy tee and a pair of loose sweats.

By the time I wander into the living area to take a picture of the flowers for Rey, Kendall stands at the kitchen counter staring at her empty mug like a zombie.

"You in there, buddy?" I tease.

She lifts a limp hand, and then sets it back down on the counter with a thud. "I slept like utter shit."

"Why?" I move the vase of flowers across the room to where the sunlight cuts through our windows.

"I should have got into bed and gone right to damn

sleep," she says as though scolding herself.

"But?" I position them just right so that the sun highlights the brilliance of the reds.

"But, I thought it would be a flash idea to stalk Toby on social media, didn't I?"

"Oh, babe. No." I snap a couple of shots from different angles. "You know that's never a good idea when you're into a guy."

"Right?" She breaks out of her daze and fills the mug. "What are you taking pictures of them for?"

"Rey wants to see how they look."

"He replied?"

I set my phone down and turn to face her, the tone of her voice concerning. She didn't say it as though surprised, like I'd expect. Nope. She sounds annoyed.

"Yeah. He said they were from him, and he wants to see that he got what he paid for." I chuckle awkwardly. "Typical ass, right?"

"Is that all he said? What time did he reply?"

"I dunno." I shrug. "Early this morning?" Truth be told, I didn't check. It was just there when I woke up. "Why?"

Kendall sighs, her face blank. "He made a right idiot of himself last night, going on a bender and smashing up some car. I sent a message to Toby, but he hasn't even read it, let alone sent one back. I figured they must all be in damage control."

"They were off to the next venue early this morning, remember?" I utter, choosing to look at the pictures I took rather than Kendall's apologetic face. "Maybe that's why he hasn't replied."

"You're ignoring the important part of what I said."

"So he went out and did stupid shit," I say all high-pitched and pathetic. "That's what rock stars do, right?" I get to my feet and whip out of the room before she can say any more.

Why I'm defending the honor of a man who's been nothing but a jackass since I met him…. Except he hasn't. Those stolen minutes alone before sound check, and the vase of roses, point toward another guy.

A private one. The kind I get the feeling not many people know.

"Tab," Kendall says softly from my doorway. "I didn't mean to be a bitch about it."

"I know." I cut my gaze to her. "Just… I don't know. The flowers were a really nice thing to do, you know? It sucks that he's more than likely another entitled idiot who thinks he can get around doing whatever he wants without any consequence."

"I know." She sips her fresh coffee. "You want me to make you breakfast?"

"No. You sort yourself out. I'm going to send him this picture and then have a long shower."

"Fair enough, babe." She takes a step back, and then disappears.

I let out my loaded breath and flick between the images on my phone. Am I that easily won over that all it takes is a few fresh cut flowers? Were there rose-tinted glasses in that bunch that I forgot about putting on?

Ugh.

I select the best image and flick it through to him with a simple message.

Hope you're satisfied.

He can take from that whatever the hell he wants. I'm done.

I choose to spend a ridiculous amount of time in the shower, simply letting the scorching hot water soothe my soul. I have to collect my stuff from the theater today between nine and midday, so considering I didn't crawl out of bed until almost ten, I really should get a hustle on.

At least I can be guaranteed a pain-free exit from the place since the band are now somewhere across town. I spare a glance at my phone as I dress and note no new messages. *Good.* I can't deny the slight pang of rejection, but at least he must have got the message, literally and figuratively.

"Do you want to come with me to pick my gear up?" I ask Kendall as I gather up my things.

She pops a slice of carrot into the hummus pot she has balanced on her lap. "No. If it's cool with you, I might hang here for the day."

"All good." I sling my black Sourpuss purse over my shoulder and do a mental inventory of the room. *Yeah, got everything.* "Need anything while I'm out?"

"When are we doing our food shop this week, babe? I've got twenty spare until I get paid on Tuesday, so I didn't know if you wanted to wait until then, or get some stuff now?"

I cross to the fridge and open the door. "Eek." It looks as though two old ladies live here, given the contents pretty much can be summed up with two words:

yoghurt and wine. "We don't have much, huh?"

"Nope." Kendall lifts her hummus. "I figured I'd start with the savory and finish with the sweet later."

"I'll pick up some basics while I'm out, then." Nobody ever got sick from eating buttered toast three times a day, did they? "I'll ring John, too, and see how long I have to wait until I get the cash from last night."

"Sure thing." Her focus sticks to the TV as I head for the door. "Enjoy!"

I chuckle. "You better not still be there when I get back."

"Or what?" Kendall calls across the room.

Or nothing. Guess I'm a little jealous that she can bum around all day while I'm on the constant hustle to get ahead, is all. "Nothing, babe. See you in a bit."

I give the roses one last glance as I head out the door, and sigh.

REY

"The Red" - Chevelle

Thankfully even though our schedule got fucked up, the gear we didn't need last night was able to carry on and arrive a day early to be set up for tonight's and tomorrow night's shows. Gave the crew a head start, which means we get down time. I sit out in what will be the general admission area, legs kicked out before me with my back against a heavy plastic bollard. Rick stares at the ground while his old man tears strips off him down in front of the stage.

Yep. Old boy Wallace caught the first available flight out here to take control.

"You've really fucked him over," Kris mumbles as he settles beside me. "Smoke?"

"Thanks, man." I reach over and pluck one from his pack.

"I heard a rumor that he's on his final warning now."

"Shit. That bad?"

Kris nods while I watch the tirade continue. I could go over and step in to defend Rick, but meh, where the fuck would that get either of us? I've made it a point not to be within arm's length of Wallace all morning for a fucking good reason.

"Ten minutes and we're back to it," Toby announces as he strides over to where we chill. "Think you can manage that?"

I flip him the bird and then lean over for Kris's light.

"You've completely overshadowed the whole point of this goddamn tour," he grumbles, thumbs hooked in pockets. "Do you even care?"

"Of course I care," I snap. "Would you like me to swallow a bottle of Valium again to show just how much I care?"

He scowls at me. Granted, that was an immature jab, but still. This is my career too; I get it.

"I'm sure old Wally-boy can get things back on track." I hold my smoke out to gesture to the guy.

The man in question finishes with Rick and then turns, eyes wild as they land on me. *Shoot.*

"Point is, he shouldn't have to," Toby digs. "When are you going to get help?"

"I don't need fucking help."

"You need something."

"A bullet?" Kris mutters.

Wallace advances at a pace I don't like all that much. At this rate, I'll be lucky to get half the cigarette down before I have to hot foot it to save myself. I chug like the little train that could, sucking as much of the legal hit as I can before I push to my feet and prepare to exit, stage right.

"Rey!"

Fuck. "Hey, Wallace." I stick my hand out for the guy.

He leaves it hanging. "What the ever-lovin' fuck got into you, boy?"

Guess it's like that, then. I shrug, and then jam my hands in my pockets while Kris makes himself scarce. Toby watches like the fucking sadist he is.

"Speak up," Wallace booms.

The guy is six-foot-plus of broad, German muscle. Rumor has it he moved to America to pursue a career in music himself, but when that didn't work out, turned his hand to managing other people's. The guy has one of the highest turnover rates for staff in the industry, so to say he's heavy-handed with his leadership style would be an understatement. The fact he still carries a strong accent after decades in the country only adds to his menace.

"It won't happen again," I say with as much conviction as I can muster. "I promise."

He leans in, thick finger pointed between us. "Your promises mean jack shit to me." The digit shunts me painfully in the chest. "I made you; remember that. I can just as easily unmake you."

And I have no doubts that he would. "I'm sorry, Wallace."

"You'll be sorry, all right. Even more so when this tour ends."

I frown at the guy. Toby crosses his arms, brow pinched, clearly waiting on the explanation also.

Wallace grins as he leans back to stand tall once more. "Rehab, Rey. You want to continue with me, you get help, boy."

Rehab. Amy Winehouse cycles through my mind.

"What? What sort of rehab?"

"The kind for destructive, arrogant alcoholics."

"I'm not an alcoholic," I grit out.

I binge when I do drink, sure. But I don't drink daily, and I can certainly say no when I want to. *Can't I?* Fuck. Still—not an alcoholic.

Wallace slices his hand through the air at my protest. "No negotiations, kid. Rehab, or it's the indie life for you."

Fuck.

I stand mute as the big guy spins heel and marches toward the stage area. Toby steps closer beside me, watching Wallace leave also.

"Told you that you needed help."

Hair, meet trigger. I spin, clutching a fistful of Toby's sleeveless tee as I do. "You fucking set this up?"

He leans back, eyes narrowed as I get right up in his traitorous face. "Nope. But wish I had thought about it now."

I release him with a shove and head for the relative quiet of the stands. Fuck sound check. If they want to test a voice, then Kris can live out his dreams by playing pretend to an empty stadium.

Rehab.

Makes me sound like I have a problem.

TWENTY

TABITHA

"My Own Summer" - Deftones

"What the fuck do you mean there are royalties owed?" I clutch my phone in a white-knuckled grip, drawing curious looks from passersby.

"You played one of their songs, Tabitha. Without permission from the recording label first. If it was an older track, something they'd released five, ten years ago, then you might get away with it. But you played one that came out last year."

"Why the hell didn't anyone tell me this *before* I did it?" I clutch a fistful of my hair, my grocery shopping at my feet.

"I guess because we didn't know?" John replies with nothing short of bitter sarcasm. "Are you sitting down, though?"

"There's more?" I cry in a pitch that borders on only being audible to dogs.

What the hell else could he drop on me?

"You used Toby in your performance."

"So?" I grimace at some nosy bitch as she makes faces

at my volume. "Is he copyrighted too?"

"He gets metered out by the hour."

I groan, slamming my free hand to my throat as I search the sky for a reason for this madness. "You have to be yanking my chain."

"Afraid not." He sighs. "His minimum is an hour."

"He was on the fucking stage for less than five minutes," I yell.

A mother gives me a scathing glare as she exits the mini-mart with her young daughter. I snatch up my bags with a huff as John answers, intending to find some-where more private.

"I know, Tabitha, but they have to make it worth-while for him, otherwise people would jerk him around for ten minutes of sweet fuck all."

"How much?" Surely we're in the vicinity of fifty for Toby and the same or thereabouts for the song?

"Seven hundred."

I'm dying. I'm fucking sure of it. Why else would breathing be this difficult? "What?"

"Two hundred for Toby, and five hundred for single use of the song."

"Since when do people have to pay that much for a song?" Jesus—my chest. "You can't tell me street buskers pay that much to do a cover."

He sighs. "Look. Wallace Bauer isn't exactly known for his philanthropy."

I sink against the side of a shop, tucked in the start of an alley. "Who the fuck is Wallace Bauer?"

"The guy who owns the band, essentially."

Damn. "Seven hundred?" I won't cry. Nope. Not going

to cry. "How much does that leave me, John? Break it to me sweet."

He chuckles softly. "Tabitha, honey—"

"Not that sweet."

He huffs in amusement. "After costs, you get a little under three thousand." *That's not so bad.* "But you still owe me for the last three months, so if I deduct that before cutting you a check, you're looking at sixteen hundred."

"Sixteen hundred?" Totally going to cry.

My share of the rent alone is four hundred and eighty a month. My credit card has a debit balance larger than the figure he just gave me.

"I know it was a big show, love, but you have to remember the few bums on seats who paid to see you were upstairs. The only reason you get so much is because they agreed to cover the full venue costs."

What did I expect? That Dark Tide would cut me in on the total ticket sales? Of course it would have been kept separate. It was just a spur of the moment deal, after all.

"Thanks, John. Message me when the transfer has been made, please."

"It'll be a few days, Tabitha."

Stab me while I already bleed out, why don't you?

"I have to wait for their PR company to wrap it all up and release our share."

"Fucking jailers, you know? That's all they are; holding our money captive."

"It's standard business."

"Yeah, well nothing about this is standard for me. Not when the cash literally means whether I eat or starve." I slam End on the call and pocket my phone.

I am *so* up shit creek without a paddle.

In a moment of petty rage I whip my phone back out and hammer out a quick message. My gut churns as it makes the sound to confirm the words have been sent. *Probably wasn't such a smart idea.* Oh well.

T: You can have your damn flowers back.

The reply is instant.

R: Why?

Was he sitting on the thing? I gather up my bags and hail a cab, giving the driver directions to the theater before I respond to Rey.

T: Why didn't anyone tell me I'd have to pay to use Toby on stage? Let alone that it costs to play your recent tracks in a paid performance?

R: What choo talkin' about, Willis?

I chuckle, earning a glance in the rearview from the cab driver.

T: I've just been informed it cost me $700 to play that cover last night.

R: Fuck off. Who by?

T: Your label.

His replies cease, not even a dancing dot or three to indicate he's formulating one. I give up waiting as the cabbie pulls up outside the theater. He takes the bill I hold out for him, my frugal grip on the note meaning he has to tug a little hard to release it from my grasp.

I can't even look at the building without wanting to go on a murderous rampage and smash every pretentious light that still spells out Dark Tide's name. The time on my phone reads 11:36. I pocket the device and head for the brass-handled doors, surprised to find that the damn things won't budge. I try the other side just in case, and find the same.

Breathe, Tab. They've probably kept it closed to the public. Look for a stage door.

Like a homeless woman staking her claim for the night, I head down the adjacent alley with my bags of groceries in hand. Sure enough, a black stage door sits two-thirds of the way down the building.

It's also locked.

Totally okay. Maybe I misheard the guy last night when he said come back tomorrow. Maybe he meant Monday? I retrieve my phone and thumb through to the theater's number. To my horror I can hear the line ringing out as I approach the front of the building again, right before the answering service picks up.

This isn't happening. Seriously—how shit can the day get?

As though rising to the challenge, the universe decides now is a good time for one of the plastic handles on my shopping bags to snap, spilling my bagged milk all over the dirty sidewalk.

My ass hits an upturned crate at the head of the alleyway. *Kill me now.* They say there's no use crying over spilled milk, but in that moment I goddamn crack a right ripper of a tantrum. There is *every* reason to cry over the puddle of creamy gold that trickles toward the drain.

I try to bring order back into my chaos by reminding myself that this isn't the first time I've wondered how I'm going to eat, but all that does is make the tears come faster when I realize how useless I have to be at this career if I'm back at square one for what, the seventh, ninth time?

How long before I crawl back to Mum and Dad with my tail between my legs and my dignity on fire behind me?

I gain a few stares from passersby, but at this time of the day the area where the theater is remains quiet. It's tucked between the business district and the industrial side of town; not much foot traffic sees these streets.

I use the hem of my shirt to dab away the remnants of my temporary lapse in sanity. An irritating trill sounds from close by, and first instinct is that I've inadvertently set off some building alarm by trying to get in. Yet my reason kicks into gear and reminds me that I've been sobbing about my spilled groceries for several minutes now, so if the alarm was to go off, it would have done it straight away.

It takes another solid minute before I realize the sound comes from somewhere *on* me. The trill stops as I reach for my phone, only to restart again. *What the hell?* I don't recognize the alert at all. Did I set an alarm without realizing it?

Rey Thomas – calling from Messenger ...

Well I guess that explains that then; I've never used Messenger to *call* someone. That just goes against my natural instinct to avoid actual human interaction wherever and whenever possible.

I touch the green icon to accept the call, careful not to nudge the video icon. "Hi."

"You sound like you're answering even though you know it's probably a scammer on the other end. Cheer up, cupcake."

"Sorry." Words fail me.

I've always marveled at how different people can sound on the phone as opposed to in person, but nine times out of ten they sound terrible down the line. Rey, though? Holy fuck, that man could make a woman weep.

"What's your bank account number?"

I scoff. "Sure. Let me just recite that from memory."

He huffs. "You do realize you can use your phone while retaining a call, huh?"

Some of us clearly don't spend as much time doing this as others. "What do you want it for?"

I swear I hear his palm hit his forehead. "Does seven hundred ring a bell?"

"You sorted that?"

"In a manner of speaking." He stays silent, presumably waiting on me to retrieve the details.

"Just a minute." I press the home button and navigate to my banking app, praying that I have enough data left to complete both this and his call. "Ready?"

"Born ready, baby."

I ignore the swimming sensation those words ignite low in my belly and recite my account number for him.

"Sweet. Got it."

"Thank you for this."

He huffs out a heavy breath. "Just wanted you to keep the damn flowers is all."

And just like that I ride the roller coaster of crazy from absolute low mere minutes ago, to a blissful high. I laugh, struggling to kill the lingering giggles as Rey chuckles in response.

"I'll keep the flowers."

"Good," he says with mock seriousness. "Because I didn't have a fucking clue how I was supposed to return them semi-used."

"How are you feeling today?"

His end of the line falls deathly quiet before he whispers, "You saw that, huh?"

"Kind of hard to miss."

"Yeah." Both of us hang in amicable silence before he adds, "I didn't know with your last message if you knew or not."

"Knew what? That you behaved like a cliché rock star?"

"One way of putting it."

I'm sorely tempted to smack the video icon now, just so I can see his face. My gut tells me it's much the same as he looked after he belted out "Descent of My Mind" last night.

"Are you decent?" I ask the question before my nerves get the better of me.

He scoffs. "Sure. Why?"

I tap the icon. The image takes a second to pixelate and become clear. "Because you don't sound like you're okay."

He drops his head so all I can see is his wild hair and jaw as his shoulders rise with his sigh. "You were the one with the issue, Tabby-cat, not me."

"I call bullshit."

His face lifts at my whispered words. Our eyes connect, and no words seem relevant. It's all there, laid out in his pained, tired gaze: he's *not* okay.

"Are they giving you a hard time about it?"

He nods. The movement draws my focus to his surroundings.

"Are you in bleachers?"

"Supposed to be doing sound check." He spins the phone to give me panoramic views of where they'll play tonight.

"Why aren't you, then?"

"I'm sulking." He returns the phone to his face and grins.

Any frustrations I had at the guy melt away. *That*, right there, was a genuine smile. I'd put my seven hundred on it.

"Tell me what happened. From the horse's mouth."

His gaze flicks past the phone, yet he holds it steady as he shrugs. "I derailed."

"Have you always had an issue with alcohol?"

"Apparently." He laughs before setting those intense grays back on me. "Can you keep a secret?"

"Who the hell am I going to tell?" I roll my eyes.

He shrugs again. "Anybody who'll pay you enough."

"Gee. Thanks for the vote of confidence."

Rey smiles again, only this time it's a lazy quirk of his lips. "I'm cracking the shits with them because our label boss told me I have to do rehab after the tour if I want to keep my career."

I should be sympathizing with him, but, "Cracking the shits?" I laugh. "That doesn't sound very American of you."

He chuckles. "Like it? I looked up Australian slang."

"I'd love it, except I'm from New Zealand, remember?"

He pulls his lips back in a grimace. "Shit. Sorry."

"Forgiven." I'm still seriously swooning that he'd do something like that just for me.

Calm down, Tab. He probably did it out of boredom. Or not....

"How do you feel about rehab, though?"

"Bummed." He frowns, seeming to search for the right words. "I don't think I have a problem that serious, but it's not as though I'm always right, is it?"

"You did smash up some cars."

"*A* car," he corrects with a raised eyebrow. "And I did that on my way to see you."

Wait. What? "To see me?"

He nods, lips twisted.

"Why?"

"Why not? You're way more fun than these clowns."

"Fun isn't a word I'd associate with me," I level.

He inclines his head in agreement. "Genuine, then."

"Sounds better." I give him a small smile. "I could

have used the pick-me-up today."

"Because of the money thing?"

"Because of this." I spin the phone to show my milk river.

His laughter echoes from the device as I turn it back around. The loud twang of a guitar sounds in the background. "What the hell *is* that, Tabby-cat?"

"My milk for the week. Let's just say Kendall will be pissed when she can't have cereal in the morning, or her cocoa at night."

"Chin up, babe. You've got seven hundred coming your way."

The deafening notes of their music crackle through my speakers. Rey frowns to the left of the screen, presumably at the stage. "I better go." He hollers to be heard over the noise. "Talk later, kitty."

My stomach ties itself in knots when he blows me a cheeky kiss before ending the call.

Rey Thomas just blew me a goddamn kiss.

I may as well have French kissed the guy on the red carpet for how I feel in this moment.

TWENTY-ONE

REY

"Bullet With Butterfly Wings"
– The Smashing Pumpkins

Yeah, Wallace told me in not so many words where I could stick Tabby's seven hundred dollars. She doesn't need to know where it comes from, just that she has it back. *Fucking raping bastards.* She's not exactly somebody who can afford that bullshit.

I jog down the concrete steps two at a time, blistering to get on stage and get my frustrations out. Toby shoots me a scathing glare as I approach the steps, much the same as he would when I dropped him in the shit with Mom as kids. I ignore the moody bastard, and weave between where he and Kris play at the rear of the stage to retrieve my guitar.

Fuck him and his self-righteous pep talks. Does he honestly think that grilling me twenty-four seven is going to do any good? Way to shove the splinter in a little deeper there, brother.

I take position at the front of the stage and stare out over the grassy area that will be alive with a sea of moving bodies tonight. Emery crosses to where I stand and knocks his foot into my calf as he strums his bass. I catch his encouraging smile and give him a sharp nod before pulling out my pick and tearing into the song.

For the next hour my worries lessen piece by piece. Each break between songs gets easier to bear, each time we play our cohesion more and more evident. By the end of the sound check I'd almost say we're back on good terms.

Almost.

"You get water backstage tonight," Toby drops casually as he pulls the dust cover over his drum set.

I set my guitar in the stand and frown. "Water?"

"Can't have a repeat of last night," he states. "Not when we have two sold-out shows that will kill us to cancel."

"And why the fuck would we cancel them?" I thrust my arms across my chest, widening my stance while he continues to avoid looking at me.

"Can't play if you're passed out, hey?"

"Fuck you." I make it halfway off the stage before he calls me back.

"You really going to place this on me, Rey?"

I spin on my heel, considering the implications of laying my brother out. "I never said any of this was your fault, Toby. So don't go putting words in my fucking mouth. I get it's my fault," I shout, throwing my arms wide. "I get that. But what *doesn't* help is you constantly making me feel like shit for slipping, okay? I'm a fuckup, yeah. I know that. *You* know that. But making me feel as though I can't ever be anything else doesn't help." I shake my head, adding before he gets a chance to speak, "You fucking label me before I have a chance to do it myself, so maybe yeah, this is a little your fault. I never was the good kid, was I?"

He says nothing, lips twisted as he stares me down. He knows I'm right. *I* know I'm right. I wasn't the good kid in the family. Toby was the all-star sportsman, our sister the academic genius that excels at everything she does. Me? I'm the misfit, the square peg in the round hole.

I never fit in. I still don't. I just figured out how to build a career around it.

"Ignore him," Kris says quietly as I pass him side of stage. "He's just being a big brother."

"Yeah?" I scoff. "Well, right now the last thing I need is my goddamn family."

He frowns, the concept seeming foreign to him. "Come on, man. Your family loves you." He swallows, and I realize what a jerk comment it was to make to him before he says the next line. "At least yours acknowledge who you are."

"Shit." I scrub a hand over my face, and then glance at Toby. "I'm sorry, Kris."

He shrugs, jerking his head to indicate we should keep walking. "No sweat. It's easy for people to forget shit about me when I hardly ever say a fucking thing, right?"

I grin at the guy, thankful for his friendship. He's a dark horse, a bit of a recluse, which is an oxymoron in itself given his career choice, but he's an all-round good guy. He cares too much, and I guess this persona of his is the only way he knows how to cope with that.

"What are we having for dinner?" I ask as we descend the stairs into the tent set up behind the temporary stage. "They ordering in here, or are we heading back to the hotel?"

"Think it's up to us." He snatches a bottle of sports drink off the free-for-all table. "What do you want to do?"

"Hide and pretend my drunken ass isn't plastered all over the interwebs at this very point in time." I collapse into one of the beanbags and look for Emery. "Where did Em go?"

Kris shrugs as Toby jogs down the stairs. He shoots me a heated stare, and then marches out the exit flap, punching the canvas out of the way as he goes.

"It'll blow over."

I shift my gaze to Kris and sigh. "Fucking better."

My phone vibrates in my pocket, still set on silent. I twist onto my left hip and dig it out. A little bit of me hopes it's Tabby. The bigger part of me knows it wouldn't be.

Still can't hurt to check.

Mom. *Shit.*

I lunge from the beanbag and stalk out the exit, much to Kris's interest. Toby stands in the middle of the grassy parking lot, phone to his ear.

"You still on the phone to her?" I holler as I approach. "Couldn't fucking let me sort this out myself?"

He turns his back to me, still talking.

"Hey!" I shunt the heel of my hand into the back of his shoulder, forcing him forward a step.

He spins on me with nothing short of murder in his eyes. "Hold on." His hand slides over the end to cover the mouthpiece. "She messaged this morning after seeing you on Facebook, so I'm doing what *you* should have and reassuring her that she doesn't need to check your fucking life insurance is up to date."

"Fuck you all." I back away, head shaking. "You're all so convinced that that's where I'm headed again, huh?"

"Aren't you?"

Maybe. I don't know. That's the glorious thing about being bipolar: you never know what you're going to get week to week. Life is literally a box of fucking chocolates.

"Should we find out?" I run for the scaffolding that supports the rear of the stage.

Toby hurriedly talks into the phone before disconnecting.

I eye the goddamn structure, breaking it down like a kid would the jungle gym, and then start to climb.

"What are you doing, Rey?"

"Seeing if I feel like trying to fly," I yell back as I make it past head height.

"Get down!"

I catch Kris in my periphery as he wanders out of the tent to see what's going on.

"All you're doing is proving how fucking immature you are!" Toby yells.

I lean off the structure, held in place by one arm hooked around the pipe steel. "That's the problem, isn't it? You think I'm a joker, always fucking around, never taking anything seriously."

"Show me otherwise," he hollers. "Get down here and fucking prove you're not."

I climb higher, my boot slipping as I take another step. Adrenaline charges my veins. I can see over the fucking back boundary fence of the stadium from here. "Ever wonder why I act like a clown?" I yell. "Ever wonder why I get blind drunk?"

Toby throws his hands up at his sides, neck craned to see me. Kris lights a cigarette.

I twist around to face them, elbows hooked over the steel behind me as I lean out over the dizzying height. "Because it's easier than being me," I say with a mixture of humor and sadness. "It's easier than having you all feel sorry for me, easier than seeing the same fucked-up pity you, Cassie, Mom, and Dad would give me when we were kids." I let my arms slide out, the thrill and the danger making my skin feel charged with electricity as I hold on to the scaffolding by just my fingertips. "It's easier to be who everyone expects you to be than what they don't understand."

"Fuck, Rey! Be careful!"

TWENTY-TWO

TABITHA

"Rx (Medicate)" – Theory of a Deadman

"You haven't moved, have you?" I give Kendall the side-eye as I walk through our apartment.

She smiles sheepishly from her position on the sofa. "I got up and went to the bathroom. Twice."

"Well done," I sass. "I'll add a gold star to your sticker chart."

"Bitch."

I blow her a kiss. "You love me." With a heave of my arms, I lift what's left of the meager groceries I picked up onto the counter.

"Hey, let me help." Kendall slides off the sofa and crosses to the kitchen. "What do I owe you?"

"Nothing, honestly."

She pauses, packet of pasta in her hand. "No, really. How much?"

"I mean it. Nothing." I sag against the counter and break the bad news. "I dropped the milk and it spilled everywhere, all over the sidewalk."

Kendall cringes. "Shoot. Do we have *any*?"

"One bag." I twist my lips in apology. "The damn handle on the shopping bag broke." I point to the plastic now tied in an assortment of knots that would make a Boy Scout cringe.

"It's okay." She returns to putting the dry food away. "I can probably fleece a jug from work if we get desperate."

"We're not thieves."

"Not yet." She gives me a wink. Her eyes track around the room as she frowns. "Where's your stuff?"

"At the theater."

Her frown deepens.

"It was locked." I put a bag of apples in the fridge. "I got there in time, but nobody was around."

"What are you going to do?"

"Wait until Monday and hope that my things are there, safe and sound."

Kendall's lips purse as she looks me over with worry. "That's pretty crap, though. If they'd said something last night we could have taken the stuff then and there."

"They did say something," I tell her. "They told me to come today between nine and twelve."

"Do you think they meant tonight?"

I stare at her a fraction too long for it to be normal. "I don't know."

She puts the last of the groceries away while I rack my brain for what *exactly* the guy said to me. Truth be told, I can't recall if he said morning or night now; I simply assumed morning.

"Don't worry about it," Kendall offers as she sets aside the fresh cheese slices and bread. "We can sort it out later. Grilled cheese?"

I nod, pouring us the first of our new bottle of wine. Yeah. We're classy as all fuck.

"Did you hear from Toby while I was out?" I take a sip from my glass, doing my best to hide any possible telltale signs that I spoke to Rey.

"I did actually."

It's not as though I want to keep it a secret from Kendall, it's more that I simply don't feel like sharing. As PG as the conversation was, it felt special—ours.

"He, um." She frowns down at the bread as she prepares it. "He said they had some more issues with Rey today. He wouldn't elaborate, clearly, because how can he trust me, you know? We've only just met. But he seemed cut up about it."

"Oh, that's not good." I take another sip, hoping my bullshit act of surprise will fly with her.

Their argument pre-practice must have been a doozy.

"Did you get ahold of John?" She layers the bread and cheese in the pan.

I nod. "Said it might take a couple of weeks for the money to come through, but I think I can manage with credit cards until then."

"If you need me to spot you a little, you know I will."

I hand Kendall her glass. "You don't have that much lying around, hon. I'll be fine."

I refrain from giving her the full story a second time. Explaining about the fees only leads on to me having to explain why I'm no longer paying them. And again, I don't want to share my conversation with Rey just yet.

"Let me know when it's ready, yeah? I'm just going to

see if I can get in touch with anyone to find out exactly what time I can get into the theater." *Liar.*

Kendall nods, ass against the edge of the counter. "Sure."

I take my wine to my room, kicking the door most of the way closed behind me as I enter. Perched on the side of my bed, I sip my drink with one hand, peering out the corner of my eye to see my phone screen in the other.

T: How did your practice go?

In all reality, it's none of my business. So we shared a moment? What does that make me now? His best buddy?

I stare at the message thread, at the little blue circle with the tick that tells me it's been delivered. Yet his profile picture doesn't slide into place. Even after the fifth time I wake the screen.

Must be busy.

"How did you get on?" Kendall edges my bedroom door open with her elbow, plates in hand. "In here, or out there?"

"Out there." I rise from the mattress, frustrated at both my empty glass and the lack of reply from Rey. "Couldn't get in touch with anyone." It's not a complete lie.

"Don't stress. I'm sure it's safe there until Monday."

"Yeah. More than likely." I accept the plate she holds out for me as I reach her, trailing behind my best buddy as she leads the way back to the living area.

"What's next for the great virtuoso?" she asks, her mouth already filled with warm bread and gooey cheese.

I shrug, balancing my plate carefully as I drop onto the sofa, one leg folded beneath me. "I guess I work on some more original pieces and see if I can get more followers."

"When are you going to start selling on something like Spotify?"

I take a bite of the grilled cheese and groan as the creamy flavor coats my taste buds. I neglected to eat before I headed out this morning, my ravenous stomach reminding me of that as it growls in appreciation at the food I currently funnel it. "Um," I mumble, finishing my mouthful. "I need to save to pay for a proper recording studio." I swallow, wiping my mouth with the back of my hand. "I need decent quality if I put it up on a site like that, not just my shitty YouTube tracks."

"Look into it," Kendall instructs with a raised eyebrow. "I'm sure there are ways around it. You can't tell me that there isn't some workaround for artists who record at home?"

I shrug as I take another bite. "Dunno."

"Babe. Finish your mouthful before you talk."

I swallow down the mouthful a little too early, eyes watering as I answer, "You're one to talk."

Kendall pulls a face as she dryly asks, "What?" with her mouth jammed full of grilled cheese.

The laughter feels good. Real good. Especially after the shitty start to the day. My thoughts drift back to Rey as we eat in relative silence, to the way he turned my day around with one simple off-the-cuff phone call. He ended it too quick for me to thank him for giving me that pick-me-up, but I guess that's what life with somebody as well known as him is like: constant snatched conversations in the brief moments of respite between the demands of a tour.

My gaze drifts to the hallway as I pop the last bite of bread into my mouth.

I'm not too proud to admit that I'm becoming addicted to the little hits of him, even after a few short days. But one thing I know for sure sets me apart from most of the other people who feel the same way is that my addiction has nothing to do with who he is in name, or what that earns him.

I don't like Rey, the lead singer of Dark Tide. He's arrogant, loud, and careless.

I like Rey, the guy who loves to play his guitar and sing about the things that torture him most.

I like Rey the artist.

Now I want to know Rey the man.

TWENTY-THREE

REY

"Bullet" – Hollywood Undead

Ever seen a security guy relive his youth? No? Then I'm telling you now, it's a fucking sight to behold.

When Toby realized that every step closer he took meant another inch I leaned out over the distant ground, he sent over Kris. Yeah, Kris. The guy who then asked if I'd like a cigarette when I got down.

I went higher—fuck them both.

And that's when they called in the big guns. The security guard, Lenny, looked to be at least fifty years old and probably the same number of pounds over his optimum weight range. Didn't stop the guy scaling that scaffolding like a motherfucking gorilla in heat, though.

Got to give the guy credit for how he managed to subdue me, all while ensuring we didn't both fall and break our goddamn necks. Shoulder still burns a little, but I think I got my point across.

"Do you ever think of anybody but yourself?"

Or maybe not.

I sigh before turning to address Toby. We have thirty

minutes until show time and he's been aiming shots at me all fucking afternoon.

"Do you?"

Two simple words that leave him shaking his head. "Just grow up, Rey. I get it; you're the baby of the family. But that's not an excuse to continue to act like a fucking child."

He storms off to the far end of our "VIP lounge," the only section of this marquee they've set up for us that has huge industrial blow heaters to ward off the cold.

Yep. It's fucking pissing down out there. Water pours from the heavens as a silent "fuck you" from life. Still, our fans are ready to go; the warm-up chants the crew has them making do their thing and build the buzz.

"Tell me you called your mom," Emery asks. He chews on a stick of jerky as he waits on my answer.

He turned up right as Lenny pinned me to the grass, a knee to the middle of my back while everyone waited on me to promise I wouldn't pull a stunt like that again. I agreed. I won't climb the scaffolding again, but I hold no responsibility for whatever else I might attempt.

"Yeah, I called her." Got the whole myriad of emotions from her: anger, worry, distress, and finally guilt.

Always the guilt.

"Good." He pops the last of the meat in his mouth before asking, "Ready?"

I nod, rubbing my hands near the side of the heater. I made the mistake of standing too close to the front earlier, and promptly learned how fucking nuclear leather and studs can get in the space of seconds.

"Fifteen-minute call, guys."

Toby waves off the crew member—Stuart, I think his name is—and goes right back to ignoring the rest of us. I eyeball the fucker as he taps his phone screen with his thumb, a small smile making his lips quirk up every so often. *Who is he messaging?* Café Girl? Nah—couldn't be. Maybe?

My gaze drifts right, and I find Emery now doing the same. Only I know whom it is he messages. He thinks we're all stupid, flicking his screen to eBay listings when we get too close. But it's her—that fucking manipulative bitch back home.

Kris reclines on a beanbag, deep in his preshow ritual of listening to the set list one last time. I figure if the three of them want to be antisocial assholes, then I can too. My fingers wrap around my phone, deep in my pocket, and I pull it free to check the notifications.

How the fuck did I miss that? I don't get message previews to my home screen anymore, not since we took off and the sheer number of old "friends" crawling out of the woodwork would clog my screen. I don't even pay mind to the fact the tiny red circle always has a "99+" in it because I never clear them all. Nope. But I do try to open the app regularly so that I catch anything important.

Anything like a message from Tabby-cat.

T: How did your practice go?

Jesus. What do I say to that? Eventful? Depressing? Same old shit, different day?

R: Run of the mill. Get the rest of your food

home safely? Or is there a Hansel and Gretel trail from where you dropped the milk to your door?

The blue circle switches to her profile pic. *Hello, kitty.* I watch the dancing dots, mesmerized by them while I alternate which hand holds the phone, and which one gets warm.

T: Shouldn't you be on stage?

My lips kick up on one side. Does that mean she's following our tour now?

R: Fifteen minutes or so. Whatchya doin?

Her dots dance, then stop, then dance. I could skip the show and happily cozy up beside this flame from heaven and watch her dots dance all night, knowing it meant another little glimpse at the girl behind the tough façade.

T: You really want to know? I promise it's not as glamorous as your life.

Oh, she has no idea. Life is never glamorous; you can just afford to mask the ugly truth better the more money you have to spend on the illusion.

R: Give me something to think about, Tabby-cat.

T: Like you'll have any time to think...

R: Maybe not for the next two hours, but I've got all night, baby.

Her dots don't show. *Too forward?* Did I push it a bit far with that one?

"Ten minutes, guys!"

I throw up a hand to show I heard, the tension melting from my shoulders as her dots begin to skip again.

T: I'm in bed, listening to music while I write my own. Leave it up to your imagination whether I sleep naked, or not ;)

Snap. There she is, that little vixen she likes to pretend doesn't simmer beneath all that anger. The text at the top of the thread changes from "Active now" to "Active 1m ago." She's switched off. Left me hanging.

Girl sure knows how to play, and she's got me holding on like a fool. I lock my phone and leave it in the secure area before giving my reflection the once-over. My hair's spiked as usual, my clothing black on black.

I'm at ease, comfortable, and entirely in my element. And thanks to Tabby-cat, horny as a motherfucker.

Going to be one hell of a show.

TWENTY-FOUR

TABITHA

"Heart-Shaped Box" - Nirvana

The snap of my neck as my head lolls forward wakes me up in a flash. Fast enough that my addled brain leaves me nauseous. I tried to stay awake until after Rey's show would be finished, I really did. But given the last few days, I'm exhausted. Heaven knows how he does it.

Probably with one or two illegal substances in his system.

I don't exactly know what I waited for, anyway. Another cheeky message? Another rub to my ego?

Don't make it out to be more than it is, Tab. He probably thinks the messages are a bit of fun: the celebrity rock star playing with the gullible pauper violinist. He taps out one harmless enough question, and I metaphorically spread my goddamn legs for him.

Leave it up to your imagination if I sleep naked.... Pfft. What the hell am I doing? I've got no interest in a guy like him. *Do I?*

Like the weak individual I am, I reach for my phone

and seek out his validation. Is my self-esteem really that low, that I'm resorting to innuendo-laden messaging with a guy who could easily tear my career to shreds with one lash of his tongue?

Yes. Yes it is.

I wake the screen, giddy to find a message waiting from Rey. Even more thrilling is the fact he sent it less than an hour ago and that he's still online. *Eep!* It must have come through as I dozed off.

R: I'm putting money on you not sleeping naked. I'm seeing a cute little tank and booty-short combo, maybe kittens with ice cream cones as the print, maybe polka dots. I can't imagine you being reckless enough to risk the paper cuts to sensitive areas if you're writing music like you say.

T: Maybe I don't write on paper? Can't get a paper cut with an iPad.

My heart matches the pace of his dots as he words a reply.

R: See, now you're starting something very, very dangerous, kitty.
R: Shouldn't you be asleep?

All manner of sex-orientated replies flit through my mind; he's left it wide open for me. Yet I hold on to the last strands of my restraint and type a simple reply.

T: Shouldn't you be out partying it up or whatever rock stars do after a show?

R: Hate to disappoint you, babe, but you shouldn't believe everything you read. I'm tucked up in bed, ready to rest up before tomorrow night's show. Leave it up to your imagination if I'm naked or not ;)

Hot damn. I fan myself with the phone. All I can hear is the sound of my blood as it whooshes through my ears. Dangerous is a mild understatement when it comes to the fine line we walk.

T: I'm picking you don't like the cold much— most pampered types don't—so you're all wrapped up in a super sexy, alluring onesie, complete with the buttoned-up butt flap.

I get a line of teary-eyed laughing emoticons in reply... right before the now-familiar Messenger alert sings out as my screen changes. *Shit.* Totally not prepared for this. I run a quick hand over my hair, and then the side of my finger under my eyes, before checking the sheet is high under my arms and tapping to answer.

"Ha!" I'm greeted with a huge grin. The fact his head and shoulders fill the screen, hair fanned out on the pillow, tells me he holds the phone above him in bed. "Knew it."

"What?" I glance down, and then back at the tiny picture in the corner that shows me what he sees.

"I figured if you took ages to answer, it meant you were naked and needed to get dressed. But you answered in five seconds, so I'm right: you wear pajamas to bed."

I cock an eyebrow. "No kittens or ice creams though."

He makes a mock sad face, shifting around in the bed to seemingly get more comfortable. "Can't have it all, I suppose."

"Well?" I square my shoulders and cock an eyebrow. "What about you?"

He smirks, the sort that I'm sure has destroyed thousands of hearts, and twists the phone to scan down his body. The blankets lift out of the way, the camera panning across his notably tattooed chest, and then down over his flat, yet undefined stomach. I suck in a sharp breath, waiting for the edge of the screen to crest past that telltale V, certain he's only winding me up because he has boxers on, yet the image blurs as he whips it back to his face with a chuckle.

"That's as far as I'm going."

"What?" I say with a laugh. "You could still be either. That doesn't answer the question."

He grins. "I sleep completely in the buff, kitty."

Lord have mercy. That glimpse just ramped itself up the hotness stakes times one hundred.

"How the fuck did our conversation go from spilled milk to this?" I muse.

He shrugs one shoulder. "Dunno. But I'm not com-plaining."

Neither. But that doesn't appease the icky feeling in my gut that says this has only got one way to go: south.

Nothing wholesome or worthwhile can come from what we're doing.

His eyes hood a little as he seems to wait on me to speak next. I slouch a little against the headboard and decide to run with honesty as the best option. "Why me?" My mother always taught me to let people know where they stand with you—I'm not about to go changing that now, just because he's famous.

"How do you mean?" Rey frowns, tossing his free arm over his head.

I pause to read the script along his forearm. *Everyone is a moon.*

"Kitty?"

I snap my attention back to his face. "Sorry."

"I asked why you said 'why me?'" His hand flexes, drawing my focus back to the quote.

It's weird. I want to know what it means, its significance.

"I, um." I frown, thrown by the ink. "You could pick anyone, Rey," I explain, my focus slowly seeping back over to my original interest. "So why chat to me?"

"Am I bothering you?" His entire mood shifts, so noticeably that I swear I feel the chill in_my room.

"No." I set the phone against my bent legs and tuck my arms under the blanket. "What's wrong?"

"Nothing."

"Don't lie to me." I had a father who lied to me for most of my childhood—I know bullshit when I hear it.

His hand flexes again, drawing my focus back to the gothic script.

"If you're going to pretend that nothing is wrong,

then at least humor me and tell me what that means." I nod toward the top of the screen.

He seems to take a moment to realize what I gesture to before he slowly brings his arm down and appears to read the words. "Everyone is a moon?"

"Yeah. What does that mean?"

"Kitty..." His lips kick up, his mood doing a complete one-eighty. "Does this mean I'm more cultured than you?"

Ugh. I roll my eyes. "For this moment, let's say yes."

He chuckles. "It's a Mark Twain quote."

"You read Mark Twain?" I lift one eyebrow.

He smiles sheepishly. "Nope. But I know some of his words. That's cultured enough, right?"

His laugh is infectious, yet not quite enough to make me forget the deeply disturbed Rey that peeked out from behind this mask mere seconds ago.

"The whole quote goes 'Everyone is a moon, and has a dark side which he never shows to anybody.'"

My gut bottoms out. There it is: the reason for that shift in mood. "Why does that mean so much to you?" I ask carefully.

"Why do you care?" he asks with nothing short of snark. "Would my answer change how you feel about me?"

"What *is* the answer, Rey?" I bite. No, it wouldn't change a thing. But it would sure explain a lot. He's been up and down like a goddamn whack-a-mole, and if I can pick that from two ten-minute Messenger conversations, then what the hell is it like to tour with him? "I'm only asking because I want to learn more about you."

"Now I'm calling bullshit," he snaps.

I hold my breath, chewing on my bottom lip as he huffs and looks away.

"Maybe it's time we both got some rest," he says in a monotone. "Good night, kitty."

His finger comes toward the screen before it cuts to black. I'm still stunned by the complete and utter shutdown, unable to think of what to say, let alone come up with anything fast enough to stop him disconnecting.

What the hell was that? So he has darkness inside of him. Don't we all? Why is he so touchy about it?

I tap on my screen to save it going to sleep, and then send a quick message before closing the Messenger app.

T: I'm sorry if I crossed a line. I was genuinely curious. I don't know enough about you to judge you. Sleep well.

Fuck knows, I won't.

TWENTY-FIVE

REY

"Black Hole Sun" - Soundgarden

The following night's show was flat, despite the fact the rain decided to hold out. The crowd was pumping; it wasn't their fault. Nope. It was all me... as usual. Hard to have a kick-ass show when the front man would rather lie on his back in a dark room and listen to Pink Floyd on repeat.

I didn't sleep much. Couldn't find it in me to relax when my mind decided to open the old albums, dust off the home videos, and show me a play-by-play of why I'm such a goddamn fuckup. "It's all in your head" is the most common response I get from people who genuinely think they're trying to help. "You need to think positive."

Trust me, fucker, I've tried. I try daily. *Fuck.* Every goddamn hour of every goddamn day. Do you know how demeaning it is to stand before a mirror and try to do the exercise laid down to you by a shrink—tell yourself five things that you appreciate about who you are—and to fail after number two? Nope? Well then I bow down to you.

I *know* it's all in my head. It's chemical, it's mental... whatever the fuck it is, the most important thing to know about a condition like this is *it doesn't go away.* You learn how to manage it, and some days you fail.

Kitty asked me a simple, honest question and I froze. I mean, fuck it, I put the fucking words on my skin so that people would see them. So why did I choke?

Why am I now sitting here six days later on a goddamn bus to our next stop on the tour, constantly waking my phone so it goes back to her message on my screen?

"Googling how to get a stick out of your ass?" Emery asks as he drops onto the narrow bench seat beside me.

I kill the screen and then slide my phone onto the small table facedown. "How much longer do we have before I can get out of this fucking sardine tin?"

He squints as though consulting some map in his head. "Less than an hour, I reckon."

"How the fuck do you know that without looking?" I tease, leaning back and spreading my arms wide across the back of the seat.

He gives me a cheeky grin while thumbing over his shoulder. "Saw the sign back there." Emery jerks his chin toward my phone. "Wanna talk about it?"

"Nope."

He shrugs. "Don't blame me then when you're chugging pills and crying for your mom." He rises out of the seat, yet stalls when I block him by stretching my leg out under the table.

"Sit down."

He drops wordlessly, allowing me his undivided

attention.

"Would the band do better with a new front man?"

He visibly pales. "What?"

"I wreck the mood, right? I want to know your honest opinion: Do you think there'd be more cohesion, that the new material would flow easier without my shit getting in the way?"

He sighs out his nose, slouching into the seat. "Is this you breaking up with me, man? Because I thought we were in this 'til death do us part."

I chuckle. "Nope. No break up, sweet cheeks." My face falls before I press again. "I really want to know what you think, though."

He pauses a moment, staring out the window on the opposite side of the bus as the scenery buzzes by. Kris sits up near the driver, knees up against his chest as he plays Xbox. Toby lies crashed out in one of the narrow beds, snoring his ass off. Turns out the rain didn't agree much with him, either, and he's got a fucking head cold.

"Look," Emery starts, drawing my focus back to him. "You are who you are, Rey. Take away the mood swings, the arrogance when you're happy, and the drama when you're not... what would be left just wouldn't be you. You get me?"

I shrug one shoulder. "I think so."

"My point is, if you're unhappy, then change what's within your control. But don't go trying to be somebody else."

"That's fucking deep for you," I tease in an effort to deflect from the fact I want to hug the shit out of his sorry ass.

He gives a soft smile as he rises again. "Sometimes I can be honest, too."

Fucker hits me right in the feels as he walks away to rib Kris. I twist my lips and stare at the phone before me. It wasn't Kitty's doing that I can't stomach talking about my issues. Not her problem that giving voice to my faults makes me loathe myself even more. Denial is a pretty flower that grows in your shade when the garden around you withers in the heat.

R: How did you learn our song so fast?

I reread the message after I've sent it and mentally slap myself for how cold and blunt it comes across.

R: I never told you how fucking awesome it sounded.

There. At least now she knows I'm asking not because I doubt her talent, but because I really was impressed.

It takes half an hour before she replies. Half an hour where I sit and replay the last few weeks through my head. If I'd looked hard enough, the signs were there that I was due to crash again. I'd hit a high. We stepped off that plane for our impromptu layover and I thought I was a fucking god among men.

I'd reached mania. And what follows mania? The slide.

T: I learn by ear.

Her reply is short, and most definitely not sweet.

Can't blame her, though, when I've been radio silent for the better part of a week.

R: I apologize for being a complete asshole.

T: I'm legit framing this message.

Emery glances over as I chuckle at her reply, concern in his eyes. I ignore the justification behind that, and settle in to talk to Tabby-cat.

R: Don't tell me you're surprised that the spoilt rock star would be such a jackass?

T: To quote my mother (shoot me now) I'm not angry, just disappointed.

Fair enough.

R: How long does it take you to learn by ear?

It's a skill I'm not that great at. Toby can pick things up, but it takes him a week before he can play start to finish without any errors. There's no way in hell she would have already been learning our work. Too much of a coincidence.

T: Depends on the piece. Your music was quite basic once I broke it down.

R: Ouch.

T: I said basic, not shit.

R: Better.

T: Why? Are you trying to learn something?

Would she teach me? I chew the end of my thumb as the bus slows for the city limits. Thank fuck this torture ride is almost over. I mean, I love these guys, but the tension lately has been off the charts.

R: Nope. Just curious. You decent?

T: Would it stop you if I wasn't?

I barely have time to read her reply before she dials through. Best part of my fucking day seeing that face when I hit Accept. I honestly thought she'd tell me to get fucked when I finally sent a reply.

"I got the tattoo when I was nineteen." I hit her with the details straight out of the gate.

Her eyes soften, yet she shows no emotion with her mouth as she softly nods. "Okay."

"I, um, read it somewhere. Can't remember where now. But it struck a chord, you know? I'd had a rough patch with my mental health and it helped me accept who I am better."

She pulls in a carefully measured breath before asking, "Do you mind if I ask what you're diagnosed with?"

I cast my eye over her tousled hair, as though she's repeatedly run her fingers through it. Her eyes are tired, and yet she looks fucking beautiful out in the natural light, seemingly somewhere open like a park.

She's not asking to hurt you. "Bipolar."

Tabby doesn't say a goddamn thing, and I can't decide if that's good or bad. She simply nods a couple of times, and then glances to her right.

"Where are you?"

"Shopping." She holds up a spiral-bound notebook. "I might have fibbed: I do write my music on paper."

Her smile fucking undoes the last six days of doubt and regret. "Ice-creams, or polka dots?"

Her lips part as her smile widens. "Polka dots." She raises her voice to be heard over my laughter. "But only on the shorts."

"How far are you from home?"

Her brow pinches, the breeze catching the ends of her hair. "A block."

"Are you headed there?"

"Soon. Why?"

"Play me something."

Her frown deepens. "When I get home?"

I nod. "Yeah. Play me one of the pieces you wrote."

Tabby ducks her chin, a low chuckle sounding from her. "Confession." She twists the phone a little, showing me her violin case beside her. "I was busking as well as shopping."

Fuck-all coins sit on the velvet. I can't explain why that makes me so mad, but it does. "How often do you do that?"

She twists the screen back to herself. "When I need to. Hang on." The picture blurs as she jostles the phone around, setting it down on the ground beside where she'd been seated on a low brick garden edging.

Her legs come into the shot, narrowing as she walks away from the phone, her violin at her side. A sense of amazement comes over me as I look at this effortless beauty, kitted out in her gray coat and white scarf to ward off the cold, her legs kept warm in black skinny jeans, a pair of heavy boots on her feet.

She pauses with the violin to her shoulder, her chest expanding on a deep breath before she begins.

I stretch my arms out before me on the table, my phone held between my hands, and watch with awe as she plays a slow, sweeping piece. The image is blocked momentarily while somebody drops a coin in her case, and I break my spell long enough to find Toby now awake. He stands in the aisle between the ends of the beds, arms stretched over his head to the curtain rail, and listens. Tabby sways with the music, her song building tempo. A flash of jealousy takes me surprise as Toby drops onto the seat beside me to watch her also.

She plays for me. This is *my* show, even if it is in the middle of a park. She didn't start the song for any of them, and she didn't start it for Toby.

She started the song for me, and I want it for myself.

I want the way she makes me feel for myself.

Damn it—I want *her.*

"She's fucking good, yeah?" Toby's fingers knit in front of his mouth, his elbows on the table as he watches her finish up the piece.

Tabby walks back toward the phone before I get a chance to tell my brother where he can stick his appreciation of my precious treasure.

"Oh. Hey," she greets as she picks up the device.

Toby lifts a hand as he slides away. "Fucking awesome, Tabitha."

"Thanks." Her gaze tracks him as he leaves the shot before I get a single raised brow. "So?"

"What he said," I grumble, still sore over sharing my things.

I'm fucking five all over again.

"Say it again, but try and convince me this time," she teases as she retakes her seat on the garden edge.

"It was beautiful." I cringe a little at such a girly affirmation coming from my mouth, but what the fuck else do you call classical music? "One of yours?"

She nods. "One of the first pieces I decided was good enough to play for an audience."

"When did you start?"

"Playing?" She flicks her hair out of her face after the breeze tangles it across her nose. "When I was seven. Dad thought it would be a good substitute for what I really wanted."

"Which was?" I frown as the bus pulls up at our digs for the night.

"Football."

My laugh escapes as a snort. "What?"

She chuckles. "I know, right? I wanted to play in the lingerie bowl, apparently."

Can't deny that'd be a sight worth watching. "We're at our destination now," I explain. "I better go."

Her lips turn down as she nods. "It was good to talk to you, Rey."

"It was good." I stare at the screen, unable to hang up just yet.

Her lips kick up on one side. "Call me whenever you need to okay? No matter the time."

Tell her you like her, you idiot. "Sure."

"Bye, Rey." Her finger comes toward the screen, and then she's gone.

"Time to get out of the sardine tin, man," Emery announces from the front of the bus. "Come stretch your legs and get some fucking sunshine or whatever it takes to cheer you up."

"Yeah, whatever."

Ain't nothing outside this bus going to make me feel any better, though. Not when the weight of the world slammed back down like five hundred pounds straight to the shoulders the minute that screen went black.

I've found what it takes to cheer me up, and it's not on this bus, let alone anywhere on this tour.

It's a thousand miles away playing for its supper without a single goddamn complaint.

TWENTY-SIX

TABITHA

"Anthem for the Underdog" – 12 Stones

I made a little over forty dollars with my busking. Not a bad effort, considering I played at the end of the workweek, and after the lunch rush. It bought us power, so there's that. Still… if I don't figure out how to turn this all around and save my flailing career before its even really started, busking will be a daily occurrence, not just a backup plan every few weeks.

"Have you seen this?" Kendall kicks her legs out to sit herself upright, eyes on her phone as she rises to join me at the kitchen counter.

I set aside the laptop, and focus on what she has to show me.

"It was only uploaded a couple of days ago, but it already has over ten thousand views."

I glance at the YouTube video as she places her phone down on the counter. "Keywords—that's why. They have Dark Tide's name in the title, plus all the band members names in the description."

"Plus yours." She lifts her eyebrows while I frown at

the screen.

Sure enough, after Kris's name is mine, plain as day in serif font. I tap the triangle icon and lean my chin on my upturned palm as the footage plays. The quality isn't too bad, clearly recorded on a phone from somewhere to the right of stage. The video cuts in at the end of the first verse of my cover. My money is on the person being surprised by my song choice and then having to get their phone out in a hurry to capture it.

It's weird, watching myself play like this. I can't help but see myself with a critical eye: did I play to the audience enough, or was I lost in the music; why did I skip through that last note; my tempo was uneven in the change.

"I guess I'm partially famous now, huh?" I sass, pushing her phone back to her.

She shoves it back my way. "Read the comments."

I shake my head, using the laptop to nudge her phone away again. "Rule one in surviving the critics: don't read what they say."

Kendall slams the phone down on my keypad. "They aren't critics, though. They're fans."

I drop a heavy sigh as I scroll up and humor her. Worst-case scenario is they point out what I already know: classical violin is a dinosaur that'll never earn me a real living. It's a niche market, one that shrinks by the day.

"Wow! I love this version!"

"Who is she? I need to see what else she's done."

"Is she touring with the band now?"

"Are they doing any more concerts with her?"

Kendall meets my gaze with a smug smile as I lift my head. "See? They love you."

I shrug, killing the video on her screen. "Doesn't matter though, does it? I haven't got any other covers like that for them to go to. They'll track me down, find what I really play, and then move on."

"Are you hearing yourself?" She snatches up her phone. "You've been given an opportunity—use it."

"*Was* given an opportunity," I correct. "This was a week ago. I fucked up the minute I forgot to take marketing material with me."

"Do another cover." She stares at me, hard-ass and clearly unwilling to let this go. "We'll pick somewhere edgy in the city to record, and I'll shoot it on my phone. So fucking what if it's not done in a studio? Snare them, Tab."

"And then what?" I close the lid on the laptop and swivel on my stool to face her. "I don't make a career out of covers. I make a career out of traditional classical compositions."

"Why?" She thrusts her arms across her chest.

"Because it's what I play," I cry, exasperated with this fucking inquisition.

"Yes. But why? Why do you play traditional classical? Why do you put yourself in that box?"

I wordlessly flap my jaw, hoping that some goddamn answer will form on its own. Yet as Kendall nods and then walks away, I realize she's won this argument.

Why do I only play traditional music? I can't say it's because that's solely where my passion lies, because it isn't. My passion is in the instrument as a whole, no matter how it's played.

What if this is the fucking universe giving me a nudge in the right direction? Will I miss my shot at making a lifetime career out of this because I'm too pigheaded to accept change?

"Where do I sell it, though?" I mumble, refusing to give Kendall the satisfaction of looking at her. "So they get hooked, and then what? I need to monetize that interest."

"Like we talked about the other night, we work out how to get you on Spotify. Google it. Now. Fuck whatever you were doing before."

Looking for regular work online. "Fine. I'm doing it."

"Good." She stays quiet a beat before adding, "I'm proud of you, Tab. Remember that. Don't forget to look back every now and then so you can appreciate how far you've come."

I glance her way, not entirely convinced; I've got so far to go.

"Remember where you were when we met?" she asks.

I suck in a deep breath and turn my stool to face where she readies her bag to head to work. "Waiting tables in the same block as the movie theater you worked at."

"Exactly." She fills her water bottle, and then twists the lid tight as she adds, "And now here you are, making music your full-time thing."

"We can barely afford to eat," I point out. "I'm literally on the verge of giving up, Kendall."

"Not yet, grasshopper." She leans over and places a

kiss to the top of my head as she makes her way to the door. "Not when that video proves that you can make a goddamn stir given the right audience."

"Love you, boo." I reach out and catch her hand as she walks away.

Her fingers slide from mine as she tosses a smile over her shoulder. "We got this babe." The door clicks as she pulls it open; I return to my laptop. "And *you* have a visitor."

"What?" I slide off the stool and walk around the half wall to see what on earth she's on about.

Kendall gives a cheeky finger wave as she slips past the last person in the world I expected to make a house call.

"Hey, kitty."

TWENTY-SEVEN

REY

"Tear Down the Wall" – Art of Dying

"What the fuck are you doing here?" she cries, brow pinched tight.

I thumb in the direction Café Girl headed. "Like me to leave?"

"No." Tabby shakes her head, finger and thumb pressed to her forehead. "Come in. Shit. I'm sorry." Her hand drops as I step inside her apartment, and I'm graced with that smile I need so fucking much right now. "I mean, I didn't expect to see you here, is all."

I shrug. "Spur of the moment thing."

"Aren't you supposed to be wowing thousands?" She chews her thumbnail as she asks the question, leaning against the wall as though she's unsure what to do.

Fuck. I don't know what to do now I'm here either; that's about where my plan ended. "Something like that."

"Something like that?" she repeats with a raised eyebrow. "I think you better sit your ass down and tell me what the hell is going on, Rey."

Her short hair bounces as she hotfoots it to the

kitchen counter and slams her laptop closed. I edge further into the place as she points to their small sofa.

"Sit."

I do as instructed, jamming myself against the rolled arm so that there's plenty of room for her. She drags the stool over and sits on it in front of the TV. *Huh.*

"What happened?" She places her hands between her knees, face neutral as she waits on me to speak.

I feel as though I'm back at the shrink, and yet I'm more relaxed at the thought of opening up than I've ever been.

This is why I'm here: because she makes me feel like *that.*

"I told them I don't want to tour anymore."

"Who's 'them'?"

"The band. Management." I stretch my arms out over the back of the sofa. "Told them yesterday."

"What did they say?" Her brow pinches, and although she may not realize it, Tabby leans forward, eager to hear the answer.

She's concerned for me—it's cute.

"Told me to do the final eleven shows and hold off on making the decision until afterward, or I could kiss another album goodbye."

Her head pulls back as she lifts both eyebrows. "Extreme."

"Not really." I shrug. "I'm fucking with their business by demanding this."

"So why do it?"

I jerk my head to the sofa. "Come sit here and I'll tell you."

A fucking lump wedges in my throat as she slides off the stool and complies. I need her so bad it physically aches. Surely she can see that? Surely it's written all over my fucking face how broken and desperate I am?

Tabby settles on the opposite end, one leg tucked up beneath her as she sits side-on to face me. "Why do it if it makes such an impact?"

Jesus. I'm not a crier. Really am not. But looking into those warm brown eyes of hers, I want to finally let go of all the anger, the frustration, and the despair. I want to let it out before it downright destroys me, and for the first time I feel as though I'm completely safe to do so.

This keeping a brave face gig is exhausting. I'm tired. I'm done. And yet, I shove that emotion down, like I always have, and swallow away the urge to let it all go.

"Hey." She reaches out and pulls my hand off the back of the sofa.

I watch with raw fascination as she sets it on her leg and toys with my ring. Such a simple, seemingly normal thing for her to do. But it's everything for me. Fucking everything.

I'm surrounded by many, adored by thousands, and yet not a single fucking person connects with me like she does.

"I can't survive what touring does to me again, kitty." I choose to stay focused on her slender fingers as she pinches the side of the metal skull between her forefinger and thumb and gently swivels it. "I struggle to live a normal life, let alone this one."

"Did you tell them that?"

I nod. "Toby's worn out. He's lived with this shit for

years. Growing up with it was bad enough, having to go without because Mom and Dad were consumed by caring for me. But now that neglect is amplified when our whole fucking entourage dedicate themselves to keeping me level."

"Is it that bad?" Her hand stills, lying flat over the back of mine.

I give her leg a gentle squeeze. "I'm an asset, kitty. I make people a lot of money, so to them the expense is worth it to keep me playing—physical expense, and monetary. They'll use me until I burn out, and by then the next big thing will be ready to take off."

"I really don't know what to say." Her hand slips around mine until she has them palm to palm, her fingers threaded between mine. "I hurt for you, so I can't imagine what it's like to *be* you."

"I'm selfish. I know the chaos I cause, and yet I still act up, let myself slide, all because I know there are people ready to catch me."

"That's a good thing though, right? Having a good support network?"

"How long until they get tired of picking up the pieces, though?" I run my thumb over the back of hers. "How long until they let me fall?"

"I don't think they'd do that. Would they?"

I shrug. "Everyone's tired of the drama. Fuck, I am the most. But how do you change who you are?"

God, I hope she has the answer.

"You don't." She tugs my hand, urging me to look at her. "Why would you want to?"

"Because I hate everything about who I am." A weight

lifts after letting that one little thing go, finally admitting the depth of my problem. And yet, at the same time I'm fucking terrified of what she'll think of me. I opened the door to my blackened heart, and now I wait with bated breath to see what she'll do with that opportunity.

Seconds pass without her uttering a single word. Fuck—she can't even look at me anymore. I prepare to pull away, to get back up and walk out that door, certain that the one person I thought might finally see me, might help me, was nothing but another case of misplaced trust.

I tug my hand from hers, and pull in a deep breath. Maybe I could walk down to the river, see how high that bridge is? Maybe I could step out into the busy morning traffic and cut out the possibility of changing my mind?

I changed it once already in the past twenty-four hours, and look where that's led me—straight to another disappointment.

I really can't take any more.

My hands shake as I rise to my feet. Those tears are so fucking close now. Is this what the end feels like? A metaphorical dead end? Where do I go from here? I'm out of options, out of reasons to—

"Rey."

I stall as Tabby stands too, her frame short and fragile next to mine.

"Just...." She doesn't say any more, simply steps forward and forces her left arm under mine to slide both of hers around my middle.

Fucking tears. There's a first time for everything, right?

Tabby forces herself against me, wrapping me tight in her hold as she also forces me to let her in. I toss out all the pretenses about how real men don't cry as the years of putting on a show, of pretending I'm somebody I'm not, take their toll and the tears silently fall.

My arm feels right against her back, her hair soft under my chin as she rests her head against my chest. We stand like that for longer than anybody should need to, her giving me everything I crave with her silent solidarity.

This is why I forced a fracture in our schedule. *This* is why three thousand people were notified the show would be canceled and their tickets transferred to tomorrow night's.

Because a thousand miles away was a woman completely unaware of the power she holds in being nothing but her true self.

Unaware of what she can do to save this dying heart.

TWENTY-EIGHT

TABITHA

"Send the Pain Below" - Chevelle

What the hell do I do now? I should pull away, but something in my gut tells me he needs this. You don't just fuck up a tour and fly however far he's come to have a chat and then leave again.

He's asking for help without saying as much. And who the hell am I to deny that?

"I'm sorry," I murmur against his chest. *God, he smells good.*

Rey's hand shifts on my back, slowly stroking down to the curve above my ass before he sets it back where he started. "Why are *you* sorry?"

"Because I don't know what to do to make you better."

His warmth leaves me as he steps away, hands lingering on my shoulders before he lets me go completely. "Yes you do."

I match his frown, unsure what the hell he means. "Really?"

He nods, the late-morning light from our front

windows catching his face and highlighting the evidence of his distress. "You're doing it now."

Okay. Now I'm totally lost. I convey as much in the tilt of my head.

"Forget it." He spins and stalks to the window. "What would you normally be doing this afternoon, kitty?"

"Don't blow me off and shut me out, Rey." I follow, wedging myself between him and the glass so he's forced to look at me. "How long are you here?"

"As long as I want, I guess."

I sigh, shoulders dropping. "How long *can* you be here before it causes more disruption?"

The downward curl of his lips makes him look like a kid who's been told they can't have the last cookie. "Tomorrow. I have to be back by four." His dark eyes shift to the people on the street below.

"Tonight we brainstorm, then." I elbow him so he looks back to me. "Pizza, and I would say beer, but I can maybe swing a bottle of soda before my budget is blown."

The resulting smirk leaves me giddy for more of this. "I can buy the pizza and beer, kitty."

I want that pure happiness from him always. I want people to see that guy, not the snarky jackass he thinks people love.

There's nothing wrong with the real Rey. Nothing at all.

"But," he adds, his face turning dour again, "we hang out. That's all. I don't want to talk about me anymore, okay?"

"Fine." He can think again if he assumes I'll let this go,

though. "We can talk about me. I need your help, actually."

"Yeah?" Rey shifts his weight between his feet, one hand going to the window frame to brace him. "How?"

"I need to know how to get my music from here"—I point to my head—"to the market. Tell me how to sell when I don't have any money. Tell me how you started recording."

My breath hitches as he lifts his free hand and gently sweeps the side of his index finger under my jaw. "I can introduce you to people who can help, Tabby."

"I don't want your charity, Rey. I want a mentor. That's all."

His jaw flexes as his fingertip trails down my throat before he pulls his hand away. "I want to help, okay? There's nothing else I can give you, so let me give you this."

Wrong—he has everything to give me. He can't see how, is all.

"We'll argue about it later." I shift my focus to the street below to save from doing anything rash.

We're so close, his hip pressed against mine. My left foot rests on the floor between his, our legs entwined as he effectively boxes me against the window, no thanks to me shoving myself in here.

Really didn't think that one through.

I could leave, slip out and walk away. But after that confession on the sofa I don't have it in me to abandon him, in any capacity. He needs me around, it seems, and I've literally got nothing else better to do with my time.

Not that I think I'd rather be anywhere else, anyway.

I feel him before I see the movement in my periphery. His breath is hot against my neck as he leans in close; his forehead and nose rest against the side of my face. It's an intimate gesture, yet strangely respectful. He could have gone for gold and kissed me, he could have been crass and copped a feel, but instead it says so much more that he chooses to be close to me in such a way.

My eyelids close as he remains there, face pressed against the side of mine. I startle when his fingers brush my hand, yet again it feels so natural, so right to let him slip his hold into mine.

"I like being with you, kitty." His whispered confession leaves a thrill tickling my spine. "It makes me feel better."

"I like having you with me too, Rey."

He was a jackass at the start. A right spoiled brat. Yet with the gift of hindsight I can see now that *that* Rey was nothing more than a mirage, a carefully constructed illusion to protect the real man behind the marketable image.

I don't lie: I like having him here. Having the *real* him here.

Suitable words won't come, the right sentiment lost in my struggle to convey within the capacity of a few short sentences how much I've grown to like him. I lose the chance all the same as he gently places a kiss to my temple, and then untangles himself from me to walk away.

"Take it the bathroom is down the end of the hall?" he calls as he steps out of the living room.

"Yeah." My lungs expand with the first full breath I've

taken since he walked in the door, the air bringing with it clarity I lost the moment he stepped into my space.

He might be the broken one, but I can guarantee by the time I've put Rey Thomas back together, it'll be me who's left in pieces. He'll go back to his gifted life, never having to want for a thing, and I'll return to mine, somewhat less whole than I was going in.

So when do we start?

TWENTY-NINE

Rey

"Suicidal Dream" - Silverchair

Dusk dulls the sky outside as Tabby-cat and I sit on her living room floor, the flyer for the local pizza shop between us. I rocked up here a little after breakfast not entirely sure what sort of reception I'd get given the way I've treated her, but I was sure of one thing—this is the right decision.

My phone's been off all day, and I've resisted the urge to check Messenger or my emails. Still, the promise of the shit storm I'll face when I return to the tour leaves me a little panicked every time the thoughts creep in.

"I have one firm rule," Tabby announces with a lift of her palm. "No anchovies."

"Deal." I nod once, rereading the list.

I can't stand the fucking things either, but if she'd said they were her deal breaker I would have gladly held my breath with each bite just to please her.

"Can't go past one stacked with meat." I point to the option that seems to cover all bases when it comes to being carnivorous.

Tabby leans forward a little to read the list of toppings. I shamelessly steal the moment to commit her to memory. She's fucking beautiful without trying. Fucking beautiful. I have no doubt that half of her appeal comes from what shines within. Where my soul is beaten and bruised, hers brings warmth with it that I don't think I could manufacture if I tried.

"Okay. We'll get that one if you'll humor me and buy the devil's food cake for after."

"Deal."

She rises to her feet, flyer in hand. "Cash or card?"

"Cash."

Tabby crosses to where she left her phone on the counter while I kick back, weight on the heels of my hands as I watch her. My gaze drops to the boots on my feet, the studs adorning the sides, and the strategic worn patches on my designer ripped jeans. For a moment there I forgot who I was while we hung out today. It's not as though we did anything special. She found some old nineties movie on the TV, and aside from that we made small talk about daily life. The only thing that reminded me I'm Rey the recognizable face, and not Rey the guy with fucking needs and wants, was when she offered to head downstairs to the pastry shop to get something sweet for lunch on her own.

She had a point: if I want to take time out, I need to stay incognito. And apparently I was recognized the last time I was here, even though I didn't see it.

"Shit." She turns to face me, still looking down at the phone in her hand. "Toby's been blowing up Kendall's phone looking for you."

Dang it. My perfect day fizzles with a pop and a bang.

"Suppose I should call him."

She frowns further, still reading. "Do they know where you are?"

"Not entirely." I roll to my side and then stretch out to pull my phone from my jeans.

I look up to find Tabby watching me with a raised eyebrow.

"I told them I needed today off and walked out of the hotel."

"And then?"

"Then nothing. I switched my phone off and jumped in the cab out front."

She sighs, clearly frustrated. "You didn't tell them where you were going at all?"

I shake my head as my phone powers up. "Didn't want them bugging me."

"Toby is apparently going nuts because he thinks you've gone somewhere to harm yourself."

Oops. "I didn't think of that."

"You know what?" She drops down onto the floor in front of me. "I looked you up the day after we met so I could learn a little about this guy who made me a crazy offer to open for his concert."

For some reason knowing that makes me like her more.

"But aside from that, I resisted doing the whole 'learning who you are through the media's eyes' thing. I didn't want other people's opinions, the dirty laundry stories they love using to cut people down, to taint my own assessment of you. I like to learn about people for myself and give them the benefit of the doubt."

"But?" I ask, unsure where she's headed with this.

"But," she says with a sigh, "I need you to tell me what the headlines about your suicide attempts referred to."

Fuck it. I really wanted to avoid this with her. Not always. Just now, and then however long I could drag it out after that.

"If you want me to help lift you up, Rey, you have to show me where you're coming from."

Christ. Why does this have to be so hard? Like she said, it's all in the media if she wanted to look it up. *But it's not.* What the media know and what *I* know are like the PG version versus the all access pass.

"Why do they worry about you so much?" she asks carefully, brow pinched.

My phone interrupts the moment with its barrage of notifications. I set it aside, figuring if they've waited twelve hours, they can wait a bit longer. Besides, Café Girl probably confirmed where I am.

"The media only know about what I've done since I started recording."

Tabby's gentle exhalation is as loaded a response as I expected.

"I first tried to end things when I was fifteen. Toby stopped me."

She settles in, folding her legs before her.

I reach out and trace my fingertip along the side of her hand, somehow disbelieving that this patient, beautiful creature is real. I don't tell people about this stuff because it hurts to. Mostly because I'm ashamed. I read the statistics; I know how many mentally affected people there are. One in four, or something like that?

Still. I don't like being weak. I hate that the failures are all based around my lack of control. I know what's wrong with me, and I understand how it works, so why can't I stop it? Why do I feel like a spectator to my own carnage-filled train wreck some days?

"You can trust me, Rey. I'm not here to judge." Her words are a quiet comfort, encouraging. "I only want to understand."

Do it. If not her, then who? Worse comes to worst, I walk away and get the lawyers to pay her a fuckload to sign a NDA. Not as though that hasn't happened already. *Thanks, Mom. Thanks, Dad.*

"I had rounds of counseling after that first attempt." I withdraw my hand. It feels filthy to touch something so pure when I'm so dirty. "They helped get me level enough that I wasn't a risk, so to speak. After a while, my family stopped asking so many questions, stopped monitoring me so close. They thought I'd beaten my demons when I got a recording contract. I'd made it, you know? So everything should have been peachy." I plaster on a fake smile, waving my hands beside my head to mimic how pleased everyone was. "Thing is, you never beat them—your demons. They play nice for a while, that's all."

"What changed?" She tucks her legs to her chest, pizza flyer and phone still in her hand as she hugs them.

"Pressure. Suddenly I wasn't on my own timeline anymore. I had people to keep happy, things I had to do before I could take care of myself. I drank a lot. That's how I tried the second time; the one you would have read about."

Tabby's brow pinches further.

"We'd come off putting together our first album. The lyrics are pretty deep in that one. I thought it was a good thing, getting all that pain out through my art, you know? But it backfired. It just held all that misery up in front of my face day after day until I couldn't face singing the songs one more time, until I wanted to avoid any chance of hearing them ever again."

"What did you do?"

I spin my phone on the carpet, ashamed to even admit it. "Got drunk and tried to base jump from our fucking hotel balcony."

She swallows hard. "What stopped you?"

I can't look at her. See how this makes her feel. Not when I know how I felt at the time was twenty times worse. "My drunk ass fell the wrong way and I cracked my head on the railing. Kris dragged me inside that time. He doesn't say anything about it, but he holds on to that grudge. I see it."

"But that's not the end of it?" She lifts her hand to wipe away a stray tear, yet her face remains impassive. She's determined to hear me out.

"I can't keep telling you this, kitty."

"You have to."

"Why?"

"Because I want you to see what I do." She gestures for me to go on.

I scoot forward and slide my legs either side of hers, reaching around her smaller body to encase her in my arms. "Are you sure?"

Tabby nods, another stray tear threatening to fall.

I rest my forehead against hers, close my eyes, and continue. "Six months later I swallowed my fresh prescription of sleeping pills. Rick's old man, Wallace, made sure that doctor never worked with us again. I've got it on file now that I get metered anything I'm prescribed." She sets her things aside with a sigh. The soft touch of her hands as they wrap around the outside of my upper arms encourages me to list the last, and most recent.

Nobody knows about it—nobody but me.

"The week before we started the tour I tried to do that again. Except when you're not allowed anything with any real strength, you have to improvise." My heartless laugh falls into the void of silence around us. Tabby sighs, hands flexing. "I thought maybe if I mixed enough painkillers—regular strength shit—with alcohol, I could get some epic concoction going. But I fucked it all up. I drank too much before I started, and so by the time I'd chugged the first packet of pills, I was so fuckin' drunk I knocked the bottle onto the floor. All I had left was top shelf, which isn't the best thing to chug when you're halfway cut on bourbon already." I frown at the vibrations that move through me from Tabby, eyes still closed to avoid her pain. "Long story short, I passed out, vomited in my sleep, and woke up with one hell of a hangover. You'd think the painkillers would have dulled it all, right?" I chuckle again, yet it's a hollow plea for forgiveness. "I was sick as a dog for four days afterward while the low-level poisoning worked its way out of my system. Told the guys I had a stomach bug so they wouldn't question why I was in the bathroom so much."

"Why were you?" Her voice is hoarse with the consequence of my regrets.

"To purge. Figured the more I could get the shit out of me, the quicker I'd get better. I lived on water and dry crackers for a week."

The familiar weight of disappointment blankets me as I sit with Tabby encased against my chest. I fucked it all up, did such a stupid thing, and what's worse is I can't say with honest clarity I wouldn't attempt it again.

I'm not sure if that's more selfish, or stupid?

"Do you see it now, though?" she whispers.

Her hands slide from my arms as she slowly pulls away.

"See what?"

"Why you do it."

I track her as she rises and walks to the counter with her things. Her hands shake as she gently sets the phone and menu down, and then wipes under her eyes with the side of her finger.

"I guess it must be a cry for help, right?"

Her face remains impassive as she fidgets with the paper.

"Kitty. Look at me. Please."

"Why?" The single word is almost imperceptible, she utters it so quietly.

I swallow back the urge to walk away, to hide and deny the truth, the pain, and the hopelessness of it all. I've done that for years, and where has it got me? "Because you make me feel ashamed of myself when you can't look at me. You make me feel as though you wish I wasn't here."

Her bloodshot eyes snap to mine; she tries so hard not to cry. "Nobody wishes you weren't here, Rey. Nobody except you."

I frown.

"That's what I want you to see," she explains, hand on the counter as though it's the only thing that holds her up. "You said Toby found you the first time. Your own brother. And yet you tried again." She holds her hand up to ask me to let her finish when I try to say something. "Then Kris found you, and although you know it hurt him deeply, and that in turn upsets you... you tried again." Her palm slides from the counter, and she slowly makes her way back over to where I sit on the floor.

My chest compresses as she places her feet either side of my thighs and sets her hands on my shoulders to brace herself as she lowers onto my lap. It takes everything in me to stay leaning back on the heels of my hands and to let her direct this. Her warm palms track up the sides of my neck until she has my jaw in her hands, her eyes wet with what can only be empathy.

"You think you do this so other people will take notice and help you."

I nod, agreeing one hundred percent.

"You do it," she whispers, "because you're waiting for *yourself* to take notice and help."

Huh? I frown, searching her eyes for more. Yet she stays rigid, waiting on me to understand.

"You think I won't help myself?"

Her head slowly moves from side to side. "Your

music, Rey. What do the lyrics talk of?"

"Hurt," I say, averting my gaze as she continues to watch me close. "Anger, and resentment."

"Where's the hope?" she asks gently, thumbs stroking my face. "Where is the line that tells of how you overcame?"

They don't exist. I sing about how trapped I feel, how hopeless. "I'm my own worst enemy, aren't I?" I search her eyes, hoping for confirmation that I understand now.

A soft smile curves her lips. She almost looks... *proud*?

"Don't underestimate yourself. Stop telling yourself you're worth nothing. Don't use your music to pet your pain, to nurture it, and to feed it. Use your music to push it out, to heal, and to encourage you."

Who the fuck is this woman? And who the fuck put her on a path with me?

Is this what divine intervention feels like? Because no way in fucking hell did we crash her concert by pure chance.

I push my hands off the floor to lean into her, Tabby having to adjust her seat on my legs to keep from falling backward. Her hands slip back to my shoulders as I loop my arms around her waist and tug her flush against me.

"Twenty-seven years of hell," I tell her as I search her face. "Almost three decades of pain before I'm finally gifted you."

Her throat bobs as she swallows, the silence in the room deafening while I wait on her to answer—to say anything.

"You have to do this yourself," she tells me carefully,

eyes flicking between mine. "I can support you, but I won't do it for you."

"Help me," I plead. "Come back with me, kitty, and show me how to write better music. Uplifting music."

She scoffs, looking away until I give her a sharp tug to bring her back. "I don't know the first thing about rock music."

"You said it yourself—it's basic once you break it down. It's layers. You know how it works." *Damn it. Come on, kitty.* "Please." She pulls in a sharp breath as I close the small space between us and place a kiss to her forehead. "I need you."

Her gaze meets mine, and for a fleeting moment I find my utopia.

I always thought it was a place, an event. But it's not. It's a feeling.

A feeling I only get from one person.

Her.

"I don't know. I—"

"Please," I whisper again, skimming my nose against the side of hers. "I'll talk to Wallace and see if we can get you on stage again. I'll make it worth your while."

She relaxes against my arms, giving me all the confidence I need to take this that one step further.

"Come be with me," I murmur as I lean in for the kill.

She sucks a sharp breath in her nose as my lips brush against hers. The hammering of my heart fills the brief second I give her before I repeat the action. *Don't reject me.* I've asked for plenty in my life, but all I hope for in this moment is for her to need me too.

Her warm breath caresses my mouth as I hold steady

a hair's breadth from her, giving her that last out, that last chance to push against me and back away. Yet she doesn't. The whole day, the disruption I caused and the pain I put Toby through is justified the moment she leans forward and gives me her wordless answer.

Her lips tease mine, soft and seemingly unsure before a switch flips. Her kiss grows hungry, her ass scooting forward as she tries to get closer, to remove any space between us while she tugs at my bottom lip with hers.

I'm not one to brag, but I've kissed plenty of willing girls over the years, yet not one of those meaningless hookups hold a candle to this.

Maybe it's Tabby? Maybe it's because for the first time ever I actually feel the unmistakable need to have a person close, to keep her with me. For once, I can't imagine why I would want to walk away.

I tilt my head a little, allowing her to deepen the kiss as she brings her hands to the sides of my face. Her breath comes fast as she finishes with a single, teasing sweep of her tongue before she pulls back and presses her forehead to mine.

"Okay."

I chuckle, stealing another brief taste of her lips. "Is that all? Just 'okay'?"

She laughs, pulling back to look me in the eye. "Okay, Rey Thomas. I'll join you. But not because you're some famous person who can show me the world, blah, blah, blah." Her eyes roll. "But because it's you." She sets a palm to my chest, over my heart. "Because you were brave enough to show me the real you, and that guy, the nice guy, the *real* guy, is the one I like." She peers up at me from under her lashes, bashful. "The one I *really* like."

"Fuck, kitty." I wrap a hand around the back of her head and pull her in for a better kiss, a more heated kiss.

The kind that tells her I *really* like her too.

"You make me feel like a horny fucking teenager all over again: awkward and a little bit insane."

She laughs, swatting at me before her face falls and she pulls in a deep breath. "I'm serious, Rey. I like the real you, and that guy I'd help any damn way I could." She dots a cute little peck of her lips on the end of my nose. "Because I want him to stick around. Always."

Fuck. For her, I might have finally found a reason to want to.

THIRTY

TABITHA

"Smells Like Teen Spirit" - Nirvana

Kendall's gaze skims over Rey as he stands at the window, phone to his ear while he seemingly talks Toby off a ledge.

"You," she hisses under her breath, finger pointing toward the hall. "Bedroom. Now."

I lead her into my room, well aware she wants privacy so she can grill me about what the hell went down in our pokey little apartment.

Truth? I kissed a guy. And it was more than just a kiss. It was... it was a reintroduction.

I met the real Rey. The vulnerable Rey. The guy who parades around with his mask of fierceness on, lest somebody see the truth: he barely holds on.

"What the fuck, Tab?" Kendall ditches her purse next to the door before starting on her coat. "Spill. Every-thing. Now."

I shrug, not ready to give her all of it. Rey shared some pretty personal things. Things that I'll keep from my best friend, even, out of respect for him. "He needed a break."

"You realize his promoters are spewing over the change." She stands staunch, arms folded. "He might be their best asset, but he needs to remember everyone can be replaced."

"No they can't," I snap. "People aren't expendable, Kendall."

You can't replace someone in their entirety. You can find a suitable substitute, sure. Somebody who can get the job done. But people are unique. Everybody holds that special mix of traits that make them who they are. And that is why we love them: because *they* make us feel a certain way, or act a certain way. You can't successfully replicate or replace a person, otherwise why would we grieve?

"What's going on here, hon?" She leans a shoulder against the doorframe, giving the hallway a quick glance.

"He needs help," I explain as my ass hits the side of the bed. "You heard him sing, heard that pain. I don't know what's going on behind the scenes with the tour, but he came here because he seems to think I can help him turn his mindset around."

"Can you?" Kendall asks softly. "And should you? You've known the guy personally all of a week."

"Almost two."

"Whatever. It's not very long, Tab. Why you?"

I shrug. I've asked myself the same question all day. Why me? "I guess only he knows that. All I know is I can't in good conscience turn away a man who is crying out for help. What kind of a person would that make me?"

Kendall sighs, her lips pressed in a flat line. "One who knows her limits, I guess." She glances to the floor, arms folded. "Where will it leave you?" Her head turns as she checks we're still in the clear. "How do *you* feel about this? Why do you want to do it, other than moral guilt?"

I study the carpet, embarrassed to admit the truth for fear it makes me sound like just another groupie. "I like the guy, Kendall. Behind all that public bullshit, there's a really genuine man."

"Or so he wants you to think."

"He said he'd talk to their boss and see if I can open some shows again." God, that sounds so lame out loud. I have no doubt he'll ask, but do I really think that a label will throw some unknown in the mix on the whim of their rebellious front man?

"You think he's telling the truth about that?"

I lift my gaze to hers. "I don't know for sure, but I hope so. I have to at least give it a try, right?"

She huffs out her nose, seemingly as torn as I am. "What now? He doesn't think he's welcome to stay here, does he?"

"I don't know. Why? Would that be a problem?" Why is she so anti-Rey? What has Toby told her?

"I'm just saying that maybe it would be in his best interest if we managed to convince him to get on a plane back to the tour *tonight*." She lifts her hands, palms showing.

"Tabby?"

"He will," I whisper to Kendall as I stand. Rey's foot-falls head our way. "He was online doing exactly that, sorting tickets, before you walked in from work."

"Did I interrupt?"

Kendall spins to find Rey directly behind her, hesitant, in the hall. "You've got a lot of people worried, you know that? Maybe you should let somebody know where you are next time you have a diva moment."

She marches toward the living area, leaving him staring at me with a surprised lift of an eyebrow. "She always that blunt?"

I nod as I turn. My bed creaks when I hit it face-first. "Ugh," I mumble into the bedspread. "Ignore her."

His chuckle draws closer, his weight making my mattress dip toward him. "Well, if it's any consolation, I think Kris and Emery talked Toby around to the idea."

"He didn't want me there?" For some reason, knowing that stabs at my gut. I'm not exactly the type who cares what people think of me—each to their own—but I don't want to be labeled as at fault for this. "He knows I had nothing to do with your impromptu visit, right?" I don't want to end up in the crossfire of a war between siblings.

"Yeah, he knows it was all me." Rey stretches out across the bed also, and then reaches out to snag me by the shirt.

I tumble against him when he pulls, my hand only just saving me from a pretty damn ungraceful collision between my nose and his shoulder. "Easy."

"Fuck easy," he mumbles, encasing me in his arm. "Tour with me, kitty, and you'll soon see there ain't much that's easy when it comes to the life and times of Rey Thomas."

I feel adored, tucked in his hold, and yet at the same

time I'm not fool enough to not recognize that I'm currently in the hands of an expert showman.

I know without a shadow of a doubt that he's about to majorly change my life, but if that's for better, or worse, I don't know. I can't distinguish the line between our reality and this illusion I seem content to be caught up in. I know what I should do, I know what the "smart" thing to say would be, but like a junkie staring down that last needle, I'm not quite ready to walk away from the danger.

The lure of the thrill that comes with his drug is too strong. One week, even one day. How amazing would it be to experience his world?

Fuck—you're only gifted one life. May as well make sure it has some memorable moments to laugh about in your old age, right?

"I'm going to regret this, aren't I?"

He smirks, pushing up on one elbow to look down at me. "Depends." Firm fingers find my chin and coax my face up toward his. He places a soft, slow kiss to my mouth, gentle and reverent as he pulls back. "I don't think I will."

I rest my forehead against his lips for a moment before I settle against his side. "Tell me. Any crazy ex-girlfriends or stalkers I need to know about? Do I need my own bodyguard?"

His chest vibrates beneath my ear with his laugh. "Fuck. I wish." He lets out an amused snort. "I haven't exactly been celibate, kitty, but no, there aren't any crazy exes."

"Really?" I push up to rest on my elbow, and frown at

him. "You haven't broken numerous hearts on your rise to fame? I find that hard to believe."

His stoic expression kills the humor. "I don't let people get that close to me, Tabby."

His switch from "kitty" to my actual name—albeit a shortened version—leaves me unsettled. He's dead serious. It intensifies the pressure somewhat, knowing that this connection, this rapid burn we're on, is new for him.

"You look worried," he muses, tracing my face with his finger.

"Because I am."

"Why?"

I pull free of his hold to sit on the edge of the bed. "What if I hurt you? What if I end up making you worse? I'm not a shrink, Rey. I know music—classical music. That's all. I'm no expert in how to help somebody who's bipolar."

The shutdown is visible as he rolls off the foot of the bed and then stands tall. "So don't treat me as *bipolar*," he grits through a tight jaw. "Treat me as fucking human."

I don't get to say another word before he storms from the room, his heavy footfalls retreating to the living room before the slam of the door echoes through the place. *Shit.* I launch from the bed and skid into the main room to find Kendall staring at me with her brow raised in a "What do you want me to do?" expression.

"I'll be back soon." I scramble to tug my boots on, whipping my coat off the back of the bedroom door before I skid back past Kendall to chase him down.

"He needs a fucking babysitter, Tab!" she hollers as I swing the door shut behind me.

My blood boils as I hit the stairs, my anger split between her ignorance and his stubbornness. Why can't she see that there's clearly a deeper reason behind his behavior other than he's a spoilt musician? And why does he always presume people believe that his labels are all there are to him?

I step out onto the sidewalk and get hit with the bite of a cool night breeze. The sun has completely gone to bed, only the glow of the streetlights giving me a limited view of the area. *Which way would he go?* I glance left, and then right, deciding on a whim to turn right since I read somewhere that men are more likely to pick that direction, which is why menswear is most often to the right of a shop entrance.

My recall of useless knowledge comes in handy when I spot him the next block over, stooped over to talk to a fan who's spotted him out alone. The girl bounces on the balls of her feet before she tucks herself into his side so she can take a selfie.

Rey's grin is wide, almost as large as the surge of jealousy that fires through me when the girl places a bold kiss on his cheek.

I bury my fists in my coat pockets and power on, catching up as she heads down the side street, suitably pleased with herself. "What are you doing?"

"I could ask you the same." His fake smile is gone, the pissed off wanker I got back at the apartment firmly in situ.

"Why did you walk out on me?"

He stares straight ahead as he strides. "It was either punch a hole in your wall, or head out for smokes. And given you're broke as fuck, I figured you wouldn't want to spring for drywall repairs."

"Um, excuse me." I cock an eyebrow as we hustle along the sidewalk. "If you punched the hole, you'd fix it."

The whisper of a smile tugs at his lips. He glances at me from the corner of his eye, and then promptly steers us into the convenience store.

"Ladies first." He pulls the door open, shoulders hunched as he waits for me to go inside.

"Why, thank you." The surge of heat from the overhead blower smacks me in the face.

It's heaven.

Rey wanders into the store, seemingly in his own little world as he heads for the drinks fridge. Me, on the other hand…. I'm stationed at the door like the fucking Secret Service, doing a sweep of the place to see if there are any other people who might recognize and accost him.

How the hell does he do this day to day? How does it not get old being unable to step out your front door without wondering if somebody will know who you are? Wondering if somebody will be there to photograph you, or upload you to social media via live stream?

Fuck fame. Being a nobody has its perks.

"You want anything?"

I snap my attention back to the man of the moment as he lifts an energy drink from the fridge. How on earth is he not freezing his ass off in only holey jeans and a T-shirt?

"No. I'm fine."

The guy behind the counter watches our interaction with dead eyes. I shake off the creepy vibe it gives me and hustle to Rey's side.

"When did you last have a cigarette?" Probably half the reason why he's so testy.

He scratches his chin with the fingers of the hand holding his bottle, seeming to think the question over. "Before the flight. So, five-ish, I think?"

"How early were you up this morning?" Is this going to be a regular part of touring too? Predawn arguments between the band?

"I never went to bed." He throws me a wink before asking the guy behind the counter for a pack of cigarettes.

I stand aside while he completes the transaction, strangely turned on by the sight of him as he then rips the pack open and uses his bottom lip to pull one out. He has that effortless James Dean look about him as he tucks the rest in his pocket and juggles the lighter with his drink.

"Here." I take the bottle from him and hold the door open.

He passes through to the street and immediately sparks the stick. The look on his face can only be described as orgasmic.

"Better?"

Rey's eyes close as he lets out a long sigh. "Fuck, yes." He flicks his gaze to me, lifting the cigarette between us. "Is this going to be a problem?"

I shrug. "Can't say I like it, but it's not a deal breaker."

He chuckles. "You know, you should have said it would be."

"Why?" I uncap his drink and pass it back to him.

He makes a face as though impressed at my service. "Because if you'd said me smoking was a problem, it would have given me reason to quit."

"Then yes, it's a problem." I smile.

He smirks, taking another pull. "No take backs."

"Asshole."

"You don't know the half of it." He waggles his eyebrows before sucking in another deep drag.

"You know." I fidget with my jacket to save from stepping into his space and suffocating myself. "I don't see you as anything other than you. You aren't a label to me, Rey. None of them."

He stares off across the road. He doesn't believe me; it's as clear as day.

"I get you think that I'm just saying what you want to hear, but maybe after we spend some time together you'll see that I mean it."

He ducks his chin, staring down at the ground as he smokes the last of the cigarette. "I want to believe you, kitty."

"But your heart won't let you?"

"My head won't let me." He matches my gaze with his own, the frustration at himself clear in the darkness of his irises. "I get I asked you to come back with me to help, but that doesn't mean we have to talk about how much of a fuckup I am every second of the goddamn day, okay?"

211

He takes an abrupt step past me to head home, punching his hands against his sides as he hugs his arms to himself. "Coming?"

"Yeah."

Although the more he fights against me, the more I wonder if he was telling me the truth about why he needs me, or if Rey Thomas was simply telling a naive girl with modest dreams what she wanted to hear so that he could get what he was after: company.

Do I even want to know?

THIRTY-ONE

REY

"I'm Not Sick but I'm Not Well" – Harvey Danger

Kendall stares at me from her spot perched on the barstool at the kitchen counter. I lean my ass against the edge of the sofa, arms folded, and eyeball her in return.

Bitch doesn't trust me.

Tabby crosses between us, fussing as she packs a bag or two to bring on the tour. My hands ping with pins and needles—the need to reach out and snag her to prove that Tabby belongs with me, intense.

"How long will you be gone for?" Kendall asks as Tabby wanders past, boots in hand.

She pauses at her friend's question, and turns to look at me for the answer.

"We have four weeks left."

I need another smoke already—this bullshit seriously pushes me to my limit. Yeah, so I walked out on the guys. Fuck it. It was either get my ass over here for a mental health break, or they could have dealt with the fun that would have been covering up my utter breakdown mid-set.

I'm done with this shit: done with the pressure, and done with the constant rush, rush, rush. Done. I want to slow down. I crave a week somewhere without the goddamn internet so I can find my fucking Zen or whatever the hell it is people do when they go recluse.

All I know, is I'm done with people. Give me a month in solitude with my guitar, and I'll give you five new tracks. But force me to play when I don't want to, force me to pretend that everything is honky fucking dory, and I swear to God the press will have a field day with the fallout.

"What about the music you were working on, Tab?" Kendall holds my eye as she calls out to her buddy.

Kitty's voice carries from her bedroom. "I'll still work on it."

"What music?" I ask, suckered in hook, line, and sinker.

Café Girl snarls as she looks me head to toe before answering. "Tabitha has a career too, you know."

Damn thing is missing in action, if you ask me. "I said I'd talk with Wally about getting her exposure, so your point is?"

"Does this really help her? Or your ego? Do you honestly think you can come in here and demand she drop everything for you?"

"I asked nicely, Kendall. Used my manners, and all." I scowl at her.

She pulls a face at me before storming off in kitty's direction. The girl's loyal—I get that. But it's not as though I strong-armed Tabby into coming with me. I may have laid on the charm a little, but that was out of sheer desperation, not ill intent.

I need the woman like I need air to breathe.

Without her I suffocate, and unless anybody has some handy tricks on how to sing when your lungs are void of oxygen, then the only way I'll make it through the rest of this tour is with my safety blanket beside me: Tabby.

"Just drop it," kitty hisses under her breath as she enters the room sans Kendall. "What time is our flight?"

"6:00 A.M."

Her lips twist as she jerks the zipper closed on the duffle in her hand. "You think there might be somewhere close to the airport with a free room?"

I frown at the frantic little thing. "Why?" Doesn't she want to stay here? "What happened to pizza night?"

Her gaze cuts to the hall before she leans in to whisper. "Let's just say things are a little chilly in here."

"Gotcha." Things are damn near arctic with that buddy of hers around. I check the time on my phone, ignoring the notifications on the lock screen. "There's literally eight hours until we leave. It's not long enough to worry about a room somewhere." As much as I'd love that alone time to pet my sexy little pussy. "We can crash at the airport if you really don't want to stay here."

"I couldn't ask you to do that."

"Why? Because I'm supposed to be handled with fancy white gloves?"

Her lips twist up on one side as the duffle falls from her hand. It hits the floor with a thud. "No. I just didn't want you drawing any unnecessary attention."

She takes a tentative step toward me, most likely still

on edge after the way I blew up at her earlier. I reach out and take her hand, tugging her against me. She falls against my leg, her feet either side of mine as she straddles me where I lean against the sofa.

"I think I drew enough attention when I forced a show to be canceled and disappeared."

"And then you reappear at an airport halfway across the country with the girl who opened your surprise show last week." She lifts a slender finger to trace my lips. "How do you think that would look?"

I nip the tip of her digit, holding it hostage for a moment before answering. "I guess it would look like that girl meant something to me."

"Yeah?" She sets her hand on my shoulder, gaze on my mouth. "What kind of something?"

"The sort of something that makes a man do crazy things like walk out on a sold-out show to be with her."

She says no more, simply smiling. I lean down to close the gap between us, my lips getting the barest tease of hers before that pain in the ass friend of kitty's ruins the moment.

"Seriously?"

Tabby pulls back as though Kendall jolted her in the ass with a cattle prod, stepping away with a flush in her cheeks. "Sorry."

"Why?" I snap, throwing my shoulders up. "Why are you sorry?"

The look I get from Café Girl is nothing short of killer.

"I didn't realize she was in here," Tabby murmurs, hands running nervously over the ass of her jeans.

"So what if she fucking is?" I push off the sofa,

throwing a hand out toward Kendall.

"Maybe I don't fancy seeing you stick your tongue down my best friend's throat?"

"Jealous?" Yeah, I'm an ass.

Kendall's eyes narrow as she slowly shakes her head. "Questioning your motives, actually."

I cock an eyebrow at her, Tabby quiet between us as she stares at the floor.

"You've known Tab for a week," Kendall explains. "Ten fucking days to be exact, Rey. Makes me wonder why you want her with you, truthfully. Is she just another bed warmer? Another person you can use up and toss aside when the thrill of the tour is over?"

"You're fucked, woman." If she'd bothered to do any research on me, looked up anything at all, she'd see that I spend most of my time alone.

"Am I?" The bitch rounds the counter, placing herself possessively beside Tabby.

That shit doesn't sit right me with one fucking bit.

"If you want me to let her out that door," Kendall levels, "then you better give me one damn good reason why I should let you have her."

"Babe," Tabby whispers to her friend.

"No, Tab. I want to hear it. What's his fucking reason for coming in here and expecting you to drop everything to jump on *his* schedule?"

I swallow hard, pissed that she's put me on the spot like this. I'm full-on when I'm invested in someone. It's all in or nothing at all, and I kind of wanted to hide that from Tabby for a bit longer before I freaked her out with my intensity.

"If I leave here without her," I explain, "then there is no tour."

"Blackmail." Kendall stares at me, head bobbing with her lips in a firm line. "That's low, Rey."

"You didn't let me finish." My fists curl at my sides. I seek out Tabby, holding her gaze as I drop the weight of it on her. "If I leave here without you, kitty, there's no more tour because there's no more me. I meant it when I said I was done. I need you. I don't know why, I just know that nothing gives me reason to look forward to tomorrow like you do."

Kendall slams a hand to her face in my periphery, yet I stay fixed on the only person who matters. Yeah, it sounded cheesy as shit, but it's also true. I couldn't get Tabby out of my head from the moment she stormed that theater, and at first it confused me. I mean, why was this literal stranger in my every waking thought? Why did I care whether her concert was ruined or not? What fucks did I have to give where she went, or what she did after she walked out of that auditorium?

But then after a while it made sense. She made me fight for her attention. She didn't gush over me, or try too hard to get *my* attention. She stayed true and genuine to who she is, and that creature, the one who stands before me chewing on her lip, is a breath of fresh air.

And God knows I need one when the tour suffocates me to the point of delirium.

"I won't be held accountable, Rey," she whispers as she takes a step toward me. "I get what you're saying, and like I told you, I want to help. I will help. But the guilt doesn't land on me. This is your fight, your victory. Don't burden me with the responsibility of keeping you around." She sets a palm on my chest, eyes locked with mine. "That stays squarely on your shoulders, okay?"

"I can't carry that weight anymore." I hang my head and chuckle. *Who is this pussy I've become?* "To tell you the honest truth, I'm scared, kitty. I'm scared of what I'll do when I hit my next low."

"Then we make sure you don't get that low, again."

"Tabitha," Kendall pleads. "He isn't your responsibility, honey."

"No," I agree, reaching for Tabby's face as I answer Kendall. "She's mine."

Fuck her roommate.

If I want to kiss this goddamn woman, then there isn't a fucking thing that's going to stop me.

THIRTY-TWO

TABITHA

"Interstate Love Song" – Stone Temple Pilots

Kendall pleaded for me to stay at home, saying that it was crazy that we were even entertaining the idea of sleeping at the airport. Yet I refused. I can't say why it was, but a part of me worried that if I had one more night in my own bed then I might overthink this whole crazy idea and change my mind.

I didn't want that chance to analyze the fun out of it. I can't remember the last time I simply up and did something on a whim, trusting my gut instinct. Every decision I've made since leaving home has been thoroughly thought out, dissected, and all scenarios taken into account.

This? It's an adventure. One I'm not likely to ever get again, and if I'm not going to get the chance to go places with my own music, then I'm hardly going to turn down the opportunity to experience what the life of a professional musician is like by living it vicariously through somebody else's fame.

"Why are you smiling?" Rey picks at the shared meal

laid out between us, a lazy smile on his lips.

We're seated on the floor facing each other near the entrance to the terminal, tucked behind the huge scales they have to check your luggage weight. The only thing open for food at this time of night was a coffee shop halfway between domestic and international. Still, our shared late-night supper of coffee and brownie couldn't be more perfect.

"I can't stop thinking about how crazy this is."

He huffs a small laugh before popping more chocolaty goodness in his mouth.

"Don't you think it's a little nuts?" I ask.

He shrugs as he swallows. "Maybe. Why, though? What's crazy about it?"

"Kendall was right." I spin my takeout cup in hand. "We've known each other a couple of weeks."

"I don't have to know you long to know that I like being with you, kitty."

"I know." I take a sip to avoid looking at him. The intensity of his gaze is bad enough without actually locking eyes with the guy. "But outside of the fact I play violin, what do you know about me, huh? What if *I'm* the one who can't be trusted?"

"If you were going to sell me out, you would have done it by now," he levels. "I trust you."

"How, when you hardly know me?"

"Why do you trust me?" He catches my eye, holding it as he pushes the last of the brownie my way. "I've had my half."

"You can have more if you're hungry."

"Eat, kitty."

I pick up a crumbling mouthful and pop it in as he watches me. *Damn.* I'm kind of glad I didn't give any up now—this is good.

"Tell me about you," Rey instructs as I continue to eat. "What should I know about this foxy little woman who knocked me on my ass?"

I grin at his jest, heated by the challenge I find in his eyes. He meant every damn word. *Wow.* Can't say I've ever been called foxy before.

"Well." I lick my fingers off one by one. "I'm an only child."

"Huh."

"Does that surprise you?" I bundle the rubbish, shoving the crumb-filled napkin back in the paper bag.

Rey shrugs one shoulder as he reaches out to take it from me. "All the people I've met who are only children have been entitled assholes."

"Really?" I know the stereotype, but I didn't think it was that honest of a representation.

"What else?" He sits up straight and pulls his arm back, lobbing the trash toward the bin behind me. It goes in on the first attempt.

"Nicely done."

"Thank you." He grins, scooting around so his back is against the wall. "What else, kitty? What made you take off to play the violin?"

My fingers walk across the fibers of the carpet as I try to summarize what pushed me to make the decision. "I hated playing at first."

"Because you wanted to play football."

I smile at his recollection of our past conversation.

"Yeah. But after a while I enjoyed how I felt when I could actually play a piece start to finish. It became my fallback on tough days, you know?"

He nods, patting the floor between his bent legs.

I scoot into the space, tucking my knees under his to sit Indian style with my back against his front.

His hands find the muscles in my back, massaging gently as I continue to give him the truncated version of events.

"Dad stepped out on Mum when I was a teenager. I was eleven when I started to question his habits. I was fifteen when it all made sense. In those years between, it was rough. He'd feed me lies so that Mum would hear them from me, and not him. I think he thought if I was spinning the yarn about where he was, she was more likely to believe it. But he slipped up, a lot. Credit card bills with unexplained charges. Constant phone calls where they'd hang up after Mum answered. And sometimes he'd forget to even tell his mates that he was using them for an alibi."

"Sounds like a swell guy."

"The best," I say with loaded sarcasm. "Anyway, at fourteen Mum could legally leave me at home alone. So one night she went to his work to wait for him. He walked out, didn't see her there, and drove straight to his mistress's. Led Mum right to the place."

"All over?"

I shake my head. "That's half the reason why I'm distant from them now. She let him stay. And he never apologized for what he did. I resent her for being so weak, and I hate him for being so cruel."

"Harsh."

"Truthful."

"How does that impact you playing violin, though?" His fingers work my shoulders as he talks, kneading, caressing, setting me alight.

"I played to drown out the sound of them arguing. I'd shut my door, pick up my violin, and play until the fingers of my left hand bore angry red indents from the strings."

"To be honest, I would have thought that would make you hate it more." He stops massaging, instead sliding his arms around my front to pull me back flush with him.

I melt into his embrace, loving how comfortable and safe it feels to have somebody literally protecting me from the world around us. The irony isn't lost on me: here I am, supposedly accompanying him to make him feel better, and so far that's all he's done for me.

"What about you?" I ask as I slide my hands over his forearms. "Why did you start to play?"

"Got told a girl I liked thought musos were cool."

I chuckle, twisting to look up at him. He grins down at me, eyes soft as he traces his gaze across my features to settle on my mouth.

"That's terrible, Rey," I tease, acutely aware his line of sight hasn't moved. "You're supposed to have some epic backstory about how it was what you were born to do."

"What can I say?" He shrugs. "I was born to be a disappointment, so it's only fitting my backstory is too."

"Don't," I whisper, turning in his hold to sit side-on. "Don't put yourself down so casually like that."

"It's easier than complimenting myself."

"Why?"

"I don't know." He frowns. "It just is."

I reach up and run my fingers along his jaw, testing the coarseness of the hair there. "How do you make it through life?" I whisper the words, not expecting an answer.

It was more of a rhetorical question. I know how heavy it feels on the days where I get down, how loaded it can be to have something disappointing happen in your life that takes the wind from your sails. But to feel that every day, without reason, purely because you're unhappy to be yourself?

I can't imagine the stress that would put on a person.

A couple walk by with suitcases in tow, headed for the exit. The spell is broken as Rey pulls his head from my touch, resting it against the wall instead. I feel unwelcome in his arms, and yet he doesn't let go, just acts indifferent by refusing to look at me, let alone talk.

It's an oxymoron for his life, it seems. On the outer, here's this guy who you'd think sheds conflict like water off a duck's back, but on the inside there's a man who hangs on to the things that mean the most to him like his life depends on it.

I guess, in a way, it does.

Content for the time being, I turn so that I face outward again, sliding his left arm up over my shoulder and against the side of my neck as I nestle into his front. He leans down once the couple has left the terminal and places a gentle kiss to the top of my head.

"Sleep, kitty. We've got a big day tomorrow."

Somehow I think it's going to be his hardest one yet.

THIRTY-THREE

REY

"Shadows" - Red

"Time to wake up, babe." I lean across and kiss her temple as the flight attendant announces we've started our descent.

We caught the red-eye flight after what can only be described as one uncomfortable as fuck evening on the terminal floor. Uncomfortable, but nice. It felt good to be needed. I felt good to have somebody happy to just be. No expectations, no schedule to keep. Just her and me, chilling, being, existing.

I never knew how much I missed that until I realized it was something I've never had.

Without a doubt, it would have been more practical to stay at Tabby's, but after the showdown last night I can't blame the woman for wanting to have the space away from her roommate. Café Girl tore me a new asshole after I shoved four hundred dollars in her bag as we headed for the door. Bitch refused to take the bills from my hand, so what else was I going to do? I can't up and kidnap her roommate and expect her to cover costs on her own.

No matter how much she doesn't approve.

I wasn't being intentionally difficult; that's just who I am.

"Kitty." I nudge her arm when she refuses to wake.

Her eyes open and shut a few times before she straightens in her seat and stretches out. "Are we there?"

"Almost. Put your belt on."

Messed up hair, and next to no makeup, she's still the best thing I've sat beside in a long time. "Feel better?"

She shrugs, eyeballing the attendant who waits on her to buckle up. "Maybe. This whole thing still feels so surreal."

"I know, but I'm happy you came." I reach out and ruffle her hair.

Not the smoothest thing to do, I know, but I'm awkward when I'm nervous. And nervous is exactly what I am. Fuck—I didn't sleep a wink last night, arms around her while I stared at the ceiling. My mind swirled like a fucking kaleidoscope, unable to focus on any one thought in particular, good or bad.

What if she freaks out under pressure and heads home?

What if the guys don't make her feel welcome? Or Wally won't let her play?

What if this whole idea is a mistake on my part and she doesn't change a goddamn thing?

Tabby doesn't say anything more as the flight attendant moves on. Simply runs her fingers through her ruffled hair and then pushes her head back into the seat to indicate she's done.

I roll my neck to face the window, watching the city grow beneath us as we come in to land. I honestly thought she'd change her mind when Kendall gave her that out. After all, I'd just wrapped up being a right asshole at the mini-mart down the street. It wasn't my conscious intention to make her mad enough to refuse to come, but maybe that's what my subconscious wanted out of it all?

Why else would I beg her to join me, and then be a right fucking bastard about it?

Am I scared of letting her get close? A little. Am I terrified of failing to get better with her guidance and merely pulling her under with me? Totally.

It's one thing to loathe the journey you're on when it's this troubled and dark, but it's a whole other level of assholery to forcibly take somebody along for the ride.

"Who's picking us up?"

I turn back to face her, smacked yet again with how fucking lucky I am. "Rick's making the trip." Why the hell a good soul like her wants to get messed up with one like mine, I don't know.

"How much trouble are you in?" She lifts an eyebrow, showing the hint of a smile.

I grin. "Loads." She makes it totally worth it, though.

A sigh falls from her lush lips as she leans her head against my shoulder. "I hope they honestly don't mind having me along. You better not be making it out to be less of a problem than it is."

I totally am, but I'm also convinced they'll soon see the method in my madness when they witness what

Tabby does for me. I've found the fucking Holy Grail. Like hell I'm letting it go over something as petty as luggage allowance.

"They love you. You made a good impression the first time they met you."

"I was a bitch the very first time we met," she says with a hint of humor.

"And I was a right cunt, so we're equal."

"Rey." Her loose fist collides with my chest. "Watch your language. There are kids on this plane."

Right. Woops.

"Guess I shouldn't make any moves on you then, huh?"

She lets out a disgruntled sigh, but I know she was thinking about it. Fuck knows I was.

The journey through the airport to get her luggage is predictably boring and even more frustrating when some idiot announces to the whole fucking terminal, it seemed like, who I am. Seriously. Half these people probably don't listen to rock music. And if they do, another half again more than likely stick to the old classics.

I'm not that much of a big deal. Not outside our tour, anyway.

"What are you doing here, man?" the guy asks as though we're old college buddies. "I saw you had to cancel a show, but didn't expect to find you here. Thought you were sick, dude."

"I'm traveling," I say bluntly.

He nods, as though I just explained the theory of

relativity. "Business?"

"Well." I rub my nose as I grimace at the fucking absurdity of this. "The rest of the band aren't here, so I'm gonna go ahead and let you work that one out for yourself."

Tabby tugs on my arm, her bags now at our feet. "Come on."

I snatch the duffle before she has a chance to grab both that and her violin case. Fuck. I travelled with the clothes on my back. Not as though I have anything to carry. Least I can do after being an asshat last night is help her out.

"Give me that one, too." I yank the case out of her hold, much to her disgust.

We make it nearly to the terminal exit before Rick shows his face.

"As if this whole asinine thing wasn't enough of a fucking pain in the ass, now you make me find parking here when it seems like every goddamn plane in the country has touched down."

Huh—Rick grew some balls overnight. "How's Wallace?" I thrust Tabby's luggage at him.

He juggles the two, allowing her to take one from him. "Murderous."

I rip the duffle bag from her and damn near throw it at Rick. "She doesn't carry anything. Got it?"

"Rey," she snaps. "Don't be such an asshole."

I forget she's only known Rick for all of a minute in the scheme of things; he hasn't had time to get on her nerves yet. "Fine." I take the bag and sling it over my shoulder. "Where's the car?"

"Parking building."

I throw the guy a blank stare. "Haven't you got a driver sitting in the fucking drop off lane?"

"No driver." He glares at me as we step out into a much warmer climate than the one we left. "Dad's making you suffer for this shit, Rey."

Fuck me gently. "Like that, is it?"

"You cost him thousands, changing the tickets to tonight."

Kitty throws me a cautionary glance. I shrug. Not much we can do about it now.

"No driver, no entertainment allowance, nothing unless he approves it first."

Jesus—guy really does have my balls in a vise. "House arrest, then?"

"Pretty much."

Kitty slides her hand in mine as we trail behind Rick to the car. His shitty little rental sits squeezed in between two hatchbacks that look like fucking SUVs in comparison.

"This all they have?" I ask as he jams her bags in the back.

His brow pinches while he takes two attempts to shut the trunk. "You aren't the only one with a new budget."

Fucking Wallace.

"You're lucky I didn't make you take a cab," he levels as he opens the passenger door for Tabby. "Ladies up front."

Only for her. Anybody else, and I'd kick up a stink about being relegated to the back. But for Tabby I'll let it slide.

"The guys are already at rehearsal," Rick explains as we all pile in. "They wanted to get a head start on things."

"Why?" Fuck me—seriously, my knees are up around my goddamn ears.

Rick tosses a glare my way in the rearview before he pulls out of the parking space. "They wanted to have a backup plan in case you didn't show."

"I've never missed a performance until now."

"You've also never skipped out without notice to fly halfway across the country on a whim." He smiles at Tabby. "No offense, Tabitha."

"None taken," she murmurs.

I twist to lie down on the back seat while Rick drives. I know I said I'm not that much of a big deal, but that doesn't mean I'm not well known enough that any paps lingering around the place wouldn't have a field day with the possibilities behind why I'm in the back seat of a fucking micro-car while my manager drives the girl who played at our impromptu show around.

"Tell me when we get to the hotel, okay? I'm going to catch a few while I'm hiding down here."

"Sure," Rick mumbles.

Kitty spins in her seat to give me a soft smile. "Hard life, huh?"

"You wouldn't know the fucking half of it."

THIRTY-FOUR

TABITHA

"Wait" - Earshot

I have never, hand to my heart, in my goddamn life stepped into a place as swanky as this. There is glass absolutely everywhere. And if it's not glass, it's crystal. And if it's not crystal, then it's shiny, reflective brass that's been polished to within an inch of its existence.

This is how the other half live. And no, I don't mean the guys from Dark Tide, because they're simply enjoying the illusion as much as I am while they're here. I mean the fact that to the right of reception is row upon row of private boxes marked "Residents."

Holy. Shit.

"You okay?" Rey smiles down at me while I scoop my jaw off the floor.

"This place is... I mean...." I chuckle. "I literally have no words."

"It's one of the better ones." He shrugs and heads for the bank of lifts where Rick already waits for a car.

One of the better ones. My apartment would fit inside this lobby.

I'm so out of my depth. My phone chimes in my pocket as I make my way over to the men.

K: You made it okay? I'm sorry, babe.

"Kendall," I explain when Rey looks down at my phone.

T: Already forgiven. We made it. I'm so in over my head. This isn't my world.

K: You'll do fine. Just be yourself. Ring me later.

She signs off with a heart emoticon. I kill the screen and pocket the phone again as our ride arrives.

The doors slide open, and I'm reflected back at myself in all my hobo glory. I opted for comfortable since it was such an early flight, but now I'm reconsidering my previously "cute and casual" leggings and Ugg boots.

"I'm a goddamn hot mess," I moan as we pile into the lift.

Rick ushers another guest out when they try to join, and then shuts the doors. He punches the button for one of the upper floors and steps back.

"You look fine." Rey slings his arm around my shoulder and pulls me in. "Don't panic."

Yeah. I'm only being reintroduced to a group of guys I've spent barely a few hours with as the girl who's on the tour to keep their lead singer in check. No pressure. None at all.

The lift doors open onto a hallway that's wide enough

to drive a freaking car down. Rick hesitates outside the lift and passes my luggage to Rey.

"I'll see you downstairs in thirty and we'll head over to rehearsal. I've told Toby you're on your way."

"Sure." Rey gives him a nod, and then steers me in the opposite direction.

I stand perfectly still, hands folded before me, while he sets my things down outside what I assume is their suite, and pulls the key card from his wallet. "Fuckers better have tidied up before they left."

I gesture to my current state of dress. "I'm not exactly high maintenance, so I'm sure it'll be fine."

He gives me a smile, and then pushes the door open.

I want to live here.

The enormous room is decorated more like a private residence than a hotel suite. Did they hire one of the empty apartments? Is that the level of pull you get being a globally recognized name?

No cliché TV mounted on the wall over a built-in shelf for your suitcase here. Nope. The large spacious living area looks out over a balcony that boasts an incredible view of the city below. The kitchen area is tucked away to the right, behind a wall so it's not the first thing you see when you walk in. And leading off the main area are one, two, three, four rooms.

"Where's the bathroom?" I stick my head in each door, unsure how I've missed it.

"Each room has its own," Rey explains as he sets my bags down in the middle of the living space.

Sure enough, empty drink bottles, food wrappers, and clothing lie scattered all over the plush furniture.

"It's just like they're at home, I imagine," I say, pointing to the mess.

Rey shoves a bunch of T-shirts aside and smiles sheepishly. "We're boys. We're messy."

"Honestly, I don't care." My hands clap together, loud in the huge room. "So where do I sleep?"

Upmarket style aside, surely one of these sofas folds out?

"With me."

I snap my gaze to Rey, suddenly all too aware it's just me, him, and a huge empty suite. "Okay?"

"Is that all right?" He rubs one arm. "I can probably arrange something else if it's not."

"No, it's fine." I mean, yeah we've kissed. So it's no big deal to share a bed, right?

This is such a big deal. Does he think I'm not here for the mental coaching, because I'm clearly down with more? But at the same time I don't want to come off as easy.

Why is this so hard? This is why I've avoided serious relationships so successfully until now. *Exactly!* Who said this was serious? Play it casual, play it cool. *Take it as it comes, Tabby.*

"Wanna let me know what's going on in there?" Rey takes a step forward, ducking to look me in the eye.

"I was in my head again, wasn't I?"

"Just a little." He smiles.

"Sorry." I take a step toward him also and slide my arms around his middle when we meet. "Kendall tells me off for it all the time. You better get used to it."

"Huh." His arms band around my shoulders, squeezing me tight. "What were you thinking, though?"

"About how out of my depth I am. I have no fucking clue what I'm doing."

"You'll do fine. You've got me." He chuckles, pulling away to look me in the eye. "Come on. I'll show you how fucking awesome the bed is." He takes off, unaware of how that sounded as he continues. "You're gonna love it after last night. It's like a fucking cloud."

I head toward the room he disappeared into, my nerves pinging as I literally step over the threshold from safe and open territory into intimate and personal space.

Rey lies on the enormous bed, one hand behind his head as he pats the mattress with the other. "Try it."

"It's a bed, Rey," I level. "I'm sure it's fine."

"Try it," he repeats, low and persuasive.

"Ugh. Fine." I kick my Uggs off and climb up.

Holy shit. It's like there's a gazillion fluffy bunnies all holding me up. "It's so soft, and yet it's not too soft, if that makes any sense."

"I know, right?"

"I want one."

"I'll buy you one." He rolls to face me, a grin splitting his face from ear to ear. "We could share it."

"Whoa." I lift both hands between us, as well as both eyebrows. "Slow down there, tiger."

"What?" He graces me with a cheeky smile before leaning in to sweep his lips over mine.

I love it, I really do. But we literally moved from twenty-first century pen pals—keeping in touch via Messenger—to… well, whatever this is in the last twenty-four hours.

"Can we just...." I slide out from beneath him and roll to my side so that we're face-to-face. "Let's get settled, get you to rehearsal, and then we can...." I wave my hand between us for lack of anything better to say.

His face falls, lines pinching his brow. "Sorry. I guess I got carried away." He slides off the bed and heads toward the bathroom. "I should get changed before we head out."

My mouth waters when he reaches over his head with one hand and then tugs his T-shirt off. The material hits the floor in a heap, while my resolve to let this develop at a more sensible pace is seriously tested. *Who the fuck am I kidding?* If I don't get to jump his bones by the end of this stint, I'm going to be seriously disappointed in myself and disillusioned in his prowess as a rock star.

Still, there's a time and a place, and the thirty minutes we have to get ready before heading out hardly seems like enough time to start *that* kind of relationship off in the right way. I don't want forever from him, but I sure as shit want more than a fleeting tap and go.

The water switches on in the bathroom while I stare at the ceiling and groan. I catch the clink of his belt before his arm appears in the doorway, jeans in hand, and he flicks them in the general direction of his T-shirt. The boxers come next.

Fucking save me.

"You're being a tease," I whine as I catch a glimpse of his naked butt in the mirror when he steps in the shower.

"I'm being an open book, kitty," he calls back. "That's

what you wanted, wasn't it?"

An open book. The goddamn thing isn't written in English, I can tell you that much. Does his non-aversion to being naked around me mean he isn't ashamed of his body? Or does he want me to join him?

I don't *need* a shower. Nope. But I do need something. Relief. And not the sort I can get here when I didn't pack *that*.

Shit.

"Come on in," he sings out in a Southern accent. "The water's just fine."

I slide off the bed with a moan, my body alive at the anticipation of what I'll find beyond that open door.

Pity I'll never know.

THIRTY-FIVE

REY

"Mudshovel" - Staind

I need a new approach. Subtle didn't work with kitty. Neither did a blatant invitation. And she shot me down when I went in guns blazing.

All I wanted was to make the most of our time alone, in private, and instead she marched her pert little ass out to the living room and waited on the sofa for me, messaging who I can only assume was Café Girl.

I don't really know what to make of it. I haven't been blown off like that in years, and the last time I was it meant the girl didn't want a fucking thing to do with me.

I know that's not the case with Tabby, but this male brain is seriously messed up when it tries to calculate what all her mixed signals mean.

She kisses me, and she gets close to me, yet she shies away when anything indicates that we could actually be something together. *Fuck.* Is she scared of commitment?

"Really could have used some help cleaning my back in there, kitty."

Her gaze lifts to me as I towel off my hair, decent in a

clean pair of boxers and fresh denim.

I'm still shirtless though. Couldn't pass up that opportunity to rev her a little before we leave.

"I'm sure you managed just fine."

"I guess you'll never really know my struggle."

Truth is, I have my shower routine down to a fine art. Takes me all of three minutes to clean head to toe. It's a case of needing to make it efficient as possible when I hate the water so damn much. Tricky fucking drips that run into my eyes—

"Would you like to eat before we go?"

I shift my focus back to Tabby to find her watching me with genuine concern. "The fridge is empty, and room service will take too long."

"Oh." She looks to the carpet and frowns. "Would you mind if I skipped rehearsal and took a walk instead? I'm kind of famished."

"We'll get food on the way."

Her jaw pulls tight as she looks toward the massive windows.

"What?" I throw the towel over my shoulder and walk closer.

"It's nothing, really."

"It's enough to make you look uncomfortable."

She returns her focus to me as I take a seat on the low table in front of her. "I don't mind being here to help you out, but I don't know anyone else. Hell, I hardly know you."

"You're shy?"

"I feel as though I'd be more comfortable letting you work things out with the guys on your own today. You need that moment as just the four of you, to talk through what went down."

"Fuck them." If they have any issues, they can talk to me about them with her there. It's not as though I have any secrets when it comes to Tabby now. "I want you there."

"Rey." Her head tilts slightly, pissing me off with her condescension.

"You're coming. End of story." I push to my feet and hustle around the table to leave so damn fast it shifts when my shin collides with the corner. "Ow. Fuck."

"Are you okay?"

Ego is a little bruised, but otherwise... "I'm fine," I snap, well aware I unnecessarily take my anger out on her, but the train's a rollin'. "I'll be better if you just do what you said you would and fucking support me through this. And right now, that means coming to rehearsal when I fucking ask you to."

Her eyes are hard, her jaw even more so as she seemingly bites her tongue and chooses to look out the windows at the skyline instead.

Jesus. Fuck. This is *not* how I wanted things to go. I march through to the bathroom and hurl the fucking towel at the floor. My knuckles turn white with the grip I take on the edge of the counter, my head low between my shoulders as I refuse to look at myself.

It's catch-22s like these that drive me fucking insane. I *need* to look in that mirror to finish getting ready to head out, but at the same time I know if I do the usual dark thoughts will take over and leave me ready to punch myself in the fucking face.

She has every right to take a fucking walk if she wants to. Who am I to stop her?

Worst of all, why the fuck can't I just go back through there and say sorry? *Pride.* It's goddamn pride that tears my relationships with people apart. If I say sorry, it validates what happened. It says, "Yes, I know I was short-tempered and out of line" and reminds me that no matter how hard I try to be better, I. Just. Keep. Fucking. Up.

Do it, you pussy bastard.

I drag my gaze along the counter, up the backsplash, and to the mirror.

Hair wax. Hands. Hair. Simple.

Two twists and I have the lid of the wax container off. I set it down a little harsher than usual, which in turn makes the fucking thing ricochet off my damn deodorant stick. The plastic disc skims over the counter before tumbling to the floor.

A twitch jerks the side of my nose as I gaze down at the tiny little error.

It's no big deal, Rey.

Except today it's everything. The straws are piling up on this camel's back: Kendall disapproves of me, we spent a shitty night in the airport to avoid her, Wallace cut off my privileges, the guys rehearse without me, and now Tabby pushes me away, rejects me... that stings most of all.

One deep breath. Two.

I lean down to retrieve the lid. My fingertips catch the white sticky wax residue and make a mess.

Something intrinsic to my state of mind snaps.

The plastic careens across the marble top with my frustration, quickly followed by the half-full tub. It skates off the end of the counter and collides with the side of the shower. The plastic tub cracks, and then falls to the carpet as my blood surges through my veins.

Fuck.

I tried so hard to keep my shit level. I really did.

But that useless plastic motherfucker....

"Fuck!"

I should leave it where it is and walk away, cool off. Take some time to wind down and then start again fresh.

But I don't have time. I've probably got ten minutes left to get downstairs if I'm lucky.

Fuck! My hands damn well shake as I reach for the cracked canister. Tiny fibers are stuck in the wax from the carpet. Tiny fibers that only bury themselves deeper when I try to swipe them out.

I. Do. Not. Have. Time. For. This.

The breaths I take leave me hysterical, whooshing out my nose like I'm some raging bull. I chuckle at myself as I fix my hair. At least by some swing of fate the hysteria helps to ease my rage.

That is, until one fucking spike refuses to play ball.

"Come on, you little fucker. Get over there."

The strand droops at the end, which wouldn't be such a problem if the rest of them weren't straight as an arrow. *Probably because your hair is wet, you fuckhead.* Of course. I'm in such a hurry I forget to do something as obvious as drying my hair first.

The plastic tub doesn't survive the second flight

across the bathroom.

"What's the matter?"

Great. And now she's here.

"Nothing." I stoop down to salvage what I can of my ruined hair product, bundling it in my palm with the dregs of my pride as I refuse to look at Tabby.

"Something's obviously wrong." She looks pointedly at the ruins in my hands, the cock of her head clear in my periphery. "Can I help?"

And there it goes—my last strand of rationality.

"I don't know, can you?" I holler at her, while my subconscious screams at me to stop, to calm down and to relax. "That's what you're here for, isn't it? Can you fix this?" I yank at my hair before messing it up with both palms.

She stands stoic in the doorway, silent while I meltdown, crying internally at myself to stop.

It's been a while. I knew it was coming. I had hoped it wouldn't be today, was all.

The tap slips in my grasp as I try to crank the water on to wash my hands. Tabby steps forward to help... forward into my lava bubble of self-hatred.

"No. I can do it."

"Just let me—"

"I said I can do it!" My voice reverberates off the shiny surfaces, deafening.

She retreats a step, watching quietly while I use a hand towel to get the tap on. The wax predictably repels the water, which means the cleanup takes a painfully long time. My heartbeat pulses through my veins.

She's not convinced I can handle this, and I don't

blame her. I can see it in the set of her eyebrows as she punches her arms over her chest.

"What?" I mutter.

"Got it out of your system yet?"

"Nope."

"What set you off?" Her question is carefully delivered.

The towel rubs hard against my skin as I scrub the last of the wax off my fingers. "You."

I turn my head to look at her when she remains silent. Her brow is pinched, the anger there to see. I get it. I asked her here, spouting off how I couldn't be without her. And I still can't. But what confuses me no end is why that is when her presence only makes me more frustrated at what I've become.

I push past her, my shoulder knocking hers as I head into the bedroom and retrieve my wallet and phone. She stays leaning against the bathroom door with her back to me while I punch them in my pockets.

"Maybe you *should* take that walk, Tabitha. Probably be a good idea if you didn't come back, either." Not when I'm like this.

Not even twenty-four hours and I've already done it.

I've already brought her down to my level.

Aaand... this is where they leave.

THIRTY-SIX

TABITHA

"Waking Lions" – Pop Evil

What the fuck have I signed up for?

My hands shake in my lap as I stare pointlessly at the coffee table before me. I dropped onto the sofa the second he slammed the door behind him and I haven't moved since. *Welcome to the tour, Tabby.*

I let him go.

What did he expect me to do? Run after him and beg for forgiveness? If so, he can think again—I don't play that game. Especially when I have nothing to be sorry for.

I mean I get it. I really do. Especially after reading a couple of firsthand accounts online from people who struggle with the disorder. He feels out of control. The mood swing takes him over, and his anger stems from his frustration at himself.

He's the product of seemingly years without proper treatment, without a proper action plan. From what he told me, the members of his support network have simply done what they had to in order to prop him up like some puppet, instead of actually dealing with the problem properly.

I can deal with that. I understand why he's so fractured.

But what I *can't* deal with is being made to feel as though this whole thing is my fault. It's like *I'm* being punished for his issues.

That's hard to get past, no matter how much I want to help him. No matter how much I know he doesn't mean to make me feel this way.

I should go out and get food, but I'm stuck with one tiny predicament: I never got a moment in that blaze of fury to ask Rey if I could use his key card. *Room service it is, then.*

I scour the apartment for the menu, finding it stashed in one of the kitchen drawers. Yet as I stare at the list of things that belong on a restaurant menu, I can't make heads or tails of the words. Nothing registers. I'm here in body, but my thoughts are across town with a man who's stuck on self-destruct.

I burn to message him, to get in touch, desperate to know how things went when he showed up to practice. Yet I know that would only give him an out for his behavior and set the benchmark. It would let him know I'm okay with him carrying on like he's always done.

And I'm not. I didn't come here for a holiday, I came here to help. And I can't help him if I enable his current defaults.

My gaze falls on my violin case as I give up on food for the time being. If I can find solace in my music, why can't Rey?

I'm such a mess. I need a reassuring voice, to talk to somebody in my corner. And there's only one person I have to do that with, despite how she feels about the man. I retrieve my phone from my purse and then navigate to Kendall's number.

"Hey, hon." Her bubbly voice leaves me tight in the chest, suddenly a little homesick.

"Hey." I return to the kitchen and lean a hip against the counter.

"What's up? You sound flat."

"Tired," I bullshit. "How are things there? No sleep-overs while I'm away, okay?"

She chuckles at my dry humor while I chew my thumbnail. "No, Mom. I'm fine, though. Little bit jealous of you living it up. You're lucky I love you, bitch."

"I promise it's not as wild as whatever you're thinking."

"Probably not, but a girl can dream." She hesitates before asking, "What have you been up to so far? Why's it so quiet? I thought you'd be getting ready for tonight, or something."

"The guys are." I fuss with the menu beside me. "I asked if I could hang back and get something to eat. We didn't have much before we got on the plane, and Rey doesn't really stop it seems."

"Well, you tell him I said he has to take good care of you, okay? He doesn't want to cross me again, trust me."

"He's just a bit stressed, I think."

"What makes you say that?"

I push off the counter and head for the windows before answering. "He lost his cool when we got in to the hotel this afternoon. Typical rock star moment."

"Ugh. Diva."

"It was worse than that, hon. He seemed like he doesn't even want to be here. Totally different from how he was at our place, that's for sure." The people and cars on the street below are merely ants from this height.

Kendall sighs down the line. "He did warn you that he was difficult."

"I know."

"And I did tell you that he's asking too much of you. He needs a shrink, not a bed buddy."

I frown at her comment, annoyed that she doesn't think I could do anything worthwhile for him. "I think I might use the time to work on some music for myself. Not every day you get some swanky hotel room to yourself, right?"

"Send me pictures. I want to see what lavishness I'm missing out on."

"Deal." I cast my eye around the place, at the things the guys have left lying around, at the strange home-liness of it. "I might have to tidy up a bit, first."

"Men are such pigs."

"Sometimes." I chuckle. "Talk later, hon."

"Miss you."

"I'll be back before you know it."

I disconnect, feeling a little better after hearing a friendly voice. Fuck knows the way Rey spoke to me cut me down, as much as I tried not to show it.

I get as far as tidying away the rubbish, and then condensing the guys' clothes to one of the sofas, before my phone chimes with a new message.

R: I'm sorry, kitty.

Sure. It's nice that he's apologized, and maybe I'm being petty, but I would have loved to hear that face-to-face.

I stare at the notification, unsure how to respond. As it stands, he doesn't know I've received it. I haven't actually opened the thread, so for all he knows I haven't seen it.

I choose ignorance until my head's in better order, and leave my phone on the table while I set up to play.

I saw this with my parents: my father would blow up and my mother would spend all her time reassuring him everything was okay. But he never apologized. He never looked my mother in the eye and told her how much he appreciated her support. Instead he searched for what he'd never find somewhere else.

Will that be me here? Am I walking down the same path; stroking the ego of a man who doesn't care, or see, what I give up to be his reassurance? Will he end up holding these arguments against me and move on to the next shiny thing?

The real question is, why after only a couple of weeks knowing each other would I care so much if he did?

I forgo using the time to compose; my head in too much of a jumbled mess to be able to focus. Instead, I take my violin to the balcony to let the mood guide me. My bow pulls across the strings, the notes lost on the breeze, yet the familiar movements, the positions that are second nature, allow me to take the concerns I have and set them into a rational order.

He needs to be clear on what he expects from this.

He needs to respect the fact that I have no obligation to be here.

And he needs to let me in.

Not simply tell me intimacies about his past. Not just explain the issues behind the outbursts.

But to take me on that journey with him.

If Rey wants me here to help him, he has to believe that he has it in him to help himself.

Until he does, there isn't a damn thing I can do that will make an ounce of change.

Not a damn thing.

THIRTY-SEVEN

REY

"Let Me Live My Life" – Saint Asonia

Rick sighs as we head past security and into the venue. "Do I need to buy her a ticket home?"

The play is broken and disjointed as we walk toward the stage. We caught a cab over here. A goddamn cab. Wallace really doesn't fuck around when it comes to punishment for the lost revenue.

I stare at his son beside me, realizing I actually don't know a fucking thing about Rick other than what he does here. "You might need to ask her that."

"How about you ask her yourself," he levels. "And while you're at it, you can apologize to the poor girl. I know saying sorry isn't your thing, but maybe just this once you can try something a little different with Tabitha." He leans forward to catch my eye before he pushes the envelope a little harder. "You might find she's worth the energy, Rey. After all, why bother flying her all the way out here if you're not going to put in any effort?"

"Just make sure you do what I asked you to, okay? She's doing this for me, so it's only fair I do something in return."

"Yeah. Okay. But don't get up my ass about it if I can't get the okay to put her onstage."

"Don't give me reason to."

Kris stands to the side of the stage as I walk on; arms resting casually on his guitar while he watches Toby and Emery bitch over who comes in first. *Fuck me.* We've only been performing the song they were playing for close to a year.

"You both cut in together, you idiots," I call out.

"We decided to change it," Emery states flatly.

Meanwhile Toby damn near knocks his fucking kit over in his haste to get off the stool. "What the fuck, you dumb cunt!"

I take a step back as he comes at me, both his palms facing outward. They connect strong and sharp with my collarbones.

"Don't you dare fucking take off like that again."

"Or what?" I taunt. "You'll do what? Fill me in here."

His mouth twists as he glares at me. "I was this close to calling Mom." He holds his forefinger and thumb an inch apart while he whispers the words. "This fucking close."

"So call her." I push past him and head for where my guitar rests on its stand.

"You know why I didn't?" he shouts across the stage. "Because I didn't know how I'd explain to her that I couldn't stop you if you *had* fucking topped yourself."

Emery takes a seat on the front of Toby's platform with a sigh.

I spin on my brother and shrug, both palms held up at

my sides. "Maybe I didn't want you to stop me?"

"You fucker." He charges across the stage too quick for Emery to cut him off.

I brace for impact; we're two ten-year-olds brawling all over again.

Kris steps out of the way as the two of us hit the deck, Toby's arm around my neck, mine around his middle. My shoulder takes most of the impact, a whoosh of air escaping him as he hits the stage on his side.

"You're selfish, Rey," he grits out through a stiff jaw as we roll and grapple. "It's all about you."

I get the heel of my right hand under his jaw and push hard, forcing him back far enough to wedge my left arm between our chests. "Then let me finish for a goddamn change, big brother. It'd be all about you if I wasn't around, wouldn't it?"

He tucks a hand over his head and swings his elbow down to knock me in the side of the head. I use my legs to roll him over, force him to his back.

"Why don't you get it?" he cries, grunting as I get an elbow into his guts. "It should be us, Rey. You and me. It should be us doing this shit together."

"What the fuck do you mean?" I straddle him, blocking his fist as he tries to give me a last shot. "We are together, you dickhead."

"He means," Emery explains from a safe distance, "he's tired of being left out of what goes on in that fucked-up head of yours."

I turn to face Em, still on top of Toby. My brother goes lax beneath me while our bassist spells it out.

"He's your blood, Rey, and you keep him in the dark."

"Because none of you fuckers want to know about it," I say, climbing to my feet. "You've all had it with me. Fuck. *I've* had it with me."

"We haven't had it with you," Kris murmurs.

Asshole hasn't moved an inch since this all started.

"We just don't know what to do anymore," he finishes.

I back up, looking at the guys with new eyes while Rick hangs back with the crew. They've all seen us blow up from time to time, but this level of physical violence is new.

"What do you want me to say?" I shrug, still retreating. "I don't have the answer, guys. I don't know either."

Toby pulls himself into a seated position, and then pushes to his feet. "Why her? Why go to Tabitha about it and not us?"

Because she's new to this. As I look around at the tired faces of my bandmates, at the concerned look on Rick's, I realize what it is that makes me feel safe around her.

It's not just that she listens without prejudice. It's that she doesn't harbor this level of frustration toward me. She hasn't been worn down by years of my shit. She hasn't had her optimism snuffed out by my repeated disrespect for her attempts to help.

I like her because she gives me a fresh chance to try again.

To try again and get it right.

Can I even do that?

"Are we going to play, or what?" I stride over to my guitar and rip it off the stand.

The guys all take their positions, quiet, shoulders down. Resigned. I've done it again. Wound everyone up with my behavior, and then left them out to dry while I shut it all out and push on as though nothing's amiss.

Emery wraps up the argument with Toby over how they were going to change the couple of bars in question while I pull out my phone and send a quick message to kitty.

I was a jackass, a complete and utter asshole. I can admit that. And yeah, Rick's right, I need to apologize to her. But it can't wait until we get back prior to the show, because if this is how far the guys are through rehearsal, I get the feeling there won't be enough of a gap in between for us to go anywhere.

It'll be a quick takeout meal backstage before we're spun through wardrobe and left to get our shit together for the show tonight.

"All set?" Em asks as he wanders past to take his usual place to my left.

"Sure." I pocket my phone and step up to kick things off.

Two taps on the mic to make sure its live and I'm right back where I should be.

Not necessarily where I want to be.

THIRTY-EIGHT

TABITHA

Help – Papa Roach

My sleep-addled brain takes a precious minute to register where I am as I blink away the remnants of my impromptu nap. The four disrupted hours I got on the airport floor with Rey didn't exactly sate my need, so it wasn't much of a surprise when I struggled to keep my eyes open watching television.

I gave in, figuring the guys would wake me up when they came back between the rehearsal and the show. Yet one look at the array of glittering lights out the darkened windows tells me that they never made it back.

I can't deny the sense of deflation that has me sinking back into the sofa cushions.

I glance at my phone where it rests beside me on the sofa. I should message Rey and ask what's going on, but that would make it seem as though I've accepted his apology and I'm already over his one-sided argument.

I guess I am, to some degree, but I'm not ready to let it blow over without talking it through first. Face-to-face.

My fingers beat a rhythm on the television remote.

What to do? The time on the corner of the television screen says a little after ten, the evening news report broadcasting something about a gridlock on the highway. I guess the only logical thing to do is have a shower and head to bed.

Not as though I have any hot invites to go out for the night. *Or do I?* I roll to the front of the sofa cushions, balancing myself precariously on the edge as I stretch out to retrieve my phone. Two new messages from Rey sit on the lock screen, as well as one from Kendall.

I unlock the device and roll to my back to check hers first.

K: You haven't sent me any updates, woman! I'm going to bed. Ring me tomorrow.

I frown, chewing on the inside of my cheek as I tap out of her thread and into Rey's.

R: We ran over with rehearsal. Sticking around here before the show. Come down, kitty. Get a cab, and I'll meet you when you get here to pay for it.

Shit. As my eyes track the first text bubble it strikes me: he messaged me. No spontaneous Messenger video call. He knew I wouldn't be up to much, yet he chose to send a text message instead.

Speaks volumes for how insecure he is underneath all that anger.

I continue on to the more recent message, sent an hour ago.

259

R: I've totally broken the no phones on stage rule by messaging you, but I've already fucked up my words twice because you didn't turn up. I didn't mean what I said, kitty. Don't leave. Don't go home.

His message brings relief—he gets how badly what he did hurt me. I'd call him, just to reassure him that I'm not going anywhere, but he'll be in the thick of it now. If they're not still on stage, they're bound to be tied up with post-show commitments.

Panic flashes through me, hot and raw as it slices a path straight through my lungs and into my heart. What if he's out drinking again? Who's he with?

Get a grip, Tab. It's none of my business who he spends his time with, or why. I've been in his life for all of a hot minute. As abandoned as I feel being here, alone, I shouldn't lose sight of the fact I've been given one hell of a privilege.

Hopefully he can do what he promised and get me on stage with them. If not, there's still the possibility that I could make some connections while I tag along on this tour. There might be something good yet to come out of it all for me.

I take the phone to Rey's room and drop onto the bed to at least send him reassurance that I'm here for him.

T: I haven't gone anywhere. I'm here. I'll be here when you get back.

The phone falls from my hand as I throw my arms wide over the bed with a sigh. I need to get prepared. If

I'm going to have all this time to myself while they're busy doing what bands do while on the road, then I'd be wise to put the hours to good use and learn a bit more about what goes on in that brain of his.

A shower to clear my head, and then I'll get started. The magic of a smartphone and free Wi-Fi at the hotel means I have endless resources available at the touch of a finger.

Maybe I *can* help him through music? Maybe I can't? But if I'm going to try, I need to give it my all.

I make a mental list of questions as I shower, things to research about his condition and what I can do to support him. I know enough not to be ignorant, but I'm one of the lucky ones who's never had anyone close in their life affected to this degree by a mental illness.

At least, not that I know of.

The hot water washes over my shoulders, easing the tension while I run through all the little tells he had leading up to that epic breakdown. With hindsight, I can see that he barely held on, but at the time I guess none of it seemed important.

I did what everyone else does and accepted it was all a part of who he is. But what if that's just it? None of that *has* to be him.

How the hell am I going to do this? How on earth do I uncover the best parts of someone with music alone? *You're delusional, Tab.* A woman with a Mother Theresa complex that's going to get somebody hurt, or maybe everybody.

I dry off and tug my pajamas on, chuckling a little when I pull the polka-dot-covered fabric up my legs. A few strokes of the brush through my hair and I'm decent enough that I don't think Rey will have a hernia when he catches sight of me in the morning.

I step out into the bedroom and immediately freeze. *What the hell?* Two men argue, far enough away that I can't quite make out whom it is. *Are they back?* Have the band returned? Arms over my chest, I edge the door open a fraction and reel as I recognize Rick's voice in the living area.

"I'm done with you blaming me for this shit. You brought it on yourself. Deal with it."

"Fuck off, Rick." *Rey.* "Just get the fuck out and leave me alone." I catch distinct footfalls as they head for the door. "And tell those backstabbing cunts they can get fucked if they think I'm going to let them in here."

"Go throw your tantrum in your room if you must, Rey," Rick scathes, "but this is *everyone's* space. If you can't deal with people right now, then get yourself another suite. The guys will be back here tonight whether you like it or not."

"Just fuck off, already!"

The door slams shut—presumably behind Rick—with a resounding boom, Rey muttering under his breath as he crosses the living space.

I step back into his room, tiptoeing across to where my sweater lies on the bed. He needs a minute to cool off, a few precious seconds to get his blood pressure down before I walk out into that minefield.

I get my arms in the sleeves before deafening vocals fill the place, the opening of the song's heartfelt lyrics sung almost solo before the music drops in. I fall to the side of the bed as the first verse resounds off the walls, my heart breaking when Rey joins in with the words at the top of his lungs.

My hands shake as I bring my phone to my lap and ask Siri, "What's this song?"

I can't hear her answer over the level of the music, but the result displays on my screen: "Help" by Papa Roach. It takes two tries, but I manage to open Google and bring up the lyrics, my chest growing tighter by the minute as Rey sings along with what is his most desperate cry for change yet.

I'm in too deep. I'm flailing, falling lower with him with every reminder that I don't have a fucking clue what I'm doing. He's on the edge, arms wind milling as he tries not to fall, and I don't know if I'm strong enough to pull him back up if he does.

My throat grows tight, air too hard to breathe, when the song restarts. Rey's voice grows hoarse as he yells the lyrics. I rise to my feet, unable to take his agony a second longer, and walk through to the living room to find him in a heap on the floor, eyes closed and pinched with pain.

The lines of the song whisper from the speakers and the man before me as the song reaches its lull, my approach hidden when the guitar and drums cut back in.

"Rey?" I step in front of him, unsure if I should encroach on his space.

His head lifts, eyes bloodshot as he stares at me with a dimpled chin. "You didn't leave?"

I step across to the dock and turn the music down. "No. Didn't you see my message?"

His maniacal laughter dissolves in a guttural moan. "Kitty, they took the fucking thing off me. Can you believe that shit? I got my motherfucking phone confiscated like I'm a goddamn kid."

It's kind of funny. "Really?"

"You're here," he repeats on a whisper. "Why?" The brief respite slides away, not a shadow of it left as he slumps onto his heels and gently rocks to the music.

The song starts again.

"Why wouldn't I be here?"

"Because everyone always leaves." His fists flex on his knees. "Everyone has enough. Everyone breaks. Mostly me."

I drop to my knees and shuffle before him, torn apart watching him self-destruct. "Talk to me. What brought you to this, Rey? Make me understand how you went from the cocky guy I met a few weeks ago to this complete one-eighty."

His jaw flexes as he swallows, his reddened eyes fixated on mine. I count the breaths he takes, praying for the patience to let him come to me in his own time. I want to shake the doubt from him, slap him with the incredible talent he possesses.

But none of that will help when he can't see it for himself through the fog of his depression.

"You wouldn't understand." He drops his head, chin tucked to his chest as he fidgets with the frayed threads on his jeans. "Fuck. It was a good show." A bitter laugh escapes. "Why am I like this, then? What the fuck is my deal?"

"Where are the others?" Something has to have

happened to send him over the edge.

"Doing interviews."

Probably a good thing he chose to come back here then. "Why are you mad at them?" I break his day down; filling in the blanks in the hopes it'll give me something to go off.

"They cut me out." His smile is beautiful in its honesty, yet ugly with its pain. "They told me to leave because I couldn't be trusted not to 'make a scene.'"

Ouch. "Who told you to leave?"

"Toby. Rick. Even Emery nodded at what they said."

"Kris?"

Rey laughs. "Fucker never says much anyway."

"Hey." I take his hands in mine, resting them on my knees. "Tell me about the show. Why was it good?"

"Fucking epic crowd." His voice is clearer as he lifts our joined hands to wipe his face with the inside of his right elbow. "I got down front with them, had them singing lines for me. It's always cool when they're so interactive."

The shift is measurable, the topic enough to pull him from his spiral. "What songs did they do for you?"

He keeps talking, recounting the night. Tells me all about a birthday girl they got up on stage to serenade with their own twisted version of "Happy Birthday." I hold on throughout, feeling the stress enter me as it melts from him.

Yet as he wraps up his retell of the concert, the darkness remains. His lips quirk up on one side apologetically as he sits in silence, only the song repeating between us.

"You're still here," he murmurs, cycling back to the start of the conversation.

I get to my feet, pulling him with me. "Not going anywhere, Rey. Except"—I tug my hands free to head for the music dock—"over here to switch this off."

He huffs a laugh, standing on the spot with his hands tucked in the back pockets of his jeans as he watches me. "You're fucking incredible, kitty. You know that?"

"Not really." I give him a sad smile. "I'm just me."

"Which is what makes you so incredible." He reaches for me, sighing when I step into his embrace. "I wish I could be more of a man for you." He huffs at the sentiment.

I pull back to shake my head at him, keeping my eyes on his. "What the hell do you mean by that?"

"It's girly, crying and shit. It's weak."

Ugh! "No, it's not," I snap. "It's never weak to admit when you need help. It's the bravest fucking thing you can do." Heaven knows I don't do it enough.

"You were on my mind all night," he says, lifting a hand to sweep the hair from my face so that he can rest his palm against my cheek. "I just wanted one more minute to talk to you. One more minute to tell you how sorry I am."

"I know you are." I allow my eyes to slip closed as I lean into his touch. "But it means nothing if you let things get this bad again."

I lift my head and hold his gaze, hoping I haven't pushed too far. Judging by the sullen look on his face, I skate the line.

His hand slips down to rest on my back. "I drove Kris

mad with how many times I screwed up one song in practice. I should have known then I'd be useless tonight. Owe him a pack of smokes for it."

Little things like that, little glimpses of their friendships remind me that behind all the fuss, they're just men. They're simply a bunch of friends who got together doing what they love.

Except now that same thing tears them all apart.

"How long have you got before we leave this place?"

"A day. We hit the road again tomorrow night."

"Tomorrow morning. You need to sit down with the guys and talk about what's going on," I level. "You can't stay angry at them, and they can't have a reason to be mad at you."

"Kitty." He steps back, the void between us physical as well as mental. "They *know* what's going on. That's the problem."

"Do they? Because I don't see them around right now. I don't see them here witnessing this."

He holds my gaze, jaw working left to right.

"What *do* they see, Rey?"

His scrutiny shifts as he heads for the bedroom.

I follow him in, standing at the door as he begins to undress. I need to hurry this conversation up if I expect to hold it without distraction. "Tell me."

He sighs, tossing his denim vest and T-shirt to the floor. "Put it this way: Toby wrestled me after I told him to leave me alone to get it right next time so that he wouldn't have to deal with me and my shit ever again."

My heart damn near stops as sickness rises. "Get what right?"

Those red eyes snap to mine as he looks over his shoulder. "You know what."

Fuck. I can't do this. I can't pretend that I'm strong enough to do this.

"I said I won't leave, and I meant it. But I'll only stay on one condition, Rey."

"Give it to me." He heads for the bathroom.

I follow him to the door, talking to his back as he flicks the shower on. "That you promise to let me know if you think of doing that again."

"Say it." His words are a cold knife against my throat. "Show me you have enough guts to say it. Don't pussy-foot around me, kitty. I don't like people who treat me with kid gloves."

"Taking your life, Rey," I grit out. "Promise to tell me if you feel like dying is the only option."

His smile is sad as he unbuckles his belt. "Guess what."

I can barely get the word out of my throat. "What?"

"I feel like that right now."

Shit. Holy shit. How the fuck do I deal with this. "Why?" My voice breaks.

"Because I miss the mania." His shoulders rise with a sigh before he drops it all; naked as the day he was born before he steps in the shower and behind the frosted glass panel. "That's the only thing about a high that great," he calls out as I literally fold to the floor. "It amplifies the low."

"I'm not leaving you."

"I wish I could promise you the same." He stops moving beneath the flow as a sigh echoes off the glass. "I really do. And you know why?"

God, don't tell me. "Why?" This is going to hurt; I know it.

"Because I think I figured out why I need you here with me."

My chest aches as I fight to control my breathing, my legs tucked to my chest.

"I think I love you."

THIRTY-NINE

REY

Ordinary – Like A Storm

She thinks I can't hear her cry, but I can, and it fuck-ing tears me apart knowing I caused that.

Water runs in rivers from my hair, slicked over my face, hiding my eyes. I like it, the pretense of a cloak to hide me from the world. I stand in the shower until my fingers wrinkle, even my dislike of water not enough to shift me from this spot.

Her sobs have stopped by the time I decide enough is enough and dry off to head through to the bedroom. She lies on the bed, curled in on herself as her fingers fidget with a fold in the sheet beside her.

"You okay?"

She snorts a bitter laugh, refusing to move. "Shouldn't I ask you that?"

I make my way to the bed wearing only my boxers, and slide on to sit beside her, my back against the headboard. "Difference is, I'm used to this. You're not."

"Your prolific phone use made a review of the show," she states flatly, sliding her phone toward me.

I skim the headline on the link to the article, not in the slightest bit interested in reading what the piece has to say. "Never mind the music, huh?"

"What were you doing?" She goes back to toying with the sheet. "You only messaged me once."

I reach down and take her hand, stilling the anxious fidgeting. "Mostly refreshing it to check if you'd replied."

She swallows, fingers flexing beneath mine.

I slide down the bed to lie face-to-face with her, and yet she still can't look at me. "Remember what I said about how it makes me feel when you can't look at me?"

She nods. And yet she fixates on the bed between us.

"Look at me."

"I can't."

"Why?"

"Because I don't want to cry for you anymore. That's not why you brought me here. I'm trying, Rey. I really am, but I don't think I'm the person you need. I'm not strong enough for this."

"You are."

"I'm not." Her eyes flick up to mine—it's a sucker punch straight to the gut. "Look at me, for fuck's sake."

"I am." She pulls in a sharp breath as I bring my hand to her face, easing the stress lines with my thumb. "The only person who has ever cried when I told them how I felt is my mom." I chuckle at how ridiculous it is to lie on a bed with a girl I'm madly in love with and talk about my fucking mother. "You know what that tells me?"

"I'm soft?" She smirks.

"You care."

Her gaze drops before she finds enough courage to

speak again. "You said you love me."

"I said I think I do." I'm not sure, to be honest. I can't trust what I think at the best of times, so how do I know this is a feeling that's going to remain and not one that'll pass with time? "I know I need you like crazy, and I can't think of any other reason why that would be."

"Because I shut out your loneliness." Her face falls as she rolls away. "I don't want to start something here if it's going to be based on dependency."

"Why is that so bad?" I follow her across the bed and lie propped up on my elbow to look down at her. Like fuck she can just take off when it gets too intense.

"Because the whole point of me being here is to help you find a way to self-soothe through your music." She shifts her gaze to mine. "We haven't touched a damn instrument yet."

My lips kick up. "I was kind of busy tonight."

She huffs a laugh. "Funny guy, huh?"

"I can be."

A sigh makes her chest swell as she looks at me. "What am I going to do with you?"

"Hopefully some pretty dirty things."

Her smile is soft, yet clearly unamused. "How the fuck do you swing from one extreme to the other like this?" Her brow pinches in a frown.

"That shit we talked about when I was in the shower? It's still there," I reassure her. "I'm not focused on it, is all."

Her hand finds my face, her fingers soft against my jaw. "I don't like that."

"Neither do I." But it is what it is, and I refuse to let it ruin what I'm doing here. "Can we start the night over?"

"How?"

I pause a moment, enjoying the feel of her hand as she trails it down the side of my neck. She doesn't appear to be touching me in a desperate attempt to seduce me, like women in the past have. Instead, it's an exploration. Her hand seems to map my skin as she traces the line of my collarbone with her thumb, reversing direction to skim lower over my chest with the heel of her hand.

I could lie here and let her do this for hours.

It's insane how good it feels to have somebody touch me as though I mean something to them, especially when all I can associate with myself at the best of times is disgust.

"I fucked up, didn't I?" I open my eyes to find her watching me, waiting.

"I think that's a little undeniable at this point, yes."

I search her eyes for any hint of fear, any sign of doubt. "I hurt you." There isn't a single sign that she wants out right now.

Yet I refuse to believe that could be possible.

"You did. Yes." Her hand skims back to my face. "But I know it wasn't the real you."

Fuck. I thought we were getting somewhere. "It is, though." I jerk free of her hand. "That is the real me, kitty. Can you deal with that?"

"If that's the real you," she challenges, pushing up to her elbow to level our faces, "then who's this right here?" Her finger jabs painfully into my chest. "Who's this guy right now? Because he isn't the one who cracked the shits at his hair. He's not the guy who pushed me away when he needed my support most. He's somebody entirely different, Rey." Her rage shows in the pinpointed black of her eyes. "So don't you give me some bullshit about how that angry motherfucker is you, because he's not." Tabby collapses onto her back with the final words, huffing out an exasperated breath as she stares at the ceiling.

I do the only logical thing.

I kiss her.

Her leg closest to me shifts as I roll on top, accommodating mine. I bear my weight on my elbows, careful not to crush her as I steal her air. I want to suck in every last bit of that pure optimism she breathes. I want to pull the purity from her soul and mash it with mine, bleed our colors together so that her light can balance my dark.

I fucking need this woman to stay more than I've ever needed anything in my life.

Her chest presses against mine as she battles to catch her breath, wide eyes fixed on mine as I hold myself over her.

There isn't a single fucking line I could deliver in this moment that would do her justice.

"I meant it," she whispers. "I won't be your fix. You've got to do this without relying on me."

"I know." I shuffle to bring my hands to her head so that I can stroke the strands from her face. "And I will."

Just not today.

FORTY

TABITHA

"The Reason" - Hoobastank

The rest of the band poured in sometime around three this morning. Judging by the ruckus they made as they found their way to bed, I'm guessing there were copious amounts of alcohol consumed in the hours between.

By that stage Rey had crashed, anyway, exhausted after a night on stage. It seems that once these guys stop, they literally come to a grinding halt.

Yeah, I was gutted that our intimate moment never really went much past first base. But the kissing... *damn*. I can't remember being that giddy over a kiss since I was twelve.

I bring my fingers to rub my lips as I lie beside him, waiting on the prince of darkness to wake. Looking back on it, I guess the fact we *did* hold off on taking our intimacy any further intensified the feelings associated. If this is his way of playing hard to get, then the guy has nailed the art of seduction.

I've never wanted somebody—literally craved

them—so damn much.

"Hey."

I turn my head toward the whisper and find Emery peeking around the door. I haven't had a chance to talk to the guy one-on-one yet, but from the things Rey's told me he's a pretty good sort, excessive drinking aside.

"Hi."

"You want coffee?" His gaze flicks to Rey, who lies spread-eagled on his stomach.

"Sounds like heaven." I slide my legs out from under the covers, checking over my shoulder that I haven't disturbed Rey. "I can make it, though."

"No." He lifts a hand, waving me back. "That grumpy fucker will wake up when he smells it, anyway. You stay there."

Seriously? Is this my life? I'm in bed with a guy women would give their left kidney to spend a night with, while another equally as sought-after offers to make me coffee.

Somebody must be feeling guilty. More than one somebody, it seems. *Odd.*

Emery slips from view, yet leaves the door ajar. I catch snippets of conversation as Toby rises and shuffles out to join him. The whole scenario is so homely, so normal. A bunch of roommates knocking around together, discussing mundane topics like how to get a stain out of a shirt. It's nothing like what I expected. Nothing like the stereotype that's given to guys like these thanks to the wild actions of a few.

To be honest, slipping out now would have been perfect to get some alone time with the other guys. I lay awake last night, resolute in the conclusion I came to after Rey's revelations: I need to know more. He tells me how *he* feels, but what about the people closest to him? The ones he should be able to lean on, not feel he has to hide from?

Is that their fault that he feels he has to bury the depth of what goes on here, or his?

"How long have you been awake?"

I look down to find Rey watching me with the one eye that's visible from where his face remains smashed into the pillow.

"A while." I scoot down and roll to face him, strangely satisfied since I don't have to wait any longer. "Rested?"

"Yeah. Much better." He rolls to his back, arms over his head as he stretches. "Fuck. Is that coffee?"

I chuckle as the clink of mugs echoes from the kitchen. "It is."

"Epic." His head rolls toward me, his smile lazy. "Morning."

"You know, Emery's a bit of a liar," I tease.

"Why?" His brow pinches, hands tucked beneath his head.

"Because he said you'd be a grumpy fucker when you woke up."

The genuine laugh that I'm gifted with is pure magic after last night. "I normally am. But I don't usually wake up beside you, so there's that."

"I'll take it as a compliment."

"You should." His smile fades, the look he gives me pure hunger. "Do we have to get out of bed today?"

I shrug. He did say they don't need to leave until

tonight. "Not for a while, I think."

"Perfect."

My skin heats when he runs a hand through my hair, brushing it off my face. This man's touch… it's not something to be taken lightly. When a person is as guarded as he is, when they struggle with so much on the inside, a show of affection as simple as the caress of his fingers around the shell of my ear—it's a gift.

"The door's open," I whisper.

"Your point is?" He pushes forward to close the space between us, teasing my lips with his own.

I soften against him, addicted already to the heady shiver his kiss incites. Only this time Rey doesn't stop there. He shuffles closer, tilting his head so that he can intensify the contact, his tongue teasing mine in a gentle caress. He takes his time, as though he's concerned that I'll spook if he rushes things. And I guess in a way I might. But this reverence, the look of sheer admiration as he pulls away to ease himself over me.

I feel loved.

I think he was right.

"I'll just, ah, close this and leave them on the table out here."

Both Rey and I turn our heads to find Emery juggling both mugs in one hand while he pulls the door shut with the other.

"Is he always so good to you?" I say with a slight laugh.

Rey's smile is lazy as he drops his head. "Only when he's been laid."

"Oh my God." I groan, totally not needing to know

that. "Way too much information."

"Hey. Just you be glad he didn't do it in front of you. Word of warning: Em has no sense of shame when it comes to... that." He cocks his head as he says it.

"Anyway."

"Anyway," he mimics with a smile.

"Where were we?" I set my hands against his ribs, acutely aware of how hard my heart beats as I run them toward his shoulders.

I'm not normally this bold. But then again, everything about this is new.

"I do believe you were convincing me why I should stay in bed this morning." My eyes slip closed as Rey runs his nose up mine, finishing with a gentle kiss to my forehead. "You can pick up where you left off anytime you like," he deadpans.

I dissolve into giggles, before the contrast of this moment steals my breath.

I'm so lost in his touch, so enveloped by the moment that I completely forgot where we were not even twelve hours ago.

"Don't slip away from me, kitty."

I snap out of my musing to find him searching my eyes with a frown.

"Where did you go?"

"Somewhere with you," I answer honestly. "Although I like this place better."

"Then stay here." He doesn't need to say any more; he gets it. I can see it in the worry that flashes in his eyes, and in the way he runs his bottom lip between his teeth.

He was there for a fleeting second, too.

"What happens after?" I whisper. "When the tour ends?"

Rey's jaw sets tight as he sighs. "Can we talk about that another time?"

"I guess."

His eyes close briefly, a frown marring his features. "It's not that I don't want to talk about it, babe, it's just...." He rocks his hips into me with an apologetic smile.

Oh. Shit. Of course.

"Can we be quiet for a bit? Just enjoy this?"

I push my fingers into his hair, tugging his face to mine as I murmur, "I think so."

If you'd asked me a month ago what I thought an encounter with a guy like this would have been like, I would have delivered some line about how rock stars all think they're God's gift to women, and that my money would have been on him being the hit it and quit it type of guy.

Consider me schooled.

Rey's modus operandi is a slow, deliberate exploration of my body as he kisses his way from my mouth—my lips left bruised—down my throat to my chest. His breath skims over my hyperaware skin, teasing me with the gentle gust that heightens my senses to the point of near pain.

I'm literally arching my back to get closer, desperate for him to rev this up. Yet he doesn't.

With a wicked smile he shifts lower, eliciting a whimper from my throat that takes me by surprise. *What is this man doing to me?*

"So impatient," he teases as his hands find the hem of my tank.

He shuffles his elbows where they're propped on the bed so that he can push the material higher. I lift up, more than eager to help him strip me down. At this point, I'm on the brink of shoving him off so I can take the reins.

I need more, and I need it now.

I bring my arms together, ready for him to guide the tank off over my head, yet he chooses not to. Instead, his rough hand, calloused from the guitar, brushes over my breast, the hem of my top wedged between his fingers. He watches me with a wolfish grin as he leaves the material bunched at my throat and runs his hand back down my body, lower, closer, skimming the line between foreplay and something more.

Something I need if I'm to survive.

"Please...." I close my eyes, ashamed at how desperate I am. Desperate enough to throw my dignity aside and beg, that's for sure.

"Please, what?" His words caress my stomach, the hot gusts of his breath doubling the heat I already possess.

"Whatever you want," I moan. "Just, please."

The satisfied rumble from his chest leaves me breathless, my bottom lip pinched between my teeth as I count the seconds until he does it. *He has to do it.* Oh fuck, he's doing it.

My pajama shorts are ripped down my legs with enough force to pull me with them, the material barely getting enough time to hit the floor before he thrusts his hands beneath my ass and lifts my hips. I'm sure the rest of the band hear my relief when Rey's mouth meets my pussy, the groan I let loose deafening in the otherwise quiet room.

I thought that tongue was a master at delivering a song, yet his talent as a singer couldn't hold a candle to this.

Holy shit. The bedding crumples in my fists, the whimpers that come from me muted by the fact I bite my bottom lip hard enough to leave imprints. My legs are jelly. His hands are literally all that hold me up as he tastes and teases.

Waiting was everything. We could have done this last night. Damn, if he had I could be as loud as I want. But the buildup to this, the tension, the need.

There's something to be said for taking things slow.

Although two weeks from strangers to this is hardly slow, by my measure.

"God, I can't...." I want to.

One word, "Come," mumbled against me before he takes me over the edge with an added finger.

It's all he has to say.

I'm fucking certain the guys out there heard me now.

Pleasure surges through me in a wave of blissful prickles. The sort of tingle you feel as your limbs come back from complete numbness.

Which is exactly what he's done: he's woken the parts of me that have been asleep for so long.

My breaths come fast and shallow as he sets me down, rearing back on his folded legs to run a palm over his mouth and chin. The smile that's revealed after he drops his hand?

God.
I think I just fell in love too.

FORTY-ONE

REY

"Stillborn" – Black Label Society

The next hotel we unload at is nowhere near as posh as the last. Tabby loves it. Says it makes her feel more at home. I told her she's what makes it feel like home. I then promptly vomited in my mouth a little at how much of a fucking pansy-ass sissy I've become because of her.

Who the fuck is this guy? It's a new type of low after the high. A strange one.

I still loathe everything about myself; can't stand seeing my image reflected back at me. But I'm calm.

I'm relaxed.

And that's totally all on her.

"Everyone paying attention while I go through this one last time?" Rick asks as he leans his hip against the back of a dining chair.

The band all nod where we're seated at a round glass table. Toby drinks his habitual bourbon-spiked after-noon coffee, while Kris listens to Rick with one ear, the set list playing in the other.

I nod, paying attention to Rick, but my focus is on

Tabby as she kicks back on the sofa.

"We've got the radio interview in an hour," Rick details, "and then you've got two small pieces with some local TV shows. Toby and Emery, you get one. Rey and Kris, you get the other. After that you're doing a run through with the sound guys, and then if it all goes to plan, you get a hour to unwind backstage before the show kicks off."

"Any other news for me?" My hands mask my question so that Tabby doesn't hear, fingers laced before my mouth as I lean my elbows on the table.

Rick's gaze shoots to the girl in question before he returns his attention to me with a shake of his head. "Not looking good. All recent events considered."

Damn it. I glance at Toby, catching his eye. He gives me a shrug, and then chugs the last of his coffee. He's the only one in the band that knows my plan, knows what I try to do for her.

I've set my pride aside and damn near begged Wallace, via Rick, to let Tabby play for us again. I even said I'd go to rehab without a fuss if he cut her in.

Asshole isn't having a bar of it. Which at least is predictable. It's more than I can say for the rest of the band.

The three of them have been strange today. Strangely kind. After the bust up preshow the other day, and then our falling out about the interviews after, I expected a little more tension between the four of us.

Instead, Emery makes Tabby and me coffee, Kris does my fucking washing with his, and Toby... well, he hasn't tried to kill me again. Also hasn't tried to talk to me one-on-one.

Kind of feels like the calm before the storm. They're a bunch of farmers fattening up the sacrificial cow before I'm sold off for the last time.

Makes me wonder if Rick knows something that I don't. I give the guy the once-over as he stands at the end of the table, absorbed in his fucking phone as usual. He seems normal, I guess. Not sweating bullets anyway, and if there was anything I should be worried about, he'd be the first giveaway.

"I'm out to get another one of these lifesavers," Toby announces as he lifts his empty coffee cup. "Anyone else want one?"

"I might come for a walk too, if that's okay?"

Five heads turn Tabby's way. She looks at each of us in turn, eyes wide as though to ask what the issue is.

I guess we're not used to company of the female kind on tour. At least, not the kind that doesn't fawn all over us and recite facts they've read from the shit published online as though each correct one scores them higher on the get-in-my-pants stakes.

"I'll come too." I push out from the table as Toby grimaces.

"Great. Right family outing, huh?"

He matches my cool stare as I make my way to Tabby. Fucker knows how to hold a grudge, that's for sure.

"If you've got other things you need to do, I don't mind going with him alone."

I take her face in my hands and lay one on her. It's becoming pretty damn apparent I can't get enough of kissing this girl. "I'll come too."

Emery clears his throat behind us; the look on Rick's face is fucking priceless. You'd think I just announced that I'm taking an oath of sobriety, with the way he seems shocked. As far as he knew, I asked Tabby here for her musical prowess only, but I guess the cat's out of the bag now.

"What?" I take a step toward him, eyes narrowed just to fuck with the guy.

"Nothing." He backs up, hands raised. "I'll wait for you here. We'll head out after you get back."

"Come on." Toby rushes for the door, shrugging his coat high around his vibrant hair. "We haven't got time to fuck around."

The walk to the coffee shop creates enough tension to rival Toby's snare. Tabby inserts herself between us as we head out the hotel entrance, seeming to feel the need to do so to defuse the situation.

"So." She looks between the two of us with a tight-lipped smile. "You guys nervous about the new album going live?"

Kitty, kitty, kitty.... Bless her heart, but small talk doesn't crack my stubborn-ass brother.

"A little," Toby answers. "You must know what it's like when you share a new piece; the worry that you won't measure up to what you've produced before."

Fuck me gently... she's done it. She split the stone wall that is Toby.

"Totally." Tabby smiles, her whole fucking face lighting up as she engages in conversation with my brother.

I watch the two of them interact as we make our way down the street to the nearest Starbucks. She has him wrapped around her little finger, pulling smiles and laughs from him without seeming to even try.

I hate it.

I thought that she only made *me* feel like that. I thought that charm of hers was for me alone. But the realization that she treats *everyone* the same way? It burns a little.

Fuck it. Okay. A lot.

Maybe I'm not as special to her as I thought?

"What are you having?" I rip her from the inane conversation they're in about childhood pets—how you go from music to that in the space of five minutes, I don't even know.

"One of those, I think." She points to a sign displaying a limited time frap deal. "But I can get it."

"Doesn't mean you have to." I step up to the counter to order, adding Toby's usual to the tail end.

Olive branch and all that shit. A coffee today, and maybe he'll have a beer with me tomorrow.

"Rey Thomas."

Fuck.

"And Toby. Holy shit." The short little guy to my right pushes up on his toes to call out across the entire fucking shop, "Margot. Check it out!"

He hitches a thumb at me and Toby, the look on his face telling me we're in for it. I love the fans, I really do. But fuck, man, can I get my coffee first?

"We're coming to the show tonight," he tells me as Tabby takes a step back to watch the shit go down.

"Cool, man. Glad to have you there." My smile is the same bullshit one I've used for years.

I've used it so often that people actually believe it to be genuine. I mean, when it's how I look all the time, why wouldn't it be? Right?

He hesitates as though waiting for one of us to announce he's won the backstage pass lottery. "Yeah. It's an anniversary treat for Margot. I can't believe we've crossed paths, man."

"Congratulations on the anniversary," Toby chips in, taking the heat off me long enough that I can pay for the coffees.

"Thanks." The guy's gaze flicks to Tabby, and I see it go down in the droop of his brow. He's lined up the equation, he's doing the math, and it's only a matter of time. "I saw you on YouTube."

Fuck.

She nods, her smile sheepish. The contrast is ridiculous: she's embarrassed by the attention, when I'm frustrated by it.

"Yeah. You played their song on your violin."

Her eyes flick to mine. She's clearly unsure what this guy's take on it is—whether he liked it or not. I give her a nod to let her know it's okay.

If he hadn't liked it, she'd more than likely be wearing his iced coffee by now. Fans—they're passionate.

"Hi." The lovely Margot reaches our group spectacle, giving a little wave.

I give her a silent nod, while Toby shakes her hand.

"Congrats." He glances between the two. "Wedding anniversary?"

Margot giggles. "No. Not yet." Her eyes soften on the short guy beside her. "We're celebrating three months together."

Three months to— What the fuck? Tabby swallows. Toby plasters on a forced smile. I fail.

Epically fail.

I manage to suppress my thoughts on the matter at first, my lips painful with how hard I mash my mouth shut. But when the guy exclaims how lucky he is, I lose it.

The entire fucking group stares at me as though I just killed a puppy when the snort erupts from me.

I just... three months. I've had hangovers that lasted longer than that.

"You okay?" Toby asks, aka "Get your shit together."

"Sorry. I just got reminded of something at the worst time." I try to bluff it off, but busty Margot isn't having it.

"Rude much?" All she needs is the finger snap to go with the wiggle, and I'd be down for the count. "Let's go, Shelly."

The guy's name is Shelly? I turn away to avoid making this worse. Kill me now.

"Have a good afternoon, guys. We'll see you there tonight," Toby calls in a lame-ass fucking attempt to salvage what's left of the situation after I've set fire to the crate of puppies. "Jesus, Rey." The heel of his hand collides with my shoulder. "You've got issues."

"Well there's a fucking newsflash." I snatch the takeaway cup from the counter and thrust his coffee at him. "Here. Enjoy."

Tabby retrieves her drink before I get a chance to,

patient and quiet as I grab my own. Fuck—I thought I had a hold on things. After yesterday morning with kitty... I was calm.

I am calm. Who the fuck am I kidding. That sated bliss I got from tasting her? It's gone. And as I look at the gorgeous creature who walks out of the shop with me, reenacting that moment is the only thing I can think of.

I want her. Now. Here. Wherever.

I just need that feeling to come back. I need that calm, that ease. I need what she can give me. All of it.

"What's going on?" Her eyes show clear concern as she peers up at me while we walk.

Toby lags somewhere behind. Fuck, he can stay there to drink his fucking coffee for all I care.

"Preshow nerves." *Fucking bullshit artist.* I shift my drink to the other hand, and then loop my arm around her shoulders. "You think we've got enough time to take the edge off for me before I head out?"

"Before *you* head out?" Her brow pinches. "Am I not coming with you?"

Fuck. So not going to get me laid. "I thought you might want to hang out where it's quiet and compose, or some shit."

"Or some shit," she mutters, sidestepping to slide out of my hold. "Sure. Why not?"

"Kitty...."

"No. It's fine." Her lips wrap around the straw of her frap, and fuck me if that doesn't have me thinking about blowjobs. She swallows and takes another stab. "It's not as though I believed you'd actually get me onstage again, anyway. I mean, how naïve would that be, right?" Her eyes are hard as she veers a little to stay out of arm's reach.

Fuck this shit. Fuck me and my goddamn mouth. Fuck having to do this, to function in society when all I want is a dark room and a pack of smokes.

Rapid cycling bipolar. I cracked a joke to the shrink when they diagnosed it, asking him if it meant I had to learn how to ride a bike. Dude didn't seem to see the funny side of things, explaining what the term meant to me anyway.

All it basically means is that unlike other forms of bipolar where the mania phase lasts weeks to months, and the resulting depression does the same, lucky me gets the entire cycle condensed down into a much shorter time frame.

The longest I've gone between peaks is four months. My average is exactly this: three to four weeks.

I'm pushing through the low like I'm in the midst of a fucking mud run, my limbs tired, my lungs burning as I put everything I have into reaching that finish line. Mania exists on my horizon, taunting me with its brilliance, with its warmth. All I have to do is survive the pot-shots my head takes at me while I wrestle those final yards and then all will be fine again, for a week at least.

I just need to push Tabby over that line first, otherwise Lord knows she'll get destroyed in my wake.

We met as I started the slide. She doesn't know me during full-blown mania, and I don't know if she'd want to.

I'm a right fucking asshole.

God complex times ten.

She punches the button on the walk signal, sipping her drink beside me while we stand in mutual silence. *What runs through her head?* Is it as messed up as mine? Or is she back thinking about childhood pets and other fun memories again?

It's fucked, really. I strived so hard to get where I am, worked my ass off to never want for a thing again, and all I did was realize that everything I did, it was all for nothing.

All the money and fame in the world can't buy me the one thing I want most: to know what it feels like to be "normal."

I reach between us and slide my hand along hers, entwining our fingers. Tabby glances down at the contact as the walk signal tells us to move, and offers a soft smile. It's the best I can do when words don't seem to suffice. Physical contact. An apology through touch.

The best and most reserved part of me: my intimacy.

It's all I can give her, and fuck, I hope it's enough.

FORTY-TWO

TABITHA

"Love the Way You Hate Me" – Like A Storm

"Can I ask a favor?" I press my hands tight in my lap as I lean toward Toby.

He sets his takeaway cup down and glances to where Rey and Kris smoke on the balcony before settling his gaze on me. "Sure."

"Do you think there'd be a way we could talk in private?"

His shoulders drop as he leans back into his seat and shifts focus to the cup. "Have you asked him?"

"Asked him what?" I say, well aware he talks about Rey.

"Whatever you want to know from me." He watches the vessel turn in his hand.

I knew this was a bad idea. After all, they're blood. Of course he'll stay loyal to Rey.

"Forget I said anything, okay?" I turn in my seat to stand, yet his hand over mine stills me.

Rey stares through the glass slider at us both and frowns.

Toby shifts, sitting tall so he can lean both elbows on the table. "Maybe I could get Rick to ask to see you so eagle-eyes over there isn't too suspicious."

I make a point of not looking toward Rey again, well aware the more I glance his way the guiltier I look. "If you're sure. If you'd rather not, I get that. I mean we hardly know each other."

He shrugs. "I don't know about you, but I can pick an asshole when I see one, and you, Tabby, aren't an asshole."

"Gosh. You're so sweet," I tease.

He chuckles. "Rey asked you here for a reason, and I know my brother well enough to trust he has the best intentions. So if I can possibly do something that helps to keep him happy as well, then I'll give it a try."

I fail at keeping my focus on the table and glance to Rey. He laughs at something Kris says, but the dull look in his eye immediately after concerns me. How much of this calm, this ease, is a put on?

He said it himself the other night: the thoughts are still there, he's just not focused on them.

"What happened that first time?" I lean my head on one hand, elbow propped on the table as I face Toby.

He sighs, thumb picking at the ridges of the card-board cup. "Have you looked us up online?"

"A little. Yeah. I read a few stories about the band."

He shakes his head. "Not us, as in Dark Tide, but us as in each of us. Our personal accounts."

"Oh." I wriggle my fingers so they thread through my hair. "Just Rey, which led me to Emery. But that's about it."

He glances my way, before returning his focus to the growing pile of cardboard dust beneath his cup. "Well, if you had you'd know that you can't find me." He presses his lips together. "I hate the internet. I tolerate it for what we have to use it for, business, but I avoid it otherwise."

"That shows some incredible self-control in this day and age," I muse.

"It's not hard," he says flatly. "Not after that first attempt you asked about."

I stay silent, allowing him the space to either continue or choose to end the conversation there without any pressure from me.

He closes his eyes and rubs a hand over his face before deciding to carry on. "He researched online how to gas yourself; carbon monoxide." Toby's gaze flicks to the balcony, most likely to check Rey still remains out of earshot. "Idiot went for a drive after school and set it all up." He shakes his head in disbelief, focus still on his brother. "I don't know why, but I just had this feeling, this gut instinct that told me something wasn't right. Rey didn't have a lot of friends in school, so it was sort of unusual for him to go anywhere for any length of time after."

"He said you found him."

Toby nods, turning his head toward the suite door when Rick rejoins the room.

"They ready?" Rick tips his head toward Rey and Kris.

Emery follows him in, pale as a ghost.

"You okay?" Toby pushes from his seat, our conversation seemingly forgotten for now.

Rick shakes his head at Emery, eyes hard. "If you can find out what the fuck he took, then good luck. He won't tell me."

"I'm fine." Em waves the two of them off, uncapping the bottle of water in his hand.

Must be bad.

My attention is drawn to Toby when he leans back over the table to whisper, "Get my number from Kendall and send yours to me. Might be easier to have this convo that way."

As though to cement his point, the slider opens and Rey calls across the room. "What are you lot talking about over there in your knitting circle?"

"Our walking chem lab," Toby quips, gesturing to Emery.

Their bassist flips the bird in return.

"Fuck, man. You look like shit." Rey rests his hands around my neck when he stops behind me. It's an odd display of dominance, yet non-threatening. Almost arousing. *I need help.* "You okay, Em?"

"Fine." Emery's shoulders drop as he accepts a packet of the mini-bar crackers from Kris. "Thanks, mom."

"Somebody has to look after you," Kris mumbles before walking out the door. "I guarantee you haven't eaten anything else."

Emery follows with a shrug, tearing the packet open as he goes.

"Come on you two." Rick jerks his head toward the door. "We need to get going."

Toby lifts his jacket from the back of a chair on his way out, silently exiting behind Rick as Rey steps to my side and tucks his fingers under my chin to coax me to face him.

I lose myself in his concentrated gaze, recognizing the doubt that clouds those grays. "Go," I urge softly. "You don't want them pissed at you for making them wait again."

"You can come too, if you want." His thumb strokes beneath my bottom lip. "I didn't mean to cut you out like that."

"It's fine." I take his offered hand and let him guide me from my seat. "Like you said, I should use the time to compose. I'll see you before the show, okay?"

He takes my face in his hands, resting his forehead to mine. "Wish I could stay here instead."

"I wish you could too." So many things I want to talk to him about, especially after his breakdown the other night. "But your fame awaits, mister rock star."

"Don't." He shakes his head gently against mine. "Don't call me that."

"Isn't that what you are?" I tease.

He pulls back, eyes hard on mine. "Not to you."

I melt into his kiss, yet push gently against his chest to remind him he has people waiting.

He steps back with a laugh. "Fine. I'm going."

"Not that I'm trying to get rid of you … but."

He grins, backing toward the sofa where he then lifts his jacket. "I'm glad you came, kitty."

"I am too." Although I still wonder if it was the wise thing to do. "I'll be here," I reassure him, sensing he needs that promise.

He nods, and then turns for the door.

I watch him leave, a weight lifting from my shoulders only to settle in my chest as he shuts the door behind him.

What the hell am I doing here? His promise of getting me onstage again has all but vanished, the theory that we'd work on music together non-existent. And yet I stay.

Why? What have I done to actually help him?

I get comfy on the sofa with the room service menu and dial Kendall on speaker.

"Hey, babe."

"Heya."

She sighs at my flat response. "How are things on the road, then?"

Lonely. "Odd."

"Odd? How?"

Because I never know what Rey I'm going to get, or what the hell I'm doing. "I've spent most of my time so far hanging out at the hotel."

Kendall sighs. "I know I was a right bitch when you left but...." She huffs. "I don't know. Something didn't sit right about him."

"I don't think anything sits right with him."

Those moments the morning after his meltdown in the last hotel room—magic. But that guy? He's the exception rather than the norm, it seems.

"Do you think it helps, though? Having you there?"

"Maybe."

He was a right jackass at the Starbucks, mocking those fans who had the guts to come up and meet him. Not to mention the cocky attitude I got on the walk back.

But then give him an hour to unwind and he's all cuddles and warmth again.

I can't tell anymore what's real, and what's not.

I just want the genuine guy to come back again, even if his honesty does scare the shit out of me.

"Babe," Kendall says with a sigh. "If this trip doesn't help him, then you've got to ask yourself why you're doing it. What about your career, huh? You've stalled it, all to tag along with his."

"I know." She doesn't tell me anything I haven't already thought over a thousand times.

"Has he done what he said he would?" she presses. "Will you get stage time again?"

"I want to say yes ..."

"But nobody's talking about it, so it's probably not happening, right?" She sighs. "Why are you doing this, babe?"

"I don't know," I whine. "I can't explain why, but I feel as though this is what I'm supposed to be doing."

Silence lingers between us. I know she's still there by the background noise, yet she seems just as stuck as I do.

"I need a favor," I say carefully. "Can you please message me Toby's number?"

"Why?" I pick up the change in sound as she switches me to speaker.

"I asked him if I could talk about Rey, and since they're always around each other, he said that might be the easiest way to do it."

"Why didn't he just give you the number himself?"

"Because we were being watched—case and point."

"Oh." My phone chimes with a message. "Sent."

"Thanks, hon."

"Hopefully he can help you decide what to do." She pauses. "You know how I feel about this whole arrangement."

"You want me to come home," I state.

"And not just because I'm going crazy on my own." Kendall laughs, the sound heartwarming. "I seriously contemplated getting a goldfish so I'd have something to talk to."

"You need to catch up with your college buddies, hon. When was the last time you went to dinner with them?"

"Pfft. When I could afford to, so that would be, like, three years ago." She hesitates. "We keep in touch on Facebook, so it's not as though I'm a complete hermit."

"Except that you are."

"Hey," she protests. "You aren't much better... usually."

"Truth."

Weekend drinks at happy hour once a month was about as adventurous as she and I would get. Even more reason why I'd hoped to tag along on some of the things the band get up to outside the shows.

"How *is* your new material coming along?"

"Slow." I push the menu around the coffee table before me. "I thought I'd get inspired being in new places, but instead I just feel... I don't know, unsettled?"

"You're distracted."

Am I what. "I told Rey he needed to have a sit down with the guys and talk through what's going on."

"What did he do?"

"Sat on the balcony and smoked until it was time for

them to go."

She snorts. "Open to change, then."

"Exactly." I push the menu aside and kick back. "It's like he knows what his issues are, yet he doesn't think he needs to do anything about it. Well, no, he wants to, he maybe can't see how? I don't know. It's confusing anyway."

"And what do the others do?" A rustle cuts through the line as she juggles the phone.

"Act as though nothing will ever change, too. Toby's real pissed at him. Have you talked to him lately?"

Her pregnant pause says it all. "He went quiet a couple of days ago. I figured I was a fun one-off thing, you know?"

"Men."

"Right?"

My fingers toy with the loose thread on the hem of my T-shirt. "What would you do, if you were me, babe?"

"It's hard to say, Tab. What does your gut tell you?"

"Stick it out." An opinion that's no doubt clouded by the epic orgasm he gave me at the last hotel.

"You don't have to tell me details," Kendall levels, "but what exactly are you two? I mean he kissed you, like, superhot before you two left. Are you...?"

"Fucking?"

She clears her throat. "I was trying to be more subtle."

"No. Not exactly."

"But you're, like, involved somehow?"

I sigh, sliding down the seat to hide my face behind my hands. "I don't know. That's just it. He keeps telling me he wants me around, but then he pushes and pulls and I really don't know where I stand with him."

"So ask him."

"I did," I cry. "I asked him what happens after the tour."

"And?"

"And he showed me what else he can do with his mouth."

"Ooh."

"Yeah." I moan, arms flailing to my sides. "How the hell can something get so complicated in the space of a few weeks?"

"Intense emotions, babe. He's mega into you."

"See, I don't know if he's into me, or—" I cringe at what I'm about to say. "—or if his bipolar is into me."

She sucks a breath with a hiss. "Damn. That's rough, especially from you."

"See my problem now? That's mostly why I want to talk to Toby and get some insight on him; I don't know Rey well enough to be able to know."

She clicks her tongue in a way that has me imagining her on our sofa, tapping her lips like she does when she thinks. "What's your biggest worry out of it all?"

"That I get attached right before he ditches me."

"There's something more, though."

She's right—there is. I get the shivers every time I think it. "What if I admit defeat and walk away, and that's his final straw?"

"You're only protecting yourself if you choose to do that, babe, and there's no dishonor in that."

"There is if it means I tip him over the edge. He's

attached. I can see that, but I think he needs to clear up in what way for himself before he can give me an honest answer."

"Give it until the tour ends," she says resolutely. "It's an easy out then if things don't clear up."

"I don't want an out, though. I like him, a lot. I just want him to be clear on what he wants from me." I sigh and reveal my biggest insecurity. "I don't want to end up being a tour bunny that keeps his libido in check."

"So tell him that," she says softly. "Lay it out, black and white. Let him know you're a person too, with your own goals that you could be chasing."

"I guess."

"Look at it this way." She huffs. "If he was Joe Blow, just some shmuck you met on the street who wasn't this uber-talented singer, what would be different?"

"I see your point." I'd be tougher on him. I probably would have run a mile when he begged me to help him.

I wouldn't have rushed headfirst into something so spontaneous.

It's Rey's passion in his music that hooked me. The same intensity I got when he hit his low our first night back on the tour. The cliché always goes that the superstar chases the girl because she's his muse. But what if he's *my* muse? I look at him and I want to explore him: his feelings, his reactions, and his experiences. I want to draw from all those things that make Rey *him* and use the knowledge as fuel for my creativity.

He's an artwork, to me: complex and yet to be fully appreciated for all its intricacies. A ballad waiting to be written.

"Thanks, babe." I scoot up the seat, newly awakened. "This really helped."

"Hey. It's what I'm here for. I just... I don't want you to come home flat and run-down after he's taken everything from you."

"I know. I don't either."

I just hope by the time I do go home that at least one of us gets something out of this arrangement.

Because right now, I struggle to see how that could be me.

FORTY-THREE

REY

"Life is Beautiful" – Sixx:A.M.

The interview preshow was hilarious. The guy Kris and I got knew his stuff, but he didn't give us the standard questions. He bantered with the two of us, cracking jokes and talking shit.

It put me in a good mood for the start of the show, and by the end of the fourth song when I'm usually fantasizing about a stiff drink and a bed to hang out in for a week, I was charging.

Fuck—I even remembered to say happy anniversary to Margot and Shelly. *Shelly—ha.* The crowd seemed to think I was grinning because I was happy for the couple, so I might have got away with that one. *This time.*

But there was only one thing that kept the buzz post show, when I usually crash, and that was Tabby's promise as I walked out the door.

"I'll be here."

It's as though she knew that's what made me stall. Is my fear of being abandoned that obvious?

"You ready to get out of here?" Kris holds his pack out

for me to steal a smoke.

"Yeah." I pull a stick and roll it between my forefinger and thumb. "The four of us came together good tonight, huh?"

He nods, lips turned down as though he hadn't really thought on it. "We've got issues with Toby, though." Kris pockets the pack, and then picks up his backpack with fuck knows whatever in it.

He takes the damn thing to every show, and after five years I still don't know what he's packing.

"What kind of issues?"

"He's been talking with Wallace about your rehab once this is all over."

Fuck. "Yeah?" *Thanks, brother.*

He nods, cigarette pinched between his lips as he ducks to the lighter.

I take a look around at the staggered city skyline beyond the stadium fence. When it comes down to it, we're all rats stuck in a race, all searching for that next crumb. Only I kind of feel like the lab techs have the walls all set out for me now; there's no escape from this.

I'm destined to follow the same old blueprint set out by generations of musos before me. Things carry on the way they are, and fuck, I might just tick all the boxes if I check out early too.

"You think he'd really shaft me from the lineup if I refused to go?" I accept the light Kris offers, his hand shielding the flame.

"Without a doubt."

"How can he though?" I bluff humor at the idea, but reality is the thought of having this all taken away before

I'm ready for it to be leaves me terrified. "There *is* no Dark Tide without me." There's no me without Dark Tide either.

There's also no comeback for most musicians after they've been dropped from the band that made them.

"Why not?" He doesn't ask the question to be an ass. "Van Halen replaced David Lee Roth. AC/DC held strong without Bon Scott."

"I get the point," I drone. I'm expendable. Fucking wonderful.

"Look." Kris jerks his head to indicate we should start walking. "I'm not trying to make you feel shit, man. I'm just pointing out that all the crap we've dealt with over the years, it never fully goes away. And I'm not only talking about you: all of us. We've all done shit to add stress to the brand. But thing is, we can say that we've wiped it all away and moved on, but after each issue there's a speck of shit that remains. Residue." He taps his smoke as we walk to shake off the ash. "After a while all that residue, all those specks, they make a mess of the mirror and we can't even see who the fuck we are anymore."

Fuck me. Some days I forget how deep these guys are. "I never really noticed that."

"But you see it, right?"

I nod, and then take a long drag of my smoke. I keep knocking us back. I know Kris said he was talking about the crap all of us have dealt over the years, but stick that shit on a pie chart, and which one of us assholes would have the largest slice? Me.

"How the fuck do we fix this?"

He shrugs. "Fucked if I know."

I slide the gate in the security fence open and let him through first, shutting it behind us. Kris gives one of the site staff a wave as we head for the road. The chauffeured vehicle Wallace hires while we're on tour is occupied taking Toby and Emery to some bar they got recommended—not that the asshole would let me use it anyway—leaving Kris and me to cab it back to the hotel.

I refused the chance to go out and live it up, eager to get back to kitty. But I've got no idea why Kris turned the offer down.

Fuck—I heard there were strippers involved. God knows the guy could use some of that kind of release.

"How come you aren't going out with the other idiots?" I ask as we near where the cab will pick us up.

He sniffs, working his jaw side to side. "Didn't feel like it."

"Everything good with you?" I get pretty damn wrapped up in myself a lot of the time, so who knows what I've missed.

Kris nods as he squints at the headlights that approach. "Not in the mood for people, man." He drops his smoke and stubs it out as the cab pulls up. "Nothing to be worried about, though. Not like your shit."

I frown as he opens the door and slides in, leaving me to follow. "Fuck my issues, dude. Don't keep quiet because of me."

Kris tells the driver where to go, and then sinks into the plush leather seat before he speaks again. "I can deal with my own shit, Rey. If I needed help, I'd let you know."

"Yeah, well make sure you do." Because I'm pretty sure his skill *isn't* expendable.

He's an uncut diamond when it comes to guitar players, and when he finds the right mentor to help smooth off those edges and hone his worth, fuck, he'll be a legend.

"An early night, a quiet room, and no fucking lights pointed at me is all I want," Kris murmurs, closing his eyes and punching both hands into the pocket of his hoodie.

"Yeah, I hear you." Half the time that's all I need to recharge too: the serenity of the dark.

Except tonight I crave the touch of a woman I barely hold on to. She's a precious keepsake, teetering on the tips of my fingers while I hold my breath, waiting to see if she'll fall.

Unlike me, I don't think she'll bounce if she hits the ground.

Kris pops his earbuds in while we travel, leaving me to stew in my thoughts alone. Every grab of downtime I've had this afternoon I've mulled over what to say to Tabby to explain the bullshit she's in for. I want to give the woman fair warning, but I don't want to scare her away. Yet I've more respect for her than to flat-out lie and leave her to be blindsided with my douchebag behavior when the mania hits.

"How was the show tonight, brother?"

I glance at our driver—an older black guy with more than a few grays in his hair. "Yeah. It was good, man. Thanks for asking." His ID says his name is Robert. "You listen to us?" Most of our fans are younger, but there are still a few that take you by surprise.

"No," he says with a hint of humor. "My daughter. She found you guys last year. It really turned her around." His gaze flicks to mine in the rearview every so often.

"How so?" I swivel to face him, settling in to the conversation.

Kris carries on with his music, eyes closed and oblivious.

"We had some issues at school," Robert says. "Bullies, that kind of thing that you get with teenagers."

"Uh-huh."

"Her mom and I were at a loss for what to do, man." He shakes his head. "But we trusted that she'd come to us if she wanted us; we gave her the space she needed. She spent a lot of time in her room with music, and you were one of the bands she'd have on repeat." He smiles in the mirror at me. "I swear by the time she came around I knew half the words to your songs, too."

I chuckle with him, yet my chest is heavy with what he's obviously been through. "Well I'm glad she's doing better."

"Yeah, me too." He nods, returning the drive to silence.

I spend the next five minutes or so catching glimpses of the guy, still a little disbelieving that we can have an impact in people's lives like that. I guess Robert is the universe's way of giving me a little nudge to say "Hey, you aren't as much of a fuck up as you think you are." He's proof I have to be doing *something* right.

Kris nods gently to his music as I reach over and slide his backpack from the floor. He carries on, unaware that

I have his prized possession in hand; hopefully there's some shit in here that I can leave with Robert for his daughter.

My hand touches card, and hopeful I've found one of our promo shots, I pull it out. Yet what greets me as I bring it into the light leaves me wondering who the fuck this guy next to me is. A picture of a girl. Our age, I'm guessing. I should shove it back in his bag, pretend I didn't see anything, yet curiosity gets the better of me and I glance over to make sure his eyes are still shut before I turn the picture over.

You're already a star to me. XX

Holy fuck—this is from before we made it. How long has he been toting this thing around?

"What the fuck are you doing?"

Shit, shit, shit. I jam the picture back in his bag, and ferret around for what I'm after. "Have you got any swag shit in here, man?"

Kris rips the canvas bag from my hands, buckling up the main compartment before tearing into a side pocket. He throws one of the picture postcards we had made at me, quickly followed by a pen.

"Just ask next time."

"Yeah, okay. Sorry." I scrawl a quick message on the blank side of the card. "Yo, Robert. What's your daughter's name?"

"Becky."

I add her name to the top, and then shove it at Kris. "Sign this."

He reads what I wrote, and nods as he add his scrawl. "Cool."

I watch him, gaze flicking to the damn bag of secrets at his feet. "Who is she?"

"None of your fucking business." The card gets thrust my way while he stashes the pen.

"You never talk about anyone from home."

"For a good fucking reason." He closes his eyes again as he pops the buds back in, shrinking down into his hoodie.

Fucking dark horse. I lean forward and tap Robert on the shoulder before I slide the postcard on the front seat beside him. "For Becky."

He glances down at it as we ease up outside the hotel, and then twists to look at me once stopped. "Hey, that's...." He sighs. "Ride is on me tonight."

"No, man. We'll pay." I nudge Kris to let him know we're here.

"No. No." Robert waves a hand. "You've just made this old man's night. I can't wait to tell her who I had as a fare when I see her tomorrow. You two go on and enjoy yourselves."

"Thanks, man." I lock hands with the guy and give it a squeeze.

Kris pats him on the shoulder as I slide out. "Have a good night."

Fuck yeah. As I look up at the glass doors into the lobby, I know that's what I'm about to get—a good night. Fucking lift can't carry me up there fast enough.

Look out, kitty, because here comes trouble.

FORTY-FOUR

TABITHA

"(I Just) Died In Your Arms" – Cutting Crew

I don't hear a damn thing before Rey comes through the door. No forewarning that he's back, no sound of guys talking in the hall before he slides the keycard in the lock... nothing.

"Catch you in the morning, Kris."

No wonder. I've barely heard a complete sentence out of the guy in the days I've been travelling with the band.

"Hey."

Rey's head snaps around as he guides the door shut. "You're awake."

"It's still before midnight; I figured I'd wait up a bit longer."

He tosses his wallet and phone on the side table as he walks in. His hair has lost the edge he gave it before they left, the casualty of too much time sweating it out under the stage lights, I imagine. The lines around his eyes show how tired he is. Yet that smile....

"Where's Toby?" We're sharing with him; Kris and Emery shacked up in the other two-bedroom suite.

"Out for the night." Rey slides onto his knees at my feet. "Just you and me, kitty." His arms push around my waist, his hands connecting behind my back as he lays his head in my lap.

I run my fingers through his hair, promptly wiping the waxy residue off on the back of his T-shirt. *Maybe not the best idea.* He chuckles when I change my tack to running my fingertips from his brow, down his temple, to his jaw.

"How was it?" I ask.

"Fucking awesome."

"How are you?"

He hesitates, the silence unnerving me. I prepare for the worst. "Okay."

"Are you sure?"

Rey rises; hands braced either side of my hips as he holds himself face-to-face with me. "I've been honest this far. I think you can rely on me to tell you the truth."

He has a point. Still.... "Okay."

"What have you been up to?" He looks at the seat around me, hands still tucked at my sides.

I rest my palms on his arms and look to where he does, at the pile of pages torn from my notebook. "I forced it." After I spent the hour they had pre-show messaging back and forth with Toby....

"You don't like it?" Rey leans over to check out the scrawled music.

"It could be better." As nice as the small talk is.... "I, um. I talked to your brother."

He drags his gaze away from the compositions and to mine, eyes narrowed. "When?"

"During your dinner break before the show."

"So that's who he was on the fucking phone with." His nose twitches, his lips tight. "Why?"

"To understand."

His arms withdraw as he rocks back to sit on his heels. "Understand what? Why do you have to ask him and not me?"

I've caught the tripwire. I'm stuck between going back and pushing forward with this, knowing both options are equally as doomed. "I wanted to hear a different viewpoint."

"On me?" His eyebrow cocks. "You think I'm a liar?"

"No." I scoot forward. "Not at all."

He retreats, swallowing. "What did you ask him?"

"About the band, how you started out, the challenges you had. You."

He stares me down, nostrils wide as he appears to breathe through his anger.

"Rey."

He looks away and shakes his head, the disgust written in the downturn of his lips. "I trusted you."

"You still can."

His gaze snaps back to mine with such intensity I physically reel. "What now, kitty? Going to write an opinion piece on me to sell for your next rent payment?"

"That's not fair—"

"What's not fair," he rages as he stands, "is being treated like some goddamn case study. If you had questions, you should have asked me."

"And would you have known the answer?" I holler, standing also. "Because it seems to me that so far you don't have a fucking clue what it is you want: from me, from your bandmates, from the tour, from anything."

"I want to be happy!" His face contorts with either anger or pain. At this stage I really can't tell anymore. "I just want to wake up one day and know what it feels like to not have to give myself a pep talk to get out of bed. I want to know what it's like," he says, hands rubbing his neck as he walks away, "to look in the mirror and feel nothing. Not hate, not guilt, not regret. Nothing."

"What do I do, then?" I drop onto the sofa again, whispering the question. "Because from what I've seen, Rey, this is way beyond me."

"Ugh!" His hands tear through his hair as he marches to the darkened windows. "Why? Is it beyond you to love? Because that's all I need." His voice falls soft. "To be loved, no strings attached."

But it's not.

Talking with Toby opened my eyes to how imbedded he is in his ways. He's had nothing *but* love for years. He's had all the love and care in the world from his support network of family, friends, and colleagues. But he refuses to see it.

Interventions. Counseling. Medication. Retreats.

You name it, he's had it. I honestly believed when Rey opened his heart to me that he'd been let down and neglected by the people who should care most. But the truth was, I only got half the story. I only got the parts his jaded mind chose to remember.

He mentioned that somebody's always there to catch him. But what he doesn't see is that once they have, he has to *hold on.*

Rey walks away.

Nobody else does.

He leaves. Checks out and shuts down until the cycle starts again.

"You're the only one who can stop this from happening over and over," I whisper as he stares stoically at the night sky. "I do love you, Rey. There's so much *to* love about you. But what good is that if it means nothing?"

"What are you saying?" He turns, eyes critical. "It means everything to me."

I sigh. Talking with him about this is the equivalent of smashing my head against a brick wall.

"Look at it this way." I rise and move toward him, yet keep a safe distance. "You're an empty vessel, wanting to be filled, right? You want the love you don't have in yourself."

He stares at me, not disagreeing, but also not accepting what I say.

It's the best I'll get.

"Problem is," I continue, "you get that love. Fuck, every day you get that love. But you sit there with your goddamn lid on tight, refusing to let it in. There's only so many times people can pour love over you, Rey, before they get frustrated with it flowing back to their feet, unwanted."

His lips twist, eyes dark and his frown deep as he studies me. "Do you regret saying yes to this? Do you regret coming?"

"Why do you ask that? Is that how I appear?"

"You're looking for an out," he says, gaze searching mine.

"I'm looking for a way in," I say gently.

He allows me to step closer, rigid as I slide my hands on his hips and stroke my thumbs over his T-shirt.

"I want to help, but I'm struggling to figure out how. *That's* why I talked with Toby."

"What else did the asshole say?"

"*Your brother,*" I scold softly, "mentioned that perhaps you use me as a crutch. That if you can kid yourself that I help, then you can justify why you refuse every other treatment option you've been given."

"I'm not kidding myself." He frowns. "You do help."

"How, though? Because if I'm being totally honest with you, I'm no cure, I'm a Band-Aid." I run my hands over his chest. "Loving me gives you something good to distract you from the bad. Am I right?"

He swallows, a sigh then rushing from his nose. "Maybe. But I think there's more to it than that."

"Why?"

He relaxes a little, one arm sliding around my shoulders to pull me close. "Without getting mad at me," he warns, "hear me out."

"You're setting yourself up for trouble," I tease.

He grins briefly. "If I wanted to be adored, not loved," he stresses, "then I could have found that anywhere, with anyone. Fuck, I could put a post up on social media right now and have twenty offers in an hour."

"Awesome," I deadpan.

He gives me a squeeze, pushing the hair from my face. "But I don't, because they aren't you." His eyes hold the truth as he runs his fingers along my jaw. "*Your* love is what I need."

I rest my head against his chest and hold on tight, hiding my face in case he can see the doubt written in my eyes.

Just like I could see the doubt in his.

He gives me a line he knows I'll love like the natural showman he is, but even he doesn't know that for sure. I make him feel good, yes, but I. Don't. Help.

And that's the problem.

Me being here? It hasn't been a catalyst for change. If anything it's been an excuse for him to justify what he does. I can see him now, standing before the guys as he argues with them "If she can accept me how I am, why can't you?"

I won't be his excuse.

"I have something I need to tell you too," he murmurs.

I lean back, hands shifting to his waist as he jerks his chin toward the sofa indicating we should sit. "What?"

"I spoke with Wallace today; about you playing."

I sigh and step away, turning toward the seat. "Look, you don't have to explain. I figured it out for myself."

He rubs a hand on the back of his neck as he follows me over. "I thought you might have."

"I'm not mad at you," I reassure as I drop onto the cushion. "It's not your fault; you tried."

"Yeah, but I kind of screwed things up, too." He stands before me, nervous as all hell. He can't even keep his eyes focused on me, his gaze darting all over the room.

"I hate today," I mutter as I sink further into the sofa.

"You know he's got my spending on a tight leash,

right?"

I nod, corners of my mouth turned down while I hear him out.

"So..." He looks to the balcony, hand brushing his pocket. "Can we do this out there?"

"Sure." I slide off the seat and make a quick detour by the bedroom to get my sweater.

By the time I return, all that's visible of Rey is the flash of his lighter and resulting glow of his cigarette as he stares out over the city.

I step out onto the balcony with him, a little at a loss with what to do with myself when he leans both elbows on the railing and looks over the edge at the road below.

A flash of panic surges through me leaving my stomach churning as it sinks to my toes. Would he think of doing that again if he felt low enough? With me here?

Pays not to think about what hasn't happened, Tabby.

I rest my hip against the glass barrier as he turns his head to look at me. Whatever he's about to say, it's not good. I can see that much in the way his fingers repeatedly flick ash that isn't there off the smoke.

"He's given you until the end of this week. Seven days."

"Until what."

Rey sighs, free hand scrubbing his face. "Until you either have to pay your own way or go home."

Oh. I hug myself, opting to peer over the rail, too, rather than meet the regret written across his face.

"I'll pay, kitty. You're not going anywhere, I just thought you should know in case you hear anyone say anything about it."

"You don't have to pay for me, Rey."

"I want to."

The reality of the fucking situation hits me right there on the twelfth floor balcony of a swanky hotel at 1:00 A.M. "I don't want you to." I shift my gaze to Rey, my hands shaking against my sides. "If you pay for me to be here, for no other reason than to keep you company between shows, then you know what that makes me feel like?"

He sucks the last of his cigarette and then tosses it over the side as he shakes his head.

"A high-priced hooker," I level. "This isn't fucking *Pretty Woman*, Rey, and I'm not goddamn Julia Roberts. Unlike her character, I actually like my career, and I'm not looking to escape from it."

He laughs bitterly, standing tall. "You think that's what this is?"

"I don't know what it is." I look to the building opposite us, not the slightest bit interested in the glow of the fucking light behind the resident's blinds, but it's better than looking at the utter repulsion on his fucking gorgeous face.

Why? Why when he does nothing but pull me into his spin, do I still want him so badly?

Because there's more to him than this. Yeah, there is, and he's still yet to give me one hundred percent, unadulterated Rey.

That man standing there, hurling insults at me as he snatches his smokes off the glass table? That's Rey the fucking prima donna rock star.

Not the man who begged me to come on tour with

him.

Not the man who listened to me spill my guts on an airport floor and reassured me that I'm somebody worth more than what I currently have in life.

And he's definitely not the man who let down every fucking wall he had to show me how bad things are when he admitted he wasn't afraid to die.

I leave my back to him and use the reflection in the glass barrier to watch as he strides around the suite, seemingly done with trying to cut me down. His long legs take him to what is essentially our room in a few quick strides, and he disappears from view. Is it always going to be like this? I feel as though I negotiate with a tantrum-throwing toddler half the time. The clang of his belt as it hits furniture tells me how pissed he is, the rumble of him muttering to himself following soon after.

I stand leaning on that goddamn rail, unable and—more so—unwilling to go after him.

He might not like what I had to say, but it's the truth. What have I got from being here? If my presence had actually done something to help Rey, then yeah, I might have let the disruption to my own career—however small it is compared to his—go without complaint.

But I can't give up on everything I've worked for just because somebody bigger and more recognized than me wants to use me as an ego-booster. Maybe it's nothing unusual for him, having people knock on your door wanting to offer their services, but I gave up submitting to agents when the "stick it on the fridge" joke became too much of a hassle. Kendall and I had so many of the damn things tacked to our small Kelvinator that at least one of them would flutter to the floor every time we opened the fridge.

So I tore them off and stashed them away in the dark recesses of my closet. Out of sight, out of mind. I also stopped searching for representation purely to salvage what was left of my self-confidence.

I could only get chipped away at for so long before I felt as though I was ready to fall.

"Screw this." I march inside and snatch up my key card from the TV cabinet before heading out the door without saying a thing to Rey.

If he can crack the shits every time things don't go how he envisioned them, then so will I.

My knuckles dance on the dark wood, my heart tight in my chest as I wait to see if he's still decent. Sure enough, the door creeps open and I'm greeted with a soft smile before Kris steps back to let me in.

"I'm sorry to crash your evening."

He simply holds out an arm to guide me through to the living area.

I drop onto the sofa, yet stay perched on the edge until I'm sure he's okay with me being here for this. "I'm at a crossroads, and I just need somebody to tell me if I'm doing the right thing."

"I wondered how long it would be." He drops into the single armchair, seeming to melt into his enormous hoodie.

The guy's quite handsome, really. High cheekbones and friendly eyes. Yet he hides behind his hair, his gaze darkened with the smudges of eyeliner left from the show.

"What's your take on this? On having me here for Rey? Is there any point to it?"

His hands fidget inside the front pocket. "He seems to think there is."

"I know what Rey thinks." This was a mistake. How do I know that everything I say here won't be repeated back the next time they all get together? "Forget it." I stand, meaning to make for the door, but Kris stops me dead.

"You're not the first."

I've never wanted to undo the past weeks of my life so bad. *Take me home.* "Pardon?" Jesus—my heart.

"He's brought a girl along on tour before, thinking it would keep him level."

Why the hell didn't I find any sign of that when I cyber-stalked the guy? "I'm a damn fool, aren't I?"

Kris shakes his head slowly. "No. He is." He indicates I should sit again with a single jerk of his head.

I don't think my legs could hold me up much longer if I tried. "When?"

"Four years back, when we were small fries."

"Who?"

"Old school buddy. It didn't work out."

"Clearly." I swear I'm going to be sick.

Kris shifts to the front of his seat, elbows braced on his knees as he clutches his hands before him. "We all thought he was an idiot when he did it last time, Tabitha. Each one of us told him to send the girl home. All she did was make him worse. But this time...." He reaches out and touches my knee before retracting his hand. "We all thought he'd finally got it right this time around."

I won't cry. I won't be weak, especially around somebody I barely know. "I still feel like a fool for believing him."

"Why? I'm sure whatever he's said to you, it's the truth."

"He told me he loves me."

Kris nods, corners of his mouth turned down. "Maybe."

"He said he needs me."

"I think he does."

"But?" I look to him, hoping for just one little olive branch. One fucking break.

"But he needs to respect what he has. He's so damn absorbed in himself that he can't piece together how you fit into it all."

He can see it too. "What do you think I should do?"

He leans back in the chair, hands back in his hoodie pocket. "What does your gut tell you to do?"

I shrug. Fuck—I'm so confused. "He said Wallace told him I either need to pay my way or go home."

"Sounds about right." He shrugs.

"It's fair, I know."

"But?"

"Rey said he'd pay to keep me here."

"And you declined." His eyes narrow as though trying to work me out.

"I told him I'm not Julia Roberts in *Pretty Woman.*" I smirk a little at how funny it sounds repeated.

He chuckles. "Bet he loved that."

"He was offended I saw it that way. Called me all manner of things under the sun and then stormed into his room, throwing his belt around and that."

He sighs. "You want me to talk to him?"

"No. I just...." I look toward Kris and sigh. "Why am I here?"

"Only you know that for sure." He flattens his lips. "Rey knows why *he* thinks you're here, but what are *you* doing this for?"

I narrow my eyes on him. "You think this is a waste of my time?"

Kris shakes his head. "No. At least, not if your goal is to make Rey happy. But is that all you want from knowing him?"

I frown.

"I'm saying"—he leans forward—"don't you think that a healthy relationship is one where the feelings are mutual?"

I'm lost. "If you're implying I don't care about him—"

"I'm implying he doesn't give a fuck about killing your career, Tabitha, if it means that he gets what he wants, which is you. *You* need to decide what's more important, which one you can live without, because Rey and other people's interests? They don't co-exist."

Jesus. He's sure as hell not holding back.

I take a moment to absorb what he's said before rising slowly from the seat. "Thank you for talking through it with me."

"I didn't do much beside point out the obvious."

"Maybe not. But it was what I needed, and I appreciate that."

He watches me in silence as I make my way to the door.

"Thanks, Kris."

"Anytime, Tabitha."

I slip out the door and into the hall, barely holding on to my composure when the latch clicks shut behind me.

There comes a point in your life, for little girls any-way, where you realize that the magic of the fairy tales you love so dearly are nothing but an illusion. That the sweet love and grand gestures they tell of never really happen in real life.

I guess standing here in the hallway of a four-star hotel while I feel no more welcome in my own room than I did in the one I just left, is my moment.

My moment where I realize that this fairy tale? This sweet love?

It's never been anything but an illusion, a show put on by one of the industry's best performers.

I merely had to stop believing to see it.

FORTY-FIVE

REY

"Always" - Saliva

Wherever she went, it wasn't far. I look at the red imprints in my palms from where I've clenched my fists so tight that my stubby nails bit into the flesh. It was all I could do to stop from tearing everything apart.

She'll walk in here to tell me she wants to leave; I fucking know it. And I don't blame her one fucking iota.

I'm a selfish cunt—always have been. I love the shit out of her, but for what she does for me. One goddamn conversation about how this all affects her and I throw my toys out of the sandpit and bully her for daring to want anything other than what I do.

Goddamn asshole. No wonder I always end up alone, huh?

Toby, Emery... they've had relationships with women throughout our years as a band. They might have been brief, but there are two motherfuckers who know how to treat a girl.

This asshole? Not so much.

"Can we talk about this now?" Tabby whispers the

question from a safe distance, arms folded as she stands in the doorway.

"When will you go?"

"Do you want me to?"

How the fuck could I let it get to this? "No."

"Why didn't you tell me you'd done this before?"

Fucking Kris. She went and spoke to that moody fucker. No doubt this is payback for me butting my nose into his business when it wasn't welcome.

"Because it didn't seem important."

"I thought you asked me to come along because we connected, Rey. I felt like I meant something to you." I don't need to look at her to know tears stain her cheeks. "What a fucking fool, right?"

"I don't think you're a fool."

"Have the decency to look at me, for fuck's sake!"

Her frustration rebounds off the walls; I've never heard her that forceful. Her face is a storm, chest heaving with her quickened breaths as I drag my gaze to hers.

"What *am* I to you, Rey?"

God, I want to touch her so bad. "Everything."

"Wrong," she barks. "What am I to you?" She repeats the question a little calmer, but also a hell of a lot less patient.

"Relief."

"Warmer."

"Why don't you tell me then, if you have all the fucking answers."

"Medication," she hisses. "I'm the drug you refuse to take. I'm your damn sedative."

Fuck off. "Whatever." I screw my face up, pissed that she's no different to anyone else.

Can't stand to be around me because of my disorder. Can't love me because of my disorder. Can't even *see* me because of my disorder.

Everything comes back to the one thing I can't fucking change.

"Fuck off, if you're just going to stand there and judge me," I scathe. "Go away."

"I don't judge you," she growls. "You judge yourself, you stubborn fucking idiot." She marches into the room, her rage seeming to give her the bravery she lacked before. "When have I ever put you down or made you feel like you're less of a person because of what you've told me?"

"You don't have to say it," I whine like the petulant asshole I am. "It's implied."

"Bullshit it is."

I damn near shit myself when she takes a fistful of my hair and yanks my head back. *Whoa, kitty.* "Fucking look at me, you coward."

"I don't want to." My damn eyeballs ache in my effort to avoid making contact with her.

"Why not?"

"Because then I'm reminded of why this sucks."

Her hand relaxes, falling away from my head to her side. "Why, Rey?"

"Because I look at you," I say, slicing my gaze to her, "and it fucking breaks me apart to admit that I'm the one responsible for losing the one thing I really love."

"Then don't push me away," she cries, seemingly as

exasperated as I am by it all. "Don't treat me like this and give me a reason to leave."

"I'd rather you left me when you're angry, than broken," I murmur, dropping my gaze again without even thinking on it. "Stay with me, and that's all you'll be—broken. I don't want to destroy you, kitty. You don't deserve that. But you and I both know that's exactly what I'm doing, isn't it?"

"Fuck you." She shunts me with the palm of her hand. "Don't give up, Rey. Don't roll over and die. Fucking fight for something for once, and stop hiding behind your mental illness as though it's at fault."

"Isn't it?" I shout. "Tell me what is to blame, then, if not that."

"*You* are. You sabotage everything to save face."

"What the fuck do you mean?" Save face how? I would have called what I do humiliating myself, since I admit over and fucking over again how weak and wrecked I am.

"God forbid you admit that you care about something, huh?" She takes a step back, and then another, staggered until she drops to her ass against the wall. "You tell me you love me, and yet you can't show it."

Is she tripping? "What the fuck was the point in kissing you, then? Why the fuck did we mess about in the last hotel, then? Wasn't that showing it?"

"No." She says the word on a bitter laugh. "That's lust, Rey. That's you seeking a natural high."

She's got it wrong. So damn wrong.

"I read up about bipolar, about how it works. I wanted to learn so that I could help. I know what you were doing. You were using me to medicate."

"You've got it wrong." I know what she means, but that hypersexuality shit comes when you're in mania. It's the God complex at work; you think you're a gift to anyone and everyone.

I wasn't at my high with her; I've only been at my lowest.

"Don't leave, okay?" I slide off the bed to sit level with her. "We'll work on this."

"When?" she whispers. "While you finish your tour, paying my way because I can't afford to, let alone service the debts I left behind when I came here?"

Now who's the one who can't look at the other?

"I need to separate myself from this so I can focus on me. I haven't been able to write shit since I've been here with you, and unlike you, I don't have a big name to fall back on. I'm still trying to find my place in this industry."

I stifle her. I'm goddamn suffocating her creativity.

I've got nothing to say. What else *can* I say when her mind is made up?

The truth, Rey.

"You know how I realized that I love you?"

She shakes her head, hands slung loosely between her bent legs.

"We haven't slept together." I laugh at how fucking ridiculous it sounds out loud. "If I didn't give two shits about you I would have found somewhere to drill you after that concert we did."

"That's really insensitive, Rey." She chuckles.

"It's the fucking truth though." I smile at her, relieved we've found calmer waters. "I craved those Messenger calls we made, because I wanted to see you. Ask the guys: I take a hell of a long time to warm up to people I don't know. But you...." I grip my hair in frustration, unable to give the sentiments the kind of words they deserve. "I've never enjoyed just *being* with a person like I have you. I mean, don't get me wrong"—I lift both hands with a chuckle—"I think about taking things to the next level with you all day, every day. But I wanted you to let me know when you were ready. I didn't want to lose the best part of you by rushing the rest of you."

She swallows hard, worrying her bottom lip with her teeth. "You're not going to make this easy, are you?"

"Don't fucking tell me you're still going. Don't."

She stares at me in silence. I count the beats of my heart.

"Stay, kitty. Please."

"Give me a reason why. And don't tell me you love me again, because I need more." She frowns. "I need you to show you care about me, about my goals too. I want to be here for you, but only if you're present for me too."

Those rich brown eyes of hers hold me captive as I cross off all the lines I could give that don't measure up to what she asks of me. Fuck—I deliver lines for a goddamn living, and yet here I am tongue-tied because the lyric I need in this moment is the linchpin to whether or not we have a future.

I've never felt performance anxiety like I do now.

So I do the only thing that comes naturally—I sing. I pull the words the only way I know how.

"The dark before the dawn, the calm before the storm. Solace is what I find with you, when the sun don't want to shine."

Love me, hold me. Tell me you're here to fix me.

Love me, hold me. Tell me, baby, please. Tell me you can fucking save me.

Her chin quivers as I sing the last lines in my head, praying she's the silver bullet I had in mind when I wrote that song.

"You added two words."

I nod. "Yeah. I did." I added "with you" to the end of the line.

When I penned the lyrics, it was the peace I found in the darkness that I had in mind. But it's her now. She brings me peace when the shadows fall.

"You still didn't give me an answer for the problem."

"Maybe I had it wrong when I asked you to help write for me," I say, hands scrubbing the carpet. "Maybe, I need to write for you?"

Her brow pinches. "Where are you going with this?"

"Maybe," I say with a shrug. "If we write something together I can, I dunno, work like a mentor or something? We'll take you indie; fuck Wallace. You give me the music, and I'll show you how to market the fuck out of it."

The rustle of her clothing brings my head up, and I find her on all fours as she crawls across the floor to where I sit slumped against the foot of the bed. She pushes my legs apart, settling herself between to sit on her heels.

"You'd do that for me?"

"I'd do damn near anything for you." Even give up my sad and pathetic life to make hers what she fucking deserves.

"I've never met somebody who messes me up like you do." She shakes her head slowly, yet with a smile. "Why do I let you do this to me?"

"Because I fucking love you, kitty." I wrap my arms around her and pull her in tight.

It fucking killed, that space between us. I hate it. It's so much more than a physical void when there are arguments involved.

"You make it hard not to love you, too, Rey."

"But you're unsure about this?" I give her space to pull back so I can see her.

"There's a lot to consider."

Yeah, there is. But no matter how messed up the puzzle in in my head, I know what the end picture is supposed to show, and it's her and me. It's going to take time to sort it all out, get the edges in and then figure out where everything else goes. But the satisfaction once complete will be worth it.

So worth it.

FORTY-SIX

TABITHA

"Wicked Game" – Stone Sour

This will break him—I know it.

I can't quantify what it is that pulls me to Rey, what it is that gives me the shivers when I think about never seeing him, talking to him again. But I need to risk that to remember who I am.

Nothing changes. Tomorrow, I'll return home. But he has to believe I'm going to stay if I can do it clean.

I hate lying. It's not who I am. But then, neither is this.

Looking into his eyes as he gently strokes my hair from my face, I know without a doubt I'd give up my hopes and aspirations for my music to make sure he continues to live his. And that right there is what tells me that no matter how painful, I'm doing the right thing.

I said to him I didn't want to start this based on dependency. I never knew I meant my own.

In the space of a few short weeks my purpose for getting up each and every day has become making sure he survives his.

That is not healthy. That is toxic love.

I'm killing myself, stripping away my own strength to give him his.

I can't do that, can't carry on down this path if I want a future where I don't resent him.

"I wish you could see what I do," I whisper. "I wish you could see how much more you are than your faults."

His smile is lazy, unconvinced. I hate that. "I like it when you tell me in your own words."

"I'll always tell you, just so you don't forget." *Even if I'm not around to do it in person.*

His eyes drop, his smile fading as he leans forward to place a kiss against my neck. I thread my fingers in his hair, holding tight as he brushes his lips down to my collarbone. It's everything I can do not to cry.

The exterior of this man is nothing but harsh and unforgiving. He'd have a person believe he's a cold-hearted asshole who cares about nothing but his own gain.

But this. As his hands press tight against my shoulder blades to keep me against him, his kisses leave a hot trail in their wake as he moves to my chest, the base of my throat.

This man is love. Pure and selfless love. He cares, so much, and it fucking hurts to see him hide such an amazing side of himself.

But I know why. I know why he does.

To protect himself.

It's what I should do now, not lean back to let him guide my shirt from my body, not set my hands on his shoulders to brace myself while he undoes my bra, all while he holds my gaze with those incredibly truthful eyes of his.

No. I should stand and walk away. I should burn this to the ground before it has a chance to finish being built. I should respect the fact that tomorrow morning, while he sleeps, I plan to betray him in the worst and cruelest way.

Doing this... it only twists that poison-laced thorn in deeper. For him, and me.

"Tell me you're ready," he whispers against my skin. "Tell me I don't have to wait any longer."

"It's okay." *It'll be okay. One day.*

"God, I love you." His hands grip my waist tight as he pushes me to my feet. "So fucking gorgeous."

It hurts.

"So fucking beautiful." His hands make quick work of the snap on my shorts.

He pulls the zipper down, but he may as well be dragging a knife through my heart. I'm selfless in this moment, in the worst kind of way. He takes his time stripping me down, his hands reverent between each article of clothing. I brace myself with my hands on his shoulders as he helps me to step out of my panties while he's still seated on the floor.

The look he gives as he tips his head back to take me in? I don't deserve it.

But I want it, and so I take it, which is what makes me such a horrible fucking person.

"Come here." He crooks his finger as he whispers the command.

I bend my knees and settle on his legs, straddling his hips. He scoots a little lower so that my knees have room before they're up against the bed.

"I don't want this night to end," he muses aloud while his palm glides across my flesh.

I thread my fingers in his hair at the back of his head, letting my forehead rest against his. "It hurts me to think you don't see how incredible you are."

He sets both hands on my hips, nudging them further around onto my ass before he takes hold. "You make me that way."

I don't. He still doesn't understand. Maybe he thinks I bring out the best in him? So what if I did? It wouldn't matter shit, what I can do, if that beauty wasn't already there inside of him.

You can't showcase what doesn't exist.

I run my hands over his shoulders, the thrill of the touch bittersweet with the sense of loss that accompanies it. I get this once, when I could have it a hell of a lot more if I stayed.

But would I still enjoy it, if I let him break me down and use me? I don't think I could.

Which is why I get to selfishly make this memory once, and make sure I do it right.

His eyes stay fixed to mine as I watch my hands trace a path over his chest. His breaths are steady, yet the heartbeat beneath my touch tells me this man is anything but in control as he holds me to him with a borderline painful grip.

I lean in and give him a chaste kiss, before moving my mouth to his ear. "I'm ready."

His right arm bands around my middle, my own thrown over his shoulders as he uses his left hand to push himself to his feet, lifting me. I cling to him, legs wrapped around his waist as he turns and sets me on the bed. His knee settles between my legs, teasing as he presses it against the junction of my thighs. I arch my back, grinding myself shamelessly against him while he hooks both thumbs in the waistband of his boxers and pauses only to give me a cheeky smile.

"What?" I try and fail to touch him, frustrated that he's just out of arm's reach.

He shakes his head, pulling his knee away to drop his clothing. "Just you, kitty. Just you."

My teeth dive into my bottom lip as he bends to push the boxers off his feet. For a fleeting second, I forget why this is such an agonizing union as he straightens out and presents himself in all his naked glory.

I'm a horrible, horrible person. But looking at the man who climbs on the bed to hold himself over me, I don't care.

I couldn't care. Not when I know that no matter how bad I regret doing this to him, I'd regret giving up the chance to go through with it ten times more.

"I love you, Tabby. And you know what?" He searches my face, arms flexed as he holds his weight. "It kind of scares the shit out of me."

"It scares me too." Mostly because the thought of what that love will do to us after tomorrow is cause for concern.

I tease my fingertips down his chest, stopping just before our bodies touch. He sucks in a sharp breath, eyes closed as his abs tense beneath my touch.

His arousal pulses against me, teasing me with how

close we are to crossing over this final boundary. I wrap my fingers around the back of his neck, pulling him to me to taste that heady mix of cigarettes and mint. Rey's hands hold me reverently as our tongues tangle, his kiss holding me captive while he rocks his hips against me.

I shuffle my butt up the bed a fraction to line him with my entrance, indicating I'm ready to skip the foreplay. I need him so badly it physically hurts, almost more than my fractured heart.

"Be right back." He leaves me with a final kiss to the tip of my nose, darting across the room to where his luggage sits on the floor.

Of course. We went into this totally unprepared.

The foil packet hits the bed next to my shoulder before Rey resumes his position over me. "Now I'm ready."

I chuckle, warmed at his use of humor. It makes this so much more relaxed, intimate even, that he feels okay enough to break from the intensity of the act.

It makes this so much harder.

"It's not much use sitting next to me though, is it?" I lift an eyebrow, taunting him.

He laughs, rearing back to kneel between my legs. I push up on my elbows with rapt attention to watch as he sheaths himself.

God, I need this man in me, like yesterday.

"Fuck, you're everything," he mutters, one hand splayed on my stomach. His touch drags lower, the heel of his hand massaging my pussy. "I wanted to take my time with you, kitty."

"I don't." My head drops back, my eyes sliding closed

as he shifts from the heel of his hand to his fingertips, his touch teasing my entrance.

"So pretty." Rey slips a finger inside, pulling it out again simply to taste me on him.

I damn near combust at the sight.

He repeats the action, massaging my pussy before each dip of his finger, adding another on the third go. He doesn't need to warm me up; I've been red hot for this man since the moment he placed his face against mine in my apartment.

I hook a heel behind his hips, urging him closer. He chuckles without opening his mouth, the sound a rumble from deep within as he leans forward to set himself chest to chest with me.

"This is it, kitty. Last chance to back out." I whimper as his cock nudges against me. "After this it's all on."

"Bring it." I hook both feet behind him and pull him toward me.

He groans as he fills me, his head dropping to my shoulder. "Fuck, that's perfect."

"You're perfect." I take his face in my hands, lifting his head as he pulls back and thrusts again, slowly, carefully. "Just as you are."

The look in his eyes is my undoing. All his vulnerabilities are laid bare as he builds a smooth rhythm. He trusts me. It's there in the dark depths of his gaze.

He trusts me, and I'm about to take advantage of that in the worst way.

I disguise my pain in my cries as he pulls my nipple into his mouth, filling me with his heat and coaxing me to the edge. His touch is heaven, and here I am, the worst demon he'll have to fight yet, masked as an angel to his eyes.

I have to do this. If I truly love this man and want the best for him, then I have to do this, no matter how I feel right now.

I wrap my arms around him, holding his head to my shoulder while I lift my legs around his hips and drive him deeper. I bind myself to him, giving him that security he seeks as he brings us both to climax.

"Fuck, Rey. Please," I beg shamelessly as he sinks his teeth into my shoulder.

Only I don't beg for the orgasm he pulls from me. I don't beg for his release as he cries out, either.

I beg, above all else, that after tomorrow he'll be okay.

That one day, he might forgive me for this.

That one day, he might understand why I had to do it.

FORTY-SEVEN

REY

"Break Stuff" – Limp Biskit

"Some of us are trying to sleep, asshole!" Toby yells to be heard over the music.

Limp Biskit's "Break Stuff" pounds through the hotel room.

Toby's eyes go wide, his head rearing back with a "Don't you dare" angle to it as he catches sight of me....

Poised in the middle of the living area with the swanky horse head ornament that usually sits on the TV cabinet.

"Put it down," he says calm and low, hands raised before him.

I lift it higher. This morning has gone to hell in a handbasket, one bottle of beer at a time.

"Rey."

The white ceramic skitters across the floor in a thousand pieces that accurately represent my goddamn heart.

"Fuck!"

Toby disappears into his room, emerging a moment

later with a pair of jeans on. He careens out the door, shirtless and shoeless, while I eye up the television. I really, *really* want to throw that fucker off the balcony, but I don't think I could take accidentally killing somebody in the street below at this point in time.

By the time Toby returns with Emery in tow, I've ripped the pretentious artwork from the wall and made a pretty picture of the space with my dot-work cutlery.

"Fuck's sake, asshole." Emery marches over and proceeds to rip them from the sheetrock. "You want to end your goddamn career? Wallace is going to have a fit."

"Who fucking cares, right?" I back up, hands thrown wide, and straight into Toby.

He bands his arms around me, which only sets me off worse. I thrash against him, twisting my shoulders in an effort to break free, but the fucker's always won when we fought since he's taller and broader than I am.

"What is the deal, Rey?" he hollers, still competing with Fred Durst.

"What's the deal?" Fuck my life—there is no deal, that's the issue. "Who's missing? Who isn't here?" I relax in his hold to play dead.

"You want me to go get Kris?"

"Who else should be out here with all the noise I've made?" I jerk my body to try and catch him off guard.

He flicks a leg around mine to put me off balance, and then slams me face-first against the wall. "What did you do?"

God—it's poetic. If only kitty could see now. "Always my fault, hey?" I say on a humorless laugh. "She played me, brother. I finally got a taste of my own medicine, and let me tell you, it's bitter as fuck."

"Christ, Rey." He lets me go to take a step back, hand scrubbing his face when I turn to look at him. "She had to have a reason. I didn't think she was like that."

"Me either." But hey, life has a pretty fucked-up way of reminding us how good it is at surprises, right?

"Have you tried calling her?" Emery parks his ass on the arm of the sofa—about the only thing that hasn't been destroyed in here.

"Fuck. No. It hadn't crossed my mind," I drawl with as much sarcasm as I can muster. "She won't pick up."

"Let me try." Toby rips his phone out of his jeans, gesturing for Emery to do the same. "Give me yours. She might answer if it's unknown."

I retreat to my room to leave them to it. He's welcome to do whatever the fuck he wants, but I already know she won't take the call. How can she when she's probably in the air?

I fall face-first onto the bed with a groan, before propping myself on my elbows to retrieve her note. At least she had the decency to give me an explanation, even if it fucking hurt like a motherfucker to read it.

This isn't me leaving you. This is me giving you space to see what's impossible to while I'm there.

I don't think there's an end to us, Rey. Maybe an indefinite pause? I don't know. But I need you to see what I could, what I couldn't tell you in my own words—at least not face-to-face.

I love that you say you find your solace in me, and

believe me, Rey, I'm fucking honored. But I want to be by your side because I support you, not TO support you. Can you see that difference? See what I mean?

I'm going home with a heavy heart, but I know it's the right thing to do. Finish the tour, do what they want you to, and give it a chance, okay? Maybe the break you'll get doing rehab is what you need? Maybe it isn't. You'll never know if you don't try.

All I know is that if I stay, I enable you. I give you an excuse to fall again and again, because why not when there's somebody there to catch you, right? You said to me at the beginning, what happens when nobody's there anymore? What happens when you fall?

To be honest, I think you'll find that once you hit the ground you'll be able to properly put your feet down and learn how to stand tall. Until then, you're floating in an endless black sea while we all hold you up, never really brave enough to test your footing.

Hit the ground running, Rey. Show me what you can do.

Do it for me. And do it for yourself.

xx

"I left her a message," Toby calls from the door.

Now that they've killed my soundtrack to life, the silence is painful. It reminds me how alone I am in this.

The guys need me to square up and act the good boy for our ringmaster. But I don't want that. I want to wallow in my anger, and I want somebody to tell me it's okay to do that.

Fuck. I've proved kitty right. I'm searching for an enabler, somebody to justify my shitty relapse.

"Read this." I thrust the letter at Toby. "Tell me if she's right."

He leans a hip against the window frame as his eyes track the lines, legs crossed at the ankle. He's shut me out, refused to talk to me all week, but I have to hand it to him: he's always been there for me when I need him most.

Why have I never appreciated that until now?

Kitty. She thinks that nothing changed while she was here, but it did, she just didn't stick around long enough to see it surface.

I rest my chin on my hands and watch the telltale signs as Toby's brow pinches, and then smooths as though he sees her point. He folds the sheet in two once he's done, and then gently sets it on the nightstand.

I flick it to the floor; just the sight of it pisses me off.

"She has valid points, bro. You do need to learn how to do this yourself."

Jesus—I fucking shake at the thought of tackling it alone. "Doesn't turn out all that well though, huh?"

"Only because you don't believe in your worth." He sighs, running a hand through his fading hair. "This is why the family have always struggled with you," he explains. "How many times did Mom and Dad tell you how much they love you, how cut up they'd be without you? How many times did I beg to have my brother back who'd play ball with me? How many times did Cassie sit with you when you were in a funk and make you laugh? You know why she did that?"

I meet his critical stare and shrug.

"Because she craved time with her brother. She missed you when you'd hide out in your room."

"This doesn't make me feel any better about myself, you know?"

"Only because you look for the negative in everything," he cries. "I bet you're lying there right now thinking 'Oh, great. He's blaming me for it all again.'"

"Pretty much." I lift an eyebrow.

"Well don't." His hand connects with the back of my head, leaving a sting in its wake. "I'm explaining to you how much you mean to all of us, you douche. I'm trying to show you how much we all love you and fucking want to you stick around and annoy the shit out of us until we're all old and gray, man."

Hit me in the feels, why doesn't he? "Do you get how lost I am trying to work out how to change this when it's all I've known for twenty-plus years?"

He nods.

"It's a hard habit to break, self-loathing."

"I know. And you won't do it in a day. But you also won't do it if you never try." He snatches up the letter and shakes it at me. "This should be motivation enough to get up and fucking push for it like you're fucking Rocky Balboa."

I chuckle at the visual of myself punching air on the steps of the Philadelphia Museum of Art. "What if I can't do it? What if I'll never be enough for her?"

He drags a palm over his face. "Did you read a fucking word she wrote?"

Twice.

"You're already enough for her," he says on his way to the door. "She wants you to be enough for yourself."

Fuck. As if this didn't seem hard enough already.

FORTY-EIGHT

TABITHA

"No More Tears" – Ozzy Osborne

I threw up before I boarded the plane, nauseous the whole way home. Kendall bundled me into bed, seemingly concerned at the fact I wasn't bawling my eyes out and surrounded by a mountain of wadded-up tissues. I told her I'd be fine, that I hadn't eaten properly while following the band around, and that all I needed was a few days of good food to set me right.

Yet, as I roll over and curse the sunshine that comes through my open curtains, the swirling in my gut reminds me of how easily I can lie these days.

Stress. It's nothing but stress. How do I know that? Because the first thing that crossed my mind, right after I realized I fell asleep last night without closing the curtains, let alone getting undressed, was whether or not I'd find a message on my phone to tell me Rey had done something drastic.

Please be okay. I can't even fathom how my life would be expected to carry on if I'd caused him to waste his. I've unloaded my trust in the three guys that love him unconditionally, Kris the only one who knows why I left, and hoped that they can continue to do what they did before Rey found me.

Or did I find him?

Gah. I don't know anymore. Nothing makes sense.

My chest feels weighted as I roll to my side and retrieve my phone off the nightstand. I silenced it last night after sending Kendall off to work, frustrated by the constant pinging of my messenger. I relegate the name at the top of the notification banners to my subconscious, blindly tapping through to see who the missed call I received yesterday is from.

Unknown Number.

Huh. I wonder if he has Rick onto me, if he's running that poor guy ragged on some ridiculous crusade to get in touch with me. *Bit full of yourself, aren't you, Tabby?* Maybe he doesn't even care? Maybe Rey has defaulted to the usual and pretends that everything's fine?

Guess I'll only know if I check my messages.

I open voice mail first, setting my phone on speaker and listening while I rub my eyes with the heel of my hands.

"Where did you go, Tabitha? Give me a ring; it's Toby. We need to talk about this, girl. You've got my number."

I don't need to discuss squat with him. I've done what none of them have been strong enough to do, it seems. I've slung Rey over that cliff edge and left him to scramble back up alone, just to prove to him that he can do it.

"Hey, babe." Kendall pops her head around my door and looks toward the phone in my lap. "I heard that so figured you were awake." She slips in the room, settling herself on the foot of my bed. "How are you feeling?"

"Rotten."

She sighs, her eyes soft as she looks me over. "You're braver than I am."

"How?" I drop a bitter laugh.

"I couldn't do it. I would have followed him around like a lovesick puppy, slowly ruining myself in the process. I don't know how you do it, switch feelings off like that."

"Because I haven't." I slide down the bed and pull a pillow over my face. "What if he tries suicide again? How the fuck do I live with that?"

"I don't know," she murmurs.

Great. I'm not the only one who can't process my current conundrum. "I did the right thing, didn't I?"

"I think so." The weight of her hand is reassuring as she rubs my leg through the blankets. "Give yourself a distraction today and go for a walk. Do some door-knocking if you're really serious about getting a day-job."

"To be honest, hon, I might do it tomorrow. I can't think straight today."

I want to cry into my cereal and pity myself for sabotaging something so real, yet at the same time I'm too proud, even now, to do it.

I left Rey to prove a point. What would he make of me if I ran back to him apologizing for standing up for what's right?

Would he even forgive me after what I've done?

"What are the plans for the day?" Kendall tugs the

blankets from my body, giving my ankle a slap for good measure. "You can't hang out in bed all day."

"Can't I?" I choke out.

Rey wanted to stay in bed all day. *Oh, God.* It begins. My stomach knots, my eyes on fire with my determination not to cry. It's no use: the stress needs an outlet. And because I deny myself the right to bawl like a little bitch over what I've done, my body picks the only other option.

I launch from the bed and barely make it to the bathroom before the remnants of last night's dinner come back up. My hands shake as I reach for a towel, the jitters never really having stopped since they began as I shut the hotel door behind me.

Why the hell am I doing this to myself? *For him.* If only he knew the price I'm willing to pay for love. He probably thinks I'm blissfully going on about my life, content with what I've done. But I'm not, and I can't decide if letting him know that this hurts me too is a good or a bad thing?

Probably bad.

"Are you okay?"

I nod, wiping my face before looking to Kendall. "Can you do me a favor?"

"Anything, babe." She edges further into the bathroom.

"Take my phone and delete the message thread with Rey." *Don't be sick again.* Everything will be fine.

"Are you sure?"

"Not really." I let slip a sad laugh. "That's why I need you to do it."

She leaves, my heart thundering in my ears as I strain to follow the sounds of her moving through the apartment. Relief mixes with the strange sense of loss I get as her footsteps track closer.

"Before I do." *Shit.* "Do you want me to tell you what the new ones say?"

I shake my head, too weak to voice my answer.

"Last chance, Tab." She stands with her thumb poised over the screen in my periphery.

"Do it."

Kendall drops a loaded sigh before whispering, "All gone, babe."

I guess this is kind of what it would feel like if he died.

 FORTY-NINE

REY

"Coming Undone" - Korn

"Jesus. What are you doing?"

I roll away from the windows as Toby tugs the heavy hotel drapes open.

"We need to leave in five fucking minutes."

"I know," I gripe, moving my sheet music to the floor on the far side of the bed so I can continue with it in relative darkness.

He snatches my acoustic guitar by the neck and marches around the foot of the bed. Scuffed boots stop perilously short of my scrap paper. "Move."

"Yeah, in a minute." I wave him off before sliding my upper half off the mattress to make an adjustment to one of the chords.

Toby sighs as Emery enters the room. "Take this." He thrusts my guitar at him.

I'm in for it now.

He takes one step forward as I awkwardly try to worm myself back onto the bed. "Fuck off, bro. I just need a bit more time."

"We don't have time," he grits out through a stiff jaw, lunging for my leg.

I crab crawl backward across the bed until my hands hit the far side.

"We already changed the whole fucking day around just for you." Toby's palm connects with my shin.

I kick at him, failing to dislodge his grip as he adds his other hand and pulls me toward him in a vise grip. "I can't do this," I cry out in a panic.

He huffs when I stop before him, bedding bunched under my ass. "You have to."

"Why?" I whine.

He sets both hands on my shoulders and squeezes. "You want a nine to five job, little brother?" His eyes are firm as he ducks his head to meet mine. "If you think this is hard, try blowing *that* responsibility off. Having to get up every day and go, not just because people expect you to like they do now, but because you have to if you want to eat."

Kitty. Is that what it's like for her to push on when life seems determined to shit on her?

"Fine. I get your point," I gripe, pushing on his chest. "I'll be out in a few; let me get dressed."

He steps back, and then promptly marches his ass to the armchair in the corner of the room.

"What are you doing?" I slip my legs off the side of the bed, hands braced either side as I narrow my eyes at him.

He drops his ass onto the seat and sets his arms on the rolled rests. "Waiting."

"Pervert."

"Just get on with it."

Fucker. He knew as well as I did I had no intention of getting dressed. I drag my sorry ass across the room and kick my jeans that lie in a heap on the floor toward the bathroom. He hoists a T-shirt at me that had been hung over the side of his chair. I catch it mid-air, and then toss it down with the jeans to kick the pile into the adjacent room.

We're doing a Thursday show. Mid-week. I mean, who the fuck wants to stay out mega late before having to drag their sorry ass to work tomorrow?

A few thousand people, it seems.

My motivation is at an all time low, my enthusiasm about as non-existent as the fucks I have to give. The thought of facing that crowd leaves my gut churning, never mind the liquid breakfast I had before I picked up where I left off with the new song last night.

Kitty won't talk to me.

Unanswered messages, and unanswered calls. *Huh. Could be the name of a song.*

I did the last two shows after she left in a goddamn zombie state, eyes glazed as I stared out over the heads of the people who paid good money to see us and flatly delivered the lines that fall from my tongue as easily as I draw my next breath.

I can't remember half of the last concert, and not just because I was drunk enough that Kris said it was a miracle I stayed upright, but because my mind was entirely elsewhere.

My cards have been put on hold, my spending money reduced to a handful of bills that Rick meters out to me at the start of each day. It was Wallace's great idea on how to ensure I don't skip out and fly to see her again.

Because I would. If only to see her face one more time before I made sure there's no way they could ever drag me back to this damn fucked up musical pageant.

The water runs hot over my hands as I stare at them in the basin. I zero in on the callouses on my palms, the thickened skin side of my fingers. My head aches while I try to drag up some feeling, some memory of who that guy was, the one who would bounce up to every goddamn show no matter how big or small with fucking stars in his eyes.

Toby once said in an interview that when you love what you do, then touring isn't as stressful as people think it is. That as long as you keep that passion, that fire, then your work will never be a chore.

I can't pinpoint where that changed—I just know it has.

I lost the passion.

My fire snuffed out a long time ago.

Now the guys drag my ashes from show to show, hoping if they huff and puff on me long enough that I'll form some sort of presentable lie.

I can't do this. I can't live this lie any longer.

How the fuck do the legends survive doing this for twenty plus years? *Simple.* Most of them don't.

My hands shake beneath the flow while my gaze slides along the counter. *There must be something in here.* There has to be a tool I can use, even if I have to improvise.

"You need help?" Toby quips from the door.

I turn my head his way, a lump in my goddamn throat as I look at the tired gaze of the one guy who has the least reason to still love me after all the shit I've put him through.

"I think I need a hell of a lot more than that."

"Fuck, man." He steps forward as my legs give out.

My wet hands drag the water down with me, the droplets running in rivers down the front of the cabinets and across my forearms, much the same as my own runs in rivers down my face.

"Hey." Toby's hands push under my arms, trying and failing to lift me off the floor.

It's no use. "Don't bother," I tell him, my voice thick with resignation. "There's nothing left to save, bro."

"There's always something left to save," he snaps, jerking harder to make me stand. "Come on you useless fuck; don't quit on me now."

Why not? I already have.

"Em!"

I roll in Toby's arms like a ragdoll as Emery appears at the door. Kris hovers behind, hands in pockets.

"We're at that point," Toby says to Em. "Get it."

I can pick the sadness in his tone, the disgust that he's allowing it to happen. He's been against this since Em suggested it the last time I got this low. Only it's never been this bad, has it?

Kris leans a shoulder to the doorframe while Em skips the room, appearing seconds later with a Corona in one hand, something I can't see in the other.

He squats down next to me, Toby kneeling behind to keep me propped up.

"Here." Em holds his hand out and offers the unconventional antidepressant. "Chuck it down ya, man."

I take the pill and throw it back, chugging the beer until the bottle is dry.

I've got no idea what he gave me, only that it's designed to keep me on my feet and fucking alive long enough to play this next show. After all, why ask questions when you honestly don't give a fuck if it kills you?

Rock, meet bottom.

FIFTY

TABITHA

"Reason I'm Alive" – Drowning Pool

My phone signals a message as I stand with coffee in hand and scour the jobs board at our local café. I haven't given up on music, simply accepted the truth that I'm further from it being my sole source of income than I'd like.

I know my limitations, and they all center on money. Taking a "real" job for a while to save up some cash to invest into an album, or a new violin, isn't giving up. It's smart business sense... at least that's what I tell myself when I freak out at seemingly going backwards.

The froth of my drink hits my lip as I hesitate over one that reads "Hours Negotiable." It turns out to be a temporary position, nothing that could sustain living costs for my foreseeable future. Aside from a couple of seasonal positions, it's all the same stuff that's advertised online—nothing I'm qualified to do.

Afternoon light paints the street in warm oranges and reds as I step out of the shop and wrestle my phone from my purse with my free hand. Kendall is at work, and over the past week I've found myself out wandering our neighborhood. What for? I don't really know. All I do know is that I'm searching for something I won't find here.

Something I left behind.

Someone.

Yet, no matter how many times the pang of regret stabs in my chest, no matter how any times my lungs grow tight when I wonder how he's doing, what happened, I won't break.

I won't cave in and search out the information that would be so readily available on the internet. Not when the only person I want to hear the news from is Rey himself.

I live with a ridiculous fantasy that after the tour ends, my Messenger will chime to let me know he's calling to say he's found himself in rehab, that he finally accepted the help he needs and he's better.

But I know that's bullshit. I know, as well as he does, that the end of the tour will mean nothing when it comes to his mental health.

Hell, all it will probably do is give him an out. Nobody there to watch him twenty-four seven. Nobody there to check his schedule, make sure he's where he's supposed to be, doing what he's meant to.

Nobody but him.

I find a seat on the windowsill of a boutique store and set my coffee at my feet to check my phone.

The name sitting proudly in bold before the preview sends my heart into chaos and my head into a spin.

Toby

I've done so well. I've managed this far. And yet one goddamn word and my subconscious catalogues how much combined cash I have between my bank account and credit card to afford another plane ticket.

Toby's message is simple, an image attached.

T: Help.

I tap on the photo: a picture of a sheet of paper with handwritten lines. I have to pinch and zoom to see what it says, but there's no doubt once I have who's written it.

Oh, babe. What are you doing to yourself?

I swallow back the restriction in my throat, determined not to cry in public. The lines are dark; darker than anything he's put out to date.

Ta: What do you want me to do?

I wait as Toby's dots dance across my screen, lifting my coffee to take a sip. People walk past, oblivious to the problem unfolding on my phone. It strikes me—is that how Rey feels when he gets up to perform? Does he stare out at all those faces, all those people who are completely unaware of what he struggles with, and get frustrated by their ignorance?

It's not their fault that they don't know his battle, but as I look at the people walk by me now, I understand how isolating that must feel.

T: We need you here, Tabby. Please.

I shake my head at Toby's reply, my heart yet to slow from the definite *prestissimo* it took on when I opened the thread.

Ta: I can't do this for him. He needs professional help.

My phone screen switches to Toby's incoming call.

"He needs more than me," I answer.

Toby sighs. "He refuses it. I'm at my wits end, Tabby. I've never seen him this low."

God. Why do they do this to me?

"You understand why I left, don't you?"

He hums. "I guess."

"If I come back now, then he uses me like a kid uses a damn cuddly toy, Toby. He'll cling to me until he feels better, and then he'll justify that this time it wasn't so bad, that me being there helps. But it doesn't."

"It does," he argues.

"Not how it needs to," I bite back. "I give him a distraction, and yeah, maybe that helps him get through this low point. But he needs to find proper help, somebody who can motivate Rey to help himself."

He sighs, a rustle cutting the line. "Are you sure you won't come back? Just for a day? Maybe you could convince him to do rehab, seek counseling, because fuck knows he won't listen to any of us."

"I'm sure." I duck my head, resting my coffee between my feet. "Don't misunderstand why I say no, okay? I care about Rey, so damn much." My words are thick with emotion. "But I can't live with myself if I enable his condition. You know as well as I do that this cycle he's stuck in, it's not sustainable. He needs change. All I do is give him an excuse not to."

"Fuck." He huffs. "I don't know what to do, Tabitha."

"He wants to stop touring," I say softly. "Can he get a break?"

"Not this close to the end of the tour." Toby groans, the muffled sound making me think he scrubs a hand over his face as he does. "We've got six shows to go. Two weeks."

"Surely your label know they need to address this if they want him to continue."

"Our label," he says scathingly, "believe that it's all a bunch of Hollywood antics and that he's fine. That a break after this tour is all he needs."

"So fucking record him and send it to them," I say. "Jesus, Toby. You would have seen him when he bottoms out; it's scary."

"Terrifying," he agrees. "Today is the first time I've let him out of my sight, and that's only because he's with Kris and Rick." He drags a deep breath. "I've hardly slept, Tabby. That's how goddamn worried I am he's planning something stupid."

Fuck. *My heart.*

"I want to help him, I really do, but I honestly believe that being there will only makes things worse."

"Please," Toby whispers. "Just to level him out until the end of the tour. Then you can go your way, we'll take him ours and get this sorted." He sighs, seeming to toss up whether to say more. "I just want my brother to stay alive, Tab, and you can help with that."

"Don't." I can barely push the word. "I know you

mean well, but honestly, dumping this on me isn't fair either."

"Is that how you see it?" he snaps. "We're 'dumping' Rey on you?"

"Not Rey," I say, exacerbated. "Whether he lives or dies." I glance up at the people who walk past, suddenly aware I'm having such a personal conversation in such a public space. "Don't put that burden on me."

"If not you, then who?" he asks. "Because, Tab? I've about had all I can take of carrying it."

"Talk to… what's his name? Your boss guy."

"Wallace?"

"Yeah. Surely if you tell him what you've told me, he'll bring in help. Can't they hire somebody to do a house call?"

"Got to be able to get to him, first."

"What do you mean?" I pick up my coffee and start walking again.

"He shuts himself in his hotel room between shows. Doesn't eat, hardly says a word. We…" He sighs.

"You what?"

"We had to give him an upper to get onstage last night."

What the hell… "You're drugging him?" I earn the wary eye of a woman I pass.

"Just the once."

"Well don't," I cry. "You know what the withdrawal from drugs like that can cause, right?"

"Tab, I'm pretty sure I'm in the prime position to know about drugs," he levels.

"So you know it could make his depression worse,

then?"

"Well aware," he snaps. "But it's a risk the rest of us are willing to take. We're locked into airtight contracts, Tab. We need him to perform."

"Even if it kills him?"

He hesitates before whispering, "Even if it kills him."

FIFTY-ONE

REY

"Sound of Madness" - Shinedown

Two weeks, four stops, and six shows since she fucking left.

And shit hasn't got any easier.

That mania on the horizon has become a goddamn vanishing point, always out of reach. Tonight we play our third show in the same venue before moving on to our second to last stop of the tour, and the whole thing is fucked.

I can see grass between the groups of people milling about with red cups in hand, waiting for us to restart.

Why the fuck can I see grass? We're supposed to be sold out.

My fairly intoxicated brain comes to one conclusion only as I stare out at those mocking patches of nature—people have left.

Ticket holders have decided that our show isn't worth staying for when light rain paints a mist across the halogen lights.

I shake my head at the bullshit and turn to grab my

drink from in front of Toby's stand. He watches me with hard eyes, sticks resting on his thighs as he waits for the cue to tear into our next song.

Emery makes his way across the stage while Kris plays whatever comes to mind in an effort to keep the crowd occupied.

Fuck the crowd.

Why should they be over the fucking moon to be here when I'd rather stick a fork in my goddamn eye than stare at those patches of grass again?

"What's the hold up?" Em snatches the bottle from my hand and takes a healthy swig.

I glare at the motherfucker, well aware he doesn't drink because he's thirsty; he drinks the contents so I can't.

Toby leans forward, pushing his mic to the side in the process. "Square your shit away, Rey. You've been off all goddamn night."

"Fuck you," I spit, tearing the alcohol from Emery. "Just follow my lead like you're supposed to."

"When this set is over you're fuckin—"

I walk away before he can finish, turning back to what remains of our goddamn traitorous crowd.

"How about this fucking weather, huh?" I holler into the mic. "What sort of fuckery is that?"

I catch a few heads turn as the patrons look to each other for guidance. I'm known for my uplifting chants, my ability to get everybody up and jumping, not this bitter bullshit.

"Fuck the rain," I yell. "Let's make some goddamn noise."

A few die-hards cheer, yet I catch all those blank stares in the mix.

The same people who seem to stare straight through me as I smash my way through one of our original tracks. Kris is on fire as usual, his playing damn near the only thing that carries us through to the end of the song.

Fuck knows it isn't me.

I give up and set my guitar down before Toby knocks out the final bars.

"Where the hell are you going?" Kris hisses as he backs across the stage and into my path, pick still working the strings.

"Anywhere but here," I snap.

I jog down the stairs side of stage and push into the tunnel that leads to the locker rooms, all to the deafening drone of the crowd's complaints.

What do I fucking care? There were two songs left on the set list before we usually pick what we'll play for the encore on the fly. Way those cunts are dead as a doornail tonight, they don't deserve a goddamn encore, let alone the rest of the show.

The pounding of boots on polished concrete gives me ample time to brace before my skull meets the painted wall of the stadium tunnel.

"Get your fucking ass back up there now." A vein throbs in Toby's temple, his forearm pressed to my throat.

I knee the bastard in the nuts and edge out of his hold as he doubles over. "Get fucked."

"I already am," he hollers after me. "You walk, we're all fucked. Think about somebody other than yourself for a change, you goddamn asshole."

My shoe squeaks on the floor as I spin on the spot and redirect course back to my brother. "I am! All I think about is *her*. And you know what?" I shout, leaning over to get in his face. "All that does is remind me how I screwed up."

"What does this achieve then?" He straightens, one hand still on the jewels. "She wanted you to fight for yourself, to prove to her that you think you're worth her goddamn time and attention. And what have you done so far? Proved her point by moping around and feeling sorry for yourself."

"That's just it." I step backward, throwing my hands wide as Rick makes his way down the tunnel. "I don't feel sorry for myself. I feel sorry for her."

Toby shakes his head as though he doesn't understand.

I grin, leaning forward to push my point. "Look at me, Toby. Look at the fucking mess I am." I laugh bitterly, checking Rick as he approaches. "She loves this?" I say disbelievingly. "I feel sorry for her because she loves such a worthless sack of shit. What a fucking idiot, right?"

What a fucking fool.

There's nothing within me, or about me, that's worth even a second of her time, and yet all I want more than anything else in this world is another second with her. One more fucking touch. One more fucking moment of her lies to believe that she was there to stay.

God, I miss her.

"Rey," Rick seethes as he passes Toby. "Pull yourself

together and get your fucking ass back on that stage before you find yourself a goddamn footnote on the bio."

"So make me one," I leer. "I dare you."

"Rick," Toby warns. "Now's not the time."

"No." He spins on my brother. "Now is the *perfect* time. I'm fucking done wearing it for everything he does. This asshole either steps up, or steps out."

"Out it is then." I thrust both middle fingers at the idiot and back away to grab my shit from the locker room.

I'm done. Finished.

Fucking over being primped and preened as Wallace's prize show pony.

What's the point of doing all this if you spend the hours between salvaging what's left of your mind to survive another round under the lights?

I want to pick up a guitar because I long to, not because I'm scheduled to.

I want to remember what it's like to do this for the love of it, to give up everything and go without because *this* is where my passion lies.

As crazy as it sounds, I fucking envy Tabby and her basic, broke life.

Because after all is said and done, at least she still has a hunger for this. A love for the music.

A fucking darn sight more than what can be said for me.

FIFTY-TWO

TABITHA

"Wish You Were Here" – Pink Floyd

The tour ended three months ago. I put Kendall in charge of my Facebook page the day they wrapped up, neglecting my profile and staying off all other social media so that I could avoid any news of what they're doing now.

How the album launch went.

If he tried again.

His name is banned in our apartment, the space my safe haven from the stress that follows me everywhere day to day. I don't listen to the radio. I'm careful not to deviate from my saved playlists in Spotify. I turn my head when I pass the magazine rack in the stores.

The closest I came was the start of one of their songs playing on the streamed radio that gets piped through the local convenience store. I set my purchases down on the nearest shelf and walked out.

It's not that I *want* to avoid him, it's that I *need* to. I kept in touch with Toby after his phone call, living the tour vicariously through his texts and calls. The bitter irony was, by the time I gave in and agreed to talk with Rey, he didn't want to talk to me.

He broke down mid show, so Toby tells me. Snapped and walked out. They had to fight to get him to play the final concerts, and even then I'm told they had to refund several hundred tickets for people who complained about the sub-standard performance and the crude things he was saying between sets.

Strangely enough, your fans don't enjoy being told they're a bunch of demanding sheep.

I screwed up. I did what I thought was right, and I totally let him down. He didn't find a reason to fight. He found a reason to give up.

I completely misjudged him.

He told me that he wanted change, and that made me think that all Rey needed was a push in the right direction. After all, when you lose the thing you love, isn't that supposed to give you incentive to fight for it?

I guess not when your mind is as fractured and incomplete as his.

It took a week before I could look at my violin after that news, another five or so days before I could string together more than a few bars. After all, how could I blissfully continue to play the very thing that had cemented my decision to walk away from Rey? I felt like a traitor loving the instrument knowing what that had done to him. But piece-by-piece, day-by-day I found that fighting girl who brought me to this point in life, and I managed to get two songs composed.

Two songs that give me hope that perhaps, just maybe, I can combine my classical training with a more modern twist and create something new and catchy.

"I'm going out tonight with Sarah from college, remember?"

A least Kendall seems to have her shit together. She slowly edges herself back into more of a social life, not letting my hermit lifestyle dictate hers.

"I haven't forgotten. Are you having dinner before you go?"

"Probably not." She flits through the living room, a dress slung over her arm. "I think I'll grab something on my way to hers if that's okay."

"Yeah. No worries." I'll probably consume my staple diet of cereal and head to bed early to try and bleed music.

"Oh, I forgot." She ditches the dress over the back of the armchair, and then dives into her purse. "I cleaned out the mailbox today and there was something for you."

"Yeah?" Another reminder for my overdue credit card, no doubt.

Kendall Frisbees the envelope onto my lap, retrieving her dress before she disappears to get ready. I lift the formal-looking correspondence, and check out the sender's address.

BMM

Who the hell is BMM?

The whine of the hairdryer starts down the hall as I slip my thumb under the lip and rip it open. A single folded sheet resides inside, and its only when I pull it out that the weight of the paper seems odd. I fold it out, my stomach knotting at the clearly music-orientated logo at the top, and then threatening to flip in on itself when I see the extra weight was a check.

What the hell?

I seriously can't breathe. The empty envelope tumbles to the floor as I rise and hustle to the cracked window for some fresh air. The figure on the check can't be right. It has way too many digits before the decimal point. Way too many.

My hands shake with such violence as I bring the letter up, that I drop it to my side again and focus on steadying my breathing. *One, two... in and out.* The page still rattles as I hold it, but at least the words aren't a blur. I skim over it, absorbing the important details.

Song title: Another Time Around

Writers: Reymand James Thomas, Tabitha Sally Reeves

What. The. Fuck.

Royalties owed for first quarter sales/streams

No. Fucking. Way.

I can't read any more.

The letter and check flutter to the ground as I narrowly avoid twisting an ankle in my haste to get to my phone. "Kendall!"

I holler her name again as I unlock the screen and punch through to the Spotify app. *Come on, come on, come on.* "Kendall!"

"I'm coming." She skids into the living room, her shoulders dropping. "Jesus. I thought you'd hurt yourself."

"I have." My thumb slips and hits the wrong song. I growl and smack the right one.

My one.

The phone clatters to the coffee table as I fail to set it

down properly, my hands shaking violently as the bars of music I wrote that last night in the hotel, the ones I trashed in a rage before I left the next day, play back at me.

Only, they're not on a violin. They're haunting in their melody, played on an electric guitar.

"Why are we listening to this?" Kendall whispers, edging closer.

Rey's voice cuts in. I lose all hope of hearing this through from start to finish the first time without losing it. "Oh my God."

"Tabitha." Kendall snatches my phone, spinning it to face her. "Why are you playing their song? Ah! You stupid girl. What are you doing, babe? This is why you've avoided it. Shit. Why we've avoided it."

"You know this song?" I blubber from the floor.

Her eyebrows peak. "Well, duh. It's only as popular as that one they played us at the theater."

"How would I fucking know?" I holler.

She shakes her head, lips flat. "True. Fuck, I'm sorry." Kendall folds to her knees, kitted out in only her lingerie. "They added it as a bonus track to the new album. Why are you playing it though?"

I scramble across the floor on all fours, shuffling back to her on my knees with the letter and check. She looks them over as my chest tears apart listening to Rey sing, her eyes slowly inching wider and wider.

"Whoa."

"Right?" I cry. "What the hell?"

"How did you not know you wrote a song? One of *their* songs?" She sets the papers on the table beside my phone.

I reach over and hit Pause, the song having moved on to the next one. "I wrote the music the day before I left, for myself. But I hated it. Told Rey I forced it, so I threw it away."

"He salvaged it."

"He had to have."

"Isn't that plagiarism or some shit?" She frowns.

"Only if he didn't give me credit, but babe"—I shake the check at her—"he gave me credit."

"Well then, tell me you're going to send him a message to say thank you," she says with a laugh, pushing to her feet. "It's the least you can do, you goose."

"I just... I can't believe he did that."

She sets her hand on her hips. "You're mad about it?"

"No! I'm blown away. I just...."

"Didn't think he'd do something that nice since you were such a bitch?" she teases.

I chuckle. "Yeah. Pretty much."

"Fuck, babe. Message him now. I mean it." She thumbs over her shoulder. "I need to get ready, but I swear to God I need to know what he says before I leave."

What the hell would I say to him? Thanks for being so awesome after I was such a cow? "I need to think on it."

"Well, don't leave it too long, because, babe, if this isn't the man confessing his love for you, then fucked if I know what is."

"He used my music. It's hardly love. He could just be an opportunist," I reason with her.

She gives me a hard stare and sighs. "Play it again, Tab, and for fuck's sake, listen to what he says."

FIFTY-THREE

REY

"Ordinary World" – Duran Duran

"First quarter payments went out yesterday," Rick tells me as he follows me into my private room. "Ironic really."

"What is?" I drop into the plush armchair by the window. *Going to miss this comfy fucker.*

"That she finds out the truth the day you're discharged."

I did the rehab. For kitty. And fuck me sideways if it wasn't exactly the break I needed. I expected a daily regime of pills and twice-weekly Kumbaya sessions. But it wasn't anything like that. Apart from the visits to the counselor every week, you'd be excused for thinking it was a compulsory stay at a resort.

"You ready to go if I duck out and do the paperwork?"

"Gagging, my good man. Get me the fuck out of here."

I said it was the break I needed, not that I enjoyed it.

"I'll go sign the gazillions of fucking forms then and meet you out front." He pulls his phone out after it starts to ring, answering as he disappears down the hall.

I survived the last week of the tour high as a god-damn kite. I barely slept, living it up in my final free days with a mainly liquid diet before signing on to become sober.

I put the band through hell, most of all my brother. Thing is, I can safely say without a doubt that if it weren't for Toby I would have found a way to try again. Jump off a balcony, walk in front of a train—with the mindset I was in, I wouldn't have given a fuck if it weren't quick and painless, as long as it worked.

But he stuck by me, going without sleep I'm told, all to make sure I didn't do anything stupid. I love that stupid motherfucker, more than I've ever told him.

One of the many things I plan to rectify once I'm on the outside of this goddamn clinic.

I have a shitload of work to do to get my career back to where it was. I sabotaged what I had, and I did it in spectacular fucking fashion. Like the shooting star I was, I burned too bright and hit that bottom kitty talked about, and fuck did it hurt. But amidst the chaos, I also wrote what I think is my best song yet.

Her song.

I drove the guys crazy, keeping them up every fuck-ing night while I sat in the hotel room with my guitar banging out the verses. I literally played until my fingers bled those first nights after she left, determined to not only get it right, but to get it perfect.

She'd cut me off, refused to answer my messages, and set her phone to send my calls direct to voice mail.

That song was my goddamn message in a bottle, and today, it washed ashore.

I pull my phone out and open Instagram to take a final shot from my room. I make it an artsy selfie, doing the whole looking-at-nothing trick as I gaze out the window. Set the filter to a black-and-white one, and fuck me if it doesn't look semiprofessional. *Got yourself a backup talent right there, you dumb fuck.*

I post the picture with the caption "Home time" and then rise to grab my bag. I hesitate when my gaze settles on the bulge created by my notebook. I wrote a dozen new pieces, some of which need polishing, but that isn't what has me undoing the zipper to pull the hardback out.

Nope. I flick through to her song and then park my ass on the edge of the chair one last time while I read it over. Only this time I don't read it with my critical eye, picking holes in my choice of words, or places where I could have tightened up the flow. I read it with her eyes. I put myself in kitty's shoes and try to imagine how she'll feel when she hears these lines. Because she will hear them. Angry, sad, or happy: however she feels when she gets that royalty check, I know she won't be able to help herself.

Back at the start again,
That's where you and I stand.
Only this time is different.
Because you won't hold my hand.

I stepped into the shadows,
Not afraid of what was to come.
You stepped out into the light,

DOWN BEAT

Said you were afraid of losing the sun.

I don't hold it against you.
I could never look at you with hate.
Only regret that when I saw your pain,
It was already too late.

One road becomes two,
Your time with me is through.
One road became two,
It was the only thing left to do.

Today I've reached the end,
Because yesterday I hit solid ground.
Tomorrow I rise again,
Because forever is where you'll be found.

Come at me running, baby,
Come at me running ...

Come at me running, kitty.

FIFTY-FOUR

TABITHA

"Angel" – Theory of a Deadman

"Best hangover cure ever," Kendall mumbles around her bowl of Fruit Loops. "How did you go?"

I cradle my second mug of coffee for the day, unable to sleep, yet also failing to find motivation to do anything with my early start.

"I didn't send him a message." I know that's all she wants to hear about.

"Why the fuck not?" She swipes the milk on her bottom lip away with the back of her hand. "What stopped you?"

"This." I set my palm over my heart. "I love him for doing this for me, babe, but it changes nothing."

"Are you sure about that?"

"Positive."

I spent the night lost in the internet black hole, looking up every scrap of information I resisted the past three months.

He relapsed. He crashed and burned, performing the last show of the tour so drunk that he forgot the lyrics to one of the songs. And even though the reports tell me he went to rehab like instructed, nothing indicates that his fire doesn't still smolder beneath the calm surface.

"Maybe in time," Kendall offers as she lifts her bowl to drink the leftover milk.

"Yeah. Maybe." I drag my phone over and tap through to check my emails.

Perhaps there was a reason why I held strong, after all? "Wow."

"What now?" Kendall asks, setting her empty bowl in the sink.

"I got an email from that agent I signed on with last month."

"And?"

"They've got me an audition for the philharmonic." Is this fate telling me to stick to the plan, to keep working on myself?

"You don't seem hugely excited by it."

I glance at Kendall as she leans her elbows on the counter beside me. "It wasn't really what I wanted."

"But it's good, right?"

"If I can get a spot, then it's steady income. Not great, but steady."

"So?"

"So, it's not the solo career I dreamed about." It's not the fantasy of working on an edgy modern mix that'll set me apart and make me successful.

She twists her lips, shoulders heaving with a sigh. "I guess you have to ask yourself what lengths you're willing to go to, to get exactly what you want."

Moreover, if I could live with settling for something

less.

"Go to the audition," Kendall suggests. "It can't hurt to see what happens."

"I guess not." Although the thought of becoming one of many, seated for the same shows over and over, already has me dying on the inside.

I'm not selfish; I just know what lit my fire. And it was that independence to play what I wanted, what I felt best suited the audience I had. It was being able to move around the stage as I played, lost to the piece. It was the freedom to express myself in a way that is true to who I am.

Still—independence doesn't pay the bills. Stubbornly holding out for that one niche opportunity doesn't feed me week to week. Sure, I've just received an unexpected lump sum thanks to Rey, but that won't last long with all the creditors knocking on our door.

Time to grow up, Tabby. Time to swallow the bitter pill that is admitting my parents were right: I can't make a career out of playing my violin.

At least not as a solo artist.

"The audition is Thursday night," I read aloud to Kendall. "Apparently I can play what I want, as long as it's one of the traditional pieces."

"Go. Knock their socks off." Kendall places a kiss to the top of my head before making her way to the hall. "It's a stepping stone, babe. Not the end."

Maybe not, but then why does it feel as though by doing this I finally shut the door on everything I worked for the past four years?

My gaze drifts to the check, sitting on the end of the

counter ready for me to bank today. I should say thank you. No matter how I feel about the guy, Rey has helped me out more than once now without any real return. Heartbreak and regret are no excuse for bad manners, really.

I exit the mail app and tap through to Messenger with my heart in my throat. The thread sits empty, reminding me that I'll never know what he said the day I left. *Although...* Kendall knows.

I slip off the stool and make my way to her bedroom, where she sits on the bed tugging her jeans on.

"You need help?" I tease.

She snorts a laugh, falling to her back to hoist her hips in the air as she yanks on the denim. "No. I've got it."

"Hey. Do you remember what the messages from Rey said before you deleted it?"

She jerks upright with a frown on her face. "Why?"

"Curious, is all."

Her lips twist as she stands to hook the stud. "I don't remember exactly what he said, but I know it was something about how you were the best liar he'd ever met. He seemed angry that you'd tricked him."

"Logical, given what I did." I lean a shoulder against her doorframe.

"It was a good thing you asked me to delete them, really." She smiles softly. "They were quite harsh, the things he said. All things considered."

Probably warranted too. I ripped his heart out by walking away when I promised I wouldn't. I became exactly like every other person that had let him down in the past.

Why did he help me, then?

"Thanks, babe."

I cross the hall to my room, nudging the door closed behind me. My violin case catches my eye as I walk in, reminding me of the decision I have to make. Do I persist? Or do I settle? My heart says to keep fighting for what I want most, yet my head says that at some point I have to admit defeat.

The issue admittedly takes some of the pressure away from messaging Rey, which is a bonus. My subconscious is so preoccupied with the decision that I don't have space to overthink what I'm going to say to him.

T: The mail brought me a bit of a surprise today. Thank you for including me. I really appreciate your generosity.

I read and reread the blue bubble that sits on my screen. God, I sound so formal. I'm right back where I started with him—cold and professional.

The screen flicks to black, the green and red icons at the bottom for me to accept or decline his video call. Fuck it all—I cry. After everything, he still wants to see me.

"Hey." I keep the camera off myself until I've finished dabbing the unshed tears from my eyes.

He drops a loaded sigh before talking. "Fuck, kitty."

Look at the screen, Tab. You can do it. My next breath catches in my throat, my heart pounding so hard I can feel the pulse point in my wrist as I pivot the phone.

Ruined. I'm utterly ruined. He has the phone propped up on something, his head in his hands, face hidden, as he leans toward the screen. Damn, I've missed this.

I've missed him.

"How the fuck are you?" he asks, fingers working through his hair as they bend and flex, bend and flex.

"How am I?" I've got no hope of stopping the tears now. None. "Why are you asking me that, after what I did to you?" I cry.

"Hey," he coos, leaning back. "No. Don't, babe. Don't do that."

God, those eyes. This is why I've avoided all news of him, any pictures, any chance at seeing a video. Because one look in those eyes and I wonder how I ever had the strength to walk away to begin with.

I set the phone down on my bed and retrieve a tissue from the box on top of my dresser as I call out, "Why did you do it?"

"Use your music?"

"Yeah." I blow my nose, ditch the used tissue in the trash, and then get another before I return.

"It was cathartic," he says simply with a shrug. "What else could I do when you wouldn't talk to me?"

"I read about what happened at the end of the tour."

"Yeah." He chuckles, looking off screen. "Right fuckup, that was."

"So why aren't you angry at me?" I whisper. "Nothing I did helped. You aren't any better." I state the fact, leaving no room to argue. "I was wrong, so damn wrong."

"What else could you have done though, right?" I

catch a glimpse of the resentment I search for. "If you stayed I would have brought you down."

"I only left because I thought it would give you reason to fight for yourself, Rey." God, my chest hurts. "Why didn't you?"

"I don't know. I wanted to." He drags both hands over his face, the sound of laughter interrupting his feed—a woman's laughter. "Every time I thought I made progress, I realized that it was all a huge fucking misunderstanding and I hadn't gone anywhere. I guess I gave up. I figured if I couldn't even get it right for you, then when could I ever?"

"And now?" I push aside the thoughts of where he is, *who* he's with.

Rey sighs, staring at the screen for a moment before he answers. "I still get dark, kitty. I still have those thoughts. But there's one thing stopping me from going through with it—and it's not myself."

"What stops you?"

His smile reaches deep inside me and pulls all the emotions attached to it out kicking and screaming. I can't go there. I can't fall for this man again. "You." I never stopped falling, did I? "Why would I want to die when you'd still be here? As long as there was a chance that I'd get to do this again"—he gestures to the screen—"then I held on."

God, this hurts.

"Nothing's changed," I say.

I wanted him. I wanted this so bad. But he's proved that there was nothing I could have done. He's accepted that this is who he is: dark and depressed. And no amount of love or light from me will ever change that.

We're fighting to reach the same boat from two different shores. We're struggling against ourselves, and when all is said and done, one of us will likely drown.

"I have changed," he argues. "Jesus—if I hadn't, then we wouldn't be having this conversation sober."

"But you're still using me as your excuse, Rey. I want to hear you say that you hold on because there's so much left of *your* life to live. Not mine. I want you to hold on because you see what you have to lose."

"I *can* see what I've got to lose," he grits out. "And I already lost it. I love you so fucking much, kitty. Give us a chance."

He trusted me to be the one thing that could help him, and I failed. I couldn't do it.

What makes him think now is any different?

"I gave us a chance, Rey. I gave us every chance." The tears return, only this time when they fall it doesn't hurt so much. It disappoints. "But you still never gave yourself one."

"Tabby," he pleads.

I shake my head, pushing the phone aside so I don't have to look at him. "This isn't about me. It never was. This has always been, and will always be, about you, Rey. And until you understand that, until you live and breathe for yourself and nobody else, then I it won't feel right to do this. I'm sorry."

Sorry that I ever said yes.

Sorry that I answered his call.

FIFTY-FIVE

REY

"Through it All" – From Ashes to New

My breath shudders from my nose as I sit on the floor of the spare room, hands massaging my thighs in a vain attempt to expel the anger that rages through me.

I *have* fucking changed. And I *do* live for myself.

Except, unlike Tabitha, I can see that I'll never *fully* live if my life isn't connected to hers.

"Hey. Mom's serving lunch."

"Be out in a minute."

My sister withdraws from the room with a nod, more used to my bullshit mood swings than any sibling should have to be.

She won't ruin this. I won't let Tabby ruin not only my day, but my fucking future. I didn't lie to her; I still have suicidal thoughts. The counselor at the rehab clinic told me that it's likely that I will never fully shake them. But unlike a few months ago, I can separate them from the moment and recognize them for what they are: my mind sabotaging my life.

What has changed is that now I have the drive to fight

back. Time was, I'd hit the low and float there, out of energy, and out of fucks to give. Now, I reach the bottom of my cycle and the shock as I hit the ground has me bouncing back.

I get angry. I get angry, and then I get even with my mind.

It will not win, and like fuck I'll let it take away the thing I deserve the most: Tabby.

"You okay?"

I look to my sis, Cassie, as I head out to join the family. "I don't understand your gender. Not one fucking bit."

She laughs, nudging me toward the dining room. "Rey, none of us understand you either. I don't think it's a gender thing."

Great. "You split up with Jack for a while, hey?"

She nods, pausing at the doorway. "Why?"

"What did he do to get you back?"

Her eyes narrow, the brightest shade of blue I've ever seen on a girl. "Why? Who are you trying to win over?" She's the best part of all of us, the little fucking ray of sunshine in our family.

Which is why she barely knows the half of how serious my issues are. It went without saying between Toby and me that we'd protect her from it. But she's a grown woman now, old enough to hold her own.

"Can I talk to you after lunch?"

"Of course." She jerks her head to indicate we should join the noisy table. "Come on. You need to put some fat back on those bones, big brother. You're skinnier than I am."

Liquid diet will do that to a person. If only she'd seen me before I went to rehab. Eish.

"Take a seat, baby." Mom pats my place setting. "Toby's ready to jump the table to get to the ribs, I think."

"You know it." He catches my eye as I take my seat, a silent question passing between us. *"What did she say?"*

I shake my head, and then turn to where Dad enthusiastically dishes out steak. "Thanks for cooking all of this."

He gives me one of his signature grunts before answering. "It's nice to see your mother happy with everyone at the table again."

"It's been years," she laments from the other end. "You boys need to come home more often. And bring the other two next time. I know Emery goes to see his folks, but I worry about that Kris boy."

Don't we all? Next week the madness starts again when we hide ourselves away for a month to work on new content. We've had our time off, a little longer than usual thanks to my stint at rehab, but we're supposed to be unwinding until we meet up again on Tuesday. Thing is, nobody's heard from Kris in close to five weeks.

Rick's holiday was cut short the minute his old man sent him out to track the guy down.

It's like a fucked-up game of Where in the World is Carmen San Diego? with Rick tracking our guitarist from the clues he leaves on social media.

"Pass your plate, Rey."

I hold it out for the old man, my arm sinking under the weight of the small calf he unloads onto my dish.

Sure as fuck won't need to eat for a week after this.

"What happens now that you're out?" Toby asks as Dad does the same for him. "Do you need to check in with anyone?"

Straight to the hard topics, huh? I stare at the asshole across the table. He called me once a week while I was in there, but it didn't take a rocket scientist to figure out he did it out of obligation.

If I thought my attempts on my life drove enough of a wedge between us, it had nothing on what I did when I fucked up that final show.

Took two and half weeks for the black eye he gave me to fully disappear.

"I've got a free pass," I answer. "Only have to call if I think I need them."

"Really?" Cassie asks as she holds her plate out for the dainty slab Dad passes her. "I thought you'd have to do AA or something."

I consider how hard it would be to swap plates while she's distracted. "Nope. Because I was a voluntary admission, I miss out on that."

"You shouldn't have needed admission at all," Dad gripes.

Here we go again.

"If you pulled your fucking head in and listened to your brother, none of this would have needed to happen."

"Clint," Mom scolds.

"Just saying it how it is," he mumbles.

"And don't we love you for your continual honesty," I snap.

Toby groans, while Cassie sighs. And just like that, our Brady Bunch moment slides into something that more resembles a scene from *Married With Children*.

Ah—home. No place like it. And Mom wonders why we don't come back more.

"Anyway," I announce loudly. "I have a few pieces to go over with you later, Toby."

"Good." The rest of his sentence is implied in his tone: *at least you got something achieved while you were there.*

I fight the urge to set my phone on the table and record this bullshit. I could send it to kitty, titled And You Wonder Why I Drink.

The meal continues in silence—at least, for me. The rest of my family unit make small talk amongst themselves, either oblivious to the fact I refuse to join in, or maybe thankful. Who would know? All I can state for certain is that without the bullshit that accompanies everything to do with me, their conversation holds a much lighter, easier feel to it.

I'm completely and utterly the black sheep, and for once, that doesn't make me feel bad. I'm okay with it. I've made my peace with it. My depression is part of who I am, but it's not everything I am.

I am my mental illness, but my mental illness is not me.

And kitty thinks I haven't changed.

"Swell meal, Mom. Thanks." I set my knife and fork on the plate, and then push out from the table.

"Where are you going?" she asks.

"People to see. Things to do." I stick my hand out for the old man. "Good to catch up, as always."

He reaches out tentatively and gives it a pump. I can see it in his eyes; he thinks I've lost it again.

Maybe I have. But this is the most right I've felt about something in a long time.

It struck me, as I sat at the table eating, that once again I'm going through the motions of life, doing what I'm told. Sit here, Rey. Do this, Rey. Say that, Rey.

Kitty wants me to fight for myself, well then welcome to the revolution, motherfuckers.

Ain't nobody going to cut me out of this box I've stuck myself in. Nope. I made that box so damn pretty that everyone around me rushes in to smooth the edges and tape it up whenever I try to break free.

Not anymore. Fuck what they think. Fuck what I think. The only person who knows what the hell they're talking about, the only person whose advice I crave, who is ready and willing to give me a high five when I finally fucking get it right, hung up on me not even a full hour ago.

And if I've got anything to do with it, then she won't be able to hang up on me again.

"See you next week," I toss Toby's way as I push my chair in and turn to Cassie. "I'll ring you later, sis."

"What do you mean next week?" Toby frowns.

"I mean I've got a fucking plane to catch." I toss a hand high in the air as I march out of the Mad Hatter's tea party. "Sayonara, fuckers."

FIFTY-SIX

TABITHA

"Never Never" - Korn

Steady income. Steady income, and no more debt *collection calls.* I repeat the reasons for doing this over and over as I wait on the cab to take me home from the audition. It went well, but I won't know the outcome until they've seen the other applicants tomorrow.

I've never wished so hard for a rejection.

My phone rings in my coat pocket, forcing me to juggle my violin case between my hands in a hurry to catch it before it stops. The agent's name flashes up on the screen, no doubt calling to see how I did.

"Hi."

"Evening, Tabitha." The guy is old school, super formal. But he knows his stuff. "You've finished your audition then?"

"I have." *Don't ask me how it went.*

"And how did it go for you?"

Damn it. "I think it went well. I find out tomorrow."

"Brilliant." I can tell by his tone of voice he's already disinterested in what else I have to say.

In a way, it's a relief. I don't want to get into the semantics of why I'm not feeling it.

"I didn't actually call about that, though."

He didn't?

"How's your evening? Is it free?"

"At this stage." As if I'd have anything to do, anyway. "Why?"

"I had a request for you to play at a private residence. Now, there are no concerns for your welfare; the parties have to fill out quite the comprehensive booking form, so we'll know where you are and what time you're supposed to leave. If you accept, then all I ask is that you phone me when you're done so I know you returned home safely."

"Is this normal?" I knew he put me up on their website as listed talent, but I seriously didn't realize people still do this.

"Quite normal. One of my other gentlemen plays at least three times a month for private functions. If you're comfortable doing such events, you can earn a nice bonus through them."

Wow. "I guess I'm thrown by the short notice, but that's fine." A girl has to eat. "What are the dress requirements? Cocktail?"

My imagination sets to work conjuring up a montage of swanky places I might be booked for.

"Casual. I'd say dress slacks and a nice blouse, but you don't need to be formal."

A nice blouse. I giggle on the inside—I don't own a blouse. "I'm happy to do it. Do they have preferences for what I play? How does this work?"

"I'll email you the particulars. You're required there in a little under two hours, so I apologize for the rush. They literally booked you this minute."

"Thanks, Don. The opportunity is much appreciated."

"I'm sure you'll blow them away, dear."

He disconnects, leaving me reeling as my cab arrives. I need to hustle if I'm going to make it in time.

My Uber Black pulls up with barely three minutes to spare. I opted to pay a little extra for the benefit of having an unmarked car drop me off. If the address had been for some stately house, or upper-class townhouse, it would have looked tacky as all hell rocking up in a Yellow Cab.

Yet as my driver double-checks the number on his GPS, I realize why I'd been asked to dress casual. The hotel gives me flashbacks to the first night with Rey. All glass and brass, and far too much class for a girl like me.

"I think you must be after one of the residences," Suresh, my driver, says with a frown. "You want me to stick around?"

Bless him. "No. I'll be okay. Thank you."

I slide out of his car, violin case in hand, and check the blouse I've borrowed from Kendall. She made me pinky promise to message her in an hour so that she knows I haven't been chopped into tiny pieces.

Seems everybody is as skeptical of people who book private sessions with violinists as I am.

I make my way into the lobby, overwhelmed by what I'm about to do. Reassuring myself that I'm just as likely to find myself playing to an upmarket birthday party in a large apartment as I am serenading some creepy guy in his small room goes some way toward calming my heart.

But only a little.

"Good evening. How many I help you?" The woman behind the front desk has the most immaculate hair.

I feel as though I just rolled out of bed in comparison.

"Hi. I've been booked to play for somebody at number 2/1078?" I lift my violin case for her, as though she needs proof that I'm legit.

"Yes. We have a note to let you up when you arrive." She glides to the far end of the desk and then returns with a key card. "You've been instructed to let yourself in."

"Thank you." I take the slip of plastic from her. "I don't need anything special to reach the right floor?"

She shakes her head ever so gently. "Only that. You'll see the directory next to the lifts."

"Thank you."

I count my steps on the way over, hoping the forced focus will settle my nerves. My phone vibrates against my thigh as I step before the brass-framed directory. I decipher which floor I need as I pull the device out, using the end of my violin case to nudge the call button.

The light above the lifts illuminates as I switch my phone to silent, and then slide it back in my pocket. It feels unprofessional having it on me, but if this had turned out to be some whacko, I wanted the option of calling for help.

The ride to the right floor breezes by, helped out by the fact I keep busy running the songs I've chosen to play through my mind. I chant the names in my head as I walk the hall, searching for the number.

It's disturbingly quiet up here. I half expected the spill of chatter from the apartment when I reached it, or at least some indication of what goes on inside. Yet there's nothing.

Overthinking again, Tab. Don wouldn't have sent me here if the details didn't check out. Hell, I doubt crazy murderers are the kind to spring several hundred on a rent-a-musician just to get their kicks.

The lock beeps with the swipe of the card, the solid clunk of the rod disengaging announcing my arrival. I push the door open, not at all surprised to find a wide-open expanse of a place on the other side. The room appears to extend to the left, all the way to the end of the building, large windows on two sides showcasing the city at night.

Aside from a floor lamp at the intersection of the two cream sofas, there aren't any lights on.

"Hello?"

I take a step forward, and still again when my boot makes a strange sound. An envelope sits under my toe, wrinkled where I've stood on it. I give the place another sweep, and then stoop to retrieve it.

- Read me.

What in the ever-loving hell?

I set my violin next to the entrance table, and slide out the card in the envelope.

- Days sober: 94. Your next card is in the same place as where we first kissed at your apartment.

404

Oh, hell to the no. "Rey?"

Cold, empty silence answers me. I cross the living space to the spot on the carpet next to the sofa. Sure enough, another glossy envelope sits waiting.

- Suicidal thoughts before you left: almost daily.
- Suicidal thoughts after you left: 7.
- Next card is where I told you I love you.

Jesus. My heart echoes my footsteps as I rush through to the bathroom. Still no sign of Rey.

- Songs written before you left: all about hate and despair.
- Songs written after you left: about you, the future, and ultimately overcoming adversity.
- Next card is where you told me you'd stay.

I stack the three cards I have in my hands, taking four short steps to see that yes, I did walk past one on the way in here. My hand shakes as I reach for the envelope propped against the wall.

- You might think I haven't changed, but not all progress can be seen by the naked eye, kitty. You wanted to know why I wasn't still angry at you after you left. Because after I lost my shit, after I cursed you out for lying to me, I realized something pretty fucking important...

I flip the card over, looking for the rest.
"You left because you love me."

Sweet baby Jesus.... "I did." I turn to face him, the rush of my heartbeat a roar in my ears.

How ironic it is that when I know the guy intimately, he makes me this nervous. I couldn't have cared less about his status the first time we met, but now... I care about everything to do with him. The stakes are that much higher now that I know what I have to lose.

"You know why I did the rehab?" Rey steps forward, dark and foreboding all kitted out in his signature black.

"Because your manager said you had to?"

He ducks his head, taking a deep breath as he slings his hands in his pockets. "Because I owed you that much. You told me you wanted me to prove that I could love myself, but you forgot something, kitty." He tilts his head, eyes critical. "I couldn't love myself when I remained the reason why you weren't there. It was a catch-22."

I guess it was. "I never saw it like that."

"You're an essential part of me, babe. I'm never as happy as I am when you're with me. And you know what? That doesn't show how dependent I am on you, it shows how fucking valuable *you* are." He edges forward again, slow as though to give me time to protest. "Is that such a bad thing, to mean so much to someone?"

The lump in my throat won't ease, no matter how many times I swallow. "No. It's not."

"So why are you running?"

Damn him. He stands before me, a simple man asking for the truth. Yet he may as well be there with a freaking mirror propped between his hands.

This whole thing, my reasons for doing this... *they*

were always about me.

"Do you remember what you said to me when I asked you why you kept pushing me away?" I ask.

"I said that I'd rather you left me angry, than broken."

I nod, the hurt I've buried these past months free-falling from my jaw in tiny droplets of truth. "You know what happened when you said that?"

He shrugs, another step closer.

"It struck me how much I cared about you, what I'd give up for you. And I told myself that it wasn't healthy having that kind of connection with somebody. That I needed some level of independence. But you know what? I lied to myself that day, right before I lied to you." He's so close now, close enough to touch. Yet still I can't. "I'm afraid, Rey."

"Afraid of what, kitty?" His breath ghosts my face as he leans in close enough to kiss me if he wanted.

"Afraid that you *would* break me. I wanted to leave before you broke me, too, but not because I was angry. I wanted to leave heartbroken knowing you were alive and living without me, before I had to leave heartbroken because you weren't."

"You were afraid of staying in case I took my life?"

I nod, too ashamed to meet his eyes. "It's selfish, I know. But it would have ruined me, Rey."

"Was it better?" he asks gently. "Living with your heart in pieces to avoid it being broken?"

I stare at him, mouth slightly parted while I try to formulate an answer. But as his lips kick up on the side I realize what he does: he's got me.

I did exactly as he said. I broke my damn heart to

avoid the possibility of it being broken in the future. I gave up on what I could have now, for what I might miss out on later.

"I told you I was no good for this," I say with a slight hint of humor.

His cheek brushes mine, and yet I don't miss the fact he keeps his hands to himself. It's deliberate, I'm sure. "No good when it came to helping me get better, sure."

I tilt my head to press it against his, frustrated when he moves away. "But?"

"I discovered that you're so much better at something else." A shiver rips through me when he drags the corner of his mouth along my temple.

"What?" His physical connection, so slight, is so damn erotic.

"Loving me for me." He places a chaste kiss to my forehead before tilting his head to rest his in the same spot. "Throughout the whole thing, kitty, you never once treated me as anyone but Rey."

I long to reach out touch him, to grab hold and force him to me. But as much as the tease drives me wild, I enjoy this. It means so much more than the rush of lust if we were to amp things up. It's so much more intimate, meaningful.

"Because that's all you are to me," I say. "That's all I need you to be."

"I promise I won't leave you." His fingers finally find my chin, tilting my face to his. "And I promise if that ever changed, if I ever found myself back there, that you'd be the first to know."

"Promise me one more thing?"

"Anything." He whispers the word against my mouth.

I try to kiss him properly, yet he pulls back.

"Promise that you'll never give up again. Promise that no matter how hard things get, how dark, you'll keep trying."

I choose my words carefully, wanting him aware that all I seek is his commitment to bettering himself. Because it was never about changing who he was, it was about shuffling the order of what parts of him got most prevalence. Accepting who he is didn't mean allowing the worst parts of him to take over. He can make peace with his illness without making it everything he is. Dark and angry Rey can be relegated to the back while I enjoy the loving man who hasn't had enough stage time.

"We'll talk about it more tomorrow. You can ask me anything." That smile I love so much graces his lips. "But tonight, I've got lost time to make up for."

"Have you now?"

He pulls back, turning his head slightly to the side as he looks at me with narrowed eyes. "Don't you dare fucking tell me after all this you'll walk again."

I shake my head, making a promise to myself that no matter how hard it is at times, I'll make it work.

If I have to suffer a few bad days to get twenty of the best, then so be it.

If I learned anything from the break I enforced, it's that I'd rather get my time with Rey any way it comes than miss out on any more searching for the perfect mix.

"Thank fuck for that," he says with a laugh as I give him a smile. "Because I didn't have a backup plan if this hadn't worked."

"It worked," I reassure him. "It definitely worked."

"Good. Now get your sexy ass over here and kiss me, woman, because watching those lips work while you talk makes me all kinds of crazy."

I step into him when he holds out an arm, letting him take my weight as he crushes his mouth to mine.

Our legs tangle in an awkward mess as he steers us to the bed, my hands making light work of his shirt.

The last time we made love, it was laced with pain and betrayal, making it a slow and deliberate act.

Yet as he shunts me up the bed, his gaze positively wild as he yanks at my clothes, I know this is something much more passionate. Primal.

It's Rey at his best. And that man? He's complicated. But I wouldn't have him any other way.

Rey has depression.

Rey has bipolar disorder.

But *having* those things doesn't make him who he *is*.

Rey is beautiful in his chaos, awe-inspiring in his strength, and above all else, madly and deeply in love with me.

And I'm crazily and obsessively in love with him too. All of him. The good and the bad.

How could I not be when each of those things makes him who he is?

Perfectly imbalanced.

POSTFACE

(A word from me to you)

I want to share something with you—a word about the themes in this book.

This note from me isn't light and heartwarming. It contains triggers, yes, but it pertains to the origins of this story and I think it's important to read.

Ready? Okay.

When I was thirteen, I stared at a knife and wondered how it would feel to run the blade across my wrist. Nope. This isn't some trick to grab your attention. I really did that.

I was diagnosed with a mental illness at around the same age. I put my mum through hell, I gave my family stress, and deep down I didn't want to cause any of that.

But I didn't know how to fight the feelings of hopelessness, of nothingness, alone anymore.

I stood in our family kitchen—fuck, I remember how it looked, the weather, everything—and I first wondered how that would feel to make yourself bleed, whether I'd actually mind the pain, before I then wondered what the people I loved would do afterward.

That thought, of what would happen after, was my light bulb moment.

I realized that self-harm wasn't the major goal to my actions, I simply wanted to shock everyone enough that they saw how serious this was for me. How little control I had anymore. ***That being mentally ill wasn't my choice.*** I wanted change, and I was sick of being told that a few counseling sessions would fix me.

Twenty-two years later, they alone still weren't enough to fix me.

At the time of writing this book, I thought that accepting depression as a part of myself was the answer. You know … the old adage if you can't beat 'em, join 'em. I thought I'd got a grip on it all by categorizing mental illness as one of my personality traits.

Oh, sweet innocent me, how wrong I was.

One month after publishing Down Beat, I burned out. Call it a mental breakdown, or collapse; it's still the same thing.

I had allowed my illness to go unchecked and given the monster a home for so long that I pushed myself into a panic-induced state of exhaustion. Ten days on a hospital ward with my resting heart rate the equivalent of being at a constant jog.

It took me a solid year—twelve months—to drag myself out of that.

I hadn't realized just how much of my current state I had written into Rey. Dudes, I don't wish that special kind of hell on anyone, but I've reached a point now where I can be thankful for the lessons that episode in my life taught me.

Amongst numerous others, it showed me how debilitating an unwell mind can be and how easy it is to justify the actions we healthier people label as "selfish" and "rash".

In case you haven't guessed it by now, I'm telling you all this because the main theme (and potential trigger) in this book was not only mental illness, but suicide. There, I said it. That ugly word that makes people gasp and clutch at their pearls.

My panic disorder was so bad that I literally wondered if I'd go to such extremes just to stop feeling scared. The days were so damn hard that, at some points, I just didn't want to do them anymore.

Life wasn't fun. And I had lost my purpose. I felt like a burden and a weight around my loved-one's ankles.

I didn't realise it at first, but all I did was feed the monster with these thoughts.

Thankfully, I have incredible friends who I cherish, and a husband who deserves a damn medal. I sought help. And yes, at first (when I was given the wrong medication) things got worse. But I persisted, and with an arsenal of treatments in my back pocket that included things I'd never considered before (like acupuncture and meditation), I got better.

I'm still getting better. And I can safely say that although I have days where I notice old habits trying to return, I am a braver, more confident version of myself than pre-burnout.

Yet, for 800,000 families every year, there is no happy ending.

The topic of suicide is discussed in Down Beat, and I wasn't afraid to do that. For too long the subject has been treated as one of those icky taboos that only a few brave dare touches because "you can't discuss it in case it causes somebody to consider it."

Trust me—I get that. At my lowest it was a trigger that would send me into a cold sweat.

And in some ways, I think putting the focus on the action itself is still the wrong way to go about it. What we should be doing, is talking about the process that takes a person from happy and healthy to considering something so against basic human instinct.

We need to greater support for people who find themselves in places they never thought they'd be. People who feel that life is so far from where they want it that quitting is the only option.

Isolation can be a debilitating disease, all on its own.

There's such a stigma around mental illness is its vast and varying forms. It's a topic glossed over at family get-togethers, it's a subject avoided in the office break room. It's an ugly fact of life that we seem so determined to eradicate through denial. *Ssh—if you don't talk about it, it'll go away.*

Ignorance may be easier, but it doesn't help.

Talking about it helps. Allowing people who suffer from mental illnesses—because these disorders are an illness you suffer—feel okay, and accepted through understanding, helps.

The biggest aid in my recovery was knowing I was not unique in my position, that I wasn't the only one.

I wrote a piece about my experiences as a way to cope during one of my lows, titled "I don't want your sympathy. I want your understanding." (One day I might publish it). That's what this book is, though.

Understanding. Education. Change.

I want to #endthestigma, and this, the story you've just read? That's me doing my part.

That's me sharing the most intimate pieces of who I am, and how I function, in the hopes that it helps people who are blessed enough never to go through this, understand. In the hopes that it lets somebody who does battle with this ailment know that they aren't alone.

That they can learn to nurture and heal the broken parts of their mind.

That there is hope.

That no matter how dark the day, there's always another, and another after that, and somewhere down the line *they do get easier.*

You've just got to get to the next one, to eventually reach the rest.

If you want to know how you can help a loved one, or

what to do about somebody who you suspect may not be coping, then I urge you to visit https://www.ruok.org.au

Max
xx

NEED HELP?

If you, or somebody you love, struggle with mental illness, remember:

It's okay to say you're not okay.

Reaching out for help isn't a weakness, it's one of the bravest things you can do to admit you have a problem that can't be ignored. Illnesses such as depression and anxiety have a great way of making you feel as though your problems are inadequate, that nobody cares because they've got issues of their own to deal with (trust me, I know this first hand.)

But depression is a liar.

People do care. Maybe it's somebody close to you, or perhaps it's a complete stranger on the other end of a helpline, but I promise you,

somebody does care.

If you're feeling overwhelmed, like there's no possible way this storm can pass, or that you can't see how things will get any better,

MAKE A CALL.

All the following organizations are waiting to help.

AUSTRALIA:

Lifeline: 13 11 14

Beyond Blue: 1300 22 4636

UNITED STATES:

National Suicide Prevention Lifeline: 1-800-273-8255

CANADA:

Alberta Crisis Line – All Ages: 403-266-4357

British Columbia Crisis Line – All Ages: 1-800-SUICIDE

Manitoba Crisis Line – All Ages: 1-877-435-7170

New Brunswick Crisis Line – All Ages: 1-800-667-5005

Newfoundland and Labrador Line All Ages: 1-888-737-4668

Nova Scotia Crisis Line – All Ages: 1-888-429-8167

Ontario Crisis Line – All Ages: 1-866-531-2600

Prince Edward Island Crisis Line – All Ages: 1-800-218-2885

Quebec National Crisis Line – All Ages: 1-866-277-3553

Saskatchewan Crisis Line – All Ages: 1-306-525-5333

Yukon Crisis Line – All Ages: 7 pm-12 am (PST) 1-844-533-3030

NEW ZEALAND:

LifeLine NZ: 0800 543 354

UNITED KINGDOM:

CHILDLINE: 0800-1111

Family Line: 0808-800-5678

Papyrus Hopeline: 0870-1704000

The Samaritans: 08457-90-90-90

Lyrics to the songs featured in

DOWNBEAT

"Descent of My Mind"

I've slipped yet again, lying cradled on the floor,
Falling harder, deeper, faster than before.
I've gone too far, I've sunk too low,
Stay a while and catch the end of the show.

I need you, I hate you.
I want you, I can't escape you.
Leave me on my own,
Yet don't walk away.
Help me, tell me,
Which way do I go?

They're talking louder.
They're talking fast.
The things they say,
I just can't grasp.
Where do I turn?
Who do I believe?
When the demons in my head,
Wear my heart on their sleeve.

I need you, I hate you.
I want you, I can't escape you.
Leave me on my own,
Yet don't walk away.
Help me, tell me,
Which way do I go?

The dark before the dawn,
The calm before the storm.
Solace is what I find,
When the sun don't want to shine.

Love me, hold me.
Tell me you're here to fix me.
Love me, hold me.
Tell me baby, please,
Tell me you can fucking save me

"Pull Me Under"

Where did you go,
When I needed you most?
You didn't show,
After I jumped from the coast.

Your whispers, like ice.
Your heart, like stone.
You pull me under, pull me under,
And I can't figure out how to swim alone.

Where did you go,
When the sorrow cut deep?
Where did you go,
When the road was too steep?

Your whispers, like ice.
Your heart, like stone.
You pull me under, pull me under,
And I can't figure out how to swim alone.

<instrumental>

Don't come back, don't you stay,
I told you to keep far, far away.
Don't you give me those three little words,
Not when I know they're tainted and cursed.

Keep running, baby.
Turn the other way.
Keep running, baby,
Find yourself and pray.

Your whispers, like ice.
Your heart, like stone.
You pull me under, pull me under,
I'd rather die alone.

ALSO BY MAX

STANDALONE

Malaise

Tough Love

Echoes In The Storm

TWISTED HEARTS DUET

Desire

Regret

Trust

ARCADIA HIGH ANARCHISTS

Good Girls

Bad Boys

Rich Riot

Loyal Love

Done Deal

FALLEN ACES MC SERIES

Unrequited

Unbreakable

Tormented

Existential

Misguided

BUTCHER BOYS SERIES

Devil You Know
Devil on Your Back
Devil May Care
Devil in the Detail
Devil Smoke

ACKNOWLEDGEMENTS

It's been a while since I've done these. And it isn't because I'm not thankful. More that I felt as though I had started to say the same thing fifteen different ways.

But this time, I have people who can't escape a mention.

First up, my beta team:

Dee Dartnell, Donna Riley-Stafford, Heather Packer, Jessica Schulze, Lisa Staples, and Tamara McLean.

You girls are always ready to give your honest and unbiased feedback, and I'm truly grateful for what you do. For Down Beat, you went above and beyond. I listened, I made notes, and without a doubt the story is what it is today thanks to your help.

Thank you, ladies.

Secondly, my mo-fos:

You know who you are. My secret squirrels, my illuminati. Everybody needs that person in his or her life who just gets it. Who knows the struggle, and who can give selfless support with no expectation of return. I'm lucky to have several, and dudes, without you I may still be rocking in a corner wondering if Down Beat would ever be good enough.

Thanks, babes.

Last, by no means least, my family:

Kids—I swear one day you'll fully comprehend what "Mum's doing her books again" means, but I love that you accept it and are patient with me when I need to finish a sentence before I can come help with something. Love you two immensely. More than I could ever find words for.

Hubs—You never doubt me. You listen, even though you don't really understand, or care much for books, and tell me what I need to hear: "Just get it done." Maybe one day you'll read one again, maybe not, but either way I'll still pop you in here just to remind you that it's you and me, babe. We got this. Mwah.

And as always:

A shout out to you, the reader. Without you my book is nothing more than a pretty cover lost in the depths of Amazon. I may write the stories *I* want to share, but I push myself to the edge with them so that *you* can love them. I love hearing how you can relate, what parts you loved, which parts made you want to toss your Kindle.

Thank you for your support. Now, and always.

Lots of love,

Max

THE MUSIC

Listen to the songs that inspired the book:
https://spoti.fi/2rdO7La

"Always" – Saliva
"Angel" – Theory of a Deadman
"Anthem for the Underdog" – 12 Stones
"Black Hole Sun" – Soundgarden
"Bottom of a Bottle" – Smile Empty Soul
"Break Stuff" – Limp Bizkit
"Bullet" – Hollywood Undead
"Bullet with Butterfly Wings" – The Smashing Pumpkins
"Coming Undone" – Korn
"Enemies" – Shinedown
"Face Everything and Rise" – Papa Roach
"Falling Away From Me" – Korn
"Fell on Black Days" – Soundgarden
"Go to War" – Nothing More
"Got the Life" – Korn
"Headstrong" – Trapt
"Heart-Shaped Box" – Nirvana
"Help" – Papa Roach
"(I Just) Died in Your Arms" – Cutting Crew
"I'm Not Sick but I'm Not Well" – Harvey Danger
"Interstate Love Song" – Stone Temple Pilots
"Invincible" – Adelita's Way
"Jekyll & Hyde" – Five Finger Death Punch
"Judas" – Fozzy

"Let Me Live My Life" – Saint Asonia
"Life is Beautiful" – Sixx:A.M.
"Love the Way You Hate Me" – Like A Storm
"Mudshovel" – Staind
"My Fight" – From Ashes to New
"My Own Summer (Shove It)" – Deftones
"Never Never" – Korn
"No More Tears" – Ozzy Osbourne
"Ordinary" – Like A Storm
"Ordinary World" – Duran Duran
"Paralyzer" – Finger Eleven
"The Reason" – Hoobastank
"Rason I'm Alive" – Drowning Pool
"The Red" – Chevelle
"Rx (Medicate)" – Theory of a Deadman
"Self Esteem" – The Offsrping
"Send the Pain Below" – Chevelle
"Shadows" – Red
"Smells Like Teen Spirit" – Nirvana
"Sound of Madness" – Shinedown
"Still Counting" – Volbeat
"Stillborn" – Black Label Society
"Stupid Girl" – Cold
"Suicidal Dream" – Silverchair
"Symphony No.7 in A Major" - Ludwig van Beethoven
"Tear Down the Wall" – Art of Dying
"Theme from Schindler's List" – John Williams, Itzhak Periman
"Through it All" – From Ashes to New
"Tomorrow" – Silverchair
"Wait" – Earshot

"Waking Lions" – Pop Evil
"Wicked Game" – Stone Sour
"Wish You Were Here" – Pink Floyd
"Would?" – Alice in Chains
"Zero" – The Smashing Pumpkins

ABOUT THE AUTHOR

Born and bred in Canterbury, New Zealand, Max now resides with her family in beautiful and sunny Queensland, Australia.

Life with two young children can be hectic at times, and although she may not write as often as she would like, Max wouldn't change a thing.

In her down time, Max can be found at her local gym, brain-storming through a session with the weights. If not, she's probably out drooling over one of many classic cars on show that she wishes she owned.

FOR ALL UPDATES AND ANNOUNCEMENTS –
SIGN UP TO MAX'S NEWSLETTER:
http://bit.ly/2mr9BUs

FOLLOW MAX

FACEBOOK – PROFILE
www.facebook.com/max.henry.9003

FACEBOOK – PAGE
www.facebook.com/MaxHenryAuthor

BOOKBUB
www.bookbub.com/profile/max-henry

GOODREADS
www.goodreads.com/author/show/
7555353.Max_Henry

TWITTER & INSTAGRAM:
@maxhenryauthor

FOR EXCLUSIVE NEWS AND EXCERPTS -
JOIN MAX'S READER GROUP, THE MADHOUSE!
www.facebook.com/groups/346994535466425/